THE OYSTERCATCHER'S CRY

THE OYSTERCATCHER'S CRY

F. K. Salwood

HEADLINE

Copyright © 1993 F. K. Salwood

The right of F. K. Salwood to be identified as the Author of the Work has been asserted by him in accordance with the Copyright, Designs and Patents Act 1988.

First published in 1993
by HEADLINE BOOK PUBLISHING PLC

10 9 8 7 6 5 4 3 2 1

All rights reserved. No part of this publication may be reproduced, stored in a retrieval system, or transmitted, in any form or by any means without the prior written permission of the publisher, nor be otherwise circulated in any form of binding or cover other than that in which it is published and without a similar condition being imposed on the subsequent purchaser.

All characters in this publication are fictitious and any resemblance to real persons, living or dead, is purely coincidental.

British Library Cataloguing in Publication Data

Salwood, F. K.
Oystercatcher's Cry
I. Title
823 [F]

ISBN 0-7472-0670-8

Typeset by CBS, Felixstowe, Suffolk

Printed and bound in Great Britain by
Clays Ltd, St Ives PLC

HEADLINE BOOK PUBLISHING PLC
Headline House
79 Great Titchfield Street
London W1P 7FN

To my grandmother

Acknowledgements

Thanks to Robert Payne's *The White Rajahs of Sarawak* (O.U.P.) for some of the background material in this novel.

PART ONE

Chapter One

'How long have I known you, Kate?' said Simon.

Kate Fernlee wondered why he had asked this question, since the answer was simple, and they both knew it to the hour.

'All my life,' she said. 'You threw a stone at me when I was five and called me names. I think that's when we first noticed each other.'

'Did I do that? I should have been whipped.'

Kate laughed. 'I think you were. At least, your father tanned your bottom for you. It was outside the church one Sunday. I remember you yelling as he dusted your pants.'

Simon Wentworth grimaced. 'I was just trying to get your attention. That's the way boys do these things.' He looked down into her eyes. 'All our lives, eh? And lots of it left to go.'

They stood on the top of a dyke which meandered along the edge of Paglesham creek like a sea-serpent heading towards the open ocean. It was the autumn of 1838 and the sky was full of godwits and peppered about with oystercatchers and plovers: the birds were wheeling and dipping in large flocks above the opalescent mudflats. A cool breeze blew across the salt marshes, rustling reeds which would soon be coated with frost.

Kate was feeling warm inside, despite the fact that she wore only a thin dress and a woollen shawl about her shoulders. The main reason for this was that the hand in hers belonged to the man at her side, Simon Wentworth.

Kate was thinking that nothing could mar this late afternoon, with its gentle colours and wide skies. Until Simon spoke to her in his country-Essex drawl, that was, the words served to spoil an otherwise perfect day.

'I am to sail with Captain Haines, for the Indian Continent, as an able seaman.'

The news upset Kate instantly, though she had been expecting it for some time. Simon had obviously been trying to soften the blow with his previous talk of spending their lives together. She felt disconsolate and wished he had not spoken until a later date. *Or never at all?* No, she had known she would hear of this sometime, but she wished it had not been this afternoon, when she had been feeling so happy. There were questions to ask now, the answers to which would make her miserable, whatever they were.

'When must you leave?' she asked with a catch in her throat.

'In one week's time.'

A fierce pang went through Kate's breast. 'Only a week?' She turned to look up into his eyes. He was miserable about it too. 'Oh Simon, can't it be longer? Can't you catch another ship, in a month's time? Next year, even?'

Simon shook his head emphatically. 'Kate, darling, I feel as bad about it as you, you know that. It's a sad thing and I wish it didn't have to happen, but it's got to be done. I have no choice. How can I make good here? So far I've survived crewing on the fishing boats, but there's so many fishermen and very few fish. There hasn't been a good season for two years now and I'm too poor to own my own boat. The sooner I go to sea the sooner I shall be back. I can't put it off for ever . . .'

'I don't see why not,' she flashed, taking refuge in anger at his stubborn disregard for their immediate future.

Instantly, though, she regretted the outburst, for she knew it would wound him for too long if they spent their last few days angry with one another. She could not do that to him, not when they were to be apart for so long. 'I mean, you needn't go at all, need you?' Her voice had a pleading note.

'I must, I must,' replied the young man, his eyes revealing the depth of his unhappiness at the prospect of their parting. 'I thought you would understand, Kate. What would you have me do: become a smuggler like my three brothers? Like my father before me? That would be a fine occupation, wouldn't it? No Kate, a man must make himself worthy of his . . . loved one.'

Kate shook her head at this ridiculous way of viewing their relationship.

'Simon, you don't need to prove anything to me. I know you to the depths of your soul – more than you know yourself – and there's not a speck of unworthiness in you. And besides, I love you, you great oaf. If you were the most worthless man in Essex it wouldn't change that fact. Don't do this to us just because you have some idea in your head – some thought that I will love you more for rising to be an officer in the navy than for what you are now. I couldn't love you more than I do.'

Simon shook his head and grasped her by the shoulders with his hands, looking deep into her eyes. 'It's more than that, Kate, you *must* know that. It's not just how you see me, but how others see me too. Your father, for instance. Others. What they see now is a man who has done nothing, has nothing, *is* nothing. I have to prove myself to them, too. I want you to be proud of me.'

She turned her head away from him so that he should not see the tears springing to her eyes. 'Oh, pride – what a stupid thing pride is.'

He let his hands drop. They were silent after that, not looking at one another. She knew he would be away for at least two years, perhaps longer, and since she was just nineteen herself, with Simon not long past his twenty-second birthday, they were young enough to feel that forthcoming months would be twenty-four forevers.

The tide was beginning to creep swiftly up the creeks now, covering the virgin sheen of the mud. It swept along like a live thing, as if it knew what it was doing, what it wanted, where it wished to go. Those birds that had been feeding on the mudflats, amongst the reed beds, took to the air. Stranded boats began to lift and bob on the incoming wavelets, turning their noses towards the sea. A sharp tang of salt was in the air.

'I shall miss you,' he said, taking her hand again. 'I want you to promise me something. The sea is a dangerous occupation—'

'Don't say it, Simon,' she cried, clinging to him.

'It must be said, Kate. There will be fighting, no doubt, for I'm sailing on a fighting ship, and there will be the sea, which shows no favour to any man. Men go missing; are shipwrecked, taken prisoner, marooned ... What I'm trying to say is, if I don't come back within three years, four at the outside, you must turn your back on me, find another. I don't want you to wait through your best years, when I might never come home.' He gave a short, false laugh. 'In four years your feelings for me will have waned enough ...'

'No!' she said, fiercely. 'Don't tell me what I must do. I'll be the judge of my feelings, not you. You must think me so fickle, Simon Wentworth.'

'Not fickle, *sensible*.'

'I don't want to be sensible. I'll wait for you, for ever if necessary. The only thing that will destroy our love is if you fall out of love with me.'

'That will never happen and you know it.'

'Then there's an end to *that* conversation,' said Kate, firmly. 'Now let's open one a bit more to the point. What am I to wait *for*?'

Simon looked uncomfortable.

'For me to come home, you know that.'

Suddenly she lost patience with him, dropped his hand, and whirled to face him.

'Simon. What is it you want to say? You have to say it *now*, because there won't be another chance. Don't make me into one of those forward girls, who throw away their pride and say it for their men. Find the words, Simon!'

His face went scarlet to the roots of his dark hair, and for one moment Kate thought she had overdone it, that perhaps she really had angered him. Then she looked into his mud-brown eyes, and realised he was just embarrassed by her outburst, embarrassed by the fact that he was going to have to put their unspoken understanding into plain English, because he had to overcome his shyness. Simon summoned the words that he had been practising for many days, words that had kept him awake at night, wondering if they were good enough.

'Kate, will you marry me?' he said in a rush, the short sentence tumbling out quite awkwardly, not at all in the serious and measured way it had during practice before the mirror. He sounded not calm and dignified, but desperate, which was closer to the truth. 'There, I've said it.'

'I'll think about it,' she said, crossing her arms under her bosom, like a fishwife ready to bargain.

'You'll *what*?' he cried.

Now he was angry.

'Yes,' she said, and threw her arms around his neck, pressing her cheek to his. 'Yes, of course I'll marry you. I love you dearly.'

'Thank God for that,' he murmured in the tones of a man who had just received a reprieve from a death sentence.

'But I hate you too,' she added fiercely.

'You hate me?'

'Of course. For going away.'

Simon asked in an exasperated tone, 'How can you hate *and* love me, woman?'

'Oh, so easily. Don't you know how it is with us Fernlees? There's love and hate side by side . . .' She kissed him savagely on the lips. 'It's called *passion*. Don't you feel it? The heat from my face?'

'I just love you,' he said helplessly. 'I don't want nothing to do with hate.'

She smiled now. 'Ah, you're a warm one, Simon Wentworth, that's why I love you, I think. My man – warm and gentle, loyal and true. You'd *better* be loyal and true, Wentworth, or you'll see the other side of my soul. But you're proud, too, more's the pity.'

'Oh, Kate, there's not another woman on the earth . . .'

They hugged and kissed as the dusk closed in around them, then turned to walk back along the dyke towards Paglesham and the sprinkling of lighted cottages that formed the East End of the village which was split in two by a wide creek. The path was too narrow for them to walk side by side, so they went in single file, the lean figure of Simon leading the way.

'When will you ask my father?' she said.

'I already did; he said he'll be glad to get rid of you.'

Kate punched him lightly in the back. 'Don't you fib me, Simon Wentworth.'

'It's true. He didn't call you a hoyden, not straight out, but I sort of sensed he wanted you off his hands quick-like, having finally managed to get you out of breeches and into dresses . . .'

She hit him again, harder this time, and he turned to look at her in the fading light. His stomach churned as he did so, as it will sometimes when a young man is confronted by beauty he never expected to possess. It was true that she had been a tomboy in her younger years, with a belligerent expression and a desire to climb trees. Now, though, Kate was like some beautiful tribal queen from the region's past.

There had been times when Simon had studied Kate: times when she had been unaware of his scrutiny. What he saw at those moments was not drawing-room loveliness, in the fashion preferred by the upper classes. Kate's shoulders were a little too broad to be termed elegant, her skin was not pale and porcelain-like, her hair was not raven. She was a wide-faced lass, with a tumbling mass of auburn hair and eyes the colour of Essex summer skies.

But it was not Kate's looks so much as her real self that attracted Simon. There was an independent spirit behind her eyes which would never have been acceptable to a viscount or lord. There was a sprinkling of freckles around the bridge of her retroussé nose which would have brought forth scorn from the mouths of barons and earls. Her figure was too generously natural to be admired by princes and kings.

To Simon though, and many other young men in the district, Kate Fernlee was as desirable as any princess. It was true she had a strong will, which could make things difficult at times, for a man likes to make his decisions unhindered by strong winds from other quarters. But she was Kate, lively and captivating, and the man who would not give an arm and an eye to have her for his own was a man without soul.

'I shall be an old woman when you come home,' she said sadly, as they walked along. 'You won't want me then.'

'Yes, you shall,' he replied with humour in his voice, 'but I will love you just the same, my darling Kate, for you will grow even older still, and be nothing but a crone when you are thirty gone – yet still I shall love you, for you shall never change in my eyes from this day on.'

'You are not supposed to say that, Simon Wentworth, you're expected to tell me I shall be beautiful until the day I go into the earth.'

He turned again, and stared at her in the gloaming. 'That's the truth of the matter, Kate my love, but I shall have to put the rumour about that your beauty will fade, or all the men in Christendom will be here to challenge me for your hand.'

'You are such a tease, Able Seaman Wentworth.'

'I'm a man in love,' he said, seriously. He took her in his arms and she buried her head in the rough shirt he wore. 'I love you so much, but I must make good my fortune, for what have I to offer? My brothers are all bound for Chelmsford prison, or worse, for they are sure to be caught one day. This way I might rise a little in the world, perhaps even become an officer. Think of that! I'm a good seaman, and the ocean is in my veins: I can feel the tides change in my blood, their courses and currents, their ebbs and flows. I know I can do well in Her Majesty's Navy . . .'

'Then go, if you must,' she said, unable to keep the touch of hardness out of her tone. 'With my love, but not my blessing.'

'Your love will be enough to see me through, and before you know it, I'll be back. You'll see.'

They parted after a final kiss outside the Plough and Sail Inn, and went their separate ways. Simon headed out into the marshes, where he lived with his brothers in a clapboard house that was ever threatened by flood and disaster from the sea. Kate went to her father's cottage, which stood in a row of such dwellings behind the inn.

Kate remained outside the doorway for a while, unwilling to enter while her thoughts were in such turmoil. She had two conflicting emotions in her breast, one of joy and one of misery, and they battled for complete possession of her. There was happiness that Simon had at last proposed to her, making definite what had been previously assumed; there was distress at having to be parted from him for so long.

'Simon Wentworth,' she said softly to herself, 'you can be such a stubborn man.'

The battling emotions were wearying and she stared out over the countryside surrounding her village, trying to lose herself in the landscape.

The smell of sea parslane, bladderwrack and saltwort drifted over the fields behind the cottage, where there were innumerable channels and ditches, sea walls and dykes, built by the Dutch engineers more than a hundred years before.

She and Simon had played on the salt marshes as children, before there were any strong feelings between them. Then one day, when she was fourteen, Simon had wiped the salt from her eyebrows with a wet finger, and a powerful tremor had gone through her body. Her feelings had frightened her. For a while after that she had been worried by him, staying out of his way, but two years later he had asked her to dance with him at someone's wedding and they had been inseparable since.

They had, after that dance, shared the salt marshes again, seeing them with new and excited eyes. Out there, in the fields, in the maze of creeks, in the saltings and marshes, were the secret creatures: bird, beast, and man. Solitary herons, like sentries, guarding their shallow stretches of water. Foxes with glittering eyes and humourless smiles. Excise men, straining their sight against the darkness, watching the waterways for stealthy-looking craft. Smugglers rubbing vegetable oil into the joints of their boats to prevent them creaking when they slipped through the labyrinth of tidal channels on their way in and out of the maze.

Kate loved this mysterious dark flatland where she had been born and raised, despite its remoteness, its narrow-eyed vision, sinister character and secretive ways. It provided her with emotional strength, for it had a sense of the eternal in its atmosphere. Long after the temporal Kate and Simon were gone, their spirits would still inhabit this place of wild birds and gentle waters.

There were prettier places in England, no doubt. She had once travelled as far as Saffron Walden, in the north of the county, where there were hills and woods; and yes, pretty enough it was too. But nowhere else had skies as big as her Essex flatlands. Nowhere else did the sea meet the land with such a rush of joy, with such a wide embrace, she was sure. Nowhere else was a bleak landscape made so appealing by such an overwhelming quantity of wildlife.

To the north-west lay the next village, Canewdon, which was a dark place indeed, and rumoured to have six witches in residence: three in cotton and three in silk. It was said that one of these creatures stole the church bell from Latchingdon. The bell sank as she tried to row it across the stormy waters of the River Crouch using a huge black feather as an oar.

Further down the river were South and North Fambridge, one on either bank. Then Ashingdon, where it was believed King Canute had built their minster a thousand years after Christ, after coming upriver with his longships and defeating Edmund Ironside in a great battle between Vikings and Anglo-Saxons.

The land was rich in rumour and tales, legends and fables, and Kate knew all the stories, true and false, which had sprung out of the East Anglian earth. She loved her flat marshy landscape with the same fervour that a Highland Scot loves his mountains and glens, or a Buckinghamshire woodlander loves his beech forests, or a Welshman his green valleys. She went to sleep at night with the odour of the salt creeks in the atmosphere of her room, and woke in the morning to the fragrance of sea lavender, and would not wish her lungs to breathe any other air.

Her father was waiting supper for her when Kate finally entered the cottage, and scolded her for her lateness. Edward Fernlee was a short stocky man, and though only in his forties, had a crop of wiry, grey-white hair. He was generally a morose man, with an outlook as grey as February, but he was also hard-working and responsible, and loved his daughters – as well as an estuary man could – without comprehending them in the least. He understood the ways of oysters better than he did those of women.

Kate's two younger sisters, Sarah and Elizabeth, were sitting impatiently, spoons at the ready, and as soon as Kate had sat down and grace had been said, they began their stew, while their father chided his eldest daughter once more for not keeping good time. Kate was hardly listening, and only toyed with the stew. She was too brimful of feelings.

Simon had, at last, asked to wed her, though it was just like him to do so with only a week to go before he sailed for some far-off land called the Indies. After all, at nineteen years old she was practically an old maid. Most of her childhood girlfriends were already wed – those that were ever going to be – some of them before they had reached sixteen. Others, the cocklers and winklers, who had had the misfortune to fall in love with men as poor as themselves and could not afford to pay the priest to wed them, were common-law wives.

'Are you going to eat that, or shall Edward throw un to the dogs?' muttered her father in his broad East Anglian accent. Since his wife had died, he had fallen into the habit of speaking of himself in the third person, as if he were not really there.

'Eat it, Father,' she said, taking a tiny mouthful of the fish stew.

Edward Fernlee sighed. A father of three daughters and their mother passed away just four years ago, of an unidentified fever caught from the mud, he felt unable to give his children the kind of understanding they needed. It took a mother to know a daughter, and he just wasn't up to their sudden mood changes and peculiar female ways. When they burst into tears, or became bad-tempered overnight, or fell to hating each other for a few days, or went silent and distant on him as his eldest daughter Catherine had now – all with no reason that he could uncover – Edward felt lost and helpless.

His daughters had urged him to marry again, but the younger two insisted on making the choice, and so far he wouldn't give an inch of bedroom to the women they had suggested. They were either great blowzy women who would boss him to death, or thin hags whose bones would surely pierce his skin in bed at night.

In any case, deep inside he was still in mourning for his Betty. They had married when both were seventeen, and she had been by his side, helping him build up his oyster-farming business since the day they had locked lives. When she had faded away from the world, literally growing thinner and thinner until she was just a wisp, most of him had disappeared along with her. If truth be told, he had no desire for a second run at it, and was content to simply drift like an oyster spat on the currents of life.

'Father, I'm getting married.'

He looked up quickly to see which one of his daughters had spoken, and was pained to see that it was, as expected, Kate who was staring fixedly at him. The other two were gawping at her, which meant the news was fresh to them too.

'Young Simon, is it?'

'He said he'd spoken to you,' replied Kate, dismayed for a moment, for she had seen her statement had come as a shock.

Edward nodded his head several times. 'Yes, yes. Edward just forgot, that's all.'

Sarah squealed in that penetrating way of hers. 'Father, how could you *forget* that someone asked for Kate? You *can't* forget something like that.'

'Can't?' he said, testily. 'If Edward wants to forget it, he jolly well will, and don't *you* forget *that*.'

Kate was determined to discover her father's motives for failing to tell her that Simon had asked him for his permission to marry her. She was fairly certain what those motives were, but she wanted to be certain. Most things her father did, even if they were not to her liking, she could forgive; but when her own future with Simon was at issue, that was a different matter. 'Father, why did you not tell me that Simon had spoken to you?'

It was obvious that her father knew he was about to enter enemy territory, for he lowered his head while he spoke, apparently attending more to his food than the conversation. 'None of your business what men talk on.'

'When it concerns me,' said Kate evenly, 'it is most certainly my business.'

Probably realising he had to face up to this attack from his daughter, Edward Fernlee told her the truth. 'Edward thought it were possible the boy might change his mind – a man's entitled to change his mind, ain't un? Atween speakin' to Edward and speakin' to you, he might've decided it weren't worth it at all, this marriaging.'

'That's what you were hoping,' said Kate.

Her father nodded emphatically. 'Edward were an' he an't ashamed of it. The business can't do without Edward's eldest daughter to run un, an' that's a fact as you could nail to the door for all to see.'

Kate said in a tight voice, 'Let me say, Father, that I think it was very bad of you – very bad.' He hung his head again. 'But as it happens,' she tilted her head in an effort to stop the tears, and was successful, 'you've no need to worry about me not helping with the oysters, at least for a while, because he's going away to sea for two years or more, and we shan't be wed until he comes home again.'

Her father looked up quickly and Kate saw the relief in his eyes.

He said, 'Well, Edward won't say he's not pleased for himself, but he's sorry for you, child. It will be a terrible hard wait, even though it be only two years.'

'*Only* two years?' cried Kate mournfully, and the girls groaned in sympathy.

'Well, it's true that two years is a fearful long time to someone as young as you, lassie, but in the oyster business, it's a snap of the fingers. Why, it takes from three to five years for an oyster to reach the table. What about that then, eh?' he cried, as if this answered all Kate's problems.

Sarah shrieked, 'Father, how *could* you compare Simon Wentworth to an *oyster*?'

Liz cried, 'And our Kate!'

Edward shrugged his shoulders helplessly. This was the kind of thing he meant about his relationship with his daughters. When he thought he was being understanding, they attacked him like harpies. He pushed his chair back, hoping to retreat to the Plough and Sail for a mug of hot brandy.

Kate said, 'Stop it, you two. Father didn't mean that – he was trying to make me feel better.' She turned to him then, with the words, 'If you're going to the inn, Father, please don't be too late back, for we have to be up early to gather tomorrow.'

'Edward knows that, Kate. Edward will be awake and ready, just as he always is.'

'And don't you go getting into any fights, Father. Last time you and that John Miggs got to arguing over whether yellow-staining mushrooms were poisonous or just plain uneatable, and you came home with mud all over your coat.'

'John Miggs pushed Edward over.'

'I'm told John Miggs was none too happy at Edward for sloshing ale down his jerkin. Now, Father, you're getting far too old to get into these capers,' said Kate. 'I won't have it, do you hear?'

Edward grumbled at her as she handed him his pipe matches.

'Your mother . . .'

'Mother doesn't come into this, she's not here and I am. We're the ones who have to do the washing and clean up the mess, Father – Sarah, Liz and me – not mother.'

A pain pierced the region between Edward's eyes when he thought of his departed wife. It was a good job he was sitting down and not standing, or he might have shown the weakness in his head. Edward had been getting these funny turns now for a year or so, though he had said nothing to the girls about them. They would just worry over him all the more and he didn't want that. On the occasions when he felt unsteady, he just said he felt tired, and sat down somewhere until the feeling passed.

'Edward's going,' he said. 'Edward will behave himself, you'll see.'

With that, he stood up and went into the scullery, taking his coat from where it hung over a dead hare on the back of the door. The hare was to be jugged once the meat had sufficiently rotted. He pulled on the coat, wrapped a scarf around his throat for protection against the mists creeping up from the river, and stepped out into the night air.

The three sisters began clearing the table. Sarah put a kettle on the range to heat the water for washing the dishes, while Liz and Kate stacked the crockery in the scullery. Kate's younger sisters chattered excitedly as they worked, plying her with questions.

'How did he ask you, Kate?' said Sarah. 'Did he go down on a knee, like a gentleman?'

'Certainly not. He'd got his best breeches on, and it was muddy.'

Liz said, 'And anyway, Simon's not gentry, he's as common as oysters.'

Kate clattered the crockery and gave her youngest sister a withering look, which was wasted, for such glares simply made no impression on Liz.

Kate said, 'Simon is not *common*. He might not be from a well-to-do family, Liz, but common means there's plenty of them around, and there's only one Simon.'

Liz was unabashed. 'Well, what words did he use? Did he say, "Darling Kate, I love you to death. You must marry me or I will die of heartache."' Liz said this in the lofty tones she imagined a suitor, even a lowly sailor like Simon Wentworth, would use for such an occasion.

'No, he did not. He said, "You are always in an oyster bed, but I would have you in mine."'

The girls' eyes opened as wide as penny coins.

'He did *not*,' whispered Sarah, a prim fifteen years of age. 'How *awful* for you.'

'Of course he didn't, you cod,' laughed Kate, gathering the dishes. She paused in the act, and added thoughtfully, 'But I wish he had.'

'Catherine Fernlee!' squealed Liz, who was just thirteen and easily impressed by such talk.

Kate had lectured both girls on the facts of life – as much as her mother had told her when she was alive – and there had been different responses. Sarah had seemed very shocked, which was understandable, while Liz had been terribly interested yet unable to stop giggling.

Kate looked hard at the two girls.

'You will not repeat that remark to Father, for he wouldn't understand.'

They promised they wouldn't, though no doubt it would be in other ears before the morning mellowed the following day.

Sarah, having burned her fingers on the handle, had fetched a dishcloth with which to carry the kettle.

'Wouldn't it be nice,' she said, as she poured the steaming water over the dishes, 'to marry someone with a position in life and an income.'

'Father has an income,' said Kate, 'but you still forget to use a rag on the kettle.'

'I don't mean that, I mean a *private* income: one you don't have to work for. Some nice handsome young man with fair hair and blue eyes, whose family has a fortune they don't want. So one could have servants who would forget to wrap a rag around the handle of the kettle . . .'

'You want it all, Sarah,' laughed Liz. 'You want love *and* riches.'

'I want it all and I want it *now*,' laughed Sarah, dancing around the scullery. 'I want to be bride of the year and have every girl jealous to death because they can't be me. Then I want to be waited on hand and foot by my adoring husband, who will be ever so grateful for just a smile from me.'

Kate, who was slightly disturbed by the way in which Sarah said this, remarked, 'I don't believe you, Sarah.'

Sarah stopped dancing and said seriously, 'You're quite right, Kate dear. I don't want to marry anyone at all. I want to be a spinster all my life.'

'I don't believe that either.'

'What then?' asked Liz.

'I believe Sarah will fall in love with an ordinary man – who'll be extraordinary to her of course – and she'll have six children and live to be a hundred.'

'How *boring*,' said Liz, wrinkling her nose.

Elizabeth was the most intelligent of the three sisters and she made no secret of it.

'I'm going to see the world first,' she said, 'before I let any man propose to me, even if I'm as old as you Kate. I'm going to become a governess and go with a fine family somewhere. Italy perhaps? Or France? I don't see why I should let some man chain me to the scullery. I'm brighter than most boys anyway. I can beat them into a cocked hat when it comes to learning.'

'Bluestocking,' sneered Sarah.

'Don't care,' snapped back Liz.

Kate said, 'You follow your head, Liz, and good luck to you. There's nothing wrong with a woman having knowledge – men who say otherwise do so because they're afraid of women who know as much as they themselves. They like women to follow their hearts, so that they can use them.'

'Kate!' Sarah exclaimed. 'You don't mean that?'

'What, about men using us? Yes I do.'

'But what about Simon?' asked Liz.

'Oh, he's not perfect either,' smiled Kate. 'Now that would be boring, Liz, to have the perfect man.'

Liz, as was her wont when she felt she was getting out of her thirteen-year-old depth, changed the subject. 'I'm to be a bridesmaid, aren't I? May I wear a lovely mauve gown with flowers embroidered around the edges?'

'If you make it yourself,' said Kate. 'You've got two years to do it in.'

'And you can find your *own* sewing basket, for you can't use *mine*,' said the ever possessive Sarah, who hated to have her things touched by the other two.

'Two years,' groaned Liz, ignoring Sarah. 'You must be dying inside, Kate.'

'Oh no,' said Kate, brightly. 'Two years is not so long – not when you get to my great age. Now let's be getting to bed, for we have an early start . . .'

Kate saw them to bed, and then settled down by lamplight to sew. The family had a reasonably comfortable life, with a good living coming in from their oyster beds. All three girls had had two years' schooling, which was twenty-four months longer than most others in and around the village. They were not wealthy, by any means, but they could pay the rent on the cottage and on the stretch of river where their oyster beds were situated, and put food on the table. They had a dog, chickens, a greengage tree, and their father had a sporting gun, with which he hunted rabbits and hares, geese in the winter when they came down from Iceland to breed, and sometimes pheasants when the squire was not around. Compared with many other estuary families, they were quite well off.

Not long ago their oysters had been the staple diet of the poor, along with cockles, winkles, whelks and mussels. Recently however, the rich summer visitors to the South End of Prittlewell (or what was commonly becoming called just simply 'Southend'), a watering-place for the gentry, were beginning to develop a taste for the local shellfish, especially oysters. With access to the natural waters of nearby Hockley Spa, Southend was trying to rival Brighton and Bath for those migrating upper classes who were finding it fashionable to copy the French aristocracy in the eating of raw oysters with a touch of lemon juice.

Kate, whose keen sense of business saw huge possibilities for the oyster trade both in Southend and London, had managed to supply the kitchens of some of these rich houses, as well as the fish market where the less wealthy bought their food. She saw no reason why her father's oyster farms could not expand to meet the needs of both the lower and upper end of the market. In this they were being rivalled by the mussel farmers, who were hopeful that the Austrian habit of cooking the shellfish as a soup would also catch on amongst the gentry; for if a dish was considered *de rigueur* at upper-class tables, it would be consumed in vast quantities.

These thoughts crowded through her mind, along with those concerning her lover and husband-to-be, until the dimness of the lamplight and her tired eyes could no longer work well enough together for her to see the stitches, and she dropped off to sleep in the chair. When she woke, the ashes in the grate were grey powder with a tiny glow to their centre. Shortly afterwards her father came home, and they locked and bolted the doors before both retiring.

While Kate was undressing her thoughts again turned to how well the business seemed to be going. She was optimistic that in the not too distant future they might be in a position to purchase a large dredging smack with which they would be able to extend their operations further into the river. Perhaps one day Fernlee oysters would be as famous as the Burnham Oyster Company, who owned more than twenty boats and whose stock was recently estimated at over £30,000. This company exported a considerable portion of their oysters to the Continent. Kate could foresee a time when she, her father and her sisters, would be in the same position. They were certainly capable enough. All it required was hard work and Kate knew they were able to invest plenty of that in their business.

Chapter Two

Jack Rockmansted was a tall, well-built man, his skin tanned the colour of leather by twenty years of working in the salt air around the Stambridge mills of the tidal River Roche, some four miles south of the River Crouch. He was a mussel farmer, who had inherited his father's firm just two years previously at the age of thirty, after the death of both his parents in an accident between a waggon and a phaeton carriage. They had been walking along the edge of the Rochford road when the haywain, forced to leave the road, had overturned, crushing them both.

Like Kate Fernlee, he too was intent on expanding the family business, and on the evening that Simon was asking Kate to be his wife, Jack Rockmansted had a meeting with one of his hired musselmen at the Cherry Tree Inn.

'Meg, I shall eat at the inn tonight,' he informed his housekeeper, an elderly village woman.

Meg came trotting in from the scullery, where she normally hid amongst greasy pots and pans hanging from dirty strings above the kitchen fire. She slept there very soundly by day, on a stool close to the flames, and her legs were covered in red weals from the heat of the coals. A yard lad would sometimes amuse himself by sneaking in and dropping dead flies and small worms into her open mouth, which she automatically swallowed without waking. At night in her bed, she tossed and turned, complaining that she was unable to get any rest in this world and would be glad to enter the narrow bed of the next.

'You don't want to eat there, master,' Meg muttered. 'You never know fresh from mouldy with that there food.'

Her toothless face was as creased and lined as old paper screwed into a ball then flattened out again. She had two shifts, both grey and grubby, which she wore on alternate days. These were never washed, unless by the rain, but always aired on the days she was not wearing them. Meg believed in the purity of air, though she never exposed her body to it, or to water.

'I'm eating at the inn, Meg,' Jack repeated, 'and I don't want no backchat. Leave a lamp burning in the porch for when I return. Where's that useless brother o' mine?'

'Atween some strumpet's legs, I shouldn't wonder,' she said with a sly glance.

'Hmmm,' Jack grunted.

The inn was just two hundred yards from Jack's house, along the lane between some sinister-looking ponds, where within Jack's lifetime a local witch had been drowned by hysterical villagers after an outbreak of cholera had been blamed on the unfortunate woman. There were ponds scattered all over Stambridge, where the water-table rose to meet the surface of the land. Around most of these stagnant pools of water covered in green algae and chickweed were bent and gnarled elderberry trees, looking as if they had just crawled from the scum and were resting their crooked limbs before moving on.

The Cherry Tree was a low-ceilinged alehouse, small and parlour-like, with only one room available for travellers. There were few who passed through this remote area of the country: those heading for open sea would have stopped at London's docks and taken a boat there, whilst those wishing to cross the English Channel to France or Holland would branch away to Southend or Harwich. The land of the poa-grass islands and saltings was not a place to which travellers needed to go, nor were any especially welcome. It was an area favoured by gypsies, but these itinerants brought their own roofs with them and had no need of inns.

As Jack ducked his head to enter the parlour, he noticed his brother Timothy, sitting amongst a group of wildfowlers and marsh farmers, a sprinkling of cockle girls amongst them, in a small alcove at the back. Timothy, like Jack, had a handsome face of roughly-hewn granite, but there was a humour in the younger brother's features that was missing from Jack's. A dispassionate observer might have said there was little difference in their looks, but a local lass would point out that Timothy's face always had a smile, whereas Jack's was usually as dull as church roof lead.

Timothy was much sought after by the women of the mudflats, the cocklers and triggers, who eked a bare existence out of collecting cockles, whelks and winkles from the estuary. Timothy noticed his brother, nodded, but neither man saw the need to speak. Although they lived under the same roof, they despised one another. Jack was contemptuous of his brother's fondness for trollops, and Timothy considered Jack a boring prig.

Jack found a table by away from the wooden door, in which the cold autumnal winds found the cracks and split into a dozen draughts, and ordered a pint of ale and some green fish from the landlord. The ale was brought immediately, but the food took longer; it had just been placed in front of him when a burly-looking man entered the inn and sat down opposite him.

Jack glared at him, and spoke. 'You're late. Be so good as to be on time in future.'

Jiz Fowler, with his distinctive wall eye and hawk nose, blinked in discomfort. 'Sorry, Jack. Got held up back there on the road.'

'See to it you *don't* get held up. I'm about to eat my supper, so you can now wait until that's done.'

The landlord, at a signal, brought a mug of hot gin for Jiz Fowler, who also ordered, 'Some of them sucklent Rockmansted mussels, done up as a soup, if you please, Harry,' and then nodded at Jack as if they were great friends sharing a secret. Jack took no notice of this grovelling: he was used to being fawned upon by people like Jiz Fowler.

'Well,' said Jack, wiping his mouth on his kerchief once he had finished, 'what have you brought me?'

Jiz Fowler leaned forward conspiratorially. 'There's a widder by the name of Jenkins, 'bout to snuff it. She's down to her last farthin'. Got a bit o' land on Foulness Island, over the hard. I reckon she'd sell, though like most of those old crones, she vowed she'd never let go of her property.'

'I know the woman. That it?'

The wall-eyed man assumed a pained look.

'Ain't it enough, Jack? I been ferritin' that out for two full days now.'

Jack reached into his waistcoat pocket and took out a crown, which he passed to Jiz Fowler and watched as it disappeared somewhere into the folds of Jiz Fowler's topcoat.

'It'll do for now,' he said. 'Keep on with your ferreting.'

Like most men in the area, especially shellfish farmers, Jack knew the state of the tide wherever he was and whatever he was doing. He had the instinct of a mussel hanging from its byssus, which opens and closes to the ebb and flow of the ocean currents. He knew exactly where the water level would be on his mussel posts, right to this very minute, and could judge a spring tide, the moon's influence notwithstanding, to a few feet, having accurately predicted the height of the terrible flood which had covered the land three years ago in 1835.

'I'll visit the woman on Foulness tomorrow,' he said to Jiz Fowler. 'By way of the hard, you say? Tide will be full out at five a.m. I'll walk across. What will she settle for, man?'

Jiz Fowler gave him a figure.

'Hmmm. I'll see if we can't reduce that. You sure you have nothing else for me?'

'Not that comes to mind, 'cept some barrels of brandy what the Wentworth brothers have got left over.'

Jack shook his head impatiently. 'You know I won't have nothing to do with that illegal contraband. I don't want no doings with the excise or the law. That's the fastest route to a hemp collar, or transportation. You play with the smugglers, Jiz, and you'll be picking mussels out of Botany Bay. You want a nice long sea voyage in the stinking hold of one of Her Majesty's ships?'

'No, Jack, but everybody does it, don't they? I mean, look at the landlord over there. His brandy comes straight from the Frenchies . . .'

'Jiz, you're a fool, they're fools, and the excise always wins in the end. Where's old man Wentworth, the father, eh? He was turned off by Jack Ketch and now lies a-moulderin' in some graveyard for hanged men. They always get caught in the end, you mark my words. If you involve me in something like that, Jiz Fowler, I'll turn *you* off, and make no mistake.'

Jiz stared into Jack Rockmansted's hard and uncompromising face, and knew he meant what he said. 'All right, Jack, no need to go on.'

'Land is where fortunes are made, not smuggling petty goods across the channel. I'll visit the widow in the morning.'

Jack took a long swig of his ale, then called to his brother. 'Timothy! I'll be away for most of the morning. You look to the mussel gathering, if you please brother.'

Timothy turned and grinned at his elder brother. 'I'll be there, sir. I'll join the little blue darlings in their beds in the mornin', but tonight I'm sharing a warmer bed . . .' He cuddled a dark-haired lass, who giggled and slapped his shoulder.

'Just see that you're there,' growled Jack as he left the inn.

Jack was up again before dawn, and went down to the scullery to find some cold porridge. The two lurcher dogs, Bess and Dagger, stirred from their nest of sacks when he went into the stone-floored room. They sensed a long walk in their master's determined manner.

Jack took with him a small bag containing pen, ink and papers already written up for the general sale of land. All he had to do was fill in some of the blanks – the location, the seller's name and address, the boundaries – and then get the old woman to sign the document. Although it required the signature of a witness who was supposed to be present at the signing, he would obtain that later from someone who would swear to have been in attendance. These were petty rules, required by the law, but impractical when engaged in the actual business of buying and selling land. How could you drag people over the marshes with you when you couldn't even be certain of obtaining a purchase? Survival in the salt marsh country depended upon getting daily tasks done on time: bandlines set, lobster pots laid, cattle moved to feeding grounds, cockles gathered. You could not take people away from these essential tasks simply on the hope of getting a buy.

The rules made in parliament by Whigs with fat bottoms, like the Prime Minister Viscount Melbourne, who sat and puffed on pipes and gave forth with their opinions, were simply an irritation to be circumnavigated out in the remote parts of Essex. Why, only just recently they had passed a law establishing prison sentences for juvenile offenders. Jack Rockmansted, and many like him, thought this a stupid law. A sound whipping was all the young thieves needed, not to be sent some place where they would learn new tricks.

Before he left the house, the day-girl, Molly, arrived, barefoot and wearing only a thin dress and shawl. She was a dark-haired, dark-eyed lass, a settled gypsy and elder sister to the yard lad. Jack used her around the house and out on the mussel beds; wherever she was useful. She worked for practically nothing, and though there were more lucrative jobs in the neighbourhood, she stayed with Jack and Timothy, fiercely loyal. Timothy kept urging Jack to raise her wages, but Jack suspected Timothy was bedding the girl, and that was the reason for his brother's philanthropic attitude towards her. Jack paid people what he thought they were worth to him, and not a farthing more. There was not a sentimental organ in his body: his heart was for pumping blood.

'You goin' out, master?' asked Molly, removing her shawl.

'Yes, out. Be sure to wake that sluggard Meg as soon as I've gone, will you?'

'Yes, Master Jack.'

Her dark eyes stared disconcertingly into his own, and he had to turn away in the end. She was not a pretty girl, being too angular in Jack's opinion, but there was a fieriness about her which stirred something in him, made him stop for a moment and lose his concentration. He was always uncomfortable in her presence, under her gaze.

'Don't you have no small tasks for me today?' she asked. 'Some sewing of your clothes?'

'You can clean my second pair of boots,' he muttered, 'though I should have thought you had enough to do without finding more.'

'I'll find the time, master,' she said, in that hissing way, like a log on the fire spurting burning gases.

Once out, on the dyke, striding towards the place where the hard went out to Foulness Island, Jack filled his nostrils with the odour of the estuary mudlands. Like Kate Fernlee, with whom he was slightly acquainted, he had a strong love of his native landscape, though others might find it dreary. There was a soft dawn light coming through the overcast sky, which fell on the flats and awoke ducks, gulls, dunlin, stints and knots. These shore birds and waders caused a commotion amongst the reeds when the two lurchers streaked past. The shrill, piping whistle of a black-and-white oystercatcher penetrated the sky as it flew off towards the wide horizons.

Jack walked along the top of the dyke, enjoying the sight of the mudflats on which his family had made a living since the times of Queen Anne. When he came within sight of the Thames estuary, around the naze, he could see sail barges and square-rigged ships moving back and forth.

India and the Far East were relinquishing their teas and spices for the benefit of the British. Earl Grey had blended some teas to form a mixture which Jack had heard was favoured by the aristocracy. In China, along the Pearl River up to Canton, the opium trade was flourishing, though the Chinese emperor was making noises of displeasure at the fact that thousands of his subjects were becoming addicts. The British were using the sea roads to make themselves rich, and Jack Rockmansted intended to grab himself a slice of those riches. He would feed the wealthy with his mussels.

He reached the hard – a stretch of mud upon which stones had been laid and marked by upturned witches' brooms – as the tide was on the retreat. At this point the waters receded up to a mile or more, and he would have to cross the hard and return before the tide came back in, or spend twelve hours marooned on Foulness Island, a place of inbred retarded folk with close-set eyes and prominent foreheads.

On crossing the mud, he reached the island, and inquired of a marsh farmer where he might find the widow's cottage. He followed the directions and came to a house made of kealy earth drawn over with lime-mortar and cruckframed with rough oak timbers. He knocked at the door, was told to enter, and inside found an old woman sitting up in bed. Since the window was small and mean, she had a lit candle by her side.

'Who be you?' she asked, peering under her nightcap. 'Thocht it were ald Jason Sperks, bringin' me brekfust.'

'No need to be alarmed, madam,' replied Jack, kicking the dogs back outdoors. 'I've come to pay you a visit. My name is Jack Rockmansted, of Stambridge, a mussel farmer by profession. I understand you have some land for purchase?'

'You understand wrong,' she spluttered. 'No land for sale in here.'

Jack smiled. 'I see. I've been misinformed . . . permit me,' he walked over to her and straightened her nightcap. 'There, pretty as a picture.'

'Don't you set out to butter me, you young spat,' she snapped, 'applesauce don't work in this dwellin'.'

Jack assumed surprise. 'Nor would I expect it to, madam, for I've been told on good authority that you're not a woman who's put in a flummox by false praise . . . I say again, the cap looks pretty, and I mean it.'

She snorted, but he could see he had pleased her.

'Well, let's hear it then, if you'm come all the way from the mainland. I never bin there meself, for I heared it were a big and fusty place, and full o' strange folk.'

Jack told her what he was prepared to offer for her land, and she snorted again. There was a fish pie on the table, so while he talked, he put it in the ashes of the previous night's fire to warm a little, before cutting a slice and handing it to her. She ate without a word, the pastry crumbs disappearing down into her bedclothes.

'That ain't much, for a good bit o' land,' she finally remarked.

'Ah, but land has come down in price over the last several years, madam, because of the wars and acquisitions, you see. Since we have got places like India and Australia, there is so much land about people are having to give it away to prevent paying the tax . . .'

'What tax?'

'The new tax – you must have heard – on land where no buildings are presently standing?' He feigned an expression of a puzzle solved. 'Of course, they will not have been here yet, for this is a remote area, and the last time I heard the tax collectors were around the Chelmsford district.'

The widow Jenkins looked worried.

Jack continued, 'When Britain was merely a small island, land was precious, but now we own practically half the earth.'

She screwed up her forehead under the nightcap. 'There's sense in them words,' she said. 'I had heard on the fac' that us'n got new lands overseas, an' I do need the money awful bad. How much did you say?'

He gave her the figure again, which was two-thirds of the price recommended by Jiz Fowler.

'Can't you make it a bit more?'

'Madam, unfortunately this is the price I must pay for the land considering its size, for the government of Her Majesty – God Bless Her – has declared a set price per acre, to prevent people like you from being cheated. I may not pay more, but then I may not pay less. With so much land lying about in the colonies, the cheapness of it has got people into a worry, so a law was passed just a fortnight gone to protect landowners from unscrupulous buyers.'

'If that's must be, I'll have to take it, an' hope to keep from starvin' for the next four year.'

Jack nodded gravely, thinking that the old biddy would probably not last more than a year or two from the looks of her, so his conscience need not be troubled on that score. It was true that the money he was giving her for the land was not a great deal, not enough to live on for half a decade, but if she was to die soon, well her inheritance would only go to some half-cousin or cockler niece who didn't deserve it. More likely, it would have to be shared amongst two dozen or so, for the island was rife with incest, and everybody was related to everybody else. The relationships were like a wicker lobster pot, all connected by this strand or that, and true lines were lost in the network.

He spoke to the widow. 'Madam, you shall not regret this decision. I have a paper here, which if you will permit me, I shall modify to suit our requirements, and then you may sign and have the money in your hand straight.'

The transaction was carried out within twenty minutes, and not a moment too soon, for as Jack was preparing to leave, another man entered the cottage. Jack decided that this must be 'ald Jason Sperks', this sturdy pepper-and-salt-haired man who stood in the doorway.

'What's all this then?' said the man, staring hard at Jack.

Jack immediately went on the offensive. 'Take your damn eyes off me, man. I don't take to being stared at like a stray dog. Me and the lady here have just finished some business, if it's any concern of yours.'

The man stepped forward, looking indignant. 'Concern o' mine? I should say so. I be her nephew, and in charge of business 'ere.'

The old woman said, 'Now don't take on, Jason, I got good money for the land . . .'

Jason Sperks' eyes opened wider.

'Land, you say?'

Jack moved towards the doorway, which Jason Sperks was blocking with his square body. The door itself had been left partially open, and the lurchers, Bess and Dagger, had squeezed themselves inside. Their slim forms now moved to Jack's side, their rat-tails wagging.

'Step aside, if you please,' said Jack.

'Not till I finds out what goes on 'ere,' said Jason Sperks.

Jack snapped out the two dogs' names in a particular way, and they lowered themselves menacingly, ready to spring immediately, stiffening their stances and baring their teeth, snarling in the backs of their throats.

The old woman started wailing and held up a bolster to protect herself.

'*If* you please,' repeated Jack in a firm tone.

The elderly man stared at the lurchers for a moment more, then stepped aside.

'You'll hear more on this,' he said softly, as Jack passed by him.

Jack did not reply. He was used to threats, the majority of which came to nothing, once people were given time to cool down and assess their situation. He knew that once he was in his own territory again, he was virtually untouchable. When he returned to the island, he would have to come with an escort, but that did not trouble him. Jason Sperks could blow all he wanted to, the deed for the land would be in Jack's hand by nightfall, and that was the important thing.

Jack crossed back over the hard, with the seagulls carking overhead, and the lean, narrow-faced lurchers chasing after any that landed on the mud. He let the dogs enjoy themselves: they had earned their play. Perhaps he would take them chasing hares tomorrow if he had an hour to spare. They deserved a blood run after today.

A grey heron went up as he crossed the salt marsh paths, and then landed again further to the north, where an area known locally as 'the dengies' lay. This was marshland which the Dutch engineers had not been able to drain, and salty old hermits lived there in the rotting hulls of stranded boats. They were wary of strangers, and were dangerous if approached by people unknown to them.

When Jack reached the house it was almost noon. He had gone by way of his mussel beds, and had Jiz Fowler mark the document as a witness to the scratched cross of the widow Jenkins.

Molly came out of the house to meet him. 'Would you have some dinner, master?' she said, wiping her hands on her apron. 'There's good rabbit stew on the fire.'

'Yes I shall, Molly, if you please. And take a generous helping for yourself, of course. It's a fine day, isn't it? A fine day.'

Her eyes sparkled at this uncommon gesture. While she could eat as she pleased of the household fare once the men had taken their fill, it was rare that Jack took the time to converse with her.

'Yes, it be, an' the river mists be gone away with the sun, an' everythin' ...' she chattered on.

Jack said no more, but strode into the house, and ordered Meg to help him off with his boots, a service which Molly would gladly have done had she been a minute earlier, but which Meg hated, because the black-and-grey slimy mud, which smelt of shellfish that had been rotting since the Creation, would work itself into the creases of her hands and stay there for a week.

After a change of boots and some rabbit stew, Jack ordered Molly to fetch him a horse from the Cherry Tree. He intended to ride to Chelmsford that very afternoon, to register the land in his own name before Jason Sperks got it into his head that he could do something to stop it.

Chapter Three

Kate Fernlee was fascinated by the history of the district in which she had been born and bred. She loved to hear stories of the past, embellished and embroidered in the telling over the years until truth became inseparable from fiction. But she also sought more reliable accounts of the region's past, and for these she turned to the men of learning, who visited East Anglia to observe the wildlife and to draw and paint in the area. John Constable, the famous artist from the north of the region who had died only last year, had travelled there to paint the ruins of Hadleigh Castle, had even eaten Fernlee oysters. Kate was not afraid to talk with such men, who were seldom unwilling to pass on to this comely but barely educated oyster girl what knowledge they had in their possession.

She learned that the oyster beds had been part of the Roche since the Romans first established them on arriving in what must have been to the legionaries a depressingly bleak and godless land. No doubt, said one of Kate's young informants, there were suicides amongst the soldiers when they were told they had to remain in occupation of the grey flatlands, where the mists obscured the sun and thick estuary mud sucked a man to his death, but the oyster beds remained. It would seem that oyster bars had been an off-duty haunt of the Roman soldier, for even now, Essexmen digging for one reason or another often came upon heaps of shells where an ancient oyster bar had once stood.

Throughout the ages oysters had served, along with other shellfish, to provide the poor of the region with a staple diet. Then, as the South End of Prittlewell became popular with wealthy visitors from London and the counties – especially when the Prince Regent relegated his Princess Caroline there to a house fronting the wide estuary of the Thames – oysters became required food on the tables of the rich, and with the new and rapidly growing railways, even inland people could now be provided with fresh seafood.

The week was almost over for Simon and Kate, and they were now three days into October. Simon was to leave the following morning, but

Kate still had her work to tend to, laying new oyster beds ready for the next summer. It was necessary to corral sections of the river, so that during the breeding season the baby oyster spats did not swim off up or down river, looking for a place to attach themselves and grow into adult molluscs. Kate had to layer the bottom of the corrals either with shells or stones, and as Simon sat on the dyke watching her, she explained to him the reasons behind the task.

'If oyster spats settle on sand or mud, there's no place for them to grip on to – and if fine grit works its way into the hinges, they can't open and close to feed and they'll die.'

Simon, who had eaten oysters all his life, was completely ignorant about how they bred, what they ate, and virtually every aspect of their life cycle. She had showed him how neatly the upper valve, or half shell, fitted into the lower one. When he had eaten them at the table, he had had no idea of up or down, and indeed would not have been interested. A diner's curiosity ended with shucking the oyster and swallowing the edible part.

'Do you have to help them breed?' he asked, quite innocently.

She looked at him quickly and laughed. 'No, they know how to do that all by themselves, same as we do.'

She was standing knee-deep in water, with her dress tied up in a knot around her thighs. When she had begun working, she had been standing in only six inches of water, but now the tide was coming in, and the salt river swirled around her legs. Her arms were wet and dripping as she toiled below the surface.

Seeing her standing there, like some water nymph just emerged from the waves, her auburn hair glinting like burnished copper in the weak October sun, Simon felt weak with love to the very bottom of his soul. Not for the first time he wondered what he was doing, chasing half-way around the world after some kind of respectability, when he should be here with his Kate. Yet he recognised in himself an insecurity – though he did not call it such – because of his family history.

They were smugglers, the Wentworths, and before that they had been pirates. His ancestors had sailed with Sir Henry Morgan, the seventeenth-century Welsh buccaneer, who was eventually made governor of Jamaica for his unofficial raids against the Spanish colonies. Subsequent sea rovers were not so highly regarded by their kings and queens, for they preyed on ships of nations friendly to the English, and did not shrink from sinking craft flying the Red Duster of the British Merchant Navy. Some of them were caught and hanged.

Given this heritage, it was not surprising that Simon felt a need to prove himself a worthy man and good citizen, but it was tearing his heart in two.

While he was thus immersed in melancholy thought, a man came along the top of the dyke, and he too paused to stare at the sight of the copper-headed girl in the water. Kate was seemingly unaware of the attention she was receiving from another quarter, but Simon broke his reverie to feel a pang of annoyance at witnessing another man appraising his wife-to-be, especially with her legs in view.

'Can we help you, Mr Rockmansted?' he asked.

Jack Rockmansted, his lurchers at his heels, broke his gaze and looked around to see Simon. He slapped his boot with a stick he was carrying, and shook his head. 'No, I need no help from you, Mr Wentworth, thank you kindly.' With that the mussel farmer moved on, striding along the top of the dyke towards Stambridge.

Simon glared after him, still rankled by the way in which Jack Rockmansted had been looking at Kate. Not for the first time Simon felt a pang of jealousy shiver through him: while he trusted his Kate, there were many men who would like to take her away from him. He felt a little under siege, and wondered whether he should marry her before he left the shores of Britain rather than on his return. Yet he still felt that gnawing sense of unworthiness that he must dispel before he could feel she was getting the man she deserved. Captain Haines had given Simon his chance, despite his family history, and it was now up to him to make good.

'I leave tomorrow, Kate,' he said.

She looked up and flushed with unhappiness. 'I know.'

'We should say goodbye this afternoon, for I still have some things to do before I go.'

Her blue eyes widened a little, and he guessed she was making an effort not to cry. She came out of the river: the brown water was beginning to swirl through the birch wickerwork corral in earnest now. When she had begun the work earlier in the day, the river had been a thin, sea-bound sliver of fresh water not over a yard wide, a silver stream in the middle of two curving banks of mud some two hundred yards across. Now it was in full flood, rushing blindly upstream, as it flowed inland with the whole force of the mighty ocean behind it. Soon the heavier salt water would be running beneath the lighter fresh water, with a brackish layer between where the two intermingled and became one.

Kate untied her frock, letting it fall to her ankles, and took Simon's hand. She knew what she wanted to do, and had planned it for a few days. She led him along the dyke towards a hut that belonged to a local marsh farmer.

She had layered the floor inside with fresh hay, and now, with the slightly bemused Simon in tow, she entered the hut.

It smelled good inside, of dry grasses and timber. There was a warm, cosy feeling about it. When she closed the door, a gentle light came through thin cracks between the planks. Kate's legs were trembling violently as she lay on the soft, cushioning hay, and tugged at Simon's hand so that he joined her at her side. He took her in his arms and kissed her eyebrows, her cheeks, her salty lips. A little slow in such matters, for he was a very young man, Simon now realised what she wanted of him.

'Kate,' he whispered in her ear, 'are you sure about this, darlin'? I shall be gone away, if something happens, and not able to do you right.'

'I don't care.' Her face felt hot, aflame. 'You can right any wrongs when you come home. And how can it be wrong, my dearest Simon, my beautiful man, when we are so much in love?'

'Some would say so . . .'

But he was now too far gone to oppose something he had no real wish to fight against. Kate was like a burning brand in his arms. They caressed each other for a while, until their passion overpowered them, and they could not find enough of each other to hold. She wanted to melt into him so that she could travel with him wherever he went over the seas.

'Be gentle with me, Simon,' she said.

'Oh, my beautiful girl, my beautiful girl,' he whispered, and then they blended like the salt and fresh waters of the river estuary, to become one warm flow.

Simon and Kate left the hut, and strolled back to the village past the church. Kate's feelings were in a turmoil. She had looked forward to this lovemaking for some time, and while it had not disappointed her, it was now over. She had formed it as a kind of barrier against contemplating Simon's leaving, deliberately not thinking about life beyond making love with Simon, her thoughts directed entirely towards this one perfect point in time, as if life stopped immediately afterwards.

Now she was facing the *afterwards*, against which she had been protecting herself, and it was not pleasant. She wanted to weep her heart out, desperately, for she felt such an agony of sadness and hurt that it was eroding her soul. She was angry, too, with him, for going when he should be staying with her. She felt an urge to tear into him with her hands, berate him with her tongue.

Instead, for his sake, she had at least to appear calm. They could not part with a terrible scene, which he would have to carry with him for two years, and which she would want to remould a million times while he was away. To give way to the tumult of feelings would be to suffer much longer-lasting regret later, that she had not been more in control when it mattered the most.

'I don't feel any different,' she said, 'not much.'

'I do,' he said, quietly. 'I feel like a prince, not a common jack tar. I can't believe we are just ordinary folk, Kate, for we seem so special . . .'

'That's just love does that. Everybody feels like that, so I'm told.'

'Well, it's good. I hope everybody *does* get the chance to feel it, for it would be a poor life without. Can you imagine dying and not having loved like this? Why, it's so wonderful, I think I have died, and am in heaven with an angel.'

She laughed, in spite of herself. 'You're getting too poetical, Simon Wentworth. When we've done it for the thousandth time, *then* you can come to me and say such things.'

'And so I shall,' he replied, earnestly. 'I think I shall see you for ever with the hay caught in your hair . . . It's a picture I can carry with me always.'

They said their last farewells standing in the tall grasses of the dyke near Kate's home, wrapped in each other's arms. To one side of them lay the river, full and brown, running seawards now that the tide was on the retreat. On the other side was a vast flatland of salt marsh, the October winds chasing shadows through the plain of reeds. The skies were dark, with heavy grey clouds rolling past overhead.

'Goodbye, my darling Kate,' Simon said. 'I don't really have the words . . . I love you terrible hard and there won't be a moment when you're not in my thoughts.'

Kate wanted to cling to him, hold him there, not let him go, but she sensed his restlessness. She wanted these moments to last for ever and Simon wanted to be gone quickly so that he could be home the sooner. That was the difference between them.

'Just a little longer,' she said, holding him tightly.

Inside she felt a hollowness growing that she knew would not be filled again until Simon returned. She knew though that if she made a great fuss and wept, it would upset him too much, so she tried to smile, hoping her expression did not look as stiff as candlewax.

She felt him stroke her hair, trying to brush away her anxieties, but they were not so easily removed.

'You will look after yourself – don't do anything silly – don't be brave – just *come home*.'

Kate clutched him as if he were going to the gallows. She noticed rain on the horizon, a slanting darkness. It seemed an ominous sign.

'I'll come home, don't you worry about that,' he said.

There was one last kiss, then he peeled her arms from around him and strode away. She watched him walk all the way along the dyke, until he came to the place where the grass wall fell away to a narrow path. Here he dropped out of sight, without turning once.

'Simon Wentworth,' whispered Kate, the tears flowing, 'why didn't you look back?'

Then suddenly, as if he had heard her, he appeared again: a tall dark figure in the distance. He stood for a moment, a still form against a back curtain of rain, to give a final wave. Then he was gone, leaving Kate with some small, sweet memories, and a grey two years ahead of her.

She woke the next morning, her pillow wet with tears after a troubled night. When Kate plummeted to despair, it was a heavy fall, but it never lasted, and already she felt determined to continue life as best she could. Kate had too much sense to mourn and mope when there was nothing she could do to change things. There was work to be done. Kate knew she had a core of toughness which affected her deepest, most tender feelings.

As if in tune with her mixed emotions, the rain was coming down like lead shot this morning, clattering hard on the roof tiles. The Fernlee cottage was built in the Dutch style, with the red-tiled roof having two smaller ridges, one on either side of the main ridge, which dropped almost vertically towards the ground, stopping just above the ground-floor windows. The upstairs windows were set in the roof itself. The house was rented from the local squire, John Pritchard, who owned most of the property in and around the mudflats. It was not the Buckingham Palace that the young Queen Victoria had been the first monarch to move into, just last year, but for working-class estuary folk it was a grand house.

Kate had her own small room adjoining the one which her sisters shared. There was not a great deal of furniture in it, but she had a small pine dressing-table with a mirror, left her by her grandmother, and a cane-back chair worn shiny with use on the seat. There was a bed, of course, which her father had made himself, also of pine. A horsehair mattress lay between her and the pine planks, as hard as a biscuit; but it was all she had ever known, and she did not think it uncomfortable.

She rose at dawn and brushed her hair vigorously before the oval mirror. Once she paused to inspect a brown stain on her face, only to find it was a fleck on the looking-glass where the quicksilver was peeling off.

She poured cold water, sometimes frozen solid in the winter months, from a china jug into a bowl, and washed herself. She was unusual in carrying out these ablutions every morning, but she had heard it was good for the complexion, and hoped one day that her efforts at scrubbing her skin would result in the removal of those wretched freckles that formed a starry band across the bridge of her nose.

When Kate was working and not seeing Simon, she tied her hair back with a strip of rag. This she did today. Then she pulled on an old frock, a faded blue that had once been the colour of cornflowers, but had paled after many washings. She had shoes, but she rarely wore them until the frosts came. Her toilet complete, she felt much better, and locked out of her mind the thought that Simon would at that moment be walking through the rain to Rochford turnpike, to catch the coach that would take him away from her.

Finally she pulled back the covers of the bed, to air it, before rapping on the wall and calling 'Time to get up, you sleepyheads!'

She waited until she heard groans coming from her sisters' bedroom, then left her own room and went down the narrow wooden staircase to the room below. Her father was already up and pulling on his boots. Kate raked the fire and found glowing embers from the night before. She put some kindling on and, once the sticks were aflame, followed this with a dry log. Soon the fire was large enough to cook on, and she hung a kettle of water over the heat.

'Edward needs his breakfast,' said her father. He was always a grouch in the mornings, which was why Kate refused to speak to him. He lit his pipe, ignoring the fact that she coughed at the smoke, waving it away impatiently.

'Edward will get his breakfast in a minute,' said Kate, turning to rebutton his waistcoat, which he had failed to do correctly, and straighten a bent-under collar. 'First things first, Father.'

'Your mother allus made her husband breakfast first – it *were* a first thing in them days.'

'That's not true, Father, and you know it. I do things in the same order as Mother did them, for she was the one who learned me how to do them. Now, will you have some cheese and bread? The bread is a little hard, but I shall soften it with some milk first.'

'If it's food, you won't find Edward complaining,' he said, which was not true either, for he loved to protest at anything and everything, especially in front of his daughters.

The two girls came down then: Liz, sleepy-eyed and frowzy-looking;

Sarah much fresher, with a bloom to her cheeks. As they ate breakfast, Kate gave them their orders for the day.

'Liz, you shall stay and clean house, for the squire is coming next week to see we are keeping his property in good order.'

Liz groaned. 'Why do I have to do all the skivvying? There's dust gets into my throat and makes me ill.'

'You're the youngest, and the youngest has to stay home and look after the house.'

Liz protested, quite rightly, 'But I'll *always* be the youngest, for there will be no more children.'

Kate sympathised with this objection. 'That's true, and once you reach fifteen, then we'll hire someone to do the housework and you can help with the oysters, but not till then.'

This seemed to satisfy Liz for the moment, though she felt obliged to add, 'Well, if I fall sick and die of something horrible, it'll not be my fault.'

Kate smiled at her young sister. 'If you die of too much house dust, then we'll not blame you for it, Liz, you can be sure. Now,' she said, turning to Sarah, 'I'll take two baskets along to the big houses on the seafront. Sarah must take another two to the trading post, and Father, you must take the bulk on your waggon to Rochford market. Sixteen baskets in all.'

'When I've taken the two baskets to the trading post,' said Sarah to Liz, 'I'll hurry back and help you with the cleaning, dearest Liz, for I know how you hate it so.'

Sarah was one of those girls who wants a household to be full of harmony and light, with everyone happy and no sign of discontent anywhere. Kate knew her middle sister was on a lost cause with Liz in the home, though, for the youngest of the sisters would complain about peace and tranquillity if she could find nothing else to criticise, for she was never satisfied. Liz was always moaning about how dull she found Paglesham, but when sent to a cousin at Canewdon for six weeks while Kate was ill the previous summer, she wanted nothing else but to return to her native village. Once back, all she could talk about to her sisters was how wonderful Canewdon was, and how she wished she could go and stay with her cousin again.

Sarah, on the other hand, fretted if people were unhappy, and spent her time trying to make them comfortable. She fussed over her father too much, and was in part responsible for him sinking into himself, for she was like her mother in this and many other ways, and reminded Edward too much of his wife.

The orders having been given, however, the family set to with their various tasks.

The Fernlee oyster beds were situated in Paglesham Creek, off the River Roche. The Roche, which feeds the River Crouch just before it meets the sea, is the smallest river in the region. Some few miles north of the Roche and Crouch lies the River Blackwater, the largest waterway in the area. The whole shoreline between is prime oyster country. Someone wrote in 1594: *Some part of the sea shore of Essex yealdeth the beste oysters in England . . . I take it to be the shore which lieth betwene St Peter's-on-the-Wall Chappell by the Blackwater and Crowche creeke on the Denge hundred.*

The nearest oyster company in the region was the one owned by Mr and Mrs John Hawkins, situated on the north shore of the Crouch estuary, which boasted ten boats and thirty or forty men. Its stock of half-ware and brood was about 14,000 tubs, each tub containing around 2,000 oysters. Most of their oysters were exported to the continent. There were other companies along the Crouch and running up through the creeks to the Blackwater, of varying sizes.

The Fernlee fishery was one of the smallest of the oyster concerns, since the Roche had not been developed as an oyster river before the Fernlees began their beds. Traditionally the Roche was a mussel farming river and there was some resentment towards the Fernlees for breaking with that tradition and farming oysters instead. In his younger years Edward Fernlee had never considered tradition to be worth worrying about, and thumbed his nose at those musselmen who looked at him sour-faced in the market place of Billingsgate.

Kate and Sarah went immediately to the oyster beds, where despite the rain three casual workers were gathering in the oysters and filling baskets. The beds themselves were not large, being rectangle corrals about ten-by-ten yards. The work was not difficult since there was not a vast area to cover.

Kate's job at that time of year was mainly to get the oysters to a local market, leaving the casual labour to tend to the beds. She had marked which beds to harvest the previous day, when she was there with Simon, and the labourers knew exactly from where the oysters needed to be gathered.

Using a handcart, the two sisters began ferrying large wickerwork baskets of oysters along the dyke to the road. It was difficult work in the wet, for the narrow dyke path was turning to soft clay, which stuck to the wheels of the cart. Every so often they had to stop and scrape the wheels clean with a piece of slate to prevent them from clogging.

Both girls were soaked to the skin within half an hour, and Kate was afraid Sarah would catch a chill, but she needed her help and dared not send her home.

'When you get to the trading post, be sure to dry out in front of the fire,' Kate told her sister.

Sarah said, 'I'm not cold,' but failed to prevent a visible shiver from running through her body even as she spoke.

While they were hauling their load, they saw a man coming along the dyke. Kate noticed a badge on his coat: it was in the shape of a silver oar. She felt a jolt of alarm go through her on recognising not the person but the office he represented.

'It's the water-serjeant,' she whispered to Sarah. 'I wonder what he wants.'

Kate knew that this visit from an officer from the Court of Conservancy might be without any definite purpose – just a stroll along the banks of his beat – but she could not suppress a feeling of unease. He carried with him always an ancient silver oyster, which represented the standard size below which oysters might not be taken from the water.

If he stopped to check the girls' harvest and found any undersized oysters, they would be in serious trouble. Kate had no reason to think there were any illegal oysters in her baskets, but nevertheless the water-serjeant's presence was worrying. He was the law along the river, and if he felt that any wrongdoing was taking place, whether innocently or otherwise, he could come down hard on those who had attracted his attention.

The water-serjeant passed them by, merely glancing down at their baskets, and tipped his finger to his cap.

Kate and Sarah glanced at each other, the relief evident in their expressions, then continued along the dyke with their load.

Edward had been along to the stables by the Plough and Sail Inn, and had hitched Damson, their gelding, to the waggon. When the girls arrived he loaded their baskets of oysters on to the back.

Once the waggon was fully loaded, Sarah took two baskets back to the trading post in the village on the handcart, while Edward and Kate climbed up on the waggon and set off for Rochford market.

They reached the market square at eight o'clock, and unloaded the waggon of all but two baskets. Then Kate left her father and drove Damson and the waggon to the seafront beyond Prittlewell. There she went from house to house, visiting the kitchens at the rear and speaking with the all-powerful cooks.

'Is cook there?' she would ask, when a boot-boy or scullery maid answered the door. Then she would wait for some imperious woman to appear. Often they would be kind, even jolly women, but cooks were used to power and responsibility, and as such expected to be treated almost as royally as the owners of the house themselves. Occasionally the cook would be a barbarian thinly disguised as a civilised woman. Such cooks should have been leading hordes of screaming Vandals and Goths against effete continental cities, but were prepared to settle for insulting a young oyster girl from the villages, whether they wanted her wares for the kitchen or not.

By three o'clock the rain had stopped, and Kate was invited into one kitchen to dry off by a stove. She chatted with the staff as they went about their various tasks, and Cook ordered one of the maids to give her a hot drink.

'Thank you, Cook,' said Kate. 'I could do with something.'

'You'm more courage than sense, young lady, goin' out in the rain like that, a-getting soaked through,' said the cook, as she chopped dried parsley with a sharp knife.

'Have to earn a living,' smiled Kate.

'A living, yes, but you'm going to earn your death if you goes about catching pewmonia.'

'Well,' replied Kate, staring around the kitchen, 'this is certainly the best place to be on a cold wet day, in a nice, well-kept kitchen by a warm stove. It must be pleasant to be so comfortable, even if you have to work long hours.'

'We thinks so,' chirruped a maid, taking a quick look at the cook for approval.

Cook grunted as she hacked and sliced.

'Long hours is right, young miss. I been up in the dark since I were a scullery girl, lightin' fires at five in the mornin'. There's not many nights I get to bed on this side of midnight, neither. At least you'm free out of doors, with your baskets of oysters to sell, not chained to no kitchen sixteen hours out of twenty-four, comfy or not.'

Kate knew this was true: she herself would hate to be at the beck and call of some grand lady with nothing but whims to occupy her mind. However, she did not say this to the cook, who was waiting for her to drop a little flattery and a few compliments.

'Well, I envy *you*,' Kate said. 'You keep a very neat kitchen, Cook. It's so *clean*. Far better than most I see in my travels . . .'

Cook was pleased with this last remark. She lifted her head and pursed her lips. 'Oh, there's some dirty kitchens about, that's for certain sure. It's a wonder there's not more in the way of typhus diseases spread about, what with the dirt some of these people cook their food in. I could tell you some stories . . .'

By the time she left for home, an hour later, Kate had sold all her oysters.

Kate felt the day had gone quite well, despite certain setbacks and disappointments due to the arrogance of the staff in some houses. That was to be expected, though, when dealing with the servants of gentry. If it had not been for the rain, it would have been one of her good days.

There was a soft grey light falling on the farmlands, picking out the solitary trees on the landscape which were now losing their leaves. Birds were finding themselves in lonely positions and swiftly seeking out roosts for the evening. Kate contemplated this world around her, while Damson trotted along at his own happy pace, needing only the flick of the reins occasionally to remind him of his direction.

Kate felt she had coped with her first day without Simon extremely well. It was only now that she had time to think that a lump formed in her throat. It worried her that she had managed to block out the sadness so effectively during the working day. Perhaps she was just an unfeeling person who could not really love someone? No, that was untrue. It was just that she had an ability to push away unpleasant emotions while she was busy at tasks, and that could only be a blessing for her at the moment. She reminded herself that she must keep as busy as possible over the next few months.

Yes, the day had gone well. The business could survive quite all right without Kate plying her oyster trade amongst the big seaside houses, but certainly this experiment with new clientele was doing them no harm. Edward would have been happy to keep to the traditional ways of selling his oysters: at the trading posts, the town marketplace and the inns. Kate, however, felt they should try new ventures, and some of her ideas were helping to expand the business. She was certainly satisfied with the results. There were times when Kate had to be in the oyster farm, laying new beds with the hired help, marking out the next day's harvest or spreading spats, but selling was her main work and she enjoyed it, for all its vagaries.

The dusk was coming in, and she wished to stop for no one on the way, but when she saw a pale, slim young man with silken blond hair, she felt impelled to offer him a lift on the waggon. He looked so weary and footsore and stared at Kate in such a dejected manner as she passed him by. When she looked back, he had stopped to sit under an oak and was taking off one of his shoes to empty it of grit into the ditch. There was an air of despondency about him with which Kate, in her own present mood, could immediately sympathise. Thin and white against the dark hedge, he seemed pathetically inadequate to the task of walking to the next village.

'Where are you going?' she called to him.

He looked up and Kate saw a shadow of hope in his eyes.

'Paglesham Church School.'

'Well, don't look so glum,' she said. 'Would you like a ride?'

He did not smile. 'I see little to be cheerful about, but under present circumstances a ride would help my physical stress, if not my soul.'

Well there's an answer that begs a volume of questions, thought Kate. This young man had a tortured spirit, it would appear, and it roused her natural curiosity. Perhaps she could help in some way? It would take her mind off her own emotional problems if she could. There was nothing like the misery of others to make your own shrink.

On reaching the waggon he looked up at her. 'My grateful thanks,' he said, giving Kate his first smile. 'My feet are just about worn to the stumps.'

He looked slightly distracted, as if he were somewhere else. Then he held up a hand as though he were waiting for someone to pull him up. Kate was having none of it, though it amused her, and she used the opportunity to study him closer.

There was an air about him of the delicate gentleman, unused to doing things for himself, and certainly his slim, waxen-looking fingers appeared never to have had a harder task than turning the pages of a book. If he wanted a ride he had to climb up himself. There seemed nothing seriously wrong with his arms, even if he was frail.

Come on my fine lad, she thought, *heave-ho*.

Eventually he broke out of his trance, realising that no assistance was coming his way; only then did he reach up to pull himself into the seat beside her. Once his weight was settled on the empty sacks on the wooden seat, Damson started to move off.

Chapter Four

As they travelled the dirt road between Stambridge and Paglesham, the young man told Kate his name was the Reverend Johann Haagan, and that he was the new teacher for the church school which lay in the centre of the triangle formed by Stambridge, Canewdon and Paglesham villages.

He did not look like a clergyman to Kate, who had been used to the fusty old men usually put out to pasture in this backwater of Essex. Young pastors avoided being sent to estuary country, a move which killed their careers stone dead, and certainly none had applied for posts before now. The Reverend William Josiah Potts, who managed the services of Paglesham church, had been there since he was seventy-five; he was now eighty-three. When he walked, he creaked like a windjammer in a squall. The priest who had taught at the church school for the poor, Gabriel Groat, had died six months previously at the age of seventy-seven. This young man was obviously here to replace the Reverend Groat, whom the children had affectionately called Billy Goat.

Johann Haagan was a slight figure of a man, no taller than five feet six inches and as thin as a gypsy's dog. His straight blond hair flopped over a pale, not unhandsome face, but it was his hands that kept recalling themselves to Kate's attention. They were slim, waxen lilies, the stamens long and tapered, which fluttered before his face in the breeze of his breath.

'I used to live in Ashingdon as a child. My forefathers were Dutch, as you can guess by my name. I was sent off to school in London. Then I went to Cambridge University. After Cambridge I spent some two years with friends I had made at college, but it's time I started to earn my own living.' He said the last few words in such a way as to make Kate suppose that they had been given birth elsewhere, probably in the mouths of his parents. 'So I haven't lived in my home county for some time now, not since I was eight years of age.'

'Now you're the new schoolteacher.'

Kate flicked the reins to tell Damson she wanted him to take the right fork, towards home, but he needed little encouragement. If left to his own devices he would have chosen that road anyway, in preference to the Canewdon one.

Johann smiled at her: it was a warm friendly smile.

'Yes, a reluctant one I'm afraid. You guessed it by my previous tone.' He hunched inside his coat, which seemed too large for him, the collar coming half-way up the back of his head. 'My friends at university, well, they are gentlemen, most of them rich. They spend their time at sport – hunting, shooting, wagering. They invited me to their fine big houses, let me ride their hunters, showed me how to fire a gun. It's difficult to resist that kind of life when someone is offering it to you.'

Kate saw Damson eyeing the lush grass by the ditch and nudged him with her toe. 'C'mon Damson, old boy, move those legs – there's hay enough in the stable when we get home.'

'Damson? Isn't that a girl's name?' asked Johann.

'Horses don't know girls' from boys' names,' said Kate, laughing at his pedantry, 'and probably wouldn't care if they did. Besides,' she added frankly, 'he's a gelding, so he's not really one or the other.'

Johann gave this attractive young country girl a sideways glance. It was not a remark he would have expected from a young lady, from one of the sisters of his friends. Even an indirect reference to sexual matters would have been considered shocking.

'So,' she said, continuing their previous conversation, 'did your fine friends get tired of you, living off them like a limpet?'

Johann frowned at this remark and gave her another quick look out of the corner of his eye. He was not used to being spoken to in such a manner, particularly by someone who was clearly below his station, someone who should show him respect. It unnerved rather than annoyed him, bringing forth the same kind of insecurities he felt with his rich friends. He felt he should admonish her in some way, but that would have been a little churlish since she was giving him a ride.

Kate, who had caught his prim glance and had recognised his disapproval, was not a woman given to flummery, however, and spoke as she found. It amused her to think that he was so easily disconcerted, though she tried not to show it in her expression. It was one thing to remark on his behaviour, but quite another to have the bad manners to reveal that she thought him rather pompous.

Johann finally broke the silence. 'You're very direct. On reflection I think I find that refreshing rather than impolite. You do it with such candour. Yes, my friends wearied of me. I committed the cardinal sin. I fell in love with one of their sisters.'

'What's wrong with falling in love?' Kate asked.

The night was well entrenched now, and though they had a lantern swinging from the side of the cart, Damson had to go slowly for fear of ending up in the ditch. Kate peered through the darkness, her knowledge of the road so good she guided the horse almost by instinct.

'There's nothing wrong with falling in love,' Johann said, 'it's with whom you choose to do it that matters.'

Kate smiled before replying, 'People don't *choose* the ones they fall in love with – it's done for them.'

Johann gave out a long, tortured sigh. 'By God, I suppose. Matches made in heaven. Well, however it's done, one of my class does not presume to announce his intention of paying court to a member of the aristocracy. The lady in question was willing, but her brother, damn his eyes, threatened to shoot my brains out. Rather than cause a terrible row, I bid the lady *adieu*.'

'You couldn't have loved her very much,' said Kate. 'My Simon would fight tooth and nail if anyone ever threatened to part us.'

'You're married?'

'No, but promised to be.'

'And where is this Simon?'

Kate reddened, realising she had led herself into a trap. 'He's ... he's gone away to sea.'

Johann nodded gravely. 'And this is the man that would fight tooth and nail for you to stay together?'

Fiercely, she replied, 'We have to earn our keep, Mr Haagan. We don't have any rich friends.'

He gave out an amused snort. 'I suppose I deserved that.'

They were silent for a few minutes, then Kate tried to make amends, hating strained atmospheres almost as much as Sarah did.

'Did you love the lady very much?' she asked.

'Well, I loved her enough to die for her,' he sighed, 'but not enough to kill for her. You see, I was the best shot among 'em. I may look a little frail, but I found myself to be a natural marksman. I can shoot the eyes out of a cock pheasant at thirty yards. If one kills a nobleman, even in a duel, it affects the whole family. My father would have been hounded by the authorities, my mother would have been distraught, and I would have brought ruin on us all.

'No, it was best to leave with dignity, the lady at the casement window weeping for our lost love, the brother with the germ of guilt which will hopefully grow into a disease and eat through his heart – and my parents none the wiser.'

Kate nodded gravely. 'I think you did the right thing.'

'But where am I now? A teacher of a school of brats in the middle of nowhere. A learned man among Philistines. I may never love again, that is certain.'

'There are plenty of pretty women about here.'

'Of that I am sure, for I have one sitting next to me, of the highest excellence of beauty,' he said gallantly. 'A nonpareil. But I'm afraid I could never marry an estuary girl.'

Kate was so astonished she almost kicked him off the cart for his insolence. Who on earth did he think he was, this feeble creature whose body was made of candlewax? What woman worth her salt, she thought furiously, would want to marry such a man, be she trigger, cockler or the rat-catcher's daughter?

When they reached the schoolhouse, she stopped the cart to let the Reverend Haagan down. He took his bags and looked up at her in the lamplight.

'I did not make a very good impression, did I? It's my arrogance, you see, it gets in the way every time. Thank you for the ride, Miss Fernlee, and forgive my impertinence. I have told you all about my occupation –' he gestured towards the dark schoolhouse – 'but I know nothing of yours. The baskets smell of fish. Do you supply the fishmongers?'

'Yes, but not with fish, with oysters.'

His eyes showed surprise. 'You collect oysters from these waters?'

'We farm them, Reverend. The Fernlees have had oyster beds here for as long as anyone can remember.'

'I see. I should like to see the beds, sometime. I've often eaten oysters, but have never stopped to consider where they came from. Perhaps I've consumed some of yours?'

She smiled at him. 'I don't know, but I'll be glad to show you over the beds, when we're not busy.'

'Thank you. I should like to talk to you again sometime, when I am in a better mood and less likely to make a fool of myself. If ever you need a friend, you will find one surrounded by grubby little pupils, picking the wax out of their ears, and paying no attention to their pompous master. Goodbye for now.'

With that he turned and walked away, a strange young man Kate thought, but one she felt she could come to like. He saw through himself clearly, which was not an easy thing for a man to do, and was ready to condemn his own faults. This, in her eyes, was worth a great deal. The remark about the estuary girls still rankled, but she was willing to forgive him for it, now that she saw he knew his thoughtless comment had been insulting. There were men who would not have deigned to talk to an oyster girl, let alone opened up their lives to her. She saw that the Reverend Johann Haagan was a man who liked to talk, about himself, about anything, and for this reason he no doubt often stumbled over his own tongue and said things which might be offensive to his listeners.

'I shouldn't wonder he'll get his bottom kicked if he goes into the inn,' she muttered to herself, as she spurred Damson into motion again. 'Come on, old thing,' she said to the horse, 'we both want our supper. Let's do the last mile as quick as we can, eh?'

There was something else about Johann Haagan though, which would have troubled her had he been a good friend. There was something that he was holding back, hiding almost, behind the talk, behind the easy manners. Kate had an instinct for these things, and she felt that Mr Haagan had a secret to keep.

'C'mon Damson,' she muttered, flicking the reins, as she heard the cold bark of a dog fox out in the fields. 'Let's get home to some supper.'

The schoolhouse was in darkness, but there was a row of cottages nearby which Johann guessed were tied to the local farm. He went to one of these and knocked on the door. A male voice called out, 'Who's a-knockin'?'

Johann would have felt very silly talking through a stout wooden door, so he rapped again, sharply.

Eventually some bolts were drawn, and a short, rugged-looking man stood before him, squinting at him. 'Yus?'

'My name is the Reverend Johann Haagan. I'm the new teacher for the school. I've just arrived and there is no light on in the schoolhouse. I wonder if I could borrow a lamp, just for a short while.'

The man stared at him for a long time, as if the question were extremely complicated, then he nodded. 'We'm only got the one lamp.'

'A candle would do.'

'We an't got no candles, neither. Oi'll tell her to wait a bit in the dark, she'm just gettin' the little 'uns to bed, and oi'll take you over to yourn meself.'

'That's extremely kind of you.'

Johann was left staring into the cottage as the man went back inside to fetch their only lamp. Shadows were moving about inside the one-roomed dwelling as the woman of the house was putting her young ones into various corners of the room. Johann was astounded at the poverty he saw. There were no beds. The only furniture appeared to be a rickety-looking table in the centre of the room. Potato sacks were strewn about on the floor, some of which were being used as bedding. A young tyke grinned at him from the far left corner through a film of grime, the detail of his features lost in dirt and shadow. He appeared to be chewing on some kind of raw beet.

'You the noo schoolie?' said the youngster. 'Me an' my brothers don't go to school.'

Johann nodded at the boy, as the father growled, 'Keep a still tongue. He don't want none of your gab.'

Finally the lamp was brought, and when Johann inquired the man's name, the other replied that he was a 'farm worker' as if this was sufficient information for the time being, thank you very much. They went round to the back of the schoolhouse, where the living quarters were situated, and found the door was unlocked. Johann was relieved, for he had no key, and had in truth been expecting someone to be there to meet him, a housekeeper at the very least.

Giving Johann the lamp, the farm worker stayed outside, refusing to enter. Johann found a Welsh dresser, which happily contained the stubs of several old candles. He lit two of these from a taper off the lamp, then returned the light to the farm worker with his thanks. Without another word, the other man went off into the night.

In the light of the candles, Johann began unpacking his bag. It was then that he noticed a folded piece of paper on the floor by the doorway. Stooping down to pick it up, he realised it was a letter which someone had pushed through the gap under the door.

His hands began shaking as he recognised the handwriting used for the address. He broke the seal clumsily, tearing the paper in the process and, holding a candle stub in one hand, read the contents of the missive.

My Dearest Johann,
They have succeeded in wrenching us apart, but they cannot stop me loving you. At least you have not gone to the West Indies, as you threatened, but are at this place called Paglesham (such a quaint name) in Essex. Congratulations on your post as curate and schoolteacher there. I am sure you will prove worthy of any position they care to bestow upon you, my dear, and you must know that your Edwina will always remember you.
I remain, your devoted Edwina.

After a moment's reflection, Johann put the page to the candleflame, holding it steady as it was destroyed, allowing it to burn his fingers as a kind of penance. His heart was leaden. Why had she written this note to him? It was all hopeless. She was to be married to another man. It were better, he thought, that she had not known the district to which he had been sent, so that she would have no address for her communications. Too late now.

He stared around him in a desultory mood.

The two rooms were furnished sparsely but adequately, and Johann put one candle in each, and familiarised himself with his surroundings. Then he took some cooked chicken he had bought on the road, and ate it, sitting on the edge of the narrow wooden bed, staring into the flickering candleflame.

How had he been reduced to this? he thought. Was this all he had to look forward to for the next twenty, thirty years? A miserable existence as a schoolmaster in some godforsaken backwater of the salt marsh country? Why, the whole landscape looked like some bleak, inhospitable Siberian plain, the type of country which travellers hurried across, not caring to stop even for a short while. Yet people actually *lived* here, spent their whole lives here – and that girl on the cart, she spoke about it as if she actually liked the place.

He suddenly dropped the chicken bone and buried his face in his hands, feeling desolate and desperately unhappy. He wept self-indulgently for a while, until the candle in the bedroom burned down to the end of its wick, sputtered, and went out. Then he rose wearily and went into the kitchen, took the lighted stub from there, and went outside to search for the lavatory. He found a privy, a doorless sentry box some ten yards from the house, his nose more help than the candlelight. There was a hole in the ground over which he was supposed to squat. It was muddy and slippery. A short bit of sacking on a dirty piece of string served as a curtain.

On his return to the house, the candle was blown out by the wind. Some unknown creature rushed past him in the darkness, stirring the long grasses around his feet and frightening him out of his wits. He found the doorway, went inside, and then retired for the night fully clothed, hoping the dawn would bring a better day.

Kate removed Damson's harness and put him in his stall. There were other horses whinnying and stamping in the stables, and some yet to come, for it was a communal building belonging to the whole village. Only the squire's horses were stabled separately. Kate got between the shafts of Damson's waggon, pulling it up alongside the stable and covering it with a sheet of flax canvas to keep it dry. Her father had already filled Damson's hay rack with feed, and the sturdy little cob was making short work of his supper. Kate went to him and stroked his nose as he ate, whispering in his ear. He tossed his head occasionally as if he understood what was being said. Then she left him, closing all doors behind her.

Kate walked back to her cottage some thirty yards away, the soft lamplight at the window guiding her. She felt warm inside, knowing she had a family behind that window who would be pleased to see her home, especially now Simon was gone.

They were waiting supper, and immediately went into hasty prayers as she entered.

'Lord, thank'ee for the repast you put a-fore us,' chanted her father. 'Edward and his daughters are grateful. A-men.'

'A-men,' repeated Kate, as she sat down. 'Father, I think you could wait grace for me.'

'Edward is hungry.'

He and her two younger sisters immediately attacked the dabs on their plates and, after a moment's hesitation, so did Kate. Between mouthfuls, she told them how much money she had made during the day, and they in their turn provided her with accounts of their activities. All except Liz, who had been in the house all the time and who now listened with a resentful look on her face as the others talked excitedly of the day's business.

Kate told them all about the young man, the new schoolteacher, to whom she had given a lift on the waggon. Her father told her he was a little disturbed that she should offer lifts to strangers, especially on the dark roads, but Kate said she would not have stopped if he had looked a bad man.

'You can't tell bad from good these days,' said Edward. 'There are cut-throats all over, with the most gentlemanly of ways about 'em.'

'But he was so frail, Father. I could have thrown him over my shoulder.'

'Is he good-looking?' asked Liz.

'In a peaky kind of way. He's very pale.'

When she thought back on his vulnerability, Kate was sorry she had been so sharp with Reverend Haagan over certain matters. It was none of her business who his friends were and what he did with them. The poor man was likely sitting in his chair thinking she was the most insensitive female he had ever met.

'I quite liked him,' she said, 'in a way.'

Edward paused in his eating. 'Daughter o' mine, you're spoken for, I think.'

'Oh, Father, stop being so foolish. I'm talking about as friend, not as a lover.'

Liz giggled, and Sarah gave a sharp intake of breath.

Edward waved his fork. 'I won't have that kind of talk at the supper table. Anyways, a lass like you can't be friends with a young man; it don't look right. What would he want to be friends with you for anyways? You got no conversation to offer a *man*.'

Kate was indignant. 'Simon likes to talk with me.'

'Simon, pah!' said Edward. 'Simon's dewy-eyed with love-sickness, an' o' course he'll let you talk along with him now, but give it a couple o' years, and you'll be talkin' to a post, you see if you ain't.'

Kate was furious with her father. She knew women were supposed to be subordinate to men – even the law of the land attested to that – but she did not *feel* inferior in any way whatsoever. She knew that among the estuary people she could match the mind of any man. It was true that those men who had had learning – such as the new schoolteacher – could make her feel as if she knew very little about the world, but then most of the men she knew would be similarly disadvantaged. Her father, for instance, had never been more than fifty miles from Paglesham, and knew little of life beyond.

'Well, the Reverend Johann Haagan enjoyed talking with me today,' she said to Edward through gritted teeth. 'I know he did, for he showed it in his manner and his face. And if you say otherwise, Father, it'll not be right, for I was there, and you wasn't.'

The two other girls watched this exchange in silence while they ate. They were used to Kate arguing with their father, for their eldest sister had a funny temper, which sometimes overflowed. Most of the time she did as she was asked, but occasionally she dug in her heels and refused to admit she was wrong. They both knew that their father's judgement was as little to be trusted as their sister's, but men ruled the world, and even when they were wrong, you did not tell them so, but pretended they were right. Kate, however, had trouble with pretending sometimes, and often got herself into a fight with her father that she could not win.

'It's Edward's opinion that this 'ere new priest is daft, if he thinks a girl's ideas are worth listening to.'

'Father,' said Kate evenly, 'you will regret that remark, for it bites into me like a cold wind. I am only a girl when I want to be such, and at other times I am a woman full-grown and capable. You were never a match for our mother, and you won't be for me, for you can't do without someone with a head on their shoulders to manage the business.'

Edward banged his spoon down on the table, making all three girls jump in fright. 'Don't you *dare* talk to me like that, you harpy. I'm your father! Your father, dammit. Edward won't be spoke to in this manner. This is *my* house, and you're a-livin' here because of *me*. Your mother, God-rest-'er, would never have spoke to Edward like this, and she'll be a-turnin' in her grave at this moment, listening to her daughter brooking her husband.'

This last part was true. No matter how much their mother had disagreed with their father, she had always shored up his weaknesses with her strength and support. She would never have allowed her daughters to tell him he was wrong.

The two sisters were right about Kate, she could never win, for Edward never fought fair. When all else failed, he fell back on household rank and privilege. He was their father, a father moreover who invoked the image of a wrathful and dutiful mother in order to get his own way. Kate always tried to fight fair and square, and had to give way to male domination supported for generations by female love and duty. She reflected on the irony that women were their own worst enemies, before she answered, 'Sorry, Father,' and bit her lip.

Kate went to bed that night still festering inside. Her father had become the aloof wounded figure he adopted when Kate questioned his authority on anything. She in turn was expected to take the role of the ungrateful daughter for a few days, mollifying and spoiling him more than usual until he deigned to come down from his sulks.

Unable to sleep she threw back the bedcovers, then opened the window and leaned on the sill with her elbows, looking out over the dark salt marshes. The moon was on the flatlands, and the breeze sent invisible boats shimmering over the sea of reeds. Kate allowed herself a few moments of misery, wondering when she would see her beloved Simon again. She said a prayer for him, asking the Lord to send him home safe to her.

Then she put a shell around those feelings, protecting herself from them, and thought instead about the new schoolteacher. He was a funny one. Despite her angry thoughts on his eligibility, she knew that the local girls would be pointing their bonnets at him in droves for, notwithstanding his pallid appearance, he was a live one, unlike past incumbents, with a comfortable living to offer a woman.

A nightjar was churring out somewhere near the farm, and Kate wondered whether the bird was sucking the milk of the goats while the farmer was abed, as they were said to do. All else was still. Ships moved along in the distant estuary waters, their lights like jewels. There would be some without lights though, running the brandy unseen.

In the beds of reeds there were secret doings, convocations of foxes, covens of stoats and weasels, and solitary cruising owls. She knew they were all out there, even if she could not see them. And the coots and moorhens would be formed into protective rafts, while the wild ducks would have found old rabbit holes in which to hide. There were wars going on, out there, in the many creeks.

Chapter Five

Winter came to the East Anglian flatlands in the teeth of winds straight from Scandinavia, which flew across the North Sea with nothing between to act as a barrier. The marsh country suffered the frosts borne by these winds with resentment, they being foreign chills with no native right to settle in the creeks. Kate had gone to bed one evening while there had been a light-brownish hue to the landscape, and had awoken the following morning to a white glistening world, as if cold powdered glass had been sifted through the clouds during the night.

Kate looked through her bedroom window to see that the air was as clear as fine crystal. The outlines of the geese, flying down in their thousands from a severe Icelandic winter, were well-defined, even sharp. The skeins of geese came in, sometimes in ragged bunches, but more often than not in perfect V-shaped formations, to land like plumb-bobs on the mud. Kate knew that hunters would be priming their sporting guns ready to fill local larders.

Kate rose and broke the thin ice in her jug of water before pouring the contents into a ceramic bowl. As she washed, the cold water brought a tingle to her skin, which she hoped was good for her complexion. Simon, she remembered, always remarked on how beautiful her skin looked on cold days.

A jolt of sadness went through her. Simon. Where was he now? The last she had heard he was in Gibraltar. It annoyed her that she couldn't imagine him there. She knew Gibraltar was a rocky island in the Mediterranean, but she couldn't picture it. And though she could sometimes recall Simon's features, his face was often hazy in her mind. It worried her a little, this inability to call forth an accurate representation of him in her mind's eye. Shouldn't his features, as the man she loved, be vivid and strong in her memory? She felt she was failing him in some way by not being able to recall his handsome face in detail.

So, mixed with the sadness was a little guilt.

Kate had found it was best not to stop and ponder too long on such things, or she fell into a feeling of despondency which might have lead to self-pity. It was best, she had decided, to go through the days and not to reflect on times past or times to come.

It was Sunday, and after breakfast Kate, Sarah and Elizabeth walked to church along the narrow path between the fields. Their father walked along behind, talking with a neighbour. The bells rang out over the furrowed land in hard, cold tones, and along the dykes came other churchgoers. The Lord's day was recognised by most in estuary country, where life-threatening floods were but a spring tide away.

When the girls arrived, they took a pew on the left side of the church, where the light was best. Edward passed them by and went down to the front to sit with the village elders. Families came in, and young single men and women, and finally the preacher began the service. This week the Reverend Johann Haagan was assisting the celebrant and preacher, the Reverend Dr Potts. Sarah and Liz, one either side of Kate, both nudged her when Johann came out of the vestry in his cassock.

'Stop that,' she whispered. 'What are you on?'

'He's better to look at than old Dr Potts,' whispered Sarah back, 'so don't be an old maid.'

'Yes, and he looks like an angel in them robes,' whispered Liz from the other side.

Kate did not know what to do with her sisters, who encouraged each other in this kind of talk and seemed never to have their minds off men.

Johann did indeed look like an angel, having lost none of the paleness of his complexion on first arriving in estuary country, and dressed in white vestments with gold trimming. The young priest knew the value of a mystical appearance when it came to impressing country folk, and he was not slow to emphasise this aspect of his profession.

The vicar began the service. 'Lord, you have taught us that all our doings without love are nothing worth . . .'

'Amen to that,' whispered the irreverent Sarah.

'. . . Send your Holy Spirit and pour into our hearts that most excellent gift of love . . .'

'And that,' whispered her impious sister, Liz.

'. . . the true bond of peace and of all virtues, without which whoever lives is counted dead . . .'

'Which will be you two in a minute,' Kate whispered back.

'. . . before you. Grant this for the sake of your only Son, Jesus Christ our Lord, Amen.'

The Reverend Haagan now took up the chant.

'And this I pray, that your love may abound yet more and more in knowledge and in all judgement; that ye may approve things that are excellent; that ye may be sincere and without offence till the day of Christ.'

'This text is taken from Philippians 1, verses nine and ten.'

The sun came out during the service, and the brighter light sent cascades of colour on to the congregation from the stained-glass windows. The phlegmy-throated old vicar rattled on from his pulpit, losing his way several times during his sermon, and once going off into a silent reverie which only ended when Johann coughed loudly and slammed a hymn book shut, bringing the vicar back to earth with a startled jump and a surprised look at finding himself before his expectant congregation. Sarah whispered that it only confirmed her suspicions that Dr Potts had died long ago, and was just walking around in an empty body, while his soul was somewhere in heaven.

They ended the service with a new hymn written by the recently dead poet William Blake, a man for whose work the Reverend Johann Haagan had unbounded enthusiasm. The tune was one that Johann Haagan had composed himself, and had tutored a reluctant organist into delivering.

Kate enjoyed the words, singing, 'And did those feet in ancient time, walk upon England's mountains green?' with great fervour, but despite her loyalty for Johann, she felt the tune lacked vital energy, and hoped that at some time someone else would add music which would do justice to the words.

After the service, the villagers milled around in the churchyard, speaking with friends and relatives. Kate spoke with Johann, still in his vestments, while other less forward single women looked on in envy. Kate had been right about Johann being pursued; but it was not merely his relative youth and steady living which appealed. The husky estuary girls clearly wanted to mother him – all the way into marriage if they could.

'You seem to have a lot of admirers these days,' Kate said to him with a smile. 'I can feel daggers sticking in my back.'

He laughed. 'I hadn't noticed.'

'That's because you feel yourself above these shellfish girls, I suppose,' she said.

He looked at her quickly. 'Oh dear, yes. I did say something like that, didn't I? The first day we met, when you gave me a ride on your waggon? The words were ill-chosen and should never have been uttered.'

'Have you changed your mind, then?'

'No, I haven't changed my mind, but I should have phrased it differently, more politely.'

Kate shook her head and wagged a finger in mock anger. 'You are such a snob, Reverend Haagan.'

He signed before replying. 'Miss Fernlee, yourself and your sisters excluded, I have not yet met a woman hereabouts who could meet the obligations of a priest's wife, for I shall not be a schoolteacher for ever. I am an ambitious man. One day I shall be given a parish, a rectory, servants – and people of quality will call on me, invite my wife and myself to grand houses for an evening of card games, even balls.

'A great many of these young ladies here today are certainly beautiful enough, in a robust way, to excite me as a man, but I must choose a wife who will know how to act when the bishop calls to take high tea. You do understand?'

She shook her head, giving him up for lost. 'Why,' she admonished, 'do you leave me and my sisters outside this group of young women you say aren't fit to make a vicar's wife? We're not any different from the rest of them.'

'Ah, but you could be trained,' he said seriously. 'With a little patience and kindness, you could be made to look tolerably civilised in proper company. The others, they are too well entrenched in their grubby little estuary manners ever to be saved from them.'

'It's a good job we're not alone, Reverend,' stated Kate firmly, 'for I would knock that halo flying in an instant if we was . . .'

'If we *were*,' said Johann with a pained look, 'if we *were* alone.'

'Whatever's right,' she said, becoming genuinely annoyed with him now and turning away to chat to a neighbour.

Johann saw this in her high colour, and knew he had overstepped the mark a little. Even though he was not wholly serious, yet he was not wholly jesting either. He had, after all, been used to people of quality, and yes, some of the manners of these rustic girls did revolt him, their ungrammatical speech jarring his nerves. Yet Kate had a natural intelligence which impressed him. She had knowledge of things that were outside his sphere of learning, especially biological facts, which she called simply 'life'.

In the beginning he had talked of the local women as cocklers and winklers – the latter known as 'triggers' he discovered early on – and had quickly been informed of his mistake. There were none of these in Paglesham, it seemed, for cockling and triggering were carried out in the

Thames estuary, the former from points of land where the tide went out the furthest, and the latter where there were rocky outcrops which were covered by the tide. The Roche was too narrow, its creeks too lean to provide good cockle beds, and there were no rocks for the winkles.

The women and girls in Paglesham were from relatively wealthy families when compared to cocklers and triggers, and had been highly insulted by Johann's mistaken assumptions, even though accidental. They were daughters of fishermen, cattle and land farmers, oyster and mussel farmers. They were from a higher level of rural society, one of the many unknown layers beneath his own. While he was familiar with those above his station, the strata below were a mystery to him. The difference between oyster girls and cockle girls, he supposed, must be the difference between himself and the lady whose hand he had once had the audacity to request in marriage.

'Forgive me, Miss Fernlee,' he murmured, once Kate had waved goodbye to her friend, 'I cannot change all at once. You must give me time to get used to your ways out here, in the wilds, for I am familiar only with families of the genteel.'

'Well, don't worry about that, Reverend,' she said, glaring at him, 'for we don't need you to change anyway.'

With that, Kate stormed off after her sisters who were already passing through the lych-gate. She despaired of the man. Father was ten paces ahead, striding out for home. Kate caught up with Sarah and Liz, and soon lost the high colour she had developed when arguing with Johann, and indeed, quickly forgave him, for he was the most silly man, standing on the fine points of his toes staring after them.

As they walked over the frosted fields, they started a hare, which went zigzagging over the bare furrows and rises. Suddenly a gunshot rang out, and the hare did a somersault before landing and kicking out its death throes. Edward and the girls watched as a tall man walked out from a copse, picked up the hare, then came towards them.

'Good day to you,' he called. 'Edward Fernlee, ain't it?'

'That's certain sure,' said Edward, 'and what be the mussel farmer doing huntin' so far from his own village, Mr Rockmansted?'

Jack Rockmansted leaned on the barrel of his gun, using it as a crutch as he nodded to each of the sisters in turn. Even though the day was cold, his arms were bared to the elbows. Kate found herself looking at the way the mass of dark hairs on his forearms curled around the white rolled-up cuffs of his shirt sleeves, and then turned her head away quickly, concerned at being caught staring.

The dead hare hung from Rockmansted's right hand, dripping scarlet blood on to the white, frosted earth.

'Oh, this and that. I've the squire's permission, if that's what you're concerned about. It's his land hereabouts, am I right?' He grinned.

'It be Squire John Pritchard's land right enough,' conceded Edward, clearly melting. 'Edward Fernlee was just arskin', you understand.'

'Of course, of course. You have the squire's interests at heart and so would I, being a man who respects the law.' Jack Rockmansted then turned to Edward's daughters. 'And these are your girls? Well, girls I say, but the eldest is a woman grown already.'

Edward puffed himself up with pride. 'These be they. First Catherine, that we calls Kate. Then Sarah, that won't be havin' any shortenin' of her Christian name, since she's given to haughty ways, and last our Elizabeth, that we calls Liz.'

'And fine ladies they are too,' said Jack Rockmansted, condescendingly. 'I expect they've each had a dozen offers to be wed? Eh?'

Liz giggled.

Edward said, 'Only our Kate. And Liz is too young.'

There was silence then, and an air of expectancy not unlike that at the cattle market, where the buyer stands surveying the beasts, and the seller waits for an offer, if one is to come. Jack Rockmansted stared at the young women, smiling over the muzzle of his gun as if it were a great game they were all playing. Finally he lifted his head, shouldered his rifle, and held out the hare to Kate.

'Miss Fernlee,' he said, 'please take the hare for your family supper, for I'm sure to shoot another before I go home.'

The breath was coming out in plumes from the mouth of this tall, strong-looking man. His eyes shone with the cold air. His dark skin, a complete contrast to the Reverend Haagan's complexion, seemed to expel the morning's efforts to whiten the world. Jack Rockmansted exuded a kind of power which frightened Kate a little.

'Take it, Kate,' said her father, 'for it is a gift offered in friendship, an' no harm in that. Mr Rockmansted knows you are spoke for, so he's not a-courtin' your favours.'

'This is sadly true,' said Jack Rockmansted, his eyes fixed on Kate's, 'and I wish it was otherwise. But since you are promised, I simply offer the hare in friendship.'

'Better you should give it to Sarah,' said Kate.

'No, not to me,' said her sister, stepping back a little, the message instantly clear that she did not want anything to do with this tall weathered man who was, in her eyes, as old as her uncles. 'I . . . I don't like dead creatures.'

This was a poor excuse, as all knew, for in the kitchen Sarah often skinned and gutted rabbits, plucked birds, and handled all manner of dead game, but Jack Rockmansted did not seem offended by her awkward display of rejection.

However, Kate saw that she had to step in quickly and accept the proffered gift, for they could not have two wilting females in the party. That would not wear at all. She took the hare from him, handing it straight to her father.

'Thank you,' she said, quietly.

'Good day to you, Mr Fernlee,' said Jack Rockmansted. 'And to you, ladies.'

With that he marched off, towards the dyke which would take him back to his own village of Stambridge. On looking down, Kate saw that she had failed to keep the hare's blood from dripping on her skirts, for there were two scarlet blobs spreading around the area of her thighs.

'That there,' said Edward Fernlee, 'is a gentleman. You girls would not go far wrong in setting your cap at that man, if you arsk Edward's advice.'

The two younger sisters exchanged looks, and Kate hurried them on before Edward noticed.

Kate herself was in two minds about whether she liked Mr Rockmansted or not. On the surface he was polite and thoughtful enough, but he seemed to lack a certain sensitivity which was a natural trait of men like her Simon, and even Johann Haagan. There was something a little brittle about Rockmansted's manner, which indeed might have been due to being somewhat out of his depth in the society of young women.

She surprised herself by finding his tough looks and hard masculinity a little exciting. She felt she should be revolted by a man with thick dark hair on his forearms and the back of his neck, rather than find him sexually attractive. It worried her, this rather deviant stirring of those desires which should be reserved for Simon alone. It was something to watch out for and control with an iron determination.

Kate had heard that Jack Rockmansted's brother Timothy was a drinker and womaniser, and that Jack himself considered his brother a waster. While she approved of men who directed their energies into worthwhile activities, Jack Rockmansted went about his business harder than most, as if he wanted to crush all his competitors without a second's thought.

Then again, she thought, she was probably doing the man an injustice. He seemed upright and strong, and though he appeared to lack gentleness, would probably make a good husband for some woman. Not Sarah though, Kate thought quickly. Sarah needed someone with a softer heart.

When she arrived home, Kate found a letter waiting for her from Simon, delivered by hand at the inn. The Royal Navy were good at distributing mail, using their own sailors who had leave on shore in various parts of the country. Kate had already received one letter from Simon, written in haste, and put on a homeward-bound ship at the island of Gibraltar. That had just been a note to say he was missing her already, but that life on the high seas was exciting and he was doing well at his seamanship. The letter she held in her trembling hands now was fuller, and had been written over a longer period of time.

My Darling Kate [it began],
I have been taking lesons to improve my poor writing skill from one of the officers for if I am to aspire to being an officer myself one day I must learn how to fill a log as well as handling the nautical divices necesary to navigate the ship.

The first thing I must tell you is how much I am missing you for I left my heart in your care. It is not with me that is certain sure. If there was no work to be done I would be feeling empty all the time but tasks aboard ship take up most of the hours doing watch and sail making and such so I have little time to feel sorry for myself. My love for you keeps me strong in this hard life for bosun has taken a dislike to me and gives me rough times but that must not worry you for I am well up to keeping myself cheerful over such things.

We had a great storm in the Bay of Biscay which I did not tell about when I first wrote. Some of the men went seasick much to the desgust of Captain Haines who likes fit men on his ship. He is a good captain which is why I do not trouble myself over bosuns. A ship with a good captain does not get into dificultes like some. I mean if the men are content and do there work without complaint then there is not a great deal to go wrong.

Yesterday we hove into the Cape of Africa. The news here is that the Boers have defeated King Dingaans Zulu savages at a battle they call Blood River.

This is all I can write to you at this time, my darling Kate, for it makes me melancoly to think we cannot be together now for such a long while. I love you my sweet Kate more than I love my life. All my best dreams are of you.

I am your loving, Simon

By the time Kate had finished reading she was in tears, and stayed in her room for over an hour, reading and rereading the letter, trying to get from it enough to feed her voracious emotional appetite for Simon. She would never succeed. It was only a letter, and not her man. Yet she felt it should mean so much. She thought how he must have laboured over the words, for he was no scholar, and such things came hard to him. She was immensely proud of the fact that he was taking lessons in writing and wished Johann Haagan were there so that she could show him what a fine man of letters her Simon had become in so short a time.

Having put the letter in a drawer for safekeeping, Kate started thinking about Jack Rockmansted again. Just recently she had seen him several times in the district, which was strange, for she had not encountered him more than a dozen times in her whole life before that. Lately he seemed to have a great deal of business to do in Paglesham. He was always quite distant towards her, never approaching before today when she was with her father and sisters, except he might lift his hat to her, or give a curt nod. Why he should take any notice of her at all bewildered her. It was a mystery.

Rockmansted was not right for either of her sisters, if that was his plan. He seemed to lack a sense of humour, which Kate thought an essential aspect of a man's personality, if he was to marry a Fernlee. For Kate and her sisters were not fashioned in the sombre sober mould of those puritan housewives who spent their time writing pious tracts to distribute around the neighbourhood. The three sisters had a sense of fun, were childlike at times, and Kate knew that marriage to someone like Jack Rockmansted would crush the spirit in Sarah or Liz.

Kate remembered the time she had brought Simon home for Sunday tea, and Sarah had put an egg in an egg-cup before him, with a slice of bread and butter. When he cracked the egg with his spoon, it splattered over everywhere, for Sarah had not boiled it at all. It had been as raw as when it first came out of the chicken. Simon, after looking round the table with dismay, had thought it a huge joke, and laughed along with everyone else.

Not every man was like Simon, and prepared to grin at a joke on himself. There were men who would have stood on their dignity, who would have been irreparably offended and would have considered they were being mocked. Many men in this day and age took themselves too seriously, and would have brought pomposity to bear on the lightheartedness of Sarah and Liz.

No, Jack Rockmansted was not for one of Kate's sisters. He was too old, too pan-faced, too dour – gentleman or not.

Chapter Six

It was an early March evening and Kate had been to the large houses along the Westcliff seafront. Damson had been put back in his warm stable. Sarah and Liz, Kate knew, were at the church, helping to decorate it for the coming Sunday. Her father was usually at the inn on a Friday, so she had not expected to see the lamplight through the window. No one should have been at home.

She peered through a windowpane, cupping her eyes with her cold hands. The scene inside at first puzzled her, then brought on a feeling of shock. Her father was sitting in the easy chair with his face in his hands. She could see his hunched back, straining against the material of his shirt. Standing before him, facing the window, was the water-serjeant, his silver oar in evidence on his coat collar.

Oh Lord, what's happened? thought Kate, beginning to panic.

She went to the door, opened it, and entered the room. The water-serjeant looked at her, but her father remained in the same crouched, almost foetal, position. The water-serjeant looked worried.

'Ah, I'm glad you're home, miss. You one of the daughters, are ye?'

'What's the matter, what's happened?' cried Kate. 'Have we been selling undersized oysters?'

The water-serjeant shook his head sadly. 'An't a simple case of that, Miss Fernlee, I wisht it was. It's much worse. People have fell sick from eating your oysters, and one has near died. A gentleman's lady from Southend. A baronet. Took the case to the Court of Conservancy, and your father's been ordered to cease trading.'

Kate felt faint at his words. '*What?* Our oysters?'

''Fraid so, miss.' The water-serjeant looked very uncomfortable and fiddled with the silver oar on his collar. 'They do say the oysters is contaminated. Some musselmen stood up in the court and said your beds should be condemned. They said it were a mussel river, in any case, and not a fitting river for oyster beds, like the Crouch. They said there's something in the mud of the Roche which don't agree with oysters, but which does good to mussels . . .'

'They said, they said,' interrupted Kate hotly, 'what about us? Why weren't we told? Don't we get a chance to defend ourselves?'

'Well, that's it, you see, your father were told. He was took to court this mornin', to plead his case, but he just stood there like a lummock and said naught. So the judge assumed he were guilty and 'ad nothing to say for hisself.' The water-serjeant gave Edward a pitying look. ''Asn't spoke since.'

Concern for her father overwhelmed everything else for a moment and Kate went to his chair. She bent down and put an arm round his shoulders. 'Father, what is it? Why didn't you speak up at the court?'

Edward remained locked tightly within himself. She gently peeled his hands away from his eyes and stared into them. They looked vacant. Her father had obviously been greatly shocked by being forcibly dragged off to court to face the charges against him. It seemed he had retreated somewhere, into the back of his mind, and would have to be coaxed out of it.

Kate's concern turned to fury and she whirled to face the water-serjeant. 'What rubbish people talk. The Roche is no different from the Crouch in its mud. Did no one speak up for us?'

The water-serjeant, who seemed a good man reluctantly doing his duty, hung his head a little. 'Not hardly, miss. I mean, Jack Rockmansted said he thought the court were being a mite hasty, but that were all. They seemed determined you should not trade again.'

'So what does it come down to?'

The water-serjeant shrugged.

Despite her concern for her father's health, and the rage she felt against the court, Kate considered their position with cold clarity. It was she who looked after the family's finances and she knew that they still owed fifty pounds for the year's rental on the oyster beds. The beds had been taken out on a three-year renewable lease. Kate's heart sank as it all suddenly came home to her.

'Can't we appeal?' she asked the water-serjeant.

The big man shook his head. 'There an't no appeal in cases like this. People was poisoned, without no doubt, an' by Fernlee oysters. Where's the point in wastin' the court's time with appeals?'

There was to be no appeal. Judgement had been passed. The Fernlee family could no longer trade in oysters. Their livelihood had been taken away from them at a stroke. She knew they had almost fifty pounds saved and, if they sold something, they could pay off their debt, but they would not have the rent for the house, nor money coming in for food and clothing. It was a disaster.

She sat down on the arm of her father's chair and stroked his head. 'Is there nothing we can do?' she asked, looking up at the water-serjeant. 'What about all those oysters we have in the beds at this moment? Some of them are almost mature. Four years we've been tending them.'

The big man shook his head and looked out of the window, as if he longed to be somewhere else.

'I can't understand it,' she said. 'What could have got into our oysters?'

She wanted an explanation, so that she could scream denials and put everything back into place. It did not seem right that their business, their livelihood, should be snatched from them like this. Her fury and despair mingled, threatening to overwhelm her cool sense.

'Maybe the tide brought something in, from further up the coast? Or from the French? These things happen,' said the water-serjeant. 'Why, I remember the time our Sally were taken ill with eating cockles. Sick near to death, she was...'

Kate stood up and steered the man towards the door.

'Thank you, serjeant. You've brought the bad news, and I know it's not your fault, but we must be alone now. You understand, don't you?'

'Yes, of course, Miss Fernlee,' he replied, obviously relieved to be on his way, 'an' if there's anything I can do...'

He lumbered through the doorway and out into the darkness.

Kate felt weary. Her mind was woolly, the news having taken away its normal sharpness. She did not know how to help her father. She needed time to think, to consider what could be done. She needed to talk to people.

'We'll manage,' she said, automatically. It could have been her mother speaking.

Her father opened his mouth at last. 'No we won't,' he said bleakly.

Those were the last words he ever spoke.

A fortnight later, Kate decided it was time to put some of her plans into action. Her whole world had collapsed around her, but she reminded herself that she still had Simon, and things could be worse. He would be home one day not so far off and they could fight the world together. In the meantime, she was determined not to bend.

During the past two weeks, Kate had been to the bailiffs again, and to the magistrate who had presided over the court, but without success. Edward Fernlee's small firm could no longer trade in oysters. No one else was prepared to help them. She must get her family over this crisis until better days were visible through the murk.

There had been floods of tears, of course, from Sarah and Liz when they learned what had happened, but Kate's eyes were dry. She had to be strong. Her father had gone even further into himself, like a turtle into its shell, after the water-serjeant's visit, and it was impossible to get anything out of him at all except grunts. He just sat by the fire, staring pathetically into the flames with a blank expression on his face. The girls were young and one could not expect too much of them; it was her father she was most concerned about.

That morning she had awoken to the sound of birds, singing in the eaves of the cottage. The sun was shining through a crack in the curtains, on to the alabaster white wall of the room, with a soft brightness. Hens were clucking in the yard below, and somewhere a pig was snorting. There was a smell of wood-smoke in the air: someone was burning hickory chips to cure herrings no doubt.

Despite the pleasant morning, and her determination to face the future squarely, it was difficult to suppress the leaden feeling in her breast as the full flood of recent events washed over her spirit once more. The spring day, which would be good to most, seemed to hold nothing but promises of gloom for the Fernlee family. Kate shook her head, trying to dismiss these doom-filled thoughts. She must be strong now. Briskly, she washed and dressed and went downstairs.

At the breakfast table, Liz began weeping again.

Kate said, 'Stop that now, Liz dear, we have to sort something out. I've been thinking it over and what I propose is this—you and Sarah should go to stay with Aunt Polly at Canewdon. You've always wanted to go back there, haven't you, Liz? Sarah will have to work on the farm full-time, and Liz part-time, for I want you to do more schooling, Liz. You're the brightest of us. Uncle Peter will be asked to supply help to the farmers, and it might as well be you as faggers coming in from the north of Essex. I shall stay here with Father.'

She looked now at Edward, who was staring at his plate. His mind seemed to have left him. Kate still hoped this was a temporary affliction, but there was no question about moving him to some other place. He had lived in the cottage all his life and to remove him now, when everything he'd known and cherished had been taken from him... Well, it had already stolen his mind; losing his home would probably kill him.

Sarah asked, 'What will you do, Kate?'

'At the very worst, I shall earn money cockling,' she said.

There was a gasp from Liz, who stopped her tears immediately, and Sarah shouted, 'You cannot!'

'I can and I will.'

She said the words, heard her own voice saying them, and they sounded firm and confident. But inside, Kate felt bleak and empty. Cockling was a punishingly hard life, especially in the winter, and a dangerous one too. It meant going two miles out on to the mud, at whatever time the tide allowed, dragging a cart on runners behind. Once out there, she would have to find a prime bed and scrape the cockles from the mud with a rake, load them into the cart, and drag it back to the shore again. This had to be done before the pincer-movement of the incoming tide cut her off in its sweeping silver arms; a great rush of water that came in faster than a man could run. All this for the pittance she would receive when she sold the cockles to one of the stall owners on the Leigh shoreline.

'Well,' she said, smiling, 'let's hope it won't come to that. I shall try to find work with the mussel farmers first, or in one of the big houses along Southend and Westcliff seafront. Perhaps I'll be lucky.'

Her optimistic tone did not fool her sisters.

Later that morning, Kate left Edward in the care of a neighbour and took the girls to Canewdon using the horse and cart. Uncle Peter and Aunt Polly had heard the news, of course, and were sympathetic. They said that the girls could stay with them in the cottage so long as they earned their keep. Peter and Polly were good people, but they were as poor as everyone else in the estuary country. Peter earned his living by travelling around the farms and doing whatever work was available for the season; he was respected by the farmers, so was often asked to gather other pickers. Kate hoped he might in this way find employment for Liz and Sarah.

'Yes, I can take the girls along,' he said, 'though there an't much at the moment, it being spring an' all. We'll find somethin' though, don't you fret, Kate. You just look arter old Edward – he's been a good brother to Polly in the past.'

She knew it was going to be hard for the girls. They were used to hard work, but not the backbreaking work they would be forced to do on the land. Liz would find it especially difficult, since she had been doing housework for many years now. They would have to learn though. Their fortunes had changed overnight. Peter and Polly had to work all hours just to put bread on the table and they could not carry passengers.

'I appreciate all you're doing for us,' said Kate to her aunt and uncle. 'Someday I'll be able to pay you back.'

'Pay us back?' snorted Polly. 'We'm family!'

After leaving the girls, Kate took Damson and the cart to Rochford market where, bidding Damson farewell, she sold both to a gypsy horse trader. This money she needed to help pay off the debt of fifty pounds for the lease of the oyster beds from the water authority. It seemed cruel that she had to pay out all they had for beds they could not use, but in fact the bill should have been paid six months previously. They had been living on credit since that time.

South Street was bustling with people as Kate went immediately to the offices of the water authority and duly paid the bill. At least now her father would not go to prison. All they had to do was find the rent for the cottage and money to put food into their mouths. *That's all!* She let out an ironic laugh, causing people to stop and stare.

She walked the five miles back to Paglesham East End, passing the church schoolhouse on the way. The doorway was open, presumably to let the spring breezes clear out the cobwebs and dust of the winter. She could see the pupils sitting on their benches, slates in hand. Johann had his back to the doorway and was writing something on the blackboard.

A musty smell of unwashed children wafted from the small classroom; some of them had been sewn into their clothes from October the previous year. They would be released from their cloth prisons when the warm weather was assured. There were those whose garments were so thin their mothers had lined them with brown paper to keep out the cold. There were boys wearing girls' smocks and girls in boys' trousers. Each had to wear the hand-me-downs of the older children in the family, without regard for gender.

Kate knew that rich people regarded the poor with distaste and pointed out how ignorant and filthy they were as reasons for their inferiority. When the majority of houses had no running water of any kind, however, and the wells were overused simply to obtain drinking water, how were these people supposed to wash regularly? They might tramp miles down to the nearest creek for freezing brackish water, but without soap the creek water made little difference and soap was a luxury only the rich could afford. Sometimes even the well water was frozen over, and someone had to be lowered down at risk to his life to break the ice. No, the priority was putting food and drink on the table, not making sure their skins were scrubbed clean.

As for being ignorant, Kate knew that certain philanthropic organisations were trying to rectify that, but there were many more poor children than philanthropists and they were not in the way of learning. Johann had told her that they first had to learn *how* to learn. They had to be given confidence in themselves.

'All their lives they have been told – and their parents and grandparents before them – that they are stupid and ignorant, and that the wealthy and well-bred are privileged by right of intellect. No one has told them they are kept that way, in ignorance and darkness, simply in order that the rich can maintain the *status quo*.'

So Johann had said only a few weeks previously, when he and Kate had been talking. He had become a good friend to her. He had been teaching her, raising the level of her knowledge rapidly over the last six months, improving on the education she had ceased at fifteen. And she had enjoyed being taught. He told her she was quick and bright, and that she grasped things with uncommon understanding. Kate felt this to be true, though a certain amount of modesty prevented her from actually admitting it to herself. She was excited by learning, by her newly won knowledge. It had raised her confidence when selling her oysters to businessmen and householders.

She had written to Simon about Johann, so that no stories reached his ears which were untrue. Johann was simply a friend, and nothing more, and though Simon had sounded a little piqued in his reply, she guessed it was simply because Johann was able to spend time with her while Simon could not. Simon could get as jealous as any man, but Kate's clear and open manner when informing him of such things would leave little room for any unjust suspicions.

She had pointed out to him that he too was trying to improve himself educationally, in order to become an officer, and there was no reason why he should have an ignorant bride. His joking reply was that he did not have a dusky maiden for a teacher, but since she had a handsome pastor tutoring her he would try to find a beautiful lady willing to take on the task of furthering his education, to square things up, and that he remained her very affectionate and loving husband-to-be.

Kate laughed at this, knowing her words had found their intended target: Simon's very vulnerable conscience. He was nothing if not a fair man, even over such traditional bastions as male domination. In fact his last letter from India had complimented her on her improvements in her writing style.

Kate saw Johann turn and catch her staring through the doorway. She heard him tell his pupils to copy the tables he had written on the blackboard and then came out to greet her.

'Kate, I've heard. Such a dreadful thing to happen. What are you going to do about it?'

She sighed. 'It seems we have no right of appeal. In any case, perhaps they're right? Perhaps we deserve it? People were poisoned by our oysters, that much is fact.'

'But it could have been an accident, something brought in on a single tide. You're not to blame, I'm sure. Sometimes I think the authorities have hearts of stone.'

She smiled at this. 'The authorities have *no* hearts whatsoever, Johann, but that doesn't mean they're not doing their work properly. If it had been some other oyster fishery – the Hawkins' say – we should have all have pronounced it was right and proper for them to stop trading.'

Johann snorted.

'If it had been the Hawkins' fishery, the authorities would have been bribed before things got this far and trading would have continued as normal.'

'I think you're being – what is it? – cynical. Yes, you're being cynical again, Johann.'

His pale face with the penetrating eyes regarded her for a moment before he asked, 'What are you going to do, Kate? You haven't answered my first question. What are your plans?'

'I shall look for work, of course. Father has fallen ill since the verdict and it's up to me to look after him.'

Johann glanced towards the schoolroom where some of the pupils were beginning to get restless. A boy, encouraged by a group of girls, was pulling another boy's hair.

'Bulman! Stop that, child!' Johann called. Then he turned back to Kate. 'I shall have to go back in there. I'll be charged with neglecting them. Look, Kate, I have a little money put aside . . .'

Kate was horrified. 'Don't say any more, Johann. I wouldn't and couldn't. People would say dreadful things about us and you know it. You'd put your position as schoolteacher at risk.'

'Some position!' he said. 'Anyway, I could loan the money to your father.'

'That wouldn't make a scrap of difference to the people around here. They would say you were lending it because I was giving you favours.'

'You surprise me both with your frankness and with your conventionality.'

'I don't know why. I'm very conventional about most things.'

He signed and shook his head. 'You're a strange mix of wildness and correctness, young lady, that's what you are. I'm sure someone understands you, but I don't.'

She smiled. 'Simon does.'

'Yes, well, Simon ought to be here, to do the understanding.'
'He will be, soon.'

Johann nodded and made his way back to the now noisy classroom, yelling for calm and order.

Chapter Seven

Kate had been to see some of the oyster farmers on the north side of the Crouch and had met with a uniform response. The reply of Mr Wilson, the Hawkins' foreman, was typical.

'If you'm been stopped by the court from trading in oysters, how do you expect me to employ you, miss? Granted you know the business, but people might say you carry the contamination with you. I hear it was typhus in your oysters. Some folks might think you was the carrier, and then were would we be?'

Demoralised but not beaten by these rejections, Kate then tried some of the mussel farmers on the Roche, but they were openly hostile to this woman who came from a family which had dared to start an oyster business on their river.

'You got a cheek, I got to say that,' said one, 'comin' here smelling of damn oysters and wanting work. Go on, get out of here, afore I sets my dogs on you...'

She remembered that Jack Rockmansted had stood up for her father in court and, according to the water-serjeant, had spoken in his favour. However, when she went to see him, he was in London on business, and she was confronted by his brother Timothy.

'You want a job?' said Timothy.

'Yes, Mr Rockmansted. I'm willing to any kind of work.'

He looked her up and down slowly, making her feel as if a flatfish had just slid over her bare skin. Tim walked around her, then moved in close and placed a large hand on top of her buttock.

'Oh, I expect we can find something for you to do,' he said softly.

Kate whirled on him. 'Take your hands off me!'

Tim smiled. 'Ow, a fiery one, eh? Red hot, this one, fresh from the flames. Burning red hair, burning red face.'

Her face growing hotter by the second, Kate strode away from the Rockmansted cottage, with Tim shouting after her, 'Come back, Kate, I was only playing with you. I didn't mean it. Look, I'm sorry. I'll give you work . . .' but there was no way she could go back to him. He sounded contrite, but Kate didn't want a job where she would have to keep watch every minute of the day. She gritted her teeth to keep the tears from flowing. God, why did she have to put up with this? All she asked for was to be treated like a human being.

'I'll give Tim Rockmansted *burning*,' she said. 'I hope he burns in hell!'

Then she stopped, shocked with herself for mouthing such a profanity, thinking it unchristian and unworthy of herself.

'I didn't mean that, God,' she said, lifting her skirts to jump a ditch. 'I expect he's going there anyway, though, that one, from what I've heard . . .'

That evening she went to the church to pray quietly, firstly for her father and his health, and secondly to gather the strength to widen her search for work, as she had guessed she would have to do. In the stillness of the church she found herself able to think more clearly, without anger, despair and frustration pulling her several different ways. It was a place where she could formulate her plans.

Johann discovered her in the gloom, as he went to snuff the altar candles for the night.

'Ah, Kate,' he said. 'Sorry to disturb your meditations.'

'That's all right,' she replied. 'I was just leaving.'

'And how is your search for work progressing?'

She gave him a wry smile. He was always so solicitous, this pale little man, forever ready to listen to her troubles, to comfort her. There was a fondness growing in her breast for Johann Haagan: a fondness of which she knew she need not be afraid. Kate would never allow it to grow into anything stronger, yet she knew they could be close friends. Kate had never had a close man-friend before now and it was a novel experience. Despite her problems she was beginning to enjoy their friendship as well as value it.

'Not too well,' she admitted, 'but I expected that. The local people know too much about why I'm looking for work. No one in this part of the estuary wants to employ someone who poisons oysters, whether accidentally or on purpose.'

'So what's the next step?'

Outside the twilight was still strong enough to bring out the colours of the stained-glass windows. Inside, though, the gloaming was thickening to darkness and the gleam of old brass and polished wood deepened in the room. Kate could not distinguish Johann's features from those of St

George, against whose portrait he was standing.

'My knight in shining armour,' she mused.

'What?'

She shook her head. 'Oh, nothing. My next step? I must go to Southend and try there.'

'That's a long way. What is it, seven, eight miles?'

'It's a long way to walk every day,' she admitted, 'even supposing I do find work, but it's got to be done. I must find someone to look in on Father, too, if I'm to leave him all day.'

'I'd be glad to call in,' said Johann.

'Thank you,' she said, 'but you have your work too. No, I was thinking of a neighbour – someone close at hand. But that's for me to worry about, not you.' She gave him a smile. 'I'll be all right, Johann, don't look so concerned.'

'It's my natural countenance,' he said.

When she left the church she felt quite strong and ready for the ordeal of tackling uninterested potential employers. When there was only a choice of either giving up and throwing herself on the charity of others, or steeling her determination and doing what had to be done, Kate always chose the latter. She had her mother's grit in her.

Kate took Simon's last letter with her and walked seven miles to Southend seafront.

She first went to an agency which supplied servants to houses throughout the town. Entering the offices of Bleaker and Thwyte, Agency for the Hire of Domestic Servants, she found to her initial dismay a row of chairs all around the outer room, filled with other applicants for work. Her feeling of disappointment was quickly followed by the thought that she was as hard a worker as anyone she knew, so why should she be concerned about a little competition? She walked straight to the desk in the middle of the room at which sat a bored-looking, narrow-faced woman in spectacles.

'Name?' said the woman, before Kate had opened her mouth.

'Catherine Fernlee,' said Kate, then attempting to lighten things added, 'How do you know I haven't come to hire someone myself?'

The woman raised her eyes and stared at Kate's frock before shaking her head slowly, as if this kind of frivolity was the last thing she wanted during a hard day at the office.

'Position?' droned the woman.

'Position?'

Again the eyes were raised from the card on which the woman was writing.

'You have been in service before?'

'No,' admitted Kate, 'but I'm willing to do anything. I can cook...'

The woman allowed herself a thin smile and Kate realised she had started at the top of the tree, whereas her inexperience dictated she begin at the bottom.

'... and clean. I was thinking perhaps a maid of some sort?'

'You're a little too old to be a scullery maid,' said the woman tonelessly. 'They don't like them over thirteen. Opinions have been formed by your age and it is our experience someone of your years is difficult to train.'

Kate, who was not at all keen on being a scullery maid in any case, said hopefully, 'Well, chambermaid?'

'Without experience? Impossible. Look around you. There are girls here who've had several years' experience as chambermaids and we still can't place them all. Southend is declining in popularity at the moment. You could go to Brighton. You'd stand a better chance there.'

'Brighton?' cried Kate. 'That's ridiculous.'

The woman blinked and did not look at all happy. Then she tore up the card on which she was writing Kate's details. There was a finality about the action.

'Is that it?' said Kate.

'There's little point in going any further,' replied the woman, 'unless you want to sit in one of those chairs and grow old?'

Kate left the employment agency with a simmering fury inside her. She realised it was silly to stay and argue that she was as able-bodied as any man or woman in the room. They had experience of being in service and she had not. It was as simple as that. If she was to find work in any of the houses, she was going to have to do it without the agency.

She began knocking on tradesmen's entrances.

They all asked her if she had been in service before, and she had to say no. 'Can't hire you then,' they said, 'we need servants with experience.' 'I can clean out the ashes from a grate,' she had cried, 'I've done that before. I can black the range, sweep the floors, dust, scrub, clean boots, brush coats... I've done *all* those before. How much experience do I need?' But they shook their heads emphatically and told her she had no experience of working in a big household, and that life below stairs was not something you could walk into just like that. They told her it was a whole new world and that she was too old to be a scullery or kitchen girl.

The last house she went to she was invited in to see the butler, who looked her up and down, just as slowly as Tim Rockmansted had done, but with a completely different expression on his face. She might have been a rat brought in by the cat the way he was staring at her with the corner of his mouth curled in distaste and his eyes as cold as a cod's.

'Where are you from, girl?' he asked her.

He was tall, thin and had a hawk nose down which he peered at Kate's forehead.

Desperate for work, she gave him a quick curtsy. 'Paglesham, sir.'

'Paglesham?' He made it sound like a backyard privy. 'If you came to live here you would need to keep to yourself the fact that you come from *Paglesham.*'

'Oh, sir, I couldn't *live* in. You see, my father's sick and he needs me to look after him.'

'Impossible,' snapped the butler, 'you would have to be here by four-thirty in the morning, and we couldn't possibly let you go home before everyone is in bed. That's quite often very late, gone midnight. No, no, you will have to live in, if it suits me to hire you, which I'm not certain would be a good idea.'

Kate thought: *I could bring Liz or Sarah back home to look after Father, if the pay is good.*

'When would I see my father then?' she asked.

'You will have one Sunday a month in which to visit relatives, providing the Family do not require your services elsewhere. You may of course be needed at the London residence, or the Worcester estate, though it's doubtful they would want to take a kitchen girl to the latter . . .'

'And what would be my wages?'

The butler mentioned a small sum.

She could see how impossible it all was, and turned from him while he was in mid-sentence. To have to take care of one of the girls, as well as Edward, on a pittance . . . It was nothing like a workable arrangement.

'I haven't dismissed you yet!' cried the butler, sounding angry, but she waved a hand at him.

'No, but I've dismissed you,' which made the boot-boy snigger behind his hand, earning himself the rage which would have been vented on Kate had she stayed to receive it.

When Kate arrived home at six o'clock in the evening, the neighbour watching her father looked cross.

'I expected you earlier,' said the woman.

'I'm sorry,' said Kate, wearily pulling off the shoes she was unused to wearing so long. 'I've had to walk miles.'

Kate's feet were blistered and bleeding and the neighbour, on seeing this, modified her mood. She gestured towards Edward. 'Well, he hasn't been any trouble, I'll say that for him. Sits there gawping into thin air, doesn't say nothing – not a sound. You wonder what's going on inside that head of his, don't you? Creepy, I find it.'

'I find it sad,' said Kate, 'but then he's my father, not yours. I agree it's very strange to have someone so quiet, just staring into space. I'm sorry you found it so disconcerting.'

The neighbour grunted. 'Dis-con-certin'? Them's big words for a backwater creek girl like you. You been seeing too much of that schoolteacher, I think. It's no business of mine,' the neighbour folded her arms under her breasts, 'but even if it's all innocent, it don't do you no good, this learning. What good's it to you, if you're scraping the mud for shellfish? Answer me that, eh?'

'Mrs Biddowing, I am most grateful for your help today, but I'm very tired now.'

'All right, I'm going, but I'm only thinking of you, dear, you know that.'

'Good day, Mrs Biddowing.'

After the neighbour had gone, Kate bathed her feet in a bucket of water. Then she made sure Edward was comfortable, packed his pipe for him, lit it, then put it between his lips. She was pleased to see his hand go to the bowl as he began to take puffs. At least he was not completely out of this world.

When she made a meal of bread-and-milk a little later, he fed himself with a spoon, slowly and deliberately. She wondered if he were fooling her with his condition, but when she accidentally dropped the bucket with a clatter behind his chair, he did not flinch in the slightest. She had to admit to herself that there was something seriously wrong with him.

After she had done some chores around the house, Kate sat down to consider her next move. She would of course continue to search for work, but in the meantime she would have to earn some money to keep the two of them alive. She decided, looking at her father's blank expression as he slumped in the chair, that she could leave him alone in bed while she went cockling at Leigh. It would take two hours to walk to Leigh and another two to walk back home, with three hours cockling between. A total of seven hours. That would be half her working day, for the tide went out twice in twenty-four hours, and she would need to be at both ebbs if she were to earn their keep. The seven hours she spent away from the house, Edward could stay in his bed.

When she got home, she could walk him round to prevent him from getting sores. Then make a meal. Then get some rest herself before the next low tide. It would not be so bad, she told herself, and in just over a year or so Simon would be home and they could make other plans. It was only work, and she was young and fit. The girls were settled at Aunt Polly's, so she had no need to worry about them. She could not afford to worry about them. They had to manage without her.

'Come on, Father,' she said, getting to her feet.

She stood behind his chair and took him under the arms to lift him up. Once she had done so, which took considerable effort on her part, he stood there solidly, not even swaying. She pulled on his top coat for him and buttoned it up before draping a shawl round her own shoulders. Then she led him to the door.

Once outside she took his arm and frogmarched him down to the dyke, where she stood looking at the creek in the dying light of the day. There were all sorts of colours on the water from the departing sun, and it looked almost beautiful. There were dragonflies and damselflies skimming the water, and swifts and martins swooping in low after insects. Frogs were croaking in the marsh reeds and crabs were scurrying through the poa grass in the creek itself. The place was alive with movement and sound.

On the other side of the creek she could see a marsh farmer herding his cattle through the shallows to the lush grazing on the Potton Island. Boats were lying at angles on the mud, the fishermen working on their nets or lobster pots, or digging in the mud for ragworm bait while they awaited the incoming tide.

It was a peaceful scene, belying any desperate struggle for existence. Yet all these men, all these creatures, had to feed themselves. As a local, Kate knew the estuary was a place which gave its people and creatures a bare living in the main, nothing too luxurious, but there was food in the opalescent mud if one cared to scrape for it. Some had made their fortunes out of it, but not the vast amounts of wealth that, for instance, ore from a mine might be expected to yield to its owners. She and her family had been comfortable, better off than most, and they had taken it for granted. She realised now just how much she had lost. It was a chastening thought that she was probably worse off than the creatures of the backwaters. The estuary supported myriad forms of life in its labyrinthine channels, from mud skippers to avocets to humans, but it didn't overfeed them or spoil them. It gave them sufficient for their daily needs and little more.

'Come on, Father, home again,' said Kate, as the darkness turned the landscape into a sinister place, despite the lamps that were being lighted.

She led him back to the cottage, where she prepared him for bed. Then, wearily, she got into her own. She had to be up early next morning to collect driftwood on the shore. She also had to make herself a cart on which to collect the cockles over at Leigh.

Still, she could get a bright, early start in the morning and once the cart was made she would be set for cockling.

Chapter Eight

As if to compensate for the disappointments of the previous day, a letter arrived for Kate the following morning. It was from Simon. She held it in her hands and looked at it for some time, savouring the mere feel and sight of the missive before actually opening and reading it.

Able Seaman Wentworth
Her Majesty's Ship Panther

My Beloved Kate,
To say that I am missing you would be foolish, for you must know that you are my world and all else outside is just an empty place. Without you I am but a shadow of a man, going about his shipboard duties, longing for the time when he is to be reunited with his Kate. I dream of nothing else. You are in my thoughts, day and night.

Yesterday I had my first taste of fighting and most confusing it was, with the guns booming and people running here there and everywhere. Our commander Captain Haines feels that Aden would make a good coaling station on the route to India and so would have it for Queen Victoria.

Let me explain a little.

Aden is an Arab fishing village on the peninsula of south-west Arabia, with the Red Sea on one hand and the Indian Ocean on the other. The territory is in the hands of one Sultan Muhsin. Captain Haines talked with the sultan who at first agreed to lease us the harbour for our purposes but then had a change of mind. So we had to fight the sultan's tribe. The marines did most of the attacking but we sailors had to help . . . [Kate's heartbeat was quickening as she read this. She didn't want to read of the dangers Simon might be experiencing. He was, however, sensible enough not to go into detail.] . . . and we won the day. The tribesmen fought bravely but they were no match for our marines and the big guns.

So here I am in this strange land of the Moor where there are tall towers on holy buildings called moskes and from these places the priests call out several times a day for the faithful to go to prayer. A little like our church steeple bells I suppose. Aden has a dead volcano with a whole village inside it making it a natural fort. There are wooded slopes on the volcano with wildlife roaming around such as gazels and baboons and many birds even herons.

It is hot here. So hot you would not believe. If you drop an egg and it breaks it fries on the ground within a few moments. There is a heavy warm dampness to the air and clothes grow mould on them quickly. We have to scrub the mould from the sails frequently. This is one of the worst jobs to do and the master-at-arms does not like me a great deal so I have to do it often. I believe the master-at-arms thinks I am trying to get above myself by learning from Lieutenant Beechy. The lieutenant is the man who is teaching me seamanship and correcting my writing mistakes . . . [Kate could see how much the latter had improved in this letter over his last.]

I stay out of the master's way for he has already had Purdy Polkinghorn – from Cornwall county – flogged for daring to complain about the rotten cheese and bread they give us that is full of maggots and weavils.

My darling I have made friends with a black man from the West Indies. His name is Winchester. He chose it himself which it seems is not so strange where he comes from. I never met a black man before but Winchester stood by me when Morgan – one of the other sailors – got a gang against me one day for reasons of his own. Winchester is not a big man but he fights like a tiger and we saw off Morgan and his cronies in very short time . . . [Kate groaned. Not only was Simon fighting foreign tribesmen but other sailors as well. She would give him a piece of her mind when he returned. Not in a letter though. They could not argue by letter, for that would do neither of them good.]

We leave for India soon . . .

The rest of the letter moved into more welcome territory: their dreams and plans for the future. This part of the letter was sprinkled throughout with endearments, each one of which Kate treasured as if it were a diamond. She liked to hear about Simon's travels, but like most young men the things that excited him were terrifying to her.

There were scenes of high seas, of waves ninety feet tall that crashed down upon the ship while the sailors were in the rigging. There were descriptions of the horrors aboard a Royal Naval fighting ship, in the form of conflicts which arose between the men. There were flippant references to the ghastly food Simon had to eat and the persecution he had to suffer under certain officers, the foremost of which was the master-at-arms.

Kate could have done without all these passages and settled for the gentle reminiscences and voicing of hopes for their future. She would have exchanged all the descriptions of hardships (which she knew were simply matter-of-fact to Simon, and had not been embellished, nor were meant to impress her) for a single endearment.

Simon was a young man on an exciting voyage and she knew he was just bubbling over with the excitement of his experiences. Kate could hardly write to him and ask him not to include these in his letters. To Simon they were probably the meat of his letters and the rest the garnish. He probably wanted to share with her all those things that were happening to him. Kate, however, was fearful for his safety; these descriptions just served to remind her that there was danger in almost every moment of Simon's shipboard existence.

Kate tucked the letter down her dress when she went to buy some expensive nails with which to make her cockle sled. She had collected the wood for it already from various places along the shoreline of the river. Her father's hammer was no stranger to her hands, for she had often had to help build corrals for the oysters, and other pieces of equipment.

The sledge took two hours to build, during which time Kate mused on the letter. She paused occasionally to take it out and reread some particular phrase that pleased her, delighting in the idea that the paper she held had not so very long before been in the hands of her loved one. She imagined him creasing his brow as he battled with pen and ink, knowing how such things came hard to him, a man who was not at all academic in his tastes.

Oh my love, she thought to herself, *we'll be together soon. Almost one whole year has gone by now. Once we face the world together, all our troubles will be as nothing to us.*

Chapter Nine

Kate knew that the oystercatcher bird does not in fact eat oysters. Instead, it devours all the shellfish it can find buried in the mud above the low-tide mark. Oysters are always in deeper water than the oystercatcher can manage. She used to watch this noisiest of shore birds stabbing at the cockles and mussels with its beak, severing the hinge that attaches the two halves of the shell together, and swallowing the mollusc inside. She thought it a very handsome bird, with its black-and-white plumage, orange legs and stout red bill.

On the day that she first went out with the cockle girls to gather cockles, however, the shrill cry of the oystercatcher seemed to be mocking her. She dragged her mud sledge over the thick sludge of the Thames estuary, trying not to mind the sharp pieces of broken shell that cut into her feet. Trying not to mind the oystercatcher's cry. Trying not to mind the hostility of the other girls, who did not like newcomers 'poaching' on their stretch of the mud.

'Wot 'ave you cum 'ere for?' cackled an old woman. 'Oysters too good for ye now, eh? Not so stuck up since you've been found pois'nin decent folks, are ye?'

There were about thirty women out on the mud. One of the younger women bent and scooped up a wodge of mud. She flung it at Kate and it splattered over Kate's old dress and up her face. Kate stopped and scraped it away angrily with her hand.

'What did you do that for?'

Kate could see that the woman who had thrown the mud was not much more than a girl of about seventeen. She had gypsy features: dark eyes, dark hair and olive skin. Pretty in a peakish way, for she was so slim as to be a shade away from being painfully thin, she had that fiery look of the gypsy with a chip on her shoulder.

'What did I do it for? To get you used to the mud, that's what. Now you see what you have to put up with – up to your knees in this stinking sludge every day. This stuff's been here since Adam tickled Eve, and if you're coming out here with us, you'd better get used to it.'

The mud did indeed have a horrible stench of rotting shellfish to it, but Kate was not going to allow this girl to get away with treating her like a townie.

'Who do you think you're talking to, you little witch?' she said. 'I've been working in river mud since I was six years of age. Just because you've stopped traipsing over the countryside in your caravan, doesn't mean you can tell me about my business.'

'Ooooh, shame, shame,' cried the old woman.

The gypsy girl's eyes flashed at these words. 'You watch your tongue, ginger-knob, or I'll cut it out at the roots.'

The girl whipped out a short-bladed knife from her waistband and several of the other women laughed when Kate flinched.

Ginger-knob? She was auburn, not ginger. Her eyes stung with the tears that started in them, but she did not let them flow. That would have satisfied the people who were baiting her. They wanted her to break down and weep. They wanted to make her miserable. Kate had heard that this was how they treated newcomers, out on the mud, to discourage them from ever coming out again. Also she knew they saw her as a 'stuck-up' oyster girl, who scorned cocklers and triggers, or so they believed.

Kate realised why they were treating her this way – the women were protecting their harvesting area – but she wasn't going to let them get away with it. She would be here at the next tide, and the next, until her circumstances changed and she did not *need* to come out on to the mud again.

Kate looked at the knife and laughed, and then continued dragging the sledge, fearful of an attack while her back was turned, but not daring to give the watchers any indication that she was at all afraid of the gypsy.

Instead, she felt the sharp sting of mud packs, as they all pelted her back with the sludge. Her thin, threadbare dress was no protection. She kept on walking, taking no notice of the catcalls. Finally the missiles ceased raining on her, for they all had work to do, and quickly, before the tide turned again.

The mud was cold and her feet soon began to get numb. Most of the time she sank only to her ankles, but occasionally she hit a softer patch and went down beneath the slick grey surface layer, up to her thighs in the black ooze of organic mush. Sometimes it took as long as five minutes to struggle free of these pits, as the sucking sludge held on to a leg, and she would have to use her cockling rake to push herself out, just as a punter on a river moves his craft. The leg would come out suddenly, with a loud *sluck*, sometimes making her overbalance. The other women had been right: she would have to get used to being covered in the smelly alluvium of the river delta.

When they finally reached the cockle beds, an exhausting journey of just over a mile from the shore, they began searching for their favourite stretches. To Kate the whole flat area of the estuary – a vast plain of shimmering mud – looked the same. But to the experienced cocklers, this was a landscape with its own contours and landmarks, and they could read it as well as a cartographer can read his own maps. The women spread out, some crossing the great gullies of mud down which the incoming tide would rush to enclose the cocklers if they were not quick enough on the return journey. Timing was all important: you didn't go back with a half-full sledge, but you didn't get caught by the tide either.

'That's my bed!' snarled the gypsy girl as Kate found a good patch of cockles. 'Go find your own.'

'I was here first,' said Kate.

Two other women came up beside the gypsy.

'That's Sally's bed,' said one. 'Out here we find our own cockles, not steal 'em from others.'

Kate wearily moved on, dragging her cart behind her, until she found another patch further out. There she began raking the surface, gathering in the cockles that were just below the slick covering. Gas bubbles belched smells as she raked, at first slowly, as she found her own pace and got used to the rhythm of the work, then more feverishly when she noticed that others were filling their carts far more quickly than she was.

She stopped once, and stared back at the shoreline. It looked a long way away. Half-way between the cocklers and the beach was a line of men digging deep holes in the mud. These were the fishermen, collecting ragworms and lugworms for their bait. Occasionally one would give a distant-sounding whoop, as he came up with a king rag which were reckoned to be the best bait in the estuary sediment. Beyond these men, in the corner of the bay, were the triggers, collecting winkles from the rocky areas. This was less dangerous work than cockling, but not so rewarding. The buyers did not pay as much for winkles as they did for cockles.

After about an hour of backbreaking toil, Kate's cart was almost full. Many of the other cocklers had already started back to the beach, the urgency in their movements suggesting that Kate ought to do the same, even though she had not collected her full quota.

She put her rake in the sledge and climbed into the makeshift harness, but when she tried to pull the cart, found it extremely difficult. The runners just seemed to stick in the mud and it would hardly budge. She heard laughter from in front and saw that the other women were watching; they had known she would have difficulty.

She gritted her teeth, dug her heels in the sludge, and heaved until her muscles screamed in agony. Finally the sledge began to move, inching its way over the mud, and Kate lifted her legs, consciously at first, then after a while automatically, trudging the long journey back to the shore.

Luckily, she only ran into one soft patch on the return journey, though the other areas were bad enough. Once or twice the cart threatened to tip sideways, and she had to redistribute the load to compensate for the change in the surface of the sludge.

The sea began racing in, creeping silently over the surface of the mud. Not for this sea the crashing Atlantic rollers of the Cornish coast, or the thunderous waves of the Scottish islands, nor even the clawing seas of the Suffolk shoreline, clattering amongst the pebbles on the beach. This sea came in swiftly, but without any obvious show of strength, as if it were pretending to be a harmless thing. In fact it was deadly, a flat, sinister sea that swept in two silver-horned currents from either side of the bay: the two crescents would soon meet a few hundred yards from the beach, cutting off anyone caught within them. It would soon be waist-deep, but impossible to wade through, for its currents went so fast it took the silt from under your feet, and the victim sank slowly in the mud, to become bogged down and held fast in its grip. The main flood tide would then rush in behind, and if that did not freeze its victims, it would soon drown them. There was little anyone on the beach could do but watch, for to fight your way out to a trapped person was to put yourself in the same position. If they were close enough to the shore, a rope might be thrown, but more often they were trapped several hundred yards from safety, and soon sank to their deaths in the liquidised mud.

Kate struggled with her load, keeping up with the stragglers, making sure she did not fall behind those with better knowledge than her of the tide's deceptive manoeuvres. Her whole body felt as if it were falling apart; everything ached, from her head to her ankles. She gasped in air, heaving on the harness, trying to keep the sledge going through its own momentum. If she allowed it to stop, it soon sank and stuck, and the effort of getting it moving again was backbreaking.

The shoreline seemed never to get any closer, and she was almost beside herself with despair when finally she felt stones beneath her bare soles, and she knew she was about a hundred yards from the beach.

It was not too soon to reach her destination. The water rushed around her ankles as she approached the shingled strand, grabbing at her in a last attempt to pull her down. Finally, she found dryness, and flopped on to the ground without even bothering to take herself out of the harness.

There was laughter from all around her.

'Not so fancy as oysters, is it?' cried Sally. 'Needs a girl with a bit of toughness to her, not some sissy maiden brought up nicey-nice.'

Kate lifted her head and stared at the dark-haired girl. 'I'll manage,' she said. 'And next time, if I reach your bed first, I'll stay there. You'll see how soft we oyster girls are, if you try me again.'

The gypsy's eyes hardened to pebbles. 'Will we now?'

'Yes, we will.'

They left it at that, but Kate knew she had made a formidable enemy. Gypsies were quick with their knives, and Kate had never been involved in any kind of violence in her life before. But she wasn't going to give in without a fight. She would show these cocklers who was a weakling and who was strong enough to put up with their heckling and tormenting.

Kate transferred the cockles to her carrying baskets, which were supported on her shoulders by a yoke, and took them to the stall holders that lined the Leigh shore. There she bargained with them. This was something she *was* used to, and they came to realise it straight away. Some of them knew her as an oyster girl, and asked what she was doing selling cockles.

Sally, the gypsy girl, heard and yelled out, 'She poisoned people with her oysters, so she can't sell 'em any more.'

The stall owners turned back to Kate and said, 'How can we trust your cockles if your oysters were no good?'

'Because they come from the same place as theirs,' snapped Kate, motioning towards Sally and her group, 'and if you're too thick-headed to understand that, you don't deserve to be selling shellfish.'

Eventually she found buyers for all her cockles, even the undersized ones, and marched past Sally and the other women with her head held high.

'Hoity-toity. You won't be back,' said an old woman, laughing.

'I'll be back,' said Kate, 'just watch me.'

Kate went back to the beach and collected her sledge, hiding it under a jetty where the tide could not reach it. She could not drag it all the way home to Paglesham, and there was no one she knew with a shed that would shelter it for her.

She walked all the way back to Paglesham and found her father still in bed: he seemed scarcely to have moved. Exhausted as she was, she helped to dress him, and took him outside to give him some air. He stood at the bottom of the yard, staring out over the creeks with a blank expression on his face.

After breakfast, Kate scrubbed the caked mud from her body, standing in a tub before the fire, and put on a fresh dress. Then she got some rest, falling into a deep sleep in the chair opposite her father's, where he sat puffing desultorily on his pipe. She woke later to the smell of burning and found he had spilled ash on his waistcoat, scorching a couple of holes in the cloth. When she had sorted out this accident, she tidied around the cottage.

Then it was time for the next tide. She took her father upstairs, getting him settled before beginning the long walk back to Leigh. She was not at all looking forward to going out on the mud again, but she knew she had to. In her head was the thought that Simon would be home in just over a year at the most, and she would have his support then. They might even start up another business, if she could save enough money in the meantime. It was not that she wanted him to keep her, for it was doubtful he would be able to even if she had, but she needed his love and inspiration to guide her through this dark time.

Chapter Ten

The third time Kate went cockling it was in the dark hours of the early morning. She walked the long lonely miles with a lantern, but on arriving at the jetty she looked underneath and found her cockling cart smashed to pieces. When she looked up from the wreckage of the sledge, she saw the faces in the light of the lamps. Sally's features were smug, with a sly smile at the corners of her mouth. The women had found the cart and had destroyed it, hoping to dishearten her enough to stop her coming again. Kate was dismayed, but tried not to show it.

'Well done,' she said bitterly, 'you've managed to rob an old man of his breakfast tomorrow. You must all be very pleased with yourselves.'

The smile left Sally's face instantly. 'You shouldn't be where you ain't wanted,' she said defensively.

Kate stared hard at the girl. 'Who put you in charge of the waterfront?'

'We don't want you here,' Sally cried.

'It doesn't matter what you *want*. If I am to put food on the table, I have to come here, whether it pleases you or not, you little madam. Or any of you. You better get used to me, because I'm not going away. And if anything like this happens again, I promise you that you'll regret it.'

'If you think . . .' began another woman, but Kate walked straight towards her, and she stumbled out of the way.

Kate continued, walking out on to the mud. The other women followed with their carts, but because she did not have to pull a sledge, Kate was out at the cockle beds long before the others arrived. She filled her apron from a prime spot, then made her way back to the beach with what she had.

The vats in the rickety cockle sheds were already on the boil and steam belched through the chinks in the boards and through the roof tiles. A row of stove chimneys with a metal cowling on each gave out smoke from the wood fires that burned within. There were over two dozen such sheds, each with its own stall in front, which lined the promenade walk to the west of Leigh. They filled the night air with their cooked shellfish odours and clouds of vapour. Out of the back hatch of these makeshift cookhouses the waste shells were thrown to form mountains on the beach.

Kate had heard that the cockles went first into a vat of sea water laced with oatmeal before they were boiled. The cockles were supposed to open to feed on the oatmeal and thereby discharge the grit inside the shell. The cockle sheds were secretive places and, when the back door was opened to the seller and a proprietor poked out his dripping head and shoulders, there was nothing to see but an interior thick with vapour and the misty shapes of vats. It was a place of mystery, where raw shellfish might have been changed into food by witchcraft.

Kate got rid of her apron-full of cockles to the first person who opened his door to her, then made her way homewards again to make a new sledge before the next tide. Dawn came up over the flatlands as she walked, following the winding lanes back to Paglesham. Kate's spirits were very low, and for the first time since the court had put them out of business, she felt like giving up. The only thing that stopped her was the certainty that it would kill her father to move him from the cottage. She hated being seen off by a bunch of stupid cocklers too. It was against Kate's nature to allow herself to be served unjust treatment. Nevertheless, her heart was heavy as she trudged along, wondering if she was going to manage to cope for at least another year.

When she finally arrived home, she had a surprise waiting for her.

Sarah and Liz had walked from Canewdon to the cottage on a short visit. They had moved their father out into the early morning sun for a while to give him some fresh air. Liz greeted Kate with a squeal of delight, hugging her eldest sister. Sarah was more reserved, but held Kate close for a moment.

'Oh Kate, dear,' said Sarah, stepping back and staring at her, 'how *thin* you've got.'

Kate laughed and brushed away a lock of hair stuck to her forehead by mud. 'I'm all right,' she said, trying to hide her weariness. 'I get sufficient for my needs.'

'And you look so tired,' Liz accused.

'A little bit of hard work didn't do anybody any harm. Anyway, you two are not exactly as fat as sows, are you?'

Liz said primly, 'I should hope not. But Kate, dearest, how are you managing? Are you still out on the cockle beds? Can't you find other work? I wish you would. Sarah has to work in the fields and that's better than cockling. Why can't you work with Sarah?'

'Because, sweet little sister,' growled Kate, cupping Liz's face in her hands, 'it wouldn't give me enough income to pay the rent of the cottage. Father would hate to move anywhere else, you know that. It would . . . it wouldn't do him any good to change his surroundings now. Anyway, I like cockling,' she lied.

Sixteen-year-old Sarah was not fooled for one minute. 'Look at you. Worn out, filthy from head to foot, and thin as a rake. How can you say you like it, Kate? You go and wash, while we carry Father inside between us, then I'll make us all some nice bread and jam sandwiches.'

'You brought some jam?' asked Kate.

'Greengage – made specially by Aunt Polly.'

Kate said it sounded wonderful, and went into the house to find a bowl. In the scullery she noticed with some relief that one of her sisters had filled the large water bucket from the pump, which would save her a tiring trip. Kate then had a luxurious wash in the cold water, making sure she got all the mud out of her hair. After drying she went upstairs to her bedroom and put on one of her best dresses.

Once she was completely dressed and had combed her hair, she felt ten times better. This visit by her sisters had revitalised her, making her feel less alone in the world. They could be silly and frivolous much of the time, but they had a lot of concern and love in their hearts. Kate felt warm and grateful towards them for turning a disastrous day into something resembling a happy one.

After they had had their bread and jam, they sat and talked, passing the day in idleness. A tide went by and Kate felt no guilt at missing it. Then, towards the end of the day, Kate asked Liz if she would stay with their father for a while.

'Why? Where are you going?'

'I have to collect some wood for a sledge. My other one . . . it wasn't strong enough. It broke up on the return journey today. I was hoping Sarah would help me make a new one before you both went back to Canewdon.'

'No,' stated Liz emphatically.

Kate's heart sank a little. 'No?'

The fourteen-year-old folded her arms. 'Sarah can stay and look after Father, while *I* help you with the sledge. I'm fed up with not doing any of the things which sound like fun, while you two enjoy yourselves. All I get to do is boring school work. You won't mind staying behind, will you Sarah?'

'Not a bit,' said Sarah. 'If you want to go looking for smelly wood along the shoreline, I'll be happy to stay here.'

Kate was delighted to have her youngest sister along with her, and the two of them chatted as they crossed the marshes to the river. There they gathered pieces of driftwood, loading them on to Kate's back, until they had enough. The evening was coming in as they returned to the house. A magenta sky drew wide lanes of purple across the marshland. The creatures were busy amongst the grasses and reeds, finding places to settle for the night. The peace slid into Kate's consciousness, filling her with a sense of calm. It was her sister who surprised her though, with her next remark.

'Listen to the birds,' breathed Liz.

Kate had always imagined that she was the only one out of the three sisters to be enthralled by the estuary country and its atmospheres. Sarah and Liz had always seemed too interested in material things to bother about the beauty of their own environment. They had until now considered a thought not connected with a new dress or an outing a thought wasted.

Now, in the twilight, she could see Liz's eyes shining with enthusiasm as they witnessed together the salt marshes, caught in the soft light of a dying sun, and listened to its creatures calling to one another.

'Isn't it wonderful?' asked Liz, quietly.

Kate, bowed over with the weight of the wood, was enjoying her sister's captivating expression of delight as much as she was the scene around her.

At least there's one of us who has not been too badly affected by our misfortunes, thought Kate, as she studied Liz's shining countenance. Thank the Lord for small mercies, at least. Perhaps Liz would come through unscathed?

Then Liz turned to her and said very seriously, 'Kate, dear, I think you're very brave. I couldn't do what you are doing, even for Father.'

A little taken aback by Liz's concern for her, Kate said, 'Oh silly, I'm all right.'

'No you're not. You hate what you're doing, I can see that – but it will come right one day, Kate. You wait and see. God will reward you...' and then more fiercely '... and if He doesn't, I will, when I get a good job and earn lots of money.'

'Oh love, *don't*,' Kate said, wanting to hug her young sister but unable to put down the wood, 'you'll have me in tears in a minute.'

'You wait and see,' said Liz, kissing Kate on the cheek.

When they reached the cottage it was time for the sisters to leave, for they had to walk back to Canewdon. There were a few tears – though not nearly as many as when they had said goodbye the last time – and then they were on their way.

Kate fetched the hammer after the girls had gone. She had rescued the nails from her wrecked sledge and these she used to fashion the new one. It was gone midnight by the time she had finished and it was time to walk to Leigh for the next tide.

She tucked her father in bed and left the house with the heavy sledge strapped to her back.

It was a long, gruelling walk, but when Kate finally dragged her sledge down the beach to the mud, she found the other women silent. Normally they would be calling her names, trying to ridicule her. If they had started their jeering, Kate would have turned and left for home, for she was at the end of her strength. The walk of seven miles with the sledge on her back had drained her of all resilience and her resistance was at its lowest since she had begun cockling.

She stared around at the silent faces, some showing scorn, some surprise, and tried herself to present an air of indifference. On one face, however, she saw something quite different from all others. It was Sally's expression that surprised Kate the most. If she could read it right, there was a look of grudging admiration beneath the glint of animosity in the girl's eyes.

'Come on then,' said Sally, after a few moments, 'what're we all waitin' for? Let's get out there. There's nothin' to hang around here for, is there?'

They all turned and began chattering amongst themselves as they pulled their sledges out on to the slick grey mud.

And so there was no attack on Kate, for which she was eternally grateful to the gypsy girl.

For the next few months, Kate worked the cockle beds without interference, though none of the other women spoke to her. She didn't mind that. She preferred to be left alone to her thoughts. It would have been nice if they had been friendly, but it seemed that this was not to be.

Kate had written to Simon about the change in her fortunes, but a letter had arrived from him a few days after she had posted it saying that his ship was about to leave India bound for Macao. Simon's captain had told the crew he had orders to subdue the pirates in the South China Sea, but there was word around the ship that the Chinese government had confiscated the British opium stores at Canton and that war was imminent.

The boatswain's mate says we're bound for the Macao Roads and the Pearl River and our true orders are to sink Chinese war junks. It seems that the emperor don't want us to sell his people any more opium, but the boatswain's mate says the Chinese merchants won't trade for anything else, so where will we get our tea, rhubarb, silk and porcelain, if not from them? I says to him, my excellent friend, how much silk and porcelain do you have in *your* house? As for the tea, why, India tea is just as refreshing as that from China. Of course we need the rhubarb, for it has medicinal properties, but for the rest the Chinese can keep them.

    I have seen opium smokers in the streets of Asia, my darling Kate, and they are so thin and wasted that their skin is stretched taut over their bones. Still, we must follow orders, the captain as well as we ordinary tars.

The letter then went on to say that once they had completed their mission in South China, they would probably go on to Sarawak in Borneo, where the Englishman James Brooke was in the process of subduing Dyak and Chinese pirates. The Sultan of Brunei had promised to make Brooke the first white rajah of Sarawak if he was successful in his endeavours to rid the area of brigands.

We are to offer Mr Brooke aid and then cross the Pacific Ocean to enter the Atlantic by way of Cape Horn. There are some stories about terrible storms around the Cape, but I am not so worried by them as by the fact that you may not hear from me again until I land in England, for there are no fast clippers coming from the Pacific. My darling Kate, do not take silence as meaning there is some concern for my safety, for you know your Simon will look to his own welfare and bring himself home to you hale and hearty. It is simply the fact that I do not know where we will be from one month to the next.

There were more reassurances, protestations of love, and the letter ended saying he 'missed her sorely'.

    Kate's heart was heavy, but she was secretly pleased he would not receive the letter she had just sent. She had deliberated with herself for a long time before writing it, not wishing to upset him and have him concern himself over the problems she was having. Finally she had written to him, describing a watered-down version of her troubles, but now the decision had been taken out of her hands. He would not receive the letter and therefore would not be made anxious.

One day, Kate was making tea when there was a knock on the door. On opening it she was confronted by Johann Haagan, who took a step backwards and exclaimed, 'Good lord!' before Kate realised she had not yet bathed after returning from her last cockling, and consequently was covered in mud from head to toe. She smiled at him through the caked dirt.

'What's the matter? Have you never seen a girl looking so pretty before?'

'Kate,' he stammered, 'I'm sorry. I didn't mean to be so rude, but you gave me a fright. You look like some monster that has emerged from the marshes.'

She laughed again. 'Thank you, kind sir. I accept the compliment.'

This made Johann feel worse, and he went red to the roots of his floppy blond hair. 'No, that was ghastly of me, I didn't mean that. I'm just not used to seeing you so . . . so . . .'

'So dirty,' she said. 'Won't you come in and share some tea? Father and I are about to have some. The mud isn't catching, you know.'

He took off his hat and ducked under the low doorway. 'Thank you, I will. I've been worried about you, Kate. You haven't been to church in months, and you've been neglecting your education. I thought we were doing so splendidly.'

'I think we were,' she said, busying herself with the cups while he sat on the other side of the fireplace from Edward. 'Unfortunately, I have no time for church or education at the moment. I must catch each tide, for the cockling, or we'll not be able to pay the rent. Here . . .' She passed Johann a cup of tea.

Johann looked nervously at Edward as Kate bent to give him his drink. He saw that the old man's eyes were vacant, and then remembered that Edward Fernlee was not so very old and this was the real tragedy of the affair.

Edward's hand reached for the cup, took it, and indeed he began to sip its contents, but there was nothing in his eyes to indicate that he knew where he was or what he was doing. It was frightening for a young curate to witness this shell of a middle-aged man, seemingly devoid of spirit or mind.

Is this what we all come to? thought Johann.

'And how are you coping?' he asked Kate, merely trying to fill the hole of silence with conversation. 'I mean, I know you're not having a good time at the moment, but are you hearing from your fiancé frequently?'

Kate who, despite the layer of mud, looked as if she had lost a few pounds, sank back into a chair beside her father, sipping her own tea. In the light from the window her eyes looked dark-ringed and hollow. She seemed to Johann to be close to exhaustion.

'Simon is on his way to the Pacific Ocean, wherever that is,' she said, 'and can't receive or send letters.'

'The Pacific Ocean,' he wagged a playful finger at her, 'is between south-east Asia and the American Continent. I showed you on the atlas last time we had a lesson.'

'I'm afraid all that seems so long ago,' she smiled faintly. 'I'm sorry I'm such a poor pupil and forget so easily.'

His heart went out to her. 'Kate, Kate, are you *sure* you won't take something from me? You look ill. You can't drive yourself into the ground like this. Let your sisters come and look after Edward while you get some rest.'

'They have enough trouble feeding themselves. I don't want to drag them down further. They need to find husbands sometime and they won't do it here. When Simon comes home, things will improve, you'll see.'

'I want to meet this Simon, who is by all accounts some kind of superhuman fellow. A man who rights wrongs with a wave of his hand. A master of life and death.'

She smiled at this. 'No, he's not a god, of course he's not, but I feel so much stronger when he's around. When you can share your problems, they seem so much less weighty.'

Johann sighed. 'I suppose you're right. I would offer myself before the altar of your dazzling beauty, if I thought for one moment you would have me, but alas I'm no match for this magnificent Simon, be he present or absent.'

Kate giggled at this compliment. 'You're such an old fraud, Johann Haagan. You don't love me and you never could. You want some highborn lady, who doesn't embarrass you with country speech and can keep you in the manner to which you would like to be accustomed. In any case, you're right. In my eyes no one can hold a candle to Simon so, handsome as you are Reverend Haagan, you would not do for me, nor me for you.'

Johann was for a very brief second tempted to argue with her, but on looking into her eyes and seeing distant seas there, he wisely remained silent. He could love her, very easily, if he allowed himself. But one didn't. One kept a tight rein on one's feelings and did not let them run downhill to make a fool of one. He had already been hurt, and had hurt someone else, once in his life. It was enough. Once was enough. The wounds were still raw from that encounter and it would take half a lifetime to heal them. The dreams still came, the remembrances were relentless, the hurt uncompromising. He had often wondered whether it was possible to suffer such agonies of mind and spirit and still remain whole. There were times when he felt he was being eaten away, from the inside, and would one day collapse like a deflated balloon.

She was right about him reaching high, too. The speech of the local women *did* grate on his nerves. He wanted – what did he want? – certainly someone whose enunciation was clear and precise, who could articulate, whose diction did not leave him inwardly wincing. He wanted someone to whom poetry was not a foreign language. Someone who could play the pianoforté with modest skill. Someone who could produce a passable watercolour painting. In short, he wanted a lady who would appreciate his finer points, his manners, his education. The local women, well they gaped at him if he quoted Wordsworth, as if he had just produced a fish from his waistcoat and was eating it raw. Not Kate, of course, for she was bright enough to know that education was good for one, and was not something to be sneered at.

'Have you made many new friends at this new profession of yours?' he asked.

Kate exploded with a violent 'Ha!' which almost had him dropping his cup of tea.

'I take it that means no,' he said.

'When you get down to the bottom of society,' she explained, 'the competition for every crust is fierce. You can't afford to make friends. You make alliances and treaties with your enemies to keep out competitors, but there is no such thing as loyalty.'

He was shocked by what she said, but impressed by the articulate way in which she said it.

'That's very profound,' he said. 'My teaching hasn't been in vain after all. Who in particular dislikes you?'

'*Hates* me. "Dislike" is not a word used by the people I have to work alongside. It's too weak and watery. I am hated. Oh, I don't know, there's this gypsy girl, Sally, not more than seventeen or eighteen years of age. She seemed to loathe me from the outset, and though she leaves me alone now, I catch her looking at me with such naked hate I wonder what's going on inside that head of hers. What does she think I've done to her?'

Johann thought for a bit, then said, 'If a lady of some consequence, not even necessarily a lady of *ton*, say the squire's wife, came down to the River Roche and started an oyster bed beside yours, what would you think? A lady invading your world, taking the bread and butter out of your mouth?'

'I'd think, "What's she doing here? Why doesn't she stay with her own kind? Why doesn't she do the things a squire's wife should be doing?" It would be wrong of me, but that's what I would think.'

'You see what I mean?'

'No,' said Kate. 'I'm not a squire's wife.'

'No, but you're an oyster farmer's daughter, which to the cockle women represents a similar social divide. To them, you are a class above theirs, and you should not be poaching on their territory. They don't realise that it only takes one stroke of the law's pen to make you into one of them.'

Kate thought about this and decided that Johann was probably right. She was ashamed to think it now, but when she asked herself whether she would have had anything to do with cockle girls before being reduced to being one herself, she had to answer 'no'. They had been creatures from another world in those days, and there would have been no need to have contact with them. Had she been asked, she would have said they were promiscuous creatures, who gave their favours to the highest bidder at the inn. This judgement had been founded on one or two observances and a great deal of hearsay. She had to admit now that they did not seem any more flirtatious than those of her own social standing: they worked too many hard, long hours in the day to have any time left to spend in taverns. One or two wayward cocklers and triggers gave the rest a bad name, that was all. And who was she to sit in judgement anyway?

'Well,' she said to Johann, 'you've told me why they hate me. Now tell me what to do about it.'

Johann shrugged. 'Nothing. There's nothing you can do about it. As you say, they don't even befriend one another, so how can you expect to gain their confidence and respect? Just do as you are doing, I suppose. Work your own way, keep out of theirs.'

Once Johann had gone, Kate bathed, finished some sewing, then put Edward to bed. It was coming on evening by the time she left him quietly in his room.

Her talk with Johann had invigorated her, making the tiredness in her bones seem less oppressive. She tied her hair back, put on her shawl, and took a walk along the narrow path by the orchard to the church.

It was a fine summer evening. The tide would not be fully out for another five hours, so she had time to spare for leisure for once. Thrushes were taking up their posts on various trees and houses, to tell others in their sweet songsters' way that they would resent any intrusion of their territory, and were prepared to battle to the death to defend it.

Behind the church, the broad reaches of the dengies swept southwards, the marsh reeds all leaning one way as if smoothed by a giant hand. Single trees dotted the landscape to the east, along the ditches of the reclaimed land, and there too the brambles and briars ran havoc around elderberry bushes. Where the reclamation had not been thoroughly effective, stagnant ponds were covered in chickweed and inhabited by coots and moorhens. These were dark forbidding stretches of water that seemed to belong to some other, darker age.

Here in the estuary country, water and earth had formed an uneasy alliance, in order to present a larger face to the vast sky which threatened to overwhelm them. It was never certain where the land stopped and where the sea began. Here the sea crept through mysterious channels, reaching into the heartland country. There were sudden appearances of islands emerging from the still waters. What was submerged today might be exposed tomorrow. What was solid ground yesterday might have been treacherous waters the day before. The face of the estuary country had many masks and disguises which it wore at random, keeping even its closest neighbours insecure. It was an unreal place and eerie to strangers, who found its people strange and its geography stranger.

Kate went through the lych-gate into the churchyard and thence to the west corner of the old stone building. There she knelt by a tomb. Her mother was buried beneath a simple gravestone, the engraved lettering of which was already beginning to fill with moss and lichen. Kate found a stick and scraped out the worst of it, reminding herself to bring a stiff brush next time she came.

She did not speak to her mother, as some did when they visited the dead, but her thoughts reached out.

Mother, I'm only barely hanging on. I wish you were here to help us through this, but it would have hurt you too much to see Father in this state. The girls are fine, though, and you'd be proud of them. Sarah is very pretty and Liz is bright and intelligent. I could not ask for nicer sisters. Mother, I miss you so much now. Anyway, since you can't be here I hope you are happy where you are. Goodbye, Mother.

When she had finished meditating, she went inside the church to pray. Jason Molar was there, just inside the doorway, chipping away at a block of stone that was needed to replace a crumbled corner of one of the chancel windows. Jason was the local stonemason, a fellow of cryptic years and a quiet disposition. The block of stone rested between his sprawled legs, one of which was wooden: Jason had fought in the Napoleonic Wars. There were gunpowder burns on his face, like dark birthmark maps, and one shoulder dropped lower than the other.

'Hello Jason,' said Kate.

'Eve'nin', Miss Fernlee,' muttered Jason. 'You want me to stop while you says your prayers?'

'No, don't worry,' she smiled. 'I don't need that much peace. We all get that in the end.'

'You'm right there,' he answered, ceasing his chiselling anyway.

Kate went to her usual pew under the south window, where the red sky was visible through the line of clear panes above the stained-glass picture of St George killing the dragon. She had often wondered what the dragon was supposed to represent. Lust? Such bold thoughts made her wonder at herself too. Was she a sinful woman to have such thoughts? At night, in her bed, she purposely pictured Simon with her, his slim hard body pressed against hers, so that she might fall asleep with him in mind and have dreams of him making love to her. Sometimes it worked and she would wake in a state of high excitement, admonishing herself for not missing the purity of his fine spirit more than his physical presence. The trouble was, she loved him with her body as much as her soul, and the remembrances of the one time they had made love together had left her wanting.

Her prayers said, Kate then went to the doorway, where Jason was about to begin his work again. 'Jason,' she said, 'you were in the Navy.'

'I was that too, miss. Admiral Nelson's Navy, and after. Fought in all sorts of battles. Left me leg in some foreign sea, but I don't miss 'er, 'cause I had one of those there ingrown toenails, which gave me gip. The fish can keep it.' This was a joke he never tired of telling.

'Had a pal,' he continued, 'what lost an arm and brought it back with 'im. Keeps the bones on his mantle, so he do – a ghas'ly skeleton hand which rattles when 'ers shook. Scares the gran'children with it on festival occasions.'

Kate smiled at him. 'You do tell some whoppers, Jason, but I've a question to ask of you. Have you heard of the Macao Roads? What is that?'

'Porteegese Macao? I have that, miss. Up around Chinee way. Dangerous waters with them Chinee pirate junkships.'

'What *are* the Macao Roads?'

'Oh, they be straits, that's all. Not like roads on land, if that's what you were thinkin'.'

'Oh, thank you. I just wondered, that was all.'

'If you'm thinkin' of your boy, the Wentworth lad, he'll be alroight, don't you fret. He's no coward but he's a careful one. He won't rush in where angels won't go, don't you worry on that young lady. It's only the daft ones what gets their heads blowed off.'

With that, Jason began chipping away again at his block of weathered limestone. Kate strolled from the church, out into the evening with its blood-streaked sky, hoping her prayers for Simon's safety would be heard.

Chapter Eleven

In the dead of night, a week after Johann's visit to Kate, three brothers set off from the French coast in their small sailing craft, bound for the Essex waterways. The names of the men were Peter, Luke and Joseph, and they were the three brothers of Simon Wentworth, notorious for smuggling contraband goods into England from foreign shores.

Peter was the eldest, at thirty, with Luke five years behind him, and Joseph the youngest in the family at twenty-one. None of the brothers had ever married, for their lifestyle was not one that a woman would want to share. Not that they had any lack of female companionship, but their love affairs tended to be fleeting, often as brief as one night.

All three men had declared a distinct lack of interest in the marital state, for Peter had instilled in the other two that while a woman might say she didn't mind what her *boyfriend* did for a living, once married they often jibed or came about sharply, wanting to run with the wind. Married women find life stormy enough, without heading into squalls for the sheer hell of it. They want to join all the other wives in a safe haven. In short, a married woman would have you jettison your old illicit ways overboard, and settle you to an honest life of fishing or transporting legal cargo, so Peter maintained.

'How's it feeling?' asked Joseph of his eldest brother, as they made their course across the channel. His voice was a whisper, for it was best to keep any noise to a minimum at all times, so that mistakes were not made during crucial periods. 'Is the sea running?'

'There's a heavy swell coming down from the Skagerrak, but she'll be all right. You just make sure them brandy barrels is lashed tight in the hold. I don't want them rolling back'ards and forrards making noises when we're in the creeks.'

'Luke's doing that now,' said Joseph, settling himself in the bow.

They carried no lights, of course, so all three brothers kept a keen watch on the night around them, for flotsam and jetsam as well as for other boats. A half-submerged log had holed the hull of their previous craft and sank it not far from the Southwold lighthouse, and they had had to swim ashore in freezing waters. All three had made it to the beach, Peter and Luke dragging the sixteen-year-old Joseph between them. Such was the hardness of these men that they had stopped to collect terns' eggs from amongst the pebbles on Southwold beach before taking the short ferry trip across the River Blyth to Walberswick where they borrowed a skiff from a fisherman they knew. They did not want to go home to their mother empty-handed: the terns' eggs were for their breakfast.

Since that night, the brothers had been more vigilant than ever in their watch for floating debris. Joseph normally sat in the bow, as he did tonight, while Luke watched to windward and Peter towards the direction from which the flow was coming, thus covering all the likely routes of dangerous flotsam.

Tonight, about a mile out from the network of Essex creeks, they spotted a Thames barge cruising along the coastline. Peter was immediately suspicious. Although the barge was well-lit and not trying to hide its presence, it was under full canvas on a night when the wind was strong, and a normally cautious barge captain would have taken in a few reefs of mainsail when navigating the bars off Maplin Sands.

The blunt, heavy craft was high in the water too, indicating an empty hold. Where was a Thames barge without a cargo thinking of going in such a hurry? While not unusual for the lug-sailed craft to come out of their mother river to visit Harwich or Felixstowe, it was uneconomical for such barges to make voyages up the coast unless loaded with cargo both ways, when less ponderous sail-boats could make the trip in a shorter time.

'They're watchin' the creeks,' growled Peter.

Luke said, 'We could make a dash for it. By the time they see us, they'll have to come about, and we'll be in amongst the creeks. They'll never catch us there.'

Joseph said, 'No, but if they've taken the trouble to hire a barge, there'll be customs and excise men thicker than wildfowl in the creeks tonight. They're after somebody, and maybe it's us. We got our enemies, don't forget. There's those who know where we're at on a moonless night.'

Peter grunted. 'Listen to your little brother, Luke. He knows what he's talkin' about.'

'So what are we going to do?' Luke grumbled. 'Dump the brandy overboard?'

Peter shook his head. 'Not likely. We'll use our old standby, St Peter's-on-the-Wall . . .'

They turned the craft back out to sea again, anxious to get further up the coast before light. They beat a passage in a lazy arc until they were off Sales Point at the mouth of the Blackwater River, then made a quick dash to shore, beaching the boat on St Peter's flats. There they unloaded their illegal cargo and stored it in the seventh-century church, St Peter's-on-the-Wall, raised by St Cedd from the stones of the old Roman fort of Othona.

The church was the first ever built on the English mainland, but had been deconsecrated and used variously as a beacon-tower, barn and cattle-shed for several centuries. The brothers had discovered it one night when they were desperate for a hiding place, and since then had used it to store their contraband temporarily, before sailing off down the coast and into the arms of the excise men carrying nothing but a few sacks of flour.

They had just finished rolling the last barrel of brandy into the old, barn-like church, when they heard a voice and the shuffling gait of cows being herded along the sea-wall path. Luke went outside to see a farm hand bringing his cows towards the church, obviously intending to use it to shelter his cattle for a while.

Luke held up his hand as the cowherd approached. 'What do you think you're on, gaffer?' he said, sternly.

The farm hand jumped back, startled, his white smock flapping round his legs. He had obviously not been expecting to see anyone emerge from the church. Then he peered through the murk at Luke. 'Whatsay?' he cried.

'I said, what do you think you're doin', eh? This old place has been took over by the excise, for watchin' the river mouth. You can't put your stinkin' old cows in here no more.'

'Whatsay?' cried the cowherd. 'I bin usin' that there barn on and off all me life.'

'Not no more, you don't. This is Her Majesty's business being conducted 'ere. This ain't no barn anyhow. It's a church. You can't put beasts in a church. It ain't . . . it's not Christian.'

'Jesus hisself were born in a barn with sheep an' cows all round his cot, so don't you give me none of that flummery,' cried the cowherd, waving his switch. 'Anyhow, my cows don't stink see, they smells the same as you and me.'

'You maybe, not me.'

At that moment Peter strode out of the church with his thumbs in his belt looking very important. He yelled back over his shoulder, 'You men keep them firearms primed, you hear? We can't be too careful, what with smugglers comin' up and down the Blackwater all the time.'

Luke heard his brother Joseph shout, 'Yes, sir,' in a very military tone.

Then Peter seemed to notice the cowherd for the first time. 'What's all this then? Somebody smuggling cattle, are they?'

Luke suppressed a guffaw. 'No sir, this 'ere is a local farm hand, honest I expect, though you never can tell.'

Peter frowned at the cowherd, who was now shuffling his feet and looking very unsure of himself. 'Oh, they always *looks* honest, don't they?'

'I be as honest as the next man,' cried the farm hand.

'And how honest is *he*, I wonder?' said Peter. 'You be off with you, fellow, and let the Queen's business be done here. I don't want to have to order my marines out.'

The cowherd blinked and then, no doubt feeling the whole thing was a bit too much for him, turned and trudged back along the path, crying, 'Oooyup, ahhh,' at his cows every so often, flicking the tail-enders with his switch.

Using a large padlock they carried for the purpose, the three brothers secured the church. Then they went back to their boat and pushed off, heading back down the coast again. Sure enough they encountered excise men as they tried to enter the mouth of the Crouch. The customs officials came at them in two small skiffs and boarded them.

'What's all this? Bothering honest men?' cried Peter.

The excise man in charge wagged a finger. 'We've been ordered to search all craft entering the river. It seems there are brandy smugglers in these parts.'

'Noooo?' cried Luke, looking at his brother Joseph as if he were one of the wanted men.

When the customs men searched the boat, they found nothing but fishing nets in the hold. They reported to their captain, who said, 'Been out all night and not caught a single fish?'

'We caught plenty,' snapped Peter, 'but we sold 'em up in Lowestoft.'

'Your nets are dry; anyway, why go all the way up to Norfolk? Don't they buy fish in Essex?'

'We dry our nets on the boom,' said Luke with disgust in his tone, 'as any *real* fisherman would know. Just as they would know that the price of fish in Lowestoft is higher than in Essex at this time, due to the fish farms in this area being overstocked. Now, will you get off our boat, or be thrown off? You've searched us and found nothing, so go an' play your games someplace else.'

The excise captain gave the three brothers a hard look, then ordered his men off the craft. Before he left, he turned and said, 'We'll catch you one of these days, don't you worry. Then I'll take pleasure in seeing you locked up, or hung, or deported to the Australian continent. All three if I can get 'em.'

Then he climbed down into one of the skiffs and was rowed to shore, leaving the three brothers smiling.

The brothers went into the Crouch, then entered the Roche, sailing down to Stambridge mills. There they moored their craft and made their way to the Cherry Tree Inn, where they knocked on the door. The landlady let them in, gave them each a noggin, and asked what they had brought her.

'The goods is hid for the moment,' said Peter, 'but we'll fetch it later. We need a waggon and horses.'

'You can use the dray,' said the landlady, 'if we gets the whole shipment.'

'We've got to agree a price first. We'll knock a bit off for the hire of the dray, o' course . . .'

They got down to bargaining and shook hands on coming to an agreement. Then the brothers applied themselves to some serious drinking, speaking mournfully about their wayward sibling, Simon, who refused to enter the family business, and was away on some damn fool errand, fighting for queen and country.

'It's such a shame,' said Peter, 'but we love 'im, God bless 'im. Here's a toast. To our honest Simon. May he come to his senses soon and join his brothers in their enterprises!'

'To Simon,' chorused the other two.

When they had been drinking for about two hours, Joseph went out the back to relieve himself. While he was absent the door burst open and the room was suddenly filled with excise men, all bearing arms.

The excise man they had encountered earlier in the day stepped forward. 'Wentworths, you're under arrest.'

Peter took a sip of his ale and sniffed. Luke shrugged. Both brothers stood up, though, slowly, their hands in full view of the arresting officers. They were confronted by seven tough men, each one pointing a firearm, and knew it would be suicide to try to fight their way out.

'Arrest?' repeated Peter. 'What for?'

'Smuggling goods from France. We found your cache, Peter Wentworth, where you stowed it this morning. Let's go – you can make any protests to the magistrate. Let me have those pistols.'

While they reached for their weapons, the excise man looked around the room. 'There should be three of them,' he said. 'Where's the other one?'

Peter dropped his pistol on to the table with a clatter, and Luke took advantage of the distracting noise. Without warning, he fired his pistol into the rafters of the ceiling, then threw the smoking gun to the floor. He grinned at the startled looks on the faces of his captors, knowing he had been within a hair's-breadth of being shot down by nervous excise men.

'Half-way to France by now, I should reckon,' he told the excise man, 'if he's heard that shot. An' my brother's got good ears, if nothing else.'

A moment later there was the sound of horses' hooves pounding the road outside. Two of the excise men ran to the doorway to pursue Joseph, while the others stayed to guard the two captured brothers.

Chapter Twelve

Kate wrote to Simon, telling him about the arrest of his brothers, hoping the letter would reach him wherever he was.

> My Dearest Simon,
> I wish I did not have to be the one to tell you, but your brothers Peter and Luke have been arrested and convicted of smuggling. We have yet to hear what the sentence is, but we are hoping and praying that they will not be sent to the colonies. Joseph managed to escape, to France we think, so at least one of your family is still free. Oh Simon, I'm so sorry. I know how this will upset you and wish I could be with you to help soothe your pain. It had to happen one day of course, for you know your brothers and how they would never have given up running goods from the French coast. It's in their blood. They take after your father, unfortunately. Peter actually laughed at the magistrate when he was taken into the dock, and told him his wig was on crooked. There is no cure for them, those brothers of yours, though I know you still love them.
> On other matters, we are all fine . . .

Kate's humdrum and weary existence as a cockler continued into autumn. Gradually, however, despite all her efforts, her hold on the cottage began to loosen. The money she earned from cockling was not enough to feed them and keep the roof over their heads, and she began to fall behind on the rent, despite the fact that she was selling pieces of furniture to supplement their income. The squire's man, Siddons, did not press her for the back rent, but she knew there would be a limit to his generosity. Siddons was a kindly man who assisted the squire in the management of his estates, collecting the squire's rents from the farmers and cottagers, and he was probably taking it on his own back for the moment, but sooner or later it would have to come to the attention of the squire himself. When that day came no doubt the squire would say, 'What's this? If these people don't pay their rent, then out they go!' Squire Pritchard was not a cruel man, but neither was he a philanthropist.

At the cockling, the women remained unfriendly, but Kate saw no reason to complain about them. She would have preferred a more amicable atmosphere but, after her conversation with Johann, she recognised the vast gulf that lay between their lives and hers, especially her former life. These people were caught in the death grip of poverty. They lived in miserable, makeshift shacks, on the shoreline between Leigh and Benfleet, that had been thrown together in haphazard fashion. Their living conditions were appalling. The shanties, constructed mostly of boxwood and tarpaulin, let in the wind and rain. In the worst weather the cocklers lit open fires inside their dwellings and were in danger of burning their flimsy homes to the ground.

She knew that few of them lived to any great age. They froze to death in their sleep, the children wasted away with malnutrition, they caught respiratory diseases and skin infections which dragged them down, eventually to the grave. The only compensation for living this kind of life was that among their own kind poverty was universal. No one was better off than her neighbour. This produced the kind of camaraderie to be found amongst soldiers living in dire conditions. They were all in the same position. They commiserated with one another, helped the neighbour in danger of going under, and felt they were not alone in the world. Consequently, when someone came along who was clearly better off than they were, they resented them. It was enough that they didn't hinder Kate now, even spoke to her occasionally; though they simply could not bring themselves to make the enormous leap from distrust to friendliness.

It was an early-dawn ebb tide, with the wind coming in sharply from the north-east. Kate walked the miles to Leigh as usual and found her cart where she had left it six hours previously. The women had not broken it again after that first time, for which Kate was thankful. She had warned them against repeating the act, though what she would have done had they ignored the threat, she had no real idea. She was one against many, and there was no law out on the mudflats.

Kate dragged her sledge out with the rest of the women. Having gained a working knowledge of the topography of the mud, she could read the surface and skirt the soft patches and avoid getting caught in the fork of two deep channels. She was also aware of where the best cockle beds were to be found, and if she got there first, her place was no longer disputed.

There was one problem which all the cockle women shared. Of late, the cockle shed owners had been lowering their prices for the raw shellfish, as if they had formed some sort of cartel to keep the prices low. Kate was convinced they had agreed a price between themselves, for it was unusually uniform. They all stuck to it, too, whichever one Kate went to with her cockles. She had asked the other women what they were going to do about it.

'Nothin',' Sally had replied. 'What else can we do?'

'Can I suggest something?' Kate had said.

'No thank you, madam. We can look after ourselves,' Sally had snapped.

'Well, we're all going to starve this winter, if nobody does anything,' Kate had finished.

She thought about this as she dragged her sledge over the pearl-hued mud, leaving slick twin snails' tracks in her wake. There *was* something they could do, but she would need the help of all the cocklers to do it. If one or two disagreed with the plan, then it would collapse. However, they did not trust her, and it was doubtful she could gain their cooperation overnight.

The grey dawn crept over the distant sea like a reluctant ghost preparing for a haunting. Out on the horizon were the ships, coming and going, past Sheppey and Sheerness and the Isle of Grain. They made her think of Simon, on his own ship, probably in some battle on the waters of the Orient. She could not picture it. Nor could she even consider that he might be killed. Kate was not a woman to dwell on horrors that might never happen. Yet she was subliminally prepared for anything. Every unexpected turn of events was a surprise to her, but nothing was a shock.

She raked the cockles and filled her cart as the light in the sky increased and a piece of red sun appeared on the horizon. The wind began to increase in strength as the women worked, until after twenty minutes it was flapping their skirts like flags. There was a danger here. A strong wind not only kept the water from completing its ebb but, once the tide turned, drove it into its flow much faster than normal, so the women had to fill their carts more quickly than usual to beat the tide back to the beach. Those children who had accompanied their mothers or sisters were sent back to shore, except for the babies in slings which remained on the mothers' backs.

The fury of the wind increased still more, and gradually women began to leave with carts only three-quarters full. Others worked desperately, trying to gather as much as they could before the race to the shore became absolutely essential. There was an urgency amongst them, for the sea was returning like a running army, rolling over the mud ripples and swallowing all in its path. Finally, the last of the cocklers turned and headed back to the beach, her feet moving at a trot in order to beat the incoming flood.

In the estuary the sea does not shuffle back and forth on its progress over the land, such as the ordinary seaside visitor expects of the ocean tide, advancing and retreating until it covers the beach. Instead it sweeps in, never going back and uncovering what it has already reclaimed, but rolling forward all the time. When a strong leeward wind is pushing it, the ocean rushes in like a torrent let loose from a breached dam, and floods the mud plain in a very short time.

Kate's cart was only three-quarters full when she began trotting back to the beach. Stronger now than when she had first started on the cockle beds, and more practised, she was able to move quickly when she needed to. The other women were yelling to one another, urging their friends to get back to the beach before they were swallowed.

'Quickly, here it comes.'

'Don't wait for me. You go on.'

Racing for her life, Kate was with the last line of cocklers, keeping pace with each other. The beach seemed a thousand miles away: a dark shoreline beyond a vast stretch of sucking mud. Like the other women, her eyes were glued to the surface of the mud, seeking out the hard patches over which her progress would be faster. The parts to avoid were bubbled and grey, whereas the stony patches had a light covering of green algae. It was the green patches that the women sought and used, avoiding the grey and brown where they could. The gullies down which the rays – the advance cavalry of the incoming tide – raced and swirled were given a wide berth.

Her legs aching with the effort and her lungs bursting, Kate kept up with the stragglers; and eventually the shore actually appeared to be getting closer instead of further away. The tearing pain in her lungs as she swallowed harsh air made her eyes water each time she sucked a breath.

The wind tore at the women's clothes and hair, and their braids whipped their cheeks and lashed their throats. There was spume in the air, the salt water stinging their eyes.

Some young men were on the shore laughing at the women as their skirts blew up over their faces. The youths thought it hilarious that caps were blowing off and sailing into the tidal rush. When a woman's cart got stuck, they yelled inane advice on how to get it moving again.

Kate's arms were almost out of her sockets when the water caught up with her, swirled round her ankles and rolled on in front of her. She felt the silt go from under her feet, but kept them moving for fear of getting stuck. The youths whooped at her distress, not understanding that they were witnessing a life and death struggle with the elements.

When she was about forty feet from the shore, she sank in the mire up to the top of her calves and had to let the cart go. By this time there was enough water underneath it to make it float and the sledge was taken in on the next wave. One of the young boys ran down and rescued it for her as it hit the beach, though some of her precious cockles tipped out and were reclaimed by the triumphantly savage sea.

The young man who had rescued her cart was laughing and waving to his catcalling friends.

She struggled to free one leg, only to have the other sink further. Then she fell forward on to her hands, letting the surf wash over her, and sliding the leg out of the sucking mud. She allowed the next wave to carry her forward, without touching the bottom. It was best, she decided, to let the cold water wash her in like driftwood, for as soon as she put a foot down it would sink in the mud. Now only about twenty feet out from the beach, and prepared to let the tide wash her in, she was suddenly aware that the women were screaming at her, gesticulating at something behind her. The young men had fallen silent, their mouths agape and their eyes staring.

The next wave washed over her head, but she managed to turn in its wake and look over her shoulder. There was a plump woman caught by the mud, some six or seven feet behind her. On the woman's face was such a look of terror that it shocked Kate to the core. The woman's head was only just above the waves and she was having to tip it back to gulp air after every wave. Even so, it seemed she must be swallowing water because she coughed and choked. Her eyes were round orbs with pinpoints of black that darted from side to side. She was clearly beyond plain fear and into a frame of mind where her reason abandoned her, leaving only stark panic behind.

The woman's arms reached up and her fingers clawed at the air as if seeking some kind of hold there.

Kate didn't hesitate: her immediate response was to turn and try to help the woman. She half-paddled, half-swam in the waist-deep water towards the woman, careful to remain out of range of her clawing fingers and to avoid putting her feet on the treacherous mud. Then she went under the surface, into the turmoil of currents below. Feeling around in the cloudy water, she eventually found the woman's skirts. As her hands tugged at the cloth, Kate realised that the woman's legs had disappeared into the mud: she was buried to her thighs and sinking deeper by the minute.

Kate began scooping at the liquidised mud, trying to free the victim, but the mud simply flowed back into the holes she made. The woman, now realising someone was under the water, began reaching for Kate in her terror to grip anything, anything that might give her some leverage to prise herself free.

Kate felt the fingers brush her back and wisely retreated. Her lungs were wrenching at her chest, needing air. She moved out of the woman's reach and surfaced, gulping down oxygen. Then she heard the screams from the beach and, turning, saw that they were unravelling a rope taken from a fishing boat. The drag of the current was pulling Kate obliquely along the shore and she had to struggle to maintain her position, her arms and legs growing more tired by the second. She was close to exhaustion, the cold current penetrating her flesh.

The first two attempts at throwing the rope were failures, but on the third cast the end of the rope slapped the water by Kate's shoulder and she grabbed it. The drowning woman was now completely under water, her grey-black hair floating on the waves.

With her chest heaving and fierce pain raking her lungs, Kate took the end of the rope between her teeth and managed to dive again. She searched in the murk of swirling silt and water, unable to find the woman at first. Using her hands, she pulled herself along the bottom, feeling her way through the turbid waters.

As the currents whipped her body back and forth, dragging it this way and that, Kate became disorientated, and began to despair of finding the woman. The eddies twisted down from the surface like corkscrews, churning the silt so that she could not see an inch in front of her face. Then, just as she was about to go up for air, a piece of skirt brushed Kate's arm, and she clutched it, pulling herself close to the trapped woman. She began to loop the rope around the woman's torso, desperate for air herself, her lungs screaming.

Suddenly Kate felt the woman's arms lock around her neck, clutching her in a death grip. She managed to tie the knot in the rope then, as blackness was overcoming her, and the pain began to slide away somewhere beyond her body, she feebly attempted to prise the woman's arms from round her neck. At the same time, the line went taut under her armpit, and began to cut into her flesh.

Frantically she tore at the woman's hands, managing to get one arm free, and took a gulp of air, but she was still below the surface and there was only water. Her agony increased: there was a red-hot iron burning a cavity in her chest and she knew she was going to die. Suddenly the woman's grip loosened, but Kate's arm was trapped between her body and the tightened rope and she could not free herself. There was movement as those on the other end of the rope heaved, but Kate could no longer hold on to consciousness. She took one more swallow, this time taking in half-air, half-water, as a trough scoured the mud from the sea bottom, then her mind collapsed.

The blackness engulfed her completely.

When Kate woke, she was lying on her stomach on the beach. She was very cold and shivering violently. Someone had put a coat over her. There were hands pummelling her back. She felt a heaving in her stomach and suddenly she was vomiting violently, bringing up a gush of warm seawater over the sand.

'That's better,' said a man's voice, 'that'll do 'er good, that will. Let 'er come lass, and keep them eyes open.'

She felt hands on her, rubbing her flesh to put warmth into her limbs. Gradually, her senses returned to normal, and she was able to sit up, though the cold was still deep in her bones and she could not stop shaking. Her teeth rattled in her head, and would not be stilled, even when a cup of hot liquid was pressed to her lips.

She looked round. 'What ... what about the other woman?' she asked.

A police constable stood over her. 'She's been took away, lass.'

Kate said, 'Was she alive?'

'Ah, think so. She were in a bad way, but her was breathin', so we hopes so. You did magnificent there, lass – these young lads tole me what you did, and you should be proud of yourself.'

Kate was now sober enough to reflect with wry chagrin on the fact that the policeman was calling her 'lass' instead of 'miss': at last she was accepted as one of the cocklers.

There was quite a crowd around her, but she could not see any of the other cocklers. No doubt they had all gone back with the woman Kate had helped to rescue. This stung a little, for Kate would have thought that one or two might have remained to see that she recovered. Still, they were a hard, unfathomable lot. Kate would not have put it past them to *resent* her for being the one to save the woman. They did not appreciate being obligated to outsiders.

She felt under her arm, where it was sore, and found a weal there which must have been caused by the pressure of the rope when the people on the beach pulled her and the other woman to safety. She wondered how the other woman felt, and thought that at the very least some of her ribs must have been broken. The mud did not let its victims go without a fight, and it would have held on tenaciously to the other woman while those on the shore tried to wrench her from its grip. Still, the policeman had said she was breathing when they took her away. That in itself was a miracle.

Kate stood up and swayed as dizziness overtook her. 'I feel a bit giddy,' she said, falling against the policeman. 'Where's my cockle cart?'

He held her up and said, 'It don't seem to be here, lass.'

'Somebody stole my cart?'

'I dunno about that, but I can't see no cart around here. Look, you better get on back to your shack with the others. You look as if you need some rest.'

It appeared the policeman was becoming embarrassed, having a cockle girl draped over him.

'I don't live there,' she said. 'I live in Paglesham.'

At that moment someone pushed through the crowd and said, 'What's going on? You're Kate Fernlee, aren't you?'

Kate looked into the face of the tall, dark-maned man and recognised Jack Rockmansted. He was dressed in a greatcoat with several collars and knee-length riding boots. In his hand was a riding crop.

The constable said, 'This lass here saved a woman from drownin'. Says she lives in Paglesham.'

Jack Rockmansted reached forward and relieved the constable of his load.

'All right, officer, I'll take her. I have a horse back there.'

Once Jack Rockmansted's strong right arm had closed around her, Kate allowed herself to stumble forward. The crowd parted for them, until they came to a young boy who was holding the reins of a horse. Jack Rockmansted gave the child a coin and then lifted Kate up into the saddle. At that moment another man came forward.

'You've got my coat, miss.'

Kate took the short coat from her shoulders and put it in the outstretched hand.

'Thank you for its use,' she said.

'S'all right,' said the man, moving off.

Jack Rockmansted then took off his own greatcoat and handed it up to Kate. He had on only a white ruffled shirt beneath, the sleeves rolled to the elbows.

'Put that around your shoulders,' he said, handing the coat up to her.

'It isn't necessary,' she protested. 'Where's my cart? I can't lose my cart.'

Rockmansted grunted. 'Do as you're told. We'll find your cart later. And if we don't I'll make you a new one myself.'

She did as she was told, without another murmur. Then the big man climbed up behind her, put one arm around her waist to hold her on the horse, and took the reins in his free hands.

'Hut!' he said, pressing his heels into the horse's flanks, and the gelding walked on.

Although feeling unwell and aware that she could not possibly have walked the distance between Leigh and Paglesham in her present state, Kate was uncomfortably conscious of the intimacy of her present circumstances. The hard, muscular thighs of Jack Rockmansted were pressed against her buttocks, his left arm around her waist, his large hand resting on her hip. She could feel the warmth of Rockmansted's body permeating into her own, and could smell the manliness of him. His coarse coat chafed her skin as she rocked to the movement of the horse, the odour of the cloth unfamiliar to her.

She also now recalled that she had not wanted Rockmansted to interest himself in either of her sisters. It seemed she might have done him an injustice, for his actions today showed him to be a gentleman. Perhaps Kate had been wrong in thinking he was not for Sarah? Maybe they would all have been better off if she had encouraged a match between her sixteen-year-old sister and this rich mussel farmer? A considerable number of estuary girls married at sixteen. Of course, there was no saying that Sarah would have liked such a match – in fact when Kate thought hard about it, Sarah had shown a distinct lack of interest in the dark-haired man from Stambridge.

She stared down at the bare, lean forearm which encircled her slim waist, remembering the last time she had been close enough to study it, when he had handed her the hare after the church service. To her anguish she felt the same feeling of excitement rising within her which had both frightened and bewildered her even then, because she was sure there was nothing about this man which attracted her spiritually. He was a large, ruggedly handsome mussel farmer, a good few years her senior, with a granite personality. When she compared him with Simon, whose inner gentleness was a quality she adored, Rockmansted was left seriously wanting. He caused no tender feelings of the kind she experienced with Simon to fill her breast. In fact, the sexual stirrings his proximity roused within her made her feel guilty and ashamed and she tried to banish them from herself.

'This is very kind of you, Mr Rockmansted,' she told him with a little difficulty, for her teeth had started to chatter again.

'It's nothing,' he said. 'What happened back there?'

'One of the other women got stuck in the mud, on the flood tide. There was a strong wind and it came in very fast. I managed to pull her out.'

'You make it sound so simple, but from the way they were talking back there, you put your own life at considerable risk. Why would you want to do that, for one of those creatures?'

Kate was a little shocked by this question, but she was too tired to investigate his reasoning. 'She was a woman in trouble.'

'That's it?' he said, with a short laugh.

'Does there need to be more?'

There was silence between them for a while, as the horse plodded on. She realised it was difficult for the gelding to trot with the two of them on its back, but she wished it would hurry itself just a little more. She did not want to remain in Rockmansted's arms for longer than necessary.

'So,' said Rockmansted after a long period of quiet, 'this is what you're reduced to, is it? A common cockle girl?'

'I have to earn money.'

'Yes, you do. But why cockling? Why not work for one of the mussel farmers, like me?'

She remembered her experience with Jack's brother, Timothy. 'I did try, but no one wanted me.'

'You could not have applied to *me*, for I remember nothing of it.'

'I asked your brother.'

'Ah. And no doubt he said yes, if there were promised favours to be had later.'

Kate was surprised at how quickly and accurately Jack Rockmansted guessed the situation. However, he was Tim's brother, and no doubt the younger Rockmansted said the same thing to all the women he employed.

'Something like that,' she said.

'I thought so. You should have waited and applied to me.'

'Would that have stopped him?'

'I could have warned him off. He knows that if he disobeys me, he'll get his philandering head knocked against a stone. It won't be the first time I've thrashed him.'

The ride took over an hour, and by the time they reached the cottage, Kate was falling asleep in the saddle. She was no longer cold, but snug inside the coat, and she found her hands gripping the forearm that had filled her with such strange and unwelcome desires earlier in the ride.

After dismounting, he helped her down from the horse, and then suggested he take her inside.

'No,' she said firmly, 'that's not necessary. I'm fine now. I'm in your debt, Mr Rockmansted.'

He swung back up into the saddle, still in his shirtsleeves, looking very much the disdainful, hard man that he was.

'Think about coming to work for me. It pays a little more than cockling and it's nearer. I'll work you hard, but I'm a fair man. I'll call for the coat later. You can give me your answer then.'

He reached into his pocket and produced a damp-looking piece of paper. 'By the way, this came out of your clothing, on the beach. It seems to be a letter.'

Kate reached up and clutched the letter. It was one of Simon's that she kept on her. She liked having something of her fiancé close to her. 'Thank you,' she said to Rockmansted.

'The ink will have run,' he muttered.

'It doesn't matter. I know it by heart.'

He grunted and turned his horse.

Kate pulled off the coat quickly, wanting to give it to him now, to stop him calling again, but he had spurred his horse forward and was cantering towards the dyke which led to Stambridge and his own house. His offer left Kate with a dilemma. There was something she did not like about him, though she could not really pinpoint why, and she felt rather guilty and ungrateful, for he had shown her nothing but kindness. For some reason, though, she did not want to work for him. It made financial sense, of course, to accept a job with the Rockmansteds, but some vague instinct warned Kate that she would come to grief if she did so.

What was she to do? Obey her common sense, or take notice of some indefinable sense of threat?

She walked towards the house, thinking she did not have to make a decision yet. It would be some days before he would call back for his coat, and even then she could hold over her answer for a while longer. What she needed now was her bed and a long rest, which she promised herself she would have, once she had fed and watered her father.

Chapter Thirteen

Kate was ill for three days following her rescue of the drowning woman. On the fourth morning, although not fully recovered, she felt well enough to make the trek to the cockling. It was a noon low tide and she set out at ten o'clock to be there in time to follow the water out. She left Edward tucked in a blanket, sitting in his soft armchair, staring through the window at the broad reaches of the marshes. She hoped that somewhere in his brain he recognised his estuary country and was able to take in the unnatural beauty of the flatlands.

On the way to Leigh, Kate was picked up by a waggoner, who was taking hay to the stables along marine parade. He was grumbling about the changes that were taking place in the world, and maintained that progress was not a good thing if it meant that horses were to become unnecessary.

'These 'ere railway things. Them's not natural, like horses. Bits of iron thund'rin along. I ain't sure I want to live in a world where bits of iron is more important than horses.'

Kate made sympathetic noises, but she had her own problems at that moment. She was not sure that she had a cockle cart at the end of the journey, and she was wondering if she could gather enough cockles in her apron to get enough money for their next meal. As she was contemplating this a blue-winged jay suddenly flew across the lane from one tree to another, startling the horse into a skittering gait, which the waggoner had to bring under control. He did so fairly quickly, using the reins and by making kissing noises.

''Course,' he said, looking hard at his mare as she fell back into her ambling walk again, 'these 'ere trains don't jump at the slightest thing. *They* don't have to be put in blinkers. *They* don't give their masters the frits when a little bird pops up in front of 'em . . .'

The wagon made its slow winding passage along country lanes, circumnavigating ponds, travelling through leafy arches where the trees met over the roadway. On the way they gathered one or two more passengers, the waggoner being happiest in company. Then the thatched cottages began to fall away and the town houses of Prittlewell appeared. Finally, the clapboard fishermen's dwellings on the cliff-line of Leigh came into view.

Kate thanked the waggoner for his kindness and jumped on to the dusty track, making her way down the slopes to the beach. There she found the cocklers preparing to go out onto the mud. They stared at her when she walked amongst them. She had a question to ask of them, though she doubted she would receive an answer.

'Did anybody see what happened to my cart?' she asked the group.

A woman pointed, and Kate saw that her cockle sledge was in the same place it always was, under the jetty.

She thanked the woman and went to the spot to collect her cart, which seemed to be intact. As she was pulling it out by the reins, Sally came up to her.

'Kate,' she said, using her Christian name for the first time, 'that was my mum you pulled out of the mud.'

Kate said anxiously, 'Is she all right? She was under the water for a long time.'

'No, she ain't all right, but she ain't dead neither, thanks to you. She's a bit sick at the moment, but me dad's lookin' after her. What I wanted to say was we sold your cockles, what was in the cart. 'Ere's the money.' The girl held out a slim hand with some coins.

Kate looked at the amount of money in the hand. 'That's too much,' she said, 'you couldn't possibly have got all that for the few cockles in my cart. I saw most of them spill out into the water when that boy rescued it.'

''Ere, take it,' said Sally, pushing the money under Kate's nose. 'I want you to have it. Please.'

Kate shook her head.

'I don't want you to *pay* me for saving the life of another human being. We're all in this together. Give me my share of the money, that's all. Please.'

Sally looked into the blue eyes of this broad-faced auburn-haired female she had once hated. She didn't know what to do: her father had told her she must reward Kate, not only for saving her mother, but for the wrongs Sally had inflicted on her. How was she to do this if Kate would not accept the money?

'It was me what smashed up your cart,' she confessed, hoping this would encourage Kate to take the money.

'I know that, but it's all in the past. Look, Sally, I was happy to help your mother . . .'

'You could've died yourself,' said Sally, the tears starting to her eyes.

'It doesn't matter. I did it without really thinking. If I had stopped to consider what I was doing, I probably wouldn't have done it. You don't need to reward me for that; it would make me feel, oh I don't know, it would be wrong. I'm proud of myself at the moment. Proud I acted like I did. But I could have easily left her, panicked, saved myself. So I don't want any reward. I'd rather just feel that we can be friends in future. Can we be friends, Sally?'

Sally burst into tears then and fell on Kate's shoulder, and the two women hugged one another. Though they were not yet *good* friends there was a promise that they might become so, and they went out on to the mud together, chattering to one another.

Sally said, 'Would you come and see me mum? She wants to thank you as well. We don't live far away. Just up the sea wall.'

'Yes, I'd like to see her,' replied Kate, 'so long as your mother doesn't start trying to persuade me to take that money.'

'I'll ask her not to say nothin' about it,' promised Sally.

'I can't stay long because my own father is sick and I have to get back to him.'

Back on the beach, all the cockle women were discussing what was happening amongst the stall owners who bought their wares.

'They've got together,' said one woman, 'an' they've agreed to one price, a low one, to cheat us.'

Sally said to Kate, 'You told us you had somethin' to say about this before. What was it?'

Kate nodded as the women huddled round her. 'Well, I don't know if it would work, but what I suggest we do is pick on one of the stall owners – any one, it doesn't matter who – and refuse to sell him cockles. We'll sell to all the others, but not to him. We'll starve him out. Then next time, we'll do it to another one, so there's two of them, then three, then we stop there, and leave these three without cockles.'

'What will that do?' asked Sally.

'In the end, the three stall owners we starve out will begin to offer us higher prices than the others, and then the others will have to raise *their* prices to meet them, and pretty soon they'll be back to their old bargaining ways again.'

She stared at the faces around her. 'There's only one problem,' she said. 'The other stall holders might sell cockles to those we starve out. I don't think they will, though, because they're in competition too, even though they've got together over dealing with us, and there's no real love lost between them. They've all got grievances, old scores to settle with one another.

'I think what will happen is that those we supply with cockles will laugh up their sleeves at those we starve out, hoping they'll go out of business. They're not in tight enough together to work out a fair way of helping the victims amongst them. One stall owner will say to himself, "Why should I sell Jones my cockles? Why can't Osborne sell him his?" and they'll be quarrelling amongst them then. I think it will all break down after a few days, and we'll have them back at each other's throats, like they usually are.'

The cocklers were very excited by this plan, and congratulated Kate on her 'sound thinking'. They settled on Walt Meckle as the man they would starve of cockles. He was the most suspicious of the group, always thinking himself hard done by, and he could be most demonstrative too. This suggestion had come from Niddy Simpson, who told them why they should choose Walt Meckle as their victim.

'You remember when he burnt down Willie Packard's shack, because Willie had told everyone Walt's cockles was bad for the blood? Got fined at the magistrate's court for that, did Walt Meckle. 'E's got a fiery temper on 'im, 'as Walt.'

'Serve 'im right if he does some'at like that again and ends up in prison,' remarked another cockler.

So, with their plan formulated, the women set forth. They accepted their payment from the various buyers without a murmur today, making sure they all stayed well clear of Walt Meckle's place. Kate saw the man in question staring out between the slits in his rickety shack, probably wondering which of the women were coming to him. He had his regulars of course, but there were those fickle ones who drifted between the shacks, always looking for a better deal.

When the women had been to all the stall holders and sold their cockles, Walt Meckle came out and complained that no one had been to his cockle shed.

'If you're not careful,' he said to his regular suppliers, Fanny Totlidge and her sister Em, 'I won't buy no more cockles from the pair of you.'

'Thasallrightthen,' said Em, sticking her nose in the air, ''cos we ain't sellin' no more to you.'

This left Walt Meckle with a stunned look on his face, although as the women walked away he seemed already to be aware that they were putting some devious plan into action because he called, 'I know what you're up to. You better bring me cockles from tonight's tide, or I'll sort the lot of you out.'

Kate and her new-found friend walked a short mile along the sea wall towards Benfleet, to the cockler's colony. There Sally took her to a broken-down shanty with a flap of sail canvas for a door. Kate tried not to show her dismay at the condition of the place as she ducked her head and entered the gloomy, fetid atmosphere within. There were gaps in the wall-boards which must have let in the inclement weather, and the floor was made of driftwood laid straight on to bare earth.

Sally's mother was lying on a bed of rags in one corner of the single-roomed shack, and she went up on to her elbow and smiled when she saw Sally and Kate.

'You brung her?' she said, struggling to sit up.

Kate said, 'Don't get up, you don't look strong enough yet. I just wanted to see how you were.'

'I'm not so bad. Be up and cockling before you know it.'

The woman actually looked wan and sickly, but Kate nodded, as if in agreement with her.

Kate stayed for twenty minutes and then told the family she had to be on her way.

'You must come and see me sometime,' she said to Sally, outside the shack. 'I'll take you over the marshes.'

'Is that good?' asked Sally dubiously.

'Well, it's *different*,' laughed Kate.

On the way home Kate thought again about Jack Rockmansted's offer to come and work for him. The pay would be more than Kate earned at cockling and Stambridge was much nearer than Leigh. There was the problem of Timothy Rockmansted, but Kate felt now that she could handle him. She had, after all, withstood months of bitter infighting with a bunch of tough women. Fending off a wolf now seemed child's play by comparison.

There was something else that worried her though. It seemed that Jack Rockmansted was being very generous in making the offer, for he could get as many people as he wanted from his own village, so was there any reason for her to feel the way she did about him? The problem was, his reputation gave lie to the idea that he was a kind, generous man. He was actually known in the district as a ruthless businessman who would sell his own mother if such an act would increase his power in the land.

So why was he being so nice to Kate, unless he wanted something from her? Since she had only one thing to offer such a man, and that was promised to another, she felt that if she did go to work for him, misunderstandings would arise from which it might be impossible to extricate herself.

Did her suspicions justify the seemingly inevitable loss of the cottage and the distress it would cause her father when they had to move? Was she being selfish, too cautious, or simply foolish? Perhaps Jack Rockmansted genuinely liked her and could see potential in her as a worker? After all, she had practically run the oyster company when they had been in business. Perhaps he had heard how astute she was in opening up the market for her oysters?

Kate couldn't shake off her doubts, though. Some instinct, faint but persistent, warned her against going to the Rockmansteds'. Perhaps eventually she would have no choice but to put aside her suspicious feelings and accept his offer in order to survive. But in the meantime she decided she would stay at the cockling.

Chapter Fourteen

Working the cockle flats was a gruelling, exhausting occupation, and it left Kate little time to reflect on her former life. However, Sarah and Liz had visited her again just after the autumn fruit picking was over.

Her two sisters were surviving, just as she was, but they had little time or money left over to assist Kate in looking after their father. Kate noticed a certain change in Sarah that had not been there the day that Kate had made her new sledge, shortly after the girls had moved to Canewdon. Sarah seemed more bitter about her new life than she had previously revealed, and less inclined to soothe the hurts of others.

They were sitting in the garden at the back of the cottage when Kate asked Liz how she was faring at school and Liz replied, 'Oh, very well, thank you, Kate, though it is hard work.'

Sarah made a snorting sound. 'Hard work!' said the middle sister. 'You should try lifting potatoes if you want hard work. Then when you've done that, try pea-picking. And after the pea-picking, see how much strength you've got left for the tree fruit . . .'

During the embarrassed silence that followed, Kate stole a look at Sarah's face, and saw the bitterness there. 'None of us are having a wonderful time, Sarah,' she said. 'Even Liz.'

'Liz will do all right,' said Sarah. 'She'll find a position somewhere, as a governess or something. You've got Simon coming home to help you. What have I got to look forward to? Who have I got? Well, I'm not going to work as a field hand for the rest of my life, you can be sure of *that*. Even if I have to marry the first man that asks me.'

Liz said, 'Sarah!' in a shocked tone.

Sarah ignored her younger sister and turned on Kate. 'I don't want any lectures from you either, Kate, on marriage, or anything. I'm . . . I'm not really interested in love. In fact I don't really believe in it. If I *like* a man well enough, that will do for me.'

'You really shouldn't be worried about getting married yet – you're very young. Oh, I know, other girls marry at sixteen and seventeen, but

Sarah, dear, you need stronger feelings than *liking* to live with someone for the rest of your life.'

Kate looked with concern at her sister, worried that Sarah had suddenly started to regard marriage simply as an escape from the drudgery of the fields. Sarah *was* very young, and Kate believed she might change her mind about her aversion to the marital bed, which had arisen in their discussions before, if she was given more time to mature. Or she might decide never to marry at all. Either way was better than marrying in the hope of a comfortable life only to live in a mental and physical hell.

Kate said softly, 'I understand you don't get on tremendously well with Aunt Polly and Uncle Peter and you used to like them well enough. When you marry you'll have someone sharing your bed as well as your brush and comb.'

'I don't *have* to go to bed with him, do I? I don't like that kind of thing anyway.'

'What kind of thing?' asked Liz.

Sarah blushed to the roots of her hair. 'Making babies. You only have to lie beside your husband once or twice in your life, don't you, if you only want one or two children? I shan't want any.'

Liz giggled and Kate told her to shush. 'Let me speak to Sarah alone,' she said to Liz. 'You go and talk to Father: it might comfort him a little to hear your voice. Go and tell him about your school.'

'But I want to hear,' pouted Liz.

'We've had this discussion about men and women before,' said Kate, 'so you won't hear anything new, Liz. What I'm surprised about is that Sarah seems to have forgotten.'

When Liz had reluctantly left, Kate turned to Sarah again. Though Sarah seemed reluctant to reopen the conversation, Kate was having none of it.

'Sarah, you're very young yet,' Kate said. 'You don't really need to get married for several years. What's all this about? Is it the thought of having a child that frightens you? There are ways to avoid having children, without having to reject your husband . . .'

'I'm not worried about that so much,' Sarah said, 'but I don't want a man doing things to me, the way you told us they do. It just *disgusts* me, that's all.'

'You may change,' Kate suggested gently. 'We all feel a bit like that when we first hear about it.'

Sarah shook her head emphatically. 'I won't change. I know it. Liz is two years younger than me and she just giggles about it. She'll be all right. I *hate* the thought of it. But I'm not going to spend my life in the fields either, so that's why it doesn't matter who I marry, so long as he can keep me. The uglier he is, the better, then he'll be grateful for whatever I let him do, even if it's just to kiss me.'

Kate was stunned at this revelation. In some ways Sarah seemed ten years older than she was herself. Sarah seemed to know herself better: know what she wanted or, rather, did *not* want. There was a fierce determination in Sarah's tone, and Kate knew persuasion was useless. There was nothing to be done, except warn her sister: 'Sarah,' said Kate, 'you may find yourself with a good-for-nothing, a drunkard or, worse than that, someone who takes his frustration out on you with his fists. There are many such men, and you certainly can't always tell who they are before you marry them. Don't you think your attitude is very foolish wanting to get married when you feel the way you do about such things?'

Sarah gritted her teeth. 'I'm not working like this for ever. I hate this way of life. My heart's turning into a prune stone. I can take care of myself, you'll see.'

The sisters had a quiet parting at the end of a too-short day, and then the two girls walked back to Canewdon, promising to visit again soon. Kate's thoughts were mostly on Sarah. Liz would do fine, as Kate had planned, but Kate had not previously given enough thought to Sarah's position. Sarah was right in some ways: she really didn't have anything to look forward to at the moment except to watch her aunt and uncle grow old. Kate had thought that Sarah would find some young farm labourer and settle down happily, but it seemed that her sister really was revolted at the thought of sex. Perhaps, Kate mused, Sarah would be able to steel herself for a few encounters beneath the sheets, or learn to just lie there and think about the next day's chores, forget about what was happening to her body. There must be many women who did just that, and some men might well be satisfied with a passive wife. Maybe she was worrying about nothing. Perhaps if Sarah met the right man, she would fall in love despite herself, and the rest would follow naturally.

The winter crackled in over the marshes, picking out the white salt flats and leaving the ground frost heavy on the reeds. The general shuffle of migrants took place, some birds departing and others arriving to take their places. The fox began to look a little hollow-eyed, and the stoat put on its winter disguise of white. The highways of both these creatures were easily discernible on the frosty landscape. So too were the rabbit runs, on which the locals placed their snares. The wind coming from the east sharpened the edge of its blade on the icy waters of the North Sea before scything over the dykes.

Out on the mudflats, the cocklers began the season of real suffering. They wrapped themselves in layers of rags and paper, but nothing could keep out that bitter wind, and their feet were always wet and frozen. Several of the more elderly women had lost toes through poor circulation of their blood. The band of cocklers trudged out on to the mud with numbed bodies to rake the bivalves that would provide them with their daily bread but not much more.

Kate's plan to destroy the price fixing amongst the cocklers had seen success towards the end of autumn. As she had predicted, old jealousies and rivalries had eventually flared up amongst the shellfish buyers: those that the women had starved of cockles eventually began offering higher prices than those who were still being supplied. This caused the situation to be reversed. The previously rejected stall owners became the favoured and those who had been supplied at the fixed price were now rebuffed. This of course encouraged more competitive bargaining and the cocklers were soon back to the old rate per bushel.

One early evening, Kate arrived back at the cottage to find the squire's man, Siddons, inside her cottage. Fear gripped her as she entered to find Siddons attempting to talk to her father, who was staring open-mouthed at the clerk. She put down a parcel of driftwood and coal and turned to face the man.

'What are you doing in here, Mr Siddons?' she asked apprehensively and with barely-suppressed vexation. She knew she was seven weeks behind with the rent, but the thought of eviction was so terrible that she had tried to put it out of her mind completely in order to concentrate on their survival. Now she feared the worst.

The tall thin Siddons straightened himself so that his head was almost touching the cottage ceiling. 'Do forgive me for entering without invitation. The door was unlocked and, receiving no answer to my summons, I entered, for I could see Mr Fernlee here through the window. I have been attempting to explain to him that he will have to vacate the cottage by noon tomorrow.'

Kate staggered, almost as if the man had struck her. So all her efforts had come to naught. They were to be ejected from the only home they had ever known. Even Edward had known no other roof over his head, for Kate's grandmother had given birth to him within its very walls.

'By tomorrow?' she said in dismay. 'My father's ill, you can see that. How can we find another place by tomorrow?'

She looked at her father, whose face bore an expression of bewilderment. His hands were on the arms of his chair, as if he were in the process of pushing himself out of it, but his joints appeared to have locked in this position. Round-eyed, Edward Fernlee seemed transfixed by the presence of Mr Siddons.

Mr Siddons coughed to regain Kate's attention. 'Unfortunately,' he said, playing with the brim of his hat, 'the squire will not listen to my persuasions any longer. He insists that Mr Fernlee, and yourself of course, must go. I'm sorry if I've upset your father –' he looked down at the old man with pity in his eyes – 'but my instructions were to give notice directly to him, not to you, Miss Fernlee. He is the tenant, not your good self, I'm afraid.'

That was true, of course. Kate had no rights whatsoever concerning the cottage, or anything else. It was Edward who rented the house, not any of his daughters, and if he was evicted then Kate had no say in it. She was simply an appendage of her father's so far as the law was concerned.

Mr Siddons himself was clearly upset over the whole business, but that did nothing to quench Kate's feeling of bitterness towards the squire and his man. She could not feel sorry for someone who had a good living and a roof over his head, when her own father was about to be thrown on the mercy of the winter. A vision of them living in a shack along the sea wall between Leigh and Benfleet sprang to her mind, and the scene horrified her. Edward would surely not survive more than a week under such conditions.

She summoned up all the dignity she could muster, and turned again to the squire's man. 'Please leave our house, Mr Siddons.'

'I'm sorry . . .'

'Just go, please,' she said wearily.

Mr Siddons went to the doorway, stooped, and passed through it, closing the door quietly behind him. Kate was left in the gloom with Edward.

She took off her shawl and draped it over a high stool. Then she knelt down before her father and prised his fingers from the arms of his chair. His knuckles were white with the effort of holding on, as if his life depended upon it, and it took all her strength to unlock his hands from their grip.

'Relax, Father,' she said, softly. 'Everything's going to be all right. Don't you worry. Simon will be home soon, and we'll work together to recover the cottage.'

Edward closed his mouth and sank back into the chair under Kate's soothing voice. Soon he had closed his eyes and seemed to have fallen asleep. Kate then made a fire using the driftwood she had brought home with her for kindling, and a little coal she had collected from the shoreline, where it had been washed up by the tide. This was soon glowing in the hearth. She washed, made them a meagre supper of green fish and cockles, and then sat by the embers.

What was she to do? There were several people who would be willing to help her, but they were no better off than she herself. Aunt Polly would make room for them, but her two-roomed place would be bursting at the seams with six of them packed within its walls. There were two other possibilities. She could go to work for the Rockmansteds, and request an advance of wages, explaining that she needed it to pay back rent on the cottage. The way Jack Rockmansted had spoken to her not long ago seemed to indicate that he would not be unwilling to help her.

Or she could go to Johann Haagan and request a loan.

If she borrowed from Johann, though, when could she pay him back? Perhaps not for years. She knew too what everyone would think of such an arrangement – a young man loaning money to a young woman – and though that was the least of *her* concerns it might harm Johann's reputation. He was, after all, a priest, and the children of the district had been placed in his care. There might be some move on the part of the Reverend Potts and other outraged parishioners to remove Johann from his post. Johann was relatively new to the area – and you had to be resident in or around the marshes for at least a generation before you were regarded as completely trustworthy and above suspicion. Until that time everything you did came under the scrutiny of local groups of men and women who saw it as their duty to guard the morals of their county. Johann's standing would just not be high enough to withstand such attacks for a long time to come.

Kate sighed and stirred the coals, staring in at them, as if she might find the answer to her problems there. She took a letter from Simon from a drawer and read it through several times, obtaining comfort from his straightforward prose. Then the letter dropped from her fingers to the floor.

She must have fallen asleep by the fire, for she woke shivering, still dressed in her muddy cockling clothes. Feeling groggy, she felt her way to the scullery and found a stub end of candle. She lit it and went back into the living-room, going straight to a cupboard for a blanket to wrap around her father, knowing he would be cold.

Turning towards her father's armchair, a sudden tremor of confusion and panic ran through her. For a moment she stood still, staring in bewilderment. The armchair was empty.

Kate called out, 'Father? Where are you? Father? Edward?' Frantically she began to search the house, room by room, but there was no sign of her father in the house. With trembling hands she lit a lamp, pulled on her shawl, and went hurrying out of the house into the night. A rapid search of the immediate surrounds yielded nothing either, and Kate desperately began knocking on the doors of neighbouring houses. Some of the men, just in from the fields and from the boats, put their boots back on and joined her in the search. The Plough and Sail was checked, but no Edward found there.

The Reverend Potts was roused from a nap by the shouting and ventured outside to see what was the matter. When he heard that Edward was missing, and knowing the elder Fernlee's fragile state of mind, he put on his frock coat and hurried down the lane to the Reverend Haagan's house. There he explained to the young man that the clergy should be involved in such a search, in case the poor elderly gentleman had met with dire circumstances, and as he himself was too old to go chasing over the countryside, Johann should bestir himself.

Johann immediately joined the search party, but finding their numbers inadequate, he went directly to Squire Pritchard and requested to borrow some of his servants.

'We've got guests,' the squire stated, 'and dinner's about to be served.'

'But there's an old man missing. He might come to harm in the marshes,' explained Johann.

'Oh, all right, I suppose the groom and stable hand won't be needed for a while, but make sure they're back in time to help hitch the horses to the coach to take my guests back to Rochford.'

'What about your valet, Albert?'

'Him too? Good lord, man. Fernlee will probably come wandering back from some inn at past midnight, drunk as a hatter and laughing at the lot of you. I expect he's annoyed with me for turning him out, and he's gone to drown his sorrows.'

Johann took this news with surprise. 'You've given him notice to vacate the cottage?'

The squire drew himself up defensively. 'He's been given enough warnings. My patience was at an end.' His tone softened. 'These people can usually find the money from somewhere if they have to, Reverend. I know them, believe me. Lived here all me life. They'll plead poverty if they think they can get away with it. You have to be hard with them or they'll take you for a fool.'

Johann felt such a fury rise within him that he wisely said nothing at all. Not a bad man, the squire, but a very stupid one. He must have been deaf, dumb and blind not to know that Edward Fernlee had lost his reason. While no one had gone up and knocked on his door and told him the situation, his servants and tenant farmers would know, and surely one of them must have passed on the information. Why, Lord Caterham; the father of Johann's university friend, John, knew everything that happened on his estates, from the birth of a litter of kittens to the death of a peasant's dog. Lord Caterham's wife would have visited the cottage months ago, partly out of curiosity but also partly out of charity, and there would no doubt have been a concerted effort on her part to 'do something for the man'. Squire Pritchard seemed ignorant of Edward Fernlee's condition.

'Did you know Mr Fernlee was sick?' asked Johann.

'Siddons kept wittering something about the man not having spoken. Doesn't mean he's ill though, does it? Might be sulking over this oyster thing.'

'I'd like the valet too, please, if you wouldn't mind, squire.'

Pritchard signed. 'Oh, very well.'

The squire's men were gathered and joined with six of Kate's neighbours in the search. They tramped over the marshes, waving their lanterns and hallooing, hoping to flush Edward from his hiding place. Kate kept saying to Johann that she was sure her father was hiding somewhere. She believed Mr Siddons' words had somehow managed to penetrate his consciousness and he was trying to avoid being evicted.

The moon came up, which made the search a little easier. Not finding him within the immediate vicinity of the cottage, the search began to widen, to take in Paglesham Church End, as well as the marshes at the back of East End. More people joined the search parties, until the animals and birds of the region were persuaded a major hunt was in progress, and that beaters were out trying to chase them into the nets and guns. One man came upon a winter nest of vipers, which frightened a few of the cottagers into ordering their children home. The youngsters, not wishing to be robbed of the excitement, made the gesture only, and returned to the search after a short interval.

It was not a member of the search party who found the body, but a fisherman walking in over the creek. The fisherman, on hearing the halloos, shouted that he had found someone in the mud and needed assistance. Soon the searchers were gathered around the corpse, lanterns held aloft, staring down on the mortal remains of Edward Fernlee.

Edward was stretched out, face buried in the black silt, on the mulch of one of the oyster beds he still owned but could not use. His arms were straight out at two and ten o'clock, so that his body formed a Y shape. In each fist he clutched some of his old oysters: those he had been forbidden to harvest and sell.

To Johann it seemed a despairing last act, as if the old man had gone to the place which had given him a good living, hoping it would yield something, perhaps enough to save his cottage? In his weak state of mind, thought Johann, Edward must have roused himself to make the last walk to his oyster beds to see if something could not be done to save his little cottage. The rest could only be surmised.

Kate was sent for, but when she arrived Johann told her to stay back. She ignored him, insisting instead on pushing through the group until she came upon her father lying face down in the mud. One of the men bent down quickly and turned the corpse over, to give the old man a little dignity before his daughter.

Edward's face was covered in the slick black sludge of the estuary. Kate knelt beside her father and wiped the mud from his eyes with her fingers. The orbs were wide and staring, his expression hardly changed from the one he had worn in the last few months of his life.

Concealing her emotion, she said, 'We must carry him back to the house.'

Once the men had moved the body to the cottage, and left Kate alone with Johann, she collapsed in tears. 'Simon,' she wailed, 'where are you when I need you?'

Johann did his best to comfort her, but she needed her man with her to share in her sorrow. Her father had been taken from her, and Simon should have been there to help her bear the pain of loss. He was not, though. Simon was somewhere in China Seas, fighting for queen and country. Instead she only had a young priest, a friend to console her. He may have wished to be more, at this moment she too might have wanted him to be more; but the designs of her heart were set in the colours they would wear until she herself died, and, her love for Simon was printed indelibly on her soul.

She rocked back and forth sitting in the armchair, hugging her knees, and only half-listening to Johann's whispered consolations. Her strength seemed to have gone for the moment, retreated somewhere into hiding. She was, when all was said and done, only a young woman of twenty, and able to bear only so much misfortune. Others would have been crushed and bowed long ago.

The night moved on into the solemn small hours, when the ticking of the clock is master of the world, and in all the houses along the estuary dykes, heartbeats had slowed to a pace not far away from death. Questions without answers spun in Kate's mind as she began to search for things she could have done to prevent the disaster, so that she could blame herself and allow guilt to feed on her grief. And when this torture was played out, there was always the agony of what she would tell her sisters. Edward had been left in *her* care and she had taken sole responsibility for him. Her sisters would have a right to expect some explanations from her as to why she had fallen so far behind with the rent, and why Edward had been allowed to wander out into the night, unescorted, to meet his death on the mudflats.

These fears were voiced, because she could not contain them and Johann dealt with them as they arrived, for he knew they had to be reeled from her gently, like cotton unwound from a spool, not torn from her leaving raw wounds behind their place. It was a painful business, for him as well as for her.

Chapter Fifteen

Finally the morning arrived in its grey garments, and Kate fell asleep, having found a certain peace within herself.

Johann remained with her, sitting quietly in a corner, observing her silent grief with some distress. The body on the floor had not yet been cleaned, and the mud had dried forming a caked deathmask on the now stiff corpse. Kate herself, draped over the arm of the chair, still had crusts of mud on her dress.

Mud unto mud, thought Johann, you couldn't escape it in estuary country. It got into everything: food, water, houses, churches, the swaddling clothes of new-born babes and, finally, the grave. You came into the world bearing the marks of stinking mud and you went out of it covered in the same substance, like some swamp creature that has emerged from the slime and then been swallowed by it at the end. That naturalist fellow Darwin who had been at the same college as Johann, though a few years before him, had recently published the findings of his voyage around the world on the HMS *Beagle*. One of Johann's other friends said this chap Darwin had some madcap ideas about the human race actually evolving from mudborn creatures, which he intended to publish in a paper once he had gathered more proof. Johann was of the opinion that this was probably heresy, and Mr Darwin had better watch out for his immortal soul: yet having lived in the Essex estuary country for a few months, he was beginning to understand the persuasiveness of such an argument.

While Kate dozed, Johann inspected Edward's body to satisfy himself that there were no marks on it which might indicate foul play or violence of any kind. There were none. He then fetched a neighbour to sit with Kate while he went to the squire.

The squire's butler let him in at once, showing him to the squire's study. Squire Pritchard was sitting at his desk, staring out at the ruins of his grandfather's Elizabethan box garden, which some enthusiastic student of the methods of Capability Brown had torn to pieces and replaced with a wild rose arbour. A famous landscape gardener of the last century, Brown had been an adherent to the view that a garden should look natural, even though of course it was not. Formal styles had been contemptuously cast aside by the followers of his gardening reforms, to be replaced by casual-looking foliage that to many eyes appeared unkempt and ill-trained. Squire Pritchard was wondering whether he dare bring back the box garden he had so loved as a child, with its little mazes and pathways, without inviting the ridicule of his friends.

The squire was suddenly aware he was not alone, and turned from the window to see the Reverend Johann Haagan standing before him. The schoolteacher was speaking.

'... Kate Fernlee has nothing, no money of any kind. Of course, no one is placing any fault with yourself, Squire, that would be quite wrong, but I think the unfortunate circumstances which have led to Mr Fernlee's untimely demise were brought about not by the Fernlees themselves, but by sheer bad luck.'

The squire brought his mind to bear on the subject, reluctantly allowing his visions of beautiful box gardens to flit into some other remote corner of his brain.

'An act of God, you mean?' he said.

'Not an act of God – an act of Fate. They are two different things. An act of God implies punishment for some moral wrongdoing. Mr Fernlee was never anything but a good neighbour, a good friend to those closest to him, and a good father. Do you consider he poisoned his own oysters on purpose? What would he have gained by such action? No, a bad tide must have come in and in the process ruined the life's work of an old man.'

From the moment Johann had entered the study he was aware he was interrupting some early morning reverie in which the squire was indulging himself. There had been a wistful expression on the stocky man's face as he stared out of the window, not vastly different from the expression which Edward Fernlee had worn when staring out of *his* window.

The squire looked thoughtful, then said, 'Perhaps not he, but one of his daughters?'

'One of his daughters *what*? I'm sorry, I don't quite follow you, sir.'

'Well, brought divine punishment on his house? That sort of thing. I expect they're good girls, they *look* decent young creatures, but perhaps they're not? You can't tell from looking at 'em, can you? The morals of the young these days leave a lot to be desired, as you know yourself, Reverend.'

Johann refrained from exploding in wrath, but wisely – not for the first time when confronted by the squire's prejudice – kept control of his feelings. If he was going to get anything out of this stupid pompous man, it was by persuasion, not by displaying anger. Johann knew that Kate would never allow him to provide her with the costs of the funeral, but there was no reason why she should not accept assistance from the man who had helped put her father into his grave.

Johann spoke very slowly. 'The sins of the fathers may be visited upon the sons, Squire Pritchard, but the sins of the daughters are not returned to either parent, not in God's eyes.'

'You know this for a fact?'

Johann snapped, 'I have studied theology, that's why they made me a priest.'

The squire was a little taken aback by this outburst. 'Yes, quite, sir. Don't mean to question your knowledge of the Bible and such. Just want to be sure I'm doing the right thing. Can't reward the girl by paying for her father's funeral if she's undergoing some sort of divine retribution for her transgressions, if you follow.'

Through gritted teeth, Johann said, 'I can assure you that no reports of misbehaviour on the part of Kate Fernlee have reached *my* ears, and the Reverend Potts has nothing but good to say of her. I think it would be a very noble gesture on your part if you were to stand the expense of the burial, and save this young woman a great deal of distress. I know you were only doing what you thought was right under the law when you gave them notice to quit the cottage, but think of the misery this has already caused the family.'

'Misery?' said the squire, looking puzzled.

'Well, what if you were to receive notice to quit this fine house? Wouldn't that upset you?'

Squire shook his head emphatically. 'Never happen. I *own* this property. Can't be turned out of my own home, can I?'

Johann sighed inwardly. The man was obviously solid oak all the way through from the outer regions of his skull to the centre of his brain, incapable of grasping any kind of theoretical concept, or sympathising with anyone else's position. All Johann could hope for was that the squire might do as he was asking on a whim.

'No, you certainly can't be evicted from the home you actually own yourself, but Miss Fernless is a respectable girl, Squire, and she has always spoken highly of you,' Johann lied, 'so I thought you might like to raise your standing in the community even higher by making this generous offer. It's just a suggestion, mind, for I'm convinced the original idea must have occurred to you at the time you learned of the old man's death.'

The squire blinked. 'Yes, yes, I'm sure it must've. So long as there's no history of impropriety in the family?'

Again, Johann felt like yelling, '*You've known them all your life, you silly man.*' Instead what he actually said was, 'No, I'm sure there hasn't been anything the church would not sanction. I will bear the responsibility for that.'

'Well, then,' said the bull-headed squire, 'I'll do it.'

Thus Johann was able to go back to Kate and tell her that she need not worry about the expenses of the funeral: that the squire was so overcome by remorse he had begged to be allowed to pay for the burial of his old tenant. Kate said she did not like the idea of accepting charity, but could see no option, and it would relieve her sisters, and her aunt and uncle, to know that they would not have to sell furniture to pay for a coffin.

'But to keep costs to a minimum,' said Kate, 'I shall dig the grave myself.'

'You shall not,' said Johann, 'for I have claimed that privilege for *myself.*'

Kate stared at this pale sensitive man for a long while, then touched a lock of his hair. Immediately Kate regretted the act. There were feelings in her breast for this man which had to be suppressed, and such gestures, innocent as they were, did neither of them any service. Was it simply that he was here and Simon was not? She tried to tell herself that her feelings for Johann were more of a fondness, a high regard. No, she corrected herself truthfully, it was *more* than that. There were things about Johann: his intellect, his artistic values, his sensitivity, which Simon did not, and never would, have. These aspects of Johann she considered priceless. She liked him, very much, and had there been no Simon she might very well have allowed herself to fall in love with him. As it was, there could only be a strong friendship between them, for Simon occupied that space in her reserved for her love.

'You're a good man, Johann.'

He smiled ruefully at her. 'You don't know my darkest secrets, or you'd never say that,' he exclaimed. 'Come, you must go to your sisters, before they're told by some other well-meaning person. Old Ben Whethers is going to Canewdon this morning with his waggon. He's promised you a ride.'

'You *are* a good man,' she repeated.

He shook his head emphatically. 'I'm not even half-way to wiping out my bad record,' he said, 'so no more of your talk, Miss Fernlee.'

He held out his hand and she took it solemnly. 'Thank you for being here,' she said.

Chapter Sixteen

Kate had thought long and hard about working for the Rockmansted brothers and, though it appeared to be the most sensible thing to do, something inside her held her back. There was the feeling that her life would develop too many complications with the two brothers around. So she decided to work out her own destiny at the cockle flats. It was an emotional decision, not an intellectual one.

So, after Edward's funeral, Kate moved into a shack at Leigh, close to the shanty of Sally and her parents. Sally was good to her, comforted her as best she could when Kate was feeling low, especially after the funeral. The shack itself was built with Sally's help, using such materials as they could find washed up on the shore, and some sail canvas begged from the fishermen to serve as a roof. The canvas was old, but once the holes had been sewn by the two women, appeared waterproof at least against normal rain.

However, the winter was bitterly cold – Kate had never known such cold before – and much of her time was spent huddled in a threadbare blanket, rubbing her feet with chapped hands, trying to keep warm. The shack did nothing to keep out the bitter east winds: it simply broke them up into small draughts which came screaming through holes between the driftwood planks.

She had brought with her an oil-lamp of course, but much of the time could not afford the oil to go in it, so long evenings and nights were spent in complete darkness. Sally came to her most evenings and they would often sit wrapped in their blankets, talking about their life so far, their fears, their hopes for the future. There was something about the vivacious Sally which warmed Kate. The girl had never had anything, and would probably end up, like her mother, still with nothing. Yet she had a shower of sparks within her which lit up her eyes as she spoke, and gave her whole personality an exciting glow. She spoke quickly and breathlessly, as if the world were going to go out like a burnt-down candle in two or three seconds, and she just *had* to say how she felt about this or that before it finally went *phut*!

Sally dreamt of travelling to foreign lands, and would sit for hours, talking about her ambition with such animation that Kate's heart bled for her, for Kate was convinced the only opportunity Sally would have to go overseas would be if she found herself on a convict boat to Tasmania or Western Australia, transportation having just recently ceased to New South Wales – even the world of the felon was shrinking.

The forthcoming marriage of Queen Victoria to Prince Albert of Saxe-Coburg-Gotha was also an endless topic of conversation for Sally, who talked of the finery that would be worn, the beautiful ladies who would be there, and the handsome great men in their uniforms covered with medals and ribbons. Kate knew that Sally envisaged such a marriage for herself. She had a young girl's dream of a knight on a white charger, who would descend from the high country, sweep her on to the mare's back, and take her away from the grinding, hopeless, sordid poverty that had her trapped.

Kate saw no reason to disillusion Sally, though the settled gypsy girl would probably end up with a man as poor as herself: a fisherman or boatman, or – at best – a cockle stall owner. Kate envisaged the bright perky Sally in ten years' time and saw a withered, sallow little woman, wrinkled by the hot stinking vapours hissing from the boiling vats, eyes protruding from sunken cheeks where the steam had wreaked its havoc, sweating over the tubs of cooked shellfish, her hair limp and stringy and already beginning to grey at the edges. Even her voice would have changed, growing thick and coarse, her throat roughened by smoke and harsh gin.

Kate did not want to shatter Sally's illusions, though, for she too had her dreams. How else could she survive while shivering in her blanket, or walking the mudflats in search of cockles, frozen to the core? Hers were more simple dreams, of a warm bed in a cottage on the marshes, with her husband Simon beside her, and perhaps a baby in a cradle in the corner of the room. It was a life where chaps and cold sores were not evident, and a good diet was to be had, and there were no dysentery pains in the middle of the night from eating raw shellfish, and her feet had shoes upon them, and her body a warm dress to clothe it. What Kate wanted was little more than what she had before, with Simon beside her to share it.

The nights were long and dreary in the shack, with little to do and certainly no entertainment. Kate still walked the miles back to Paglesham and Canewdon occasionally, to see her family and friends, especially Johann, who winced involuntarily every time he saw her and then told her, much too quickly, how well she was looking. He tried to persuade her to accept money from him but she would not hear of it. Under Victoria, England had taken on a high moral tone, where the slightest infringement of a virtuous code brought condemnation from the rest of the community. This code was only surface deep, like the hard white crust on the salt marshes, while underneath there was slime and muck aplenty. But Kate was careful on Johann's behalf.

Kate was always hoping for a letter from Simon. She had heard there was a war going on in China and she suspected Simon would be involved; she knew if he were that he would have no time to write to her. As it was she frequently reread those letters she did have, savouring the words.

The Government, under Rowland Hill's guidance, had introduced adhesive postage stamps, along with a wrap-around cover for each letter called an 'envelope' and Kate wondered how this would affect her mail. Previously she and Simon had used friends and other sailors to carry their letters for them. She would give a letter to someone who knew someone whose cart was travelling to London or Southampton or Portsmouth, and they would promise to give it to some sailor going east. How the letters ever got to Simon was a mystery: she suspected that often they did not. Some of her precious words were no doubt tucked away, forgotten, in some dirty pocket of a waggoner's coat, or at the bottom of a jack tar's chest; or had perhaps ended up in some far-flung, fly-ridden harbour, in the hands of a stranger.

One day, after an exhausting early-morning cockling, Kate told Sally she was going to walk to Paglesham to see her friends and family.

Sally cried, 'Oh, let me come too. I want to meet your folks. I ain't seen nobody you know yet, have I?'

Kate hesitated long enough for Sally to pout and say, 'I know you don't think I'm good enough for them, but I am, see. I can behave as good as any oyster girl.'

Kate shook her head. 'Sally, I wasn't thinking that way, honestly I wasn't. Of course I'm not ashamed of you. Why should I be? You're brighter than most people I know, anyway. I was just thinking that we'd had a long day and it's a fair walk to Paglesham. Are you sure you're not too tired?'

'Fit as a cat what's slept a week,' cried Sally, her eyes lighting up at the thought of adventure.

They set off into the grey winter day, leaving the shanty town behind them, climbing first up past the ruined castle of Hadleigh, until they reached the main highway. There they begged a lift from a carter to Rochford, travelling through the winding country lanes where hawthorns were peppered with winter birds: sparrows, of course, the occasional robin, stonechats, blackbirds and thrushes. The Brent Geese flew in skeins over the flat landscape, not venturing into the ploughed fields of the farmlands, but dipping low behind humps crowned with blackthorns, and settling somewhere on an out-of-sight creek.

Kate, ever the country girl, pointed out poisonous plants to Sally, knowing they would excite her imagination. The spindle tree, white and black bryony, and the guelder-rose whose succulent looking red berries last all summer and are the fear of mothers whose young go out to pick blackberries and sloes. Sally was eager to learn and asked the name of many plants, some of the names of which, to her consternation, Kate did not know.

'What's the name of that tree?' asked Sally, pointing.

'Beech, I think,' she said.

The carter cleared his throat.

'That be a horny-wood tree, miss. What's used for butcher's chopping blocks and mallets an' such like that. Hard it is, though often mistook for beech, I have to say, due to its same smooth bark and like shape. Lot's of 'em up in Eppin' Forest way.'

'Oh,' said Kate, 'thank you.'

'You're welcome, miss.'

From that moment on, Sally directed all her questions at the carter, who seemed quite happy to take over from Kate as the natural history expert of the region. Kate in her turn was allowed to sit and dream as the bare hedgerows flowed past them. They left the cart at Rochford and continued on foot through Stambridge to Canewdon.

Canewdon village crowned a knoll above a low, wide valley which swept alongside the River Crouch and rose again up to another knoll on which Ashingdon village was perched. The two churches, with their old stone towers, stood on the two highest points of the knolls, glaring across the valley at each other like old warriors too lazy to fight. In the valley between them, the Viking King Canute fought and won, battling against the Anglo-Saxon King Edmund Ironside: Canewdon was named after him. Danes occasionally turned up in both villages, searching for their lost heroes, and receiving short shrift when they pried too closely into the history of the region: the English, whether of Viking, Saxon or Norman descent, invariably sided with the underdog.

Sally was taken through the village, where the stocks still stood, used unlawfully on rare occasions when the inhabitants felt rough justice was deserved by certain members of the community, to an old stone house at the end of a terrace. There she was introduced to Kate's sisters, who raised their eyebrows at Kate behind the girl's back. What was their elder sister thinking of, bringing this tatty gypsy to see them?

Kate took no notice of the arched brows, reminding herself that she would have to take Sarah and Liz to task when Sally was not there for giving her such a reception.

Sarah had news, for she was courting Tom Weeks, a cider-maker from Ashingdon, across the valley.

'He's quite well off, Kate,' said Sarah, 'and he's a nice man in his mid-twenties. He's taken the cider-making business over from his father, and is doing quite well. We aim to get married in a year or so's time, if you agree.'

'Me?' cried Kate, startled at the family status she seemed to have attained since Edward's death. 'Why do I have to agree?'

'That was my thinkin',' said Uncle Peter, tapping the ash out of his pipe on the heel of his boot, making a pile of grey dust on the floor and getting a glare from his wife Polly in the process. 'It's a man must give his permission for you to marry, not a female.'

Uncle Peter was a warm person, and Kate liked a lot about him, but this was more than she could bear.

'Uncle Peter,' she said evenly, 'our father brought us up to trust our own judgement. It's not up to me or to you whether Sarah should marry this man. It's up to her. She's sensibly decided to wait for a while, for she's quite young still, but if in the end she does decide to marry him, she needs no permission from you or me.'

Uncle Peter looked so uncomfortable at these words, muttering something about 'rights and privileges', that Kate was sorry she had been so forthright, and quickly changed the subject.

Later, before she left, Kate made an excuse to speak to Sarah in private in her bedroom. 'Sarah, what about your problem? With the marriage bed?'

Sarah snapped, 'It's not my problem, it's Tom's.'

Kate sighed. 'Now you know that's not true. If anything, it will make things difficult for both of you. Have you spoken to him about it?'

'Yes,' said Sarah, 'and he says he understands.'

Kate said, 'He may be hoping that by the time you actually do get married you'll feel differently.'

'Perhaps, but I don't think I will.'

'I was afraid of that. What if I don't give you my blessing? What if I forbid you to marry?'

Sarah started to sound impatient. 'It's only a formality, Kate. I thought it would please you to be asked. We'll be marrying anyway, whether you like it or not.'

Kate sighed again. 'Well, there's nothing more to be said then, is there?'

'No.'

They returned to the group downstairs and Kate turned her attention to Liz.

Liz was still too young to marry, and she declared she wanted to 'flirt a bit' before settling down with one man, which made her aunt fall back in her chair apoplectically, saying she would rather have the hoyden she had at the moment in the house than the hussy she might have next year. Kate laughed, knowing that her younger sister still had a lot of growing up to do and would probably do nothing of the sort.

Kate and Sally left them around midday and followed the road down to the schoolhouse, south-east of the village. Kate remained disturbed about Sarah's plans, but she could not really interfere. In any case, Sarah and Tom might very well have a happy married life and all Kate's fears might come to nothing.

Sally's voice broke into her thoughts. 'Who are we going to see now?' she asked.

'A friend of mine. A man friend. But you mustn't mind if he seems snobbish. He's all right when you get to know him.'

'Is he a very great gentleman then?'

'He believes he is,' laughed Kate.

Kate knocked on the door of the schoolhouse, then stood a little to the side. Sally remained boldly in front of the door, obviously curious to see this 'man friend' of Kate's. Nothing very much frightened Sally, especially not other people.

The door was flung open by Johann, who stood rubbing his eyes and looking at Sally in bemusement. He wore a frill-fronted shirt, which was open to half-way down a pale, hairless chest of almost ivory quality. In his dark tight breeches he looked a most romantic figure, like some young poet disturbed in his meditations. Johann had indeed been writing poetry, a pastoral verse with religious undertones, and his hand still held the pen. He brushed away a lock of blond hair which had flopped over his face and remained staring at Sally, who stared back at him with candour.

Kate, standing to the side of the step, moved slightly, and Johann's attention switched to her. His eyes lit up and he cried, 'Kate! I'm so sorry to appear such a halfwit. I was scribbling one of my silly verses and not expecting you at all. Come in, come in.'

Once they were in the small, cramped living-room of the schoolhouse, he turned to Sally. 'I don't believe we've met?'

Kate said, 'This is Sally Mayar. We collect cockles together. Sally, the Reverend Johann Haagan is an ordained priest and our schoolteacher, but he's quite harmless really. He thinks us working girls a little beneath his station, but he'll talk to us if we encourage him.'

'Without a trace of condescension,' confirmed Johann, managing to smile at Sally and glare at Kate almost at the same time, 'or contempt for the working woman.'

Sally, to Kate's amazement, did a little curtsy. 'Please t'meecha,' she said. 'Kate's spoke about you ever so much, sir.'

'Johann. Please call me Johann. Here, take a seat.' There were too few to be had, and his pale features became a little flustered. 'Well, I'll sit on the edge of the bed, and you, Kate, take the stool if you please, while Miss Mayar can have the chair. There, now we're all comfortable. I'll make some tea in a moment. Do you like toasted crumpets, Miss Mayar? The stove is well stocked with coals and the crumpets would toast in a moment . . .'

In all this time he had not once taken his eyes from Sally's face. She in turn seemed flushed and excited, presumably because she was in a man's house and was unused to such surroundings. Kate found herself feeling rather superfluous to the company.

Johann discreetly buttoned his shirt and put on a smoking jacket of Chinese red silk. Then he busied himself with the making of the tea and crumpets while the women asked him questions.

'You the schoolteacher then?' asked Sally, rather pointlessly, Kate thought.

'Yes, I knock some education into the little monsters. But I do other things as well. I act as curate to the rector of the local church, as Kate will confirm, and I write a little . . .'

'You write things? What things?'

'Poetry, a little prose. I am an admirer of Mr Coleridge and his mysterious verses, some of which I am told are the result of his opium addiction. Poems like *Kubla Khan*. Do you read Coleridge at all, Miss Mayar?'

'Can't read,' said Sally, with that open frankness and honesty Kate so much admired in the girl. 'Never learned.'

Johann straightened from his task. 'Can't . . . ? Well, Kate, you should teach her.'

'No time for learnin' stuff like that,' laughed Sally. 'We got to get the cockles in. 'Sides, books wouldn't last long in our place. Damp would get to them.'

'Yes,' said Johann, the consternation showing in his expression, 'yes, I suppose it would. Crumpet?' He offered the plate. 'There's butter and jam on the table.'

The two women helped themselves to the crumpets, spreading butter and jam on them quite liberally, while Johann watched, fascinated by this wild little creature Kate had brought with her from the cockle sheds. She looked, what? Irish? Hungarian? Something very earthy anyway, very raw and natural, like a child reared by wolves or something. *Mayar*. Probably Hungarian. Such black eyes, like unripe sloes. The thin, almost pointed features and raven hair. Born surely on some vast, mid-continental plain during the dead of winter, while the wolves looked on if they did not actually take part in the rearing. He imagined her swathed in furs, those dark eyes vying with the northern nights for the deepest pitch.

'Another crumpet, Miss Mayar?'

'You don't have to keep callin' me Miss. Sally will do for me. I ain't too posh, you know.'

'Yes, Sally. A nice name. A very *beautiful* name.'

Surely some warlord had driven her parents from their homelands and, though already itinerants, they now had to travel far from the place of their birth, across the seas, to settle on the shores of Albion.

'Thank you.'

'You're very welcome.'

Johann suddenly saw the sheet he had been working on lying on the table by the jam. He picked it up and said animatedly, 'Shall I read you my lines?'

'What lines?' said Sally, frowning.

Kate whispered, 'He means his poetry.'

'Oh, does he? Well, why didn't he say so? All right.'

Johann cleared his throat, struck a pose, and began:

> *'The leaf saw the wing gliding free:*
> *Envied its colours, compared their bladed forms,*
> *Then called to itself shades of fire and molten metal*
> *and once, before death, flew.'*

'Very nice,' said Sally. 'No more crumpets left?'

The two women stayed for over an hour, then left together to take the road to Paglesham. Kate showed Sally where she had lived when her father was alive, and Sally was impressed.

'Never been in a house that big,' she said.

'It's only a small cottage.'

'It might be, but I just never been in one.'

They walked from East End to Church End, and then took the path along the sea wall, following it round to Stambridge. There they managed to pick up a lift from a waggoner heading to St Mary's church in Prittlewell. He told them he was a part-time gravedigger and there was a hole to be dug before the next morning.

'I dursn't dig in the dark, and the burying's early in the morn, so I'll do it afore the even comes in.'

They sympathised with his fear of churchyards after dark: Sally said she wouldn't go near one if her life depended on it, not at night. They exchanged supernatural stories then, Sally telling Kate that there was a statue of a Viking in the Leigh churchyard, that if you ran round it three times it came to life and chased you with its battleaxe. The waggoner, listening in, then announced that he was glad he was going to St Mary's, where that sort of thing didn't go on.

'No statues there,' he said. 'Only these angels on top of the tombstones.'

'Ones with wings?' asked Sally.

The waggoner nodded. 'Some of 'em.'

'They're the worst kind,' said Sally. 'They flits around the place at night, like stone bats, looking for gravediggers to eat up.'

The waggoner visibly started out of his seat, then became angry when the two women began laughing at him.

'You shouldn't do that to an old man,' he complained. 'It ain't proper.'

Sally apologised, but couldn't help giggling, and finally the waggoner started to laugh too, and they kept up their jolly mood all the way to Prittlewell, where the women left the old man to his shovel and went on their way to catch the next tide.

Chapter Seventeen

After Sally's visit to Kate's village, the gypsy girl insisted that Kate come home with her again. Kate was not unwilling to socialise with her newly made friends, and went with Sally to her shack after the cockling one day. There Kate asked about Sally's origins: where she and her family came from. After a little encouragement, Sally's father talked about where they had once lived.

'We was once a family what travelled the Europe continent,' he said, smoking his pipe as he talked. 'Right in the middle we lived, not from no country so to speak, for we was gypsies even in them days – 'ave been since Adam and Eve. We didn't follow no flag, nor have no borders, see. We was just a tribe on the move the whole while. We was always gettin' caught up in wars of some sort or another, even though we never fought none. Gypsies is used to bein' knocked about a bit, this way and that.'

'How did you come to be in England?' asked Kate.

Mr Mayar took another puff on his pipe before replying. 'Well, that's a mystery that is, but a few grandfathers ago, the tribe was pushed out of the middle of the continent by some ruffians or other – Vandals or Goths which were barbarian folk movin' west. Buggers on wild horses just out to kill and take what they could get their 'ands on. We couldn't see 'em off, we wasn't strong enough, so we always moved on. Comes a time when we're standin' on the edge of the seashore, with nowhere else to go to.'

'So you took a boat to England?'

'Well, not *me* 'xactly, but me grandfather's people. I says *we* because we still feels like a people, if you understand me, what are out on their own here. A separate tribe, so to speak.'

He nodded and looked contemplative until Kate interrupted his meditations with another question. 'Why did you stop moving around, here in England, I mean?'

'Bless you, you've got a few of them questions, ain't you? I never got asked these things before, not outside the family. Well, it happened like this. When Sally was born we was still on the road, travellin' and tradin' in horses. Then one night me brother killed a man in a knife fight outside an inn. Me brother was arrested and sent for trial at the Old Bailey Street court. The family had to rally, don't you see and get 'im out of that damned prison.

'So I hires us a lawyer to defend me brother, selling everything we'd got to pay the legal fees and makin' us dirt poor into the bargain. The trial was lost, me brother 'anged in Newgate Prison, and the family left without a penny. We 'adn't even homes no more, for the caravans was sold along with the horses . . .'

Kate was astounded at their selflessness. They had sacrificed everything they owned for one man, Sally's uncle. They would have done so, she knew, for any member of the family.

She heard how the whole extended family of thirty-one individuals walked from the streets of London, down through Essex, to the beach at Leigh, and there became shellfish collectors. There was a dream amongst them that one day they would be horse traders again, but their numbers were whittled down fairly quickly. Some of the children died of the cold that first winter, Sally being one of those tough enough to make it through. The elderly fell away too, of rheumatic fever, hypothermia, tuberculosis, and various other ailments. Some just faded away, depressed and spiritless, when they realised they would never go back on the road again.

By the time Sally was fourteen, there was only her mother and father, two of her uncles, and three female cousins left in Leigh. The others had mostly died, but those who had not had gone on the road on foot: something most gypsies would find as repugnant as exile. To become a common tramp was worse than death: it was to sell one's honour.

To Sally, who had known no other life, the cockling was as good a way to earn a living as any. She did it with a cheerfulness that had other cocklers looking at her sourly. She was still young and fit, full of dreams, and nothing very much troubled her beyond her parents getting sick. The salt air, far from ravaging her features, seemed to be good for them. Her complexion was of course not the soft peach owned by many English girls, but a darker, more resilient olive which seemed to thrive on inclement weather, taking on a sheen that made her face appear to glow in the wind and rain. Her thick black hair, which she sometimes wound in a shining coil that hung down her back served to emphasise her high cheekbones, her slim, aquiline nose and her long, slender, elegant neck.

Johann Haagan knew nothing of the exotic history of Sally Mayar, but had certainly been captivated by her beauty. On the night following the visit of Kate and Sally, he lay in his bed, tossing and turning, wondering why the world seemed so different all of a sudden, knowing and yet not wanting to admit it. There was an excitement in his breast never felt before, at first like the stirrings of life in a desert region, then a full-blooded blossoming of forests of flowering trees. He had fancied himself in love before, but it had been nothing like this; nothing so powerful and unrestrained had inhabited his heart before this afternoon.

He got out of bed at three o'clock, having barely closed his eyes for four hours. He lit the lamp and went to sit on the step in the cold night air, staring out into the void where not even a star was visible. How could this be? he asked himself. How could he find such a woman so irresistible? She was illiterate, ignorant, with no appreciation of any of the things he valued so much. She had no refinements, no social graces, no *anything*. A guttersnipe. An urchin.

He told himself he was surely smitten only temporarily. It was true that her beauty was like something out of Xanadu: a mysterious dark loveliness from the Asian heartland. Sally might have looked a queen, but she was a cockler. She was crass and stupid – no, that was wrong of him. Just because she was ignorant did not make her stupid. Kate had told him she was very bright, and Kate's judgement was certainly to be trusted.

But still, he argued with himself, one could not educate her into being a lady. A lady was born and bred, not made from materials already formed into some crudely fashioned gypsy-cum-cockle girl. No matter how much education he stuffed into her, she would still be of inferior stock, a common mud dabbler. The ladies Johann knew would not touch mud with someone else's walking stick, let alone their own hands.

And a lady was what Johann had always wanted, wasn't it? Of course it was. Ever since he could remember he had been impressed by style, *ton*, class. He wanted an accent that was as smooth as warm milk, not a deep throaty voice that dropped aitches and emitted appalling grammatical errors. How could he live with a woman like that? How could he introduce her to his friends? What would she look like in a stylish crinoline dress by Swinthorpe's of London?

'What would she look like? She would look like a damned *princess*,' he growled at the night.

He had to admit that the Reverend Johann Haagan had not bargained for this. God was playing games with him. The Johann Haagan he knew looked at women coolly, judging them by their appearance, their gestures, their sweet voices. He wanted a pretty young woman named Edwina, with small dainty feet, trim waist, eyes of cornflower blue and a sweet smile that took his breath away. This was a woman who had to be helped over a low stile when out walking, offering him her gloved hand, chiding him when he tried to put his arm around her waist. Such a woman stirred his protective instincts, made him feel like a strong man, a gentleman, full of tender feelings.

Sally, on the other hand, stirred no such feelings. What she aroused in him was frantic excitement. He didn't want to help Sally over stiles, he wanted to grab hold of her, ravish her, lock naked legs with her in the tall grass of some meadow.

When he did imagine her naked before him, his mind began spinning like a vortex and a sandstorm raged through his breast. He had never felt such a passion, a desperation in his life before. Was that love, or simply lust? Or love of a certain kind? He didn't want to hurt her, that was for sure. His fantasies of deflowering her were simply overstimulation of his imagination. Johann knew that when it came to the act itself he could be as tentative and shy as a maiden. Yet she enflamed his thoughts to such an intensity that anything seemed possible!

Could he live on without ever having her, that was the question. One thing was certain, he couldn't go to *sleep* without the thought of another meeting. If he did not see Sally once more, he might never rest again but be doomed to a life of insomnia.

He had always imagined that love was something quite different from what he felt now. In fact he had fancied himself in love with Edwina, for whom he had wanted to care. Edwina had invited solicitous behaviour: like a vulnerable faun whose large eyes, forever brimming with moisture, had brought forth from him tenderness and gentle inquiry.

This dark girl aroused within him an urgency, as if everything in life were suddenly vital. The world crackled with electricity when she smiled. He wanted to take her hand and say, 'Let's take a boat to the Americas, build a log cabin and fend off Red Indians together.' She needed no protector, that much was certain, for she was full of her own confidence. Physically she looked as fragile as porcelain, but spiritually she appeared as strong as obsidian. He could not imagine her coming to him weeping uncontrollably because she had stubbed her toe on the root of a tree, or full of anxiety at having mislaid a purse, or fearful because a man had 'looked at her' while she had been admiring the milliner's window display.

He had to see her just one more time to rid himself of these strange fascinations.

* * *

A week after Kate and Sally had visited Johann, Kate was busy bargaining for her cockles with a stall owner. Steam billowed out of the open doorway of the cockle shed, its warmth welcome to Kate, who was wet and cold from head to foot, standing in the freezing drizzle with her cartload of shellfish. She was just putting the money into a pouch tied around her waist when she felt a tap on her shoulder. She turned and found herself facing Johann Haagan.

'Johann! What are you doing here?'

He was dressed in an oilskin cape with a sou'wester to fend off the rain. The water ran in rivulets from his face. He had obviously been out in the open as long as Kate, though she was dressed only in a thin dress and a canvas smock, which was simply a piece of sail with a hole in it for her head to go through.

'Forgive me for appearing without an invitation,' he said, sounding stiff and formal, and not at all like his usual self, 'but I thought it time I came to visit you.'

He was clearly nervous in this area where the lowest peasants were in the majority. Cocklers and triggers were staring at him, running their eyes up and down his body, watching curiously as if he were an alien from exotic climes, as if he had made some terrible social error in joining their throng.

Johann looked around him at the inquisitive stares. 'I feel a little out of my depth,' he said with a false laugh. Then he turned back to Kate and said in a whisper, 'My God, young woman, what are they doing to you? Is this the way you live?'

'You haven't *seen* where I live,' she replied. 'I'll take you there.'

After stowing her cart in its usual spot under the jetty, she walked him along the sea wall towards Benfleet, where the fishing smacks were coming in. The sea was rising now, kicking up white horses which rolled and crashed against the earthen wall that kept the water from running over the flat area fronting the shallow cliffs. Gulls were being thrown around in the air, some dipping down to the waves to rest for a moment on the turbulent surface. Further inland a large grey heron rose from a patch of reeds and, like a flying cross, sailed over the cliffs to seek refuge from the storm that seemed to be sweeping in from the ocean.

When they reached the shanties, Kate found her own shack and threw back the canvas door, motioning Johann to enter. He went inside and found a fish crate to sit on. In the gloom within he opened his cape and took out a parcel.

'Some bread and meat,' he said.

As they ate their simple meal, Johann looked around the interior of the shack, which was letting in water in various places.

'So this is your little home?' he said.

'Not so much a home as a place to rest my head.'

'Yes, I can see that. It must be very cold in here when the wind comes over that wall.'

'Bitterly.'

They continued in silence after that, Kate wondering when he was going to come to the real reason for his visit. She had guessed what it was, of course, for Johann had never given any indication that he would like to visit her, and she doubted he had even thought of doing such a thing before now. Yet here he was, on a wet and windy day, having tramped all the way from Paglesham to Leigh, and without a thing to say for himself.

Finally Johann cleared his throat and said, 'Where does that other girl live? What's her name? Sally something?'

'You know very well what her name is,' said Kate, 'and we both know she's the reason why you're here. Sally is looking after her sick mother at the moment and I'm not sure I should let you see her. What do you want with her, Johann?'

He seemed crushed with embarrassment. 'Oh, I don't know,' he shrugged, staring out of the doorway rather than into Kate's eyes.

'She's my friend, Johann. I won't have you playing with her like a toy. She may seem very worldly, but she still has a lot of the child in her. If you use her simply to satisfy some male vanity, I'll never speak to you again, and what's more, I'll make certain you suffer for it. Do you understand?'

Johann drew himself up and looked at her stiffly. His eyes burned with fury. 'How dare you talk to me in that manner? You would do well to remember that I'm a gentleman and a priest, young woman. I have influence in the community—'

Kate could have taken offence at this curt speech, but she knew Johann was trying to bluster his way out of an embarrassing situation. Instead she decided to get down to the roots of the matter and cut him short.

'You're in my house – don't sneer, Johann, it may be a few driftwood planks, but it's still my house – and I know you're up to something. Since you're under my roof, you'll listen to me. You're my friend, Johann, even if you are a priest, but you're still a man and you men believe you can take what you want and remain respectable. You can't, not here. These people may look poor and pathetic creatures, but Sally's father is a proud man, a gypsy. The gypsies have a code of honour just like you gentleman priests, and if you shame one of their daughters, they'll kill you.'

'What are you doing, Johann? You're a gentleman, who says he's revolted by anything lower than the daughter of an earl, yet here you are in a cockle girl's hut.'

The fury in Johann's eyes had not abated when someone darkened the doorway of the shack. It was Sally, who came right in without being invited, and sat down opposite Johann. Her eyes were sparkling. 'You came to see *me*, din't you?'

Johann glanced at Kate. 'Well, I just thought I might visit my friend Kate . . .' he began, but Sally shook her head.

'No, you come to see me. Think I don't know? I never seen someone look at me like you do before. You want me, don't you?'

Johann was speechless before this onslaught. He tried to dismiss the girl as horribly vulgar and terribly forward: a peasant girl with the manners of a strumpet. Yet somewhere beneath the dignified priestly veneer rose a feeling of admiration for this young woman. She was not being ill-mannered, not in her terms. She was being forthright and honest, laying everything down as she saw it. She was not trying to embarrass him or put on a shocking demonstration to draw attention to herself: she was simply telling the truth as she saw it.

The barrier Johann drew up between his horror of indelicacy and uncouth behaviour and the awe in him aroused by her frankness, served to prevent him from saying anything in return. Instead he looked to Kate for help and found those blue eyes unyielding.

Finally he managed to open his mouth. 'Miss Mayar, I feel you're like the cavalry who knows my every tactic. You're thundering up to my defences and threatening to break them down with a direct attack . . .'

Kate interrupted him here. 'Stop hiding behind – what is it you call them? – *metaphors*? Tell Sally what you're really thinking and feeling for once, instead of sheltering behind these screens of words.'

He stared about him helplessly, then looked into Sally's face. There was no hussy there. She was a simple innocent girl who wanted straight answers. Was he capable of such things? All his life he had employed the vague and the obscure, using his education to weave ambiguous replies to awkward questions, using the mystery and magic of his profession to confuse his listeners, using pomposity and position to put down those who were below his station. Was he now expected to bare his soul to this eighteen-year-old gypsy girl? And could he really promise, as Kate wished him to do, that he would not discard her once her purpose had been served?

Surely it was too much to ask. But the more he stared into her face, the more he felt himself swirling in some monstrous maelstrom, drowning, drowning, drowning.

'Yes, I came to see *you*, Sally,' he heard himself saying. 'I have to admit I have not slept since I saw you last. I believe I am in love with you, though I have no idea what to do about it. I do not know you. I have met you only once, very briefly. But this much I have admitted to myself. I am as confused as you probably are on hearing myself say this.'

There, the secret which was no secret was out in the open.

Sally nodded gravely. 'I can see it's hard for somebody like you. You're a Christian preacher and high above my class of person. But I knew when you was lookin' at me that you was wanting me.'

'How . . . how do you feel about *me*?' Johann asked a little faintly, dreading the answer.

'I like you,' she said with her usual candour. 'You seem a nice person and I think you're nice looking. If you wanted to marry me, I don't suppose I would say no.'

'Marry you?' gasped Johann, half-rising.

Kate had to stifle a cough at this point, her face buried in her hands, and Johann realised that it was still up to him to offer some kind of response to what Sally had said. Kate's fears, at least, were unfounded, for it was clear that marriage was the only arrangement that Sally would countenance. He sat down hard on the box. Marry her? He needed time to think. He felt hot and a little out of breath. His heart was racing like a hare's at a coursing. Marriage?

Sally said at last, 'I can see you ain't thought much about that, but if you want me, that's the only way. I'm willin', and that's what I wanted to tell you.' She stretched out her arm, and Johann rose again to shake her hand, feeling the slimness nestling in his own. The palm was not soft, but the touch of Sally's skin sent shivers up his spine.

'Thank you for being so candid with me, Miss Mayar.'

'Candid? What's that?'

'Sincere, honest.'

'Oh, that's all right.' Sally stood up and straightened her ragged clothes with her hands as if they had been fashioned from the finest fabrics money could buy. She seemed completely composed, and gave Kate one last smile, before leaving Kate and Johann alone.

Johann broke the silence that followed. 'She certainly doesn't use any feminine wiles to trap a man into wedlock, does she?'

Kate laughed. 'You noticed?'

He raised his eyebrows. 'I am given the plain choice. No frills around it. Life or nothing.'

'I warned you, Johann. If Sally hadn't insisted on it, then I would have done my best to do so.'

Johann shrugged, wiping away a track of water which was dripping down on to his face through a slit in the canvas roof. He had not expected anything. He had merely come for a second look at the woman who was haunting his hours so much. Certainly he had not expected to be confronted and given the choice of matrimony or exile. Events were moving at a remarkable pace: too fast for a man who liked to study matters at leisure, turn them over and over in his mind, weigh them, inspect them for fissures, open all their drawers, sniff their contents, test them for durability. It was like being offered illicit goods in the street. *Do you want them or don't you? Quick, make up your mind, for I shall be gone away in a second and you shall not see me again.*

'When she says she likes me,' Johann asked, 'does she mean it?'

'Of course. You've surely realised by now she doesn't say anything she doesn't mean?'

'But what does she mean by it?'

Kate smiled at him. 'There's no hidden language in Sally. There's no signals to look for. She means what she says. If she grows to love you, which I'm sure she will, you will have no wife more faithful, no wife more loving, no wife more loyal. Perhaps she will love you long after these feelings you have for her have died.'

'You think my feelings shallow?'

'I think them different from what they have to become if you are to love her for herself.'

'You think I could grow to love her soul?'

'I think you could grow to love her *all*, everything about her – even the way she speaks – if you shed your prejudices.'

He smiled ruefully. 'I have taught you too well, Kate. You use words against me now that would have never entered your head when I met you.'

'I don't use them against you, Johann,' said Kate, taking his hand in hers. 'I'm trying to help you.'

He nodded dumbly, humble before this young woman whose education had been but a fragment of his own, yet in a way was so much more complete.

When Johann had gone, Sally came back to talk to Kate about the visit.

'I told you he likes me,' said Sally. 'Someone don't come seven miles just for a chat, do they?'

Kate, who really did not know what to make of these events, was worried for both Johann and Sally. That a tempestuous sea of emotion had suddenly appeared between them, she had not the slightest doubt, but she was anxious that they should not cross it too early. Heavy storms have a way of subsiding very quickly, and she was afraid that if they leapt in and swam towards each other now, they might regret it later.

'Sally,' she said, 'you must make absolutely sure of your feelings before you really commit yourself.'

Sally laughed. 'Oh tosh,' she said. 'You sound like me mum and dad. Look, nobody's ever *absolutely sure*, Kate. You just got to go by how you feel. There ain't no other way of doin' it, now is there? Even those people who can read an' write can't sit down with a paper and pencil and list all the rights and wrongs of it an' then make a decision, can they? That's daft. You just got to hope everythin's all right. Look at you an' your Simon.'

'What about us?' said Kate.

'Well, you don't know you're goin' to feel the same way in ten or twenty years' time, do you? Maybe you love him so much because you can't have him at the moment. Maybe it's because you're kept apart that you feel so loving towards him?'

Kate felt a little flare of annoyance in her. How dare Sally judge her feelings towards Simon? 'I don't think my feelings towards Simon are any concern of yours, Sally.'

Sally cocked her head to one side, folded her arms, and said with a little smile, 'I s'pose it's quite a different thing from discussin' my feelings about Johann?'

This stopped Kate dead in her tracks, and after a few moments she mumbled, 'You're right, I'm sorry. I didn't mean to sound snooty. I'm feeling a little sensitive at the moment. It seems such a long time since Simon went away. It frightens me that I can't recall his face – not in any detail. Sometimes I think Simon's slipping away from me, gradually, and I'm not doing enough to hold on to him.'

'That's silly,' Sally said. 'You an' him will be together soon and these couple of years he's been away will seem like two weeks, you'll see.'

'I'm worried about me, though. My feelings... and will he still love *me* when he sees me again. After all, I'm nothing special and he's probably meeting all sorts of fine oriental women on his travels...'

'You're worried because you think you don't love him as much as he deserves. Well, that's daft for a start, because he don't deserve nothin' for goin' away like that, so whatever you've got left is good enough, an' he'll know it. An' as for him falling out of love with you, well you can't do nothin' about that, but you can be sure of one thing: there ain't no oriental woman who could hold a candle to you, Kate, and he'll know it. Come on love, I'm sure Simon's breakin' his neck to get back here to you.'

Kate allowed herself a wan smile. 'I hope so.'

'If he's not he needs a good kick up the backside – pretty lady like you waitin' on him! But I'm sure he is, 'cause all the things you've told me about him, well, he sounds luvely, don't he?'

'He is lovely – but he wouldn't like to hear me call him that. He'd be embarrassed. He likes me to tell him he looks handsome, but *lovely?* No, that would worry him.'

Sally laughed. 'I know. They're such vain creatures, men, ain't they? Always puffin' themselves up with pride, bein' a *man*, stuffed to the gills with honour and all that. Yet you try to give 'em a compliment an' they go all stiff and starchy on you. Daft really, init?'

'Sometimes you do wonder whether they're worth all the attention,' agreed Kate.

'Yet you've got to give it to 'em, or they pine away like puppy dogs, don't they? You love 'em, but they're such babies when it comes down to it. Without us women they'd be lost for the praise they need so much, wouldn't they? Can you imagine it, a world just full of men, goin' round sayin', "By George, you look a fine figure of a man today, Simon." "Thankyou, Johann, I particularly like the way you're dressed yourself today." Course not. They'd just walk around goin', "Hmm, ahh, good morning Simon." "Ahhh, mmmm, and good morning to you too, Johann." An' that would be it. Load of stuffed shirts dyin' for someone to praise 'em, but scared to do it to each other for some reason. Women tell each other how nice they look, but men would rather die.'

Kate laughed uproariously at the gruff tones Sally used to imitate the men, the tension in her unravelling in the company of this young woman. They were so close now. Kate realised that for the first time in her life she had allowed herself the luxury of a female friend. Until now she had only had her sisters; other women had been mere acquaintances. No one had been receptive to Kate's most inner fears. Her younger sisters had needed her to be strong and in complete control, had looked to her to provide security and stability; whilst her acquaintances would have regarded such revelations as an imposition. Now she had someone in whom she could confide fully, without fear of being rejected or misjudged in any way, and it felt very good.

* * *

The next Sunday the two women went to the church service at Paglesham. When he first saw them, sitting three pews back, Johann wanted to bolt. He felt a great panic surging through him. Why had she come here? To judge his performance as a minister? Old Potts was in failing health now, and much of the service was dependent on Johann himself. He was the preacher most of the time, while Potts remained the celebrant. It seemed the cockle girl had come to see how good the preacher actually was, whether he could do his job properly, whether he was just another boring droner, or a genuine orator with something to say, something to offer. Did he have substance, or was he a fraud inside the cloth?

I can't do it, he told himself. *I can't go out there and pretend to be a great speaker. I'm not. I'm just an ordinary priest with no special calling. She'll think I'm a pretender, a man who does this simply for a living.*

The next moment he rejected all this as stuff and nonsense. He had to prove himself to no one. His honour was intact. He was Johann Haagan, and certainly not concerned about how he appeared in the eyes of a mere cockle girl. His pulpit presence had dazzled far more beautiful women than Sally Mayar. Why, there had been great ladies who had fawned on him after hearing him preach, telling him he was gifted. He himself did not believe he was so good a speaker, but his congregation often thought otherwise.

Then came the time when he actually had to step up to the pulpit, and his heart failed him once again. He stood speechless for an embarrassingly long time, staring into those black eyes just a few feet away, and quaking in his shoes. Sally looked stunningly beautiful in a pretty white frock, her raven hair coiled around her head and wearing a pair of lace gloves. He found himself wondering where the clothes had come from. A family heirloom, perhaps? He had read somewhere that gypsies were inclined to hoard clothes long after their other valuables were lost. Then someone, Farmer Billings in the front pew, coughed impatiently and brought Johann back to earth.

'Today,' he began, 'our thoughts are on Christian fellowship . . .'

His voice sounded unusually high, even squeaky, and his hands would not stop trembling as he turned the pages of his sermon. It took a thousand years, a million years, to get it said, and then finally he stepped down and the service continued.

Afterwards, he waited outside to shake hands with the congregation as they left the church, and Farmer Billings said in a grateful voice, 'Nice short sermon there today, vicar. Like to see it. Get to the point, I say. Cut all this wiffle-waffle and pare it down to essentials.'

Johann glanced at the clock on the church and realised his sermon had only lasted twelve minutes. *Twelve minutes*! They were usually twenty to thirty minutes long at least. Yet it had seemed like a millennium up there in the pulpit.

When the two women came out, he invited them back to the schoolhouse for tea and cake. They accepted graciously. He went to the vestry and changed before escorting them along the lane.

'Well,' he said to Sally as they walked, 'how did I measure up?'

'Beg pardon?' said Sally.

'My sermon?'

'Oh, *that*,' replied Sally. 'To tell you the truth I wasn't listenin' much. You looked so beautiful in your robes and stuff I just couldn't take me eyes off you.'

Kate stifled a giggle and Johann glared at her. 'You mean,' said Johann with candour, 'I worried myself silly and ruined my sermon for *nothing?*'

'Did you? I dunno. I loved the sound of your voice, all dark and syrupy, so I don't think it was wasted, not on me anyway. I could 'ave given meself to you right there and then, in front of all those people.'

Johann stopped in his tracks, stunned by this vulgarity. Was he seriously thinking of a liaison between him and this young woman, who said such awful things? It was impossible. Impossible. He would have to make some excuse to get out of the tea and cakes.'

He turned to confront her and found his tongue tied in a knot. His eyes must have conveyed how he felt, however, for she stopped smiling when she looked into his face.

'I've done it, ain't I?' Sally said, her black eyes staring into his. 'I've shocked you somethin' terrible. Well, what would you want me to say? That you was magnificent? Well, you was, but not in the way you wanted to be. Would you want me to say I felt all giddy and sick, just sittin' there watching you? Well I did, but a bit stronger than how you wanted me to be, that's all. You made me legs go all weak and me heart was going so fast I thought the rest of me wouldn't never catch up with it. If that's shockin', well, I can't help it, 'cause that's the way I felt, your Reverence.'

Again, this woman had outfenced him. He did not know what to say. Her honesty was remarkable and he had nothing with which to combat it.

'Don't call me "your Reverence",' was all he could muster.

'It was a joke,' said Sally, winking at Kate.

Johann felt weak himself now, and continued down the lane in silence, wondering if he was going to find enough strength in him to say goodbye to this woman for ever at the end of the morning.

What he found himself doing, after the tea and cakes, was begging them to stay for the Evensong service, and asking Sally if he could visit her again at Leigh. The women said they couldn't stay for the service, for they had a tide to catch, but Sally added that she would love to see him again.

'Could you wear your robes, for me mum and dad to see?'

'Certainly not,' Johann said.

'Oh well,' said Sally, 'never mind. You look so nice in your cassock thing, it would have given 'em a treat. Maybe they'll see you sometime.'

'I'm sure they'll benefit greatly from the experience,' he was able to joke himself now, 'but we mustn't rush it.'

'No,' she said, smiling. 'Might blind 'em to your faults, mightn't it? Can't have them thinkin' you're some sort of angel, can we?'

'Wouldn't do at all,' agreed Johann.

After the women had gone, Johann fell on to his bed in a cold sweat. What was he doing, throwing himself at this creature? He had to stop it now, before it was all too late. He would write to Kate and ask her to intervene for him in this matter, and let Sally out gently by the back door. No, perhaps that was the coward's way out. He *would* visit, but he would do so with the intention of making it plain it was his last visit, and that he could ill-afford the time to see Sally again. That's what he would do . . .

Instead, Johann found himself a regular visitor at the Mayars' shack. Then one day he discovered himself talking about how much he admired Sally – her forthrightness and honesty – and how she would make someone a good wife.

They understood exactly what he meant, and there was an exchange of looks between Sally's mother and father. A flushed Sally whispered endearments into his ear. The funny thing was, Johann did not feel distressed. He felt quite elated. He knew Kate was concerned by the speed of the thing – he was concerned himself – but who was timing it? Man? God? Or the priest of love? It was really something of little consequence: how fast one fell in love and acknowledged it.

There was a moment, as he spoke briefly with Sally's father alone afterwards, when he learned something which had not occurred to him before now.

It was a salutary lesson.

As the two men stood on the beach and stared out over the mouth of the Thames, Sally's dad took his pipe out of his mouth and said to Johann,

'You know, we don't like our people to marry outsiders.'

'Outsiders?' said Johann, not quite catching what was being said to him.

'People like you, who ain't travellers.'

It still took Johann a few moments to realise he actually needed to obtain approval – approval that was not easily given to outsiders such as him – before he could marry this gypsy girl. Such a thing had not entered his head: that he might not be accepted by the family of a group of lowly cocklers. Until now, he had considered himself more than worthy of Sally, thinking he was the one who had to approve of *them*. That he was not good enough for an aristocrat's daughter was one thing, but not good enough for a cockler's girl? Life was certainly full of pitfalls for a gentleman of the middle classes.

Suddenly Sally was indeed a dark princess from an alien land, an alien people, perhaps unobtainable after all? It was at this moment he realised how badly he wanted her.

'Will it . . . will it be a problem?' he asked.

Sally's father sucked on his pipe a moment. 'It would have been, at one time, but now we're settled it's bit easier. My girl loves you a great deal, a blind man could see that, an' I wouldn't want to see her unhappy. I don't know you. You seem a good enough man, but I don't know you, if you understand me. I expect you to treat her right, you hear?'

'Naturally.'

'Well, it ain't so natural, once you've got to live with someone, but I'm going to trust you with her, precious as she is to me. I'll put my weight behind you, at the meeting, when the family gets together to talk about it.'

'Thank you,' said Johann, humbly.

And he meant it.

Chapter Eighteen

The wedding took place, appropriately, in the spring. The wild geese had flown back to their northern climes and the summer winged visitors were beginning to come in. The Essex fishing and shellfish industries were busy with a new season, in and around the mouths of the rivers. Further up the coast, around Maldon, the salt gatherers were hard at work, using windmills to pump the seawater on to the flats where it was allowed to evaporate, leaving behind a white, crystalline crust. Around Tollshunt D'Arcy, the raspberries and strawberries were being nurtured, while at Jaywick Sands, near Holland-on-sea, they were battling against the spring tides which annually invaded the countryside.

On the eve of the wedding, Johann had been conducting a service at Paglesham Church End. It was a baptism, and when he had ushered out the last of the family, he found himself alone in the church, except for Jason the stonecutter, who was working outside, chipping away at a block of granite. The rhythmic *chink, chink, chink* of Jason's chisel on stone imbued the evening with a sense of tranquillity. It was the kind of sound that enhanced quietude, endowing the scene with a more pronounced peace than no noise at all.

The sunlight through the vestry window, below which Jason was working, would provide enough light for Johann to change out of his canonicals. In the heart of the church it was quite dim, though the altar candles still burned. These would be snuffed out by one of the church wardens when they did their rounds as a last duty of the evening.

Instead of changing out of his robes immediately, Johann went out on to the steps and stared up at the sky. It was not yet dark, but the solitary Evening Star shone gently from its lone position in the vault of the sky, like a single candle bravely trying to light the whole universe. Soon it would be joined by a vast array of God's nightlights.

Johann sighed. Tomorrow was his wedding day, to a young woman he considered his social inferior. He had wanted to marry above himself, not below, and he was still not sure he was doing the right thing. These heightened feelings he had for this woman might very well be the result of some insidious fever that had worked its way into his bones and was now manifesting itself in the guise of love. Did he actually believe that? No, no, he told himself, it was useless to blame it on some malady. He *was* in love, but was it genuine love, or some passion instilled in his frame by the Devil? The Devil? These were unworthy thoughts, he reprimanded himself. Sally was no instrument of Satan. She was good and lovely and if she turned the blood in his veins to fire ... well it was because he found her intensely desirable. But was that good for him? Should an ambitious clergyman not choose a love that was cool and calm? A love that would further his career by being a model of conformity? A love that was sweet and clean to observers? Not this passion unleashed from some furnace. It must be obvious to everyone that he could not keep his eyes, or even his hands, off his intended bride. It must be clear to all onlookers that he burned for her touch and that his body was inflamed simply by a look from those black eyes of hers. Well, so be it, he sighed to himself, whether I go to hell or heaven it shall be fulfilled in matters of carnal discovery and experiences.

Chink, chink, chink, came the sounds from Jason's tools.

Out on the marshlands, the dying light of the sun had caught the reeds and had set them afire with its trailing veils of scarlet. Birds were beginning to go to their rest, frogs were starting to awaken. There was a warm wind coming from the south, stroking the reeds gently.

Johann went inside the church and to the vestry. He was about to remove his surplice when he heard the sound of footsteps on the stone flags of the aisle. He thought it was the church warden until he heard Sally's voice calling him softly, 'Johann, where are you?'

Sally was staying at the Plough and Sail with Kate, in a room paid for by Johann, so they would be able to get to the church more easily in the morning. The inn was quite close, but he was still surprised that she should seek him out, seemingly alone, when she should have been preparing herself for the wedding the next day.

'In here,' he called back, a little perturbed. 'In the vestry.'

There was a red velvet brass-ringed curtain separating the vestry from the main part of the church, and Sally ducked around the end of this, and closed the small gap she had made behind her. He saw that she was dressed in a plain black frock, very simple, with short sleeves and a shallow neckline. She wore nothing on her feet, which were dusty from her travels. Her wild hair fell about her shoulders like a waterfall of jet, and her eyes were sparkling with something ... what was it? He studied her face for a moment in the gloaming. There was something decisive in Sally's expression, as if she had finally made up her mind about something that had been concerning her. She looked slightly afraid, but at the same time determined. There was a fluidity about her movements as she moved closer to him: a liquefaction that disturbed him.

'Johann,' she said, in the back of her throat. 'You're still in your holy robes.'

She stretched out her slim hand and laid a spread of olive fingers on the front of his white surplice, as if she were gently pushing him away.

'What are you doing here, Sally?' he said nervously. 'Good Lord, child, we are to be married tomorrow. You should be resting, preparing yourself.'

'Don't talk, darling. Just be quiet a minit. You're always talkin',' she said huskily.

'What . . .? What are you doing, Sally?'

She had wormed her hand down between the neck of his surplice and his throat. Her cool hand was on the bare flesh of his upper chest. He felt her fingers flexing, gently clawing at his breast, and he was almost instantly aroused. His breath began to quicken to match hers, which smelled musty and hot to him. Her eyes were on his, high-points of light in them, flashing signals.

'Kate's out walkin'. I came looking for you, darlin',' she murmured. 'I had to see you. I just had to. I ain't never done nothin' like this before, I promise. I'm only eighteen, just gone. But see, gypsy girls, darlin', they need to know before the wedding. If you don't like me, you can stop the weddin' then, see?'

Now he could see what was in her expression. It was *passion*, perhaps even lust? This shocked him, for he was unused to females who pressed him for action. He had always been able to go at his own speed as a lover, the piper calling the tune, the commander controlling the pace of the march. What did she want of him? Some passionate response, naturally, but would a fierce kiss be enough, or what? What did she really expect from him?

'Johann,' she said again, the word coming out urgently, like the sound of some animal in need. 'It's because you might not like me, and then you can call it off, and I won't mind.'

Johann was conscious of Jason, just outside the stained-glass window of the vestry, now working by lamplight, and of the eternal sound of his iron chisel working against stone, cutting hallowed blocks from the base material, sculpting sacred shapes from its grey mass.

'We're in *church*,' he whispered.

175

She seemed not to hear this but began to tear at his vestment with her fingers, pulling it up, running her hands over his hips and buttocks. He groaned, unable to help himself. He grabbed at the black dress, raising it, finding her hipless figure naked beneath. His fingertips touched her thighs, caressed her abdomen, skirted the periphery of that small area which was the opening bud of her womanhood.

Sally trembled violently under his gentle touch, her slim, sylph-like form pressed against him. His vestments were rucked, gathered up around his chest now, billowing under his armpits. There were no undergarments to worry her, for he rarely wore them once winter was over, and her fingers were all around his lower waist, as if she were trying to gather him, but had not hands enough. She was kissing his face, dozens on dozens of quick, urgent kisses. Her loose raven hair was in his eyes, in his mouth.

He responded, kissing her eyelids, her lips, her nose, her cheeks, her forehead – raining showers of kisses upon her beautiful skin with its tanned complexion. Despite his wan skin, Johann's body was smooth and hard, like marble. Hers, dark, soft and silken, like some rare eastern fabric. When they pressed, one against the other, both the man and the woman moaned softly at the ecstatic sensation it aroused in them.

Like two tall flowers, one with a pale white stem, the other with an olive stem, their clothes gathered up beneath their arms to form the folds of petals – a black rose and a white rose – they trembled violently together. In the beginning, simply touching was enough; almost too delightful to bear. Johann had to reach out with his left hand and hold a cool stone pillar to support them both.

Then they could not bear just to touch, and finally he entered her.

Her eyes opened wide and she gave out a little cry, possibly of pain, then she relaxed a little and gripped him strongly around the waist, pulling him into her.

Chink, chink, chink. At first they moved to the rhythm of the stonecutter's chisel, but then Jason's careful workmanship became too slow for them, and soon they left the old man's regular cadence behind as they raced ahead of him, still showering kisses on each other, clawing at each other's thin bodies, desperate to gather in the whole carnal harvest with one reaping. At the height of their combined passion, a voice called from the chancel, 'Is anyone here? Is that you Reverend Haagan? Are you here?'

Even this, though it stabbed at some tiny corner of Johann's brain, could not interrupt his passion. He swiftly stuffed the lace hem of his surplice in his mouth to stifle his own sounds of ardour, while Sally bit his shoulder, through the white cotton, into the flesh. Though the pain was intense, Johann merely let out a slow, shallow sigh, and finally she released him to bury her face in the folds of cloth around his neck. They continued in silence, as the footsteps walked maddeningly up and down on the stone flags not a few feet from their hiding place, stopping occasionally as if the owner were listening to some sound out in the galaxies of the stars.

Then came the sound of someone at prayer as the intruder muttered orisons in the hollow of the chancel, begging forgiveness for sins, asking for a pure spirit to dominate the weak flesh.

Johann used this opportunity to cover up the sound of his own passion. Sally was making noises in the back of her throat, her face still buried in the flesh of his neck, but Johann was too far along the road to ecstasy himself to warn her to be quiet. How loud they actually were, in the end, he never really knew, for he was beyond himself.

Then, almost too soon it was over, and they relaxed against each other.

'Darling, darling, my dearest lady,' murmured Johann in her ear, as softly as the sound of a moth brushing its wings together, as quietly as dust settling on velvet. 'I want us to stay like this for ever.'

Dusk finally completed its task of filling the world with its tidal shadow.

Then the candles were snuffed on and around the altar by the unseen intruder, the footsteps walked the length of the aisle and died, leaving the pair of lovers clinging to each other in the darkness. They remained together for a very long time, until their bodies cooled and eternity came to an end.

Jason's chisel finally ceased its clinking.

The wedding was held, not at Paglesham Church End, for the Reverend William Josiah Potts was unwell. Instead, it took place at the small minister of St Andrew's, in Ashingdon. Sally's mother was well enough to attend, and the gypsy family walked from Leigh to Ashingdon village to be present.

Sally's mother and father were not used to formal church weddings. Although the family was Christian they had their own sect, which leaned towards Catholicism without allegiance to Rome. As nomads they carried their own altars, their own icons, their own statues of the Virgin and Child.

The gypsy way was to have weddings within the encampment, an elder presiding, and not concern themselves with civil niceties. Their church tended to be a woodland clearing, and they were not interested in signing pieces of paper at the end of the day.

Thus they tended to be a bit overawed by and impatient with the formality of the ceremony and the rituals involved, and were lost with regards to etiquette. After a necessary rehearsal they had said, between themselves, that on the whole it seemed all bit rigid and complicated for their tastes. Sally's father reckoned that far fewer words could be used, less dabblings and doings, and the whole thing could have been over in ten minutes, so they could get on with the dancing.

Johann's quite elderly parents also came to the wedding, but intended to stay only a short while at the feast afterwards, which was to be held behind the church itself on a patch of green that had not yet been taken over by the dead.

Kate was one of three bridesmaids, the other two being Leigh cockle girls. Though not a wealthy man, Johann had a healthy income, and he bought new dresses for each of the bridesmaids in a pale lilac; a smart jacket and breeches for Sally's father; and a dress of calico for her mother. The feast was also at Johann's expense, for Sally's father had no money for such things. There were village musicians too, consisting of a fiddler, an accordion player, and a man who whistled and sang country dancing songs.

Sally, used to outdoor services of a simple kind, led by a lay preacher, confessed to Kate that she found the inside of any church a little frightening.

'It's all so holy, init?' she said, as they stood in the doorway waiting for the cue to walk down the aisle.

Kate realised that she meant awe-inspiring, though in fact the minster of St Andrew's, built in 1020, was a small village church with no pretensions to grandeur.

Johann had given Kate and Sally a grand tour of the church interior during the wedding rehearsal two days before, pointing out the historical significance of several parts of the church.

The altar was made of carved oak and was a gift from the Cowley Fathers of Westminster. The stained-glass window above the altar had been donated by Moon's Farm, and the centre light of the window showed Christ in Glory, wearing a crown and holding a sceptre. The right-hand light showed St Andrew, and the left-hand light the Blessed Virgin. Below these, smaller lights showed the Danish King Canute and St Cedd. There was also a light depicting the River Crouch and boats.

On the south side was the tiny 'leper window', unglazed, which let in a modicum of light. Another window showed the first rector, Stigand, (later to be archbishop) as he appeared on the Bayeux Tapestry, wearing the pallium bestowed on him by the pope in recognition of his outstanding abilities. The north side had the door with a coat of arms opposite: the red rose of England, the Prince of Wales' feathers and the thistle of Scotland.

The two women had been impressed by Johann's knowledge and Sally, who had a superb memory for things that interested her, had retained all of it.

'S'all very nice though,' said Sally, clutching her bouquet of forget-me-nots, dusty miller daisies, herb roberts and other woodland wildflowers. Sally's mother had made the bouquet in the old way of the gypsies, who scorned cultivated blooms. 'I like musty old places like this.'

Kate replied, 'Yes, I like these ancient stone churches with their high wooden beams. They could have come from some Viking longboat, couldn't they?'

'Hmm. Me and Johann chose the hymns in here. I made him sing some of them, so I knew what was what.'

They had settled first on a new Welsh hymn, 'Immortal, invisible, God Only Wise', the tune of which was rousing, and whose words could be thundered out by the wedding guests and any villagers who stood outside the doors, as they were wont to do on fine wedding days, feeling themselves at liberty to join in most of the proceedings, undeterred by the stone walls between them and the actual ceremony. After all, a wedding was an event and entertainment hereabouts was sparse.

The second was Johann's old college hymn, 'Captains of the Saintly Band, Lights Who Lighten Every Land . . .', the words of which were written by J.B. de Santeuil. It was a hymn full of brightness, promising the banishment of darkness, which Johann felt appropriate for both himself and Sally, in that they were putting their dark years behind them.

Sally's face, during the ceremony, was suffused with happiness and, seeing her so joyful, Kate could not help but yearn for the return of her own man. Her feelings were tinged with envy as the service proceeded.

Johann, wonderfully smart in grey and black, his blond hair flowing over the starched collar of his shirt, seemed both rigid and relaxed at the same time. No doubt, thought Kate, he had some idea in his head of looking the English nobleman, the honourable gentleman: a figure he was known to admire. He appeared to wince once or twice. Perhaps that was because a clearly nervous Sally was gripping his arm so tightly that her fingernails must have been penetrating the cloth of his suit?

'Dearly beloved, we are gathered here in the sight of God,' intoned the priest, 'to join this man and this woman in holy matrimony . . .'

Throughout the service, the gypsies fidgeted like little children, staring round them as if bored by the ceremony, sighing as their eyes alighted on the high windows letting in the sunshine, shuffling their feet, inspecting the hassocks before they kneeled on them, their big rough hands running over the smooth wooden pews, tracing the dips in the worn backs.

When it came to the singing, the gypsies and the other cocklers excelled themselves with volume, bellowing out the words with only scant attendance to the melody, thoroughly enjoying the noise they were making. In contrast, Johann's side of the family, demure and gentle, were drowned in the flood. Kate noticed a look of spiritual pain go over Johann's mother's features, as one neighbouring cockler even began stamping her foot to the rhythm of the hymn as if it were a jig.

Kate lost herself in reverie some of the time, dreaming of the day when she would stand where Sally stood, with Simon by her side. She ached for that time, and it was all she could do to keep back the tears.

Kate had received a letter at last from Simon, brought to England by a private sloop. Simon was now off the shores of Sarawak in Borneo, helping James Brooke to subdue rogue Dyak and Chinese pirates of the region. It was a long letter, explaining how he had been in a great battle on the Pearl River, against Chinese war junks. The emperor had ordered the destruction of the opium stocks and thus began the Opium Wars.

> These Chinese soldiers don't know how to surrender, though, for when we attacked the forts and had them at our mercy instead of telling us 'enough' and showing the white flag they kept on fighting and we had to massacre them to put a stop to it. When they fell in the water they rather drowned than be saved by us. I felt sick to my stomach with it all and wondered what we were doing there in the first place. All these deaths for a few sticks of rhubarb and some tea? It did not seem right, Kate.
>
> Then some new British ships came up the river. They were steamships not sailing vessels like ours and the Chinese thought them dragons. There was such a rout that the Chinese Admiral, name of Kwan, lost his red cap button which was his badge of office from the emperor. He was much distressed and sent a messenger asking us to look for it. We found the red button on the deck of a captured war junk and our officers returned it to him. This was perhaps the only humane touch in the whole war. I was glad our ship was sent off once the steamers arrived. We was sent to help James Brooke off the coast of Borneo.

Simon explained that Brooke was every schoolboy's idea of a swashbuckling adventurer and was about to be made Sultan of Sarawak by the King of Brunei. '... Brooke is a man whose heart is lost to Sarawak, with its scheming Malay princes, its Chinese merchants and its headhunting tribes of Dyak Indians.' According to Simon, Brooke was well respected by the local population, who needed an outsider to rule them in order that the sultan remain impartial to the internal petty jealousies that raged between the three main races that dwelt within its tropical shores.

Brooke had apparently survived several assassination attempts, mostly from Malay princes, but one from the pirates themselves, fed up with his continual raids on their fortified harbours. Simon, whose skill at writing had improved immeasurably since the first letter to Kate, described the incident in his letter. Kate read it out loud to Sally as they sat on the grass drinking apple wine after the wedding ceremony was over. Johann was busy attending to the rest of his guests.

James Brooke was sitting at tea in his modest bungalow when a band of about a hundred Dyak pirates burst in on him. First he demanded to know what they were doing there, and they laughingly replied they had come to kill him. Brooke coolly asked if he might have a last drink with the pirates before they cut off his head and they agreed, whereupon Brooke handed round cigars and called to his servant in English asking for whisky to be brought, but added (knowing the pirates did not speak the English tongue) that the servant should run to fetch Datu Patingi, a Malay Chieftain.

The pirate chief Lingire, suspecting nothing, settled to drinking the whisky with Brooke, who asked the man about his exploits, whereupon the proud Lingire began telling Brooke about his feats of courage and strength at great length. After a long while, when they were on their third bottle, the Datu Malays stormed the bungalow, and killed some of the pirates, chasing the rest down to their canoes. Brooke had previously forbidden the interior tribes to hunt heads, as is their custom, but they seized this chance to stock up on their store of enemy skulls. Some Iban Indians pursued the pirates, who tried to paddle upriver rather than out to sea, and left a trail of headless corpses through the jungle, as they went about collecting the trophies which they take home to their village to give as gifts to their brides.

'There, you're lucky you aren't an Indian,' said Kate to Sally, 'or you might have received a severed head for your wedding present from your husband, instead of that nice ring.'

'A chopped-off head?' mused Sally, still clutching her precious bouquet which she had kept herself, according to gypsy custom, and refused to throw to the bridesmaids. 'That sounds useful. Could put it on the doorstep to scare people away when you don't want 'em.' The bride blew upwards from her mouth at the white ribbon that was apparently tickling her forehead. Kate thought she looked absolutely beautiful, like some eastern princess from a tale, yet Sally seemed completely unconscious of her loveliness. She had the demeanour of a young woman who had not long given up climbing trees with her brothers and, though she was beginning to feel at home in her ribbons and bows, could well have tossed them aside without a second's hesitation.

Kate folded the letter and put it away in a pocket. Then she said to Sally, 'How do you feel? Like a wife?'

'I don't feel like nuthin' much, at the minute. Got a bit of headpain, from bein' nervous, I suppose. Don't feel like I'm married at all. Strange, init?'

'You will, soon enough,' said Kate. Her voice dropped to a whisper so that others around them on the grass would not be able to listen in. 'What about tonight?'

Sally glanced at her. 'What, you mean the marriage bed?'

'Yes. Is that worrying you?'

'No, we've already done it,' she said with her usual candour. 'Last evening. Din't want *that* to worry about today.'

Kate was at first shocked, then reminded herself that she had no right to be judgemental.

'Well, then,' she said without thinking, 'any practical advice I have to offer will arrive too late, won't it?'

Sally turned and looked at her friend and raised her eyebrows.

A voice from behind them said, 'Any advice you have to offer, Kate, should not be practical at all, but most certainly theoretical in nature.'

Kate whirled to see Johann bearing down on them carrying two plates of sweetmeats: she felt herself colouring immediately. She thought about chastising him for sneaking up on them like that, but realised this would not do at all. She had spoken without consideration, and both Sally and Johann now knew her secret. She felt mortified, not by the contents of the revelation itself, but because she had given herself away in public, by accident. It would have been better to have told Sally in private than to be caught out like this.

Sally laughed. 'You should see your face, Kate Fernlee. I could toast a bit o' bread on it.'

'You have no room to talk,' snapped Kate, which only made Sally laugh the louder.

Johann sat down with the ladies on the grass, offering a plate to each. The fiddler was playing a lively air now, and guests and villagers were dancing around the gravestones, quite unconcerned by the fact that they were stamping on the horizontal bodies of their ancestors. As Tom Sparkit shouted to his cousin, if his old grandpa didn't like it, he could come up and join them.

'We could do wi' a couple o' skelitins,' returned his buxom cousin, 'to rattle along wi' the band.'

The gypsies changed behind the yew trees and holly bushes, relieved to get out of their sober church clothes and into brightly coloured garments which flowed as they danced. Sally's dad borrowed the fiddler's violin and the music became even more lively as gypsy airs came racing out from bow and strings, making the dancers breathless with exertion and excitement. Sally leapt to her feet and performed a most provocative dance, which both aroused and concerned her new husband.

'That was not very becoming,' he said to her in mild admonishment when she ran to him afterwards, breathless and full of glee.

'Becoming what?' she asked, with a puzzled look.

'Well,' he tried to whisper, 'you're a respectable married woman now.'

'That's right,' she said ingenuously, 'so it don't matter if I dance like that, does it? Couldn't have done a dance like *before* I was married. Might've given the men ideas, eh? But now they know I'm taken, they can just lick their lips and curse themselves for not being you. Bet they're jealous as anything of you right now . . .'

'No, no, that's not the point . . . I mean, it was bad enough when you were showing the whole of your leg with that fast tune, but then the slow sinuous dance that followed . . .'

'Liked it, did you?' she murmured, kissing his ear.

He shuddered with resignation and threw his hands into the air.

Kate came to him during a brief moment when he was alone and said, 'I know what you think, Johann, but never mind the tongues. She's entitled to enjoy herself in the way of her people. You'll have plenty of time to tame her later.'

'That's just it,' he said, feeling Kate had pinpointed his problem, 'she's so *wild*.'

'It's what makes her so attractive,' suggested Kate.

Johann sighed again, deeply. 'I suppose so. The vicar's wife... What if someone reports this to the bishop? The vicar's wife, doing some sort of a fandango dance in front of the village yokels, not just her ankles but practically the whole of her legs on view. The vicar's wife...'

'You'll find respectability again!'

He smiled then as a warm wash of feelings came over him, not only for his new bride, but for Kate and the whole of mankind. He was a fortunate man, having the safety of his profession to keep him in employment, and at the same time a wife who would see that he never lacked for excitement.

'This will not be a boring marriage,' he murmured to Kate, 'that's for certain.'

Others were tucking in to the repast laid out on tables overlooking the valley towards Canewdon, where that other church sat brood and sulking, jealous at the grand time its enemy was having in full view of its tower. Elizabeth was standing at the table, talking to her aunt Polly. Sarah had brought Tom Weeks, the cider-maker, and was showing off a little by clinging to his arm and occasionally kissing his cheek – actions which clearly shocked her uncle, who was frowning in displeasure.

Kate ignored this behaviour, wondering whether this public show of affection masked a private problem. It was best, Kate decided, to leave Sarah to her harmless if slightly unseemly conduct. Beside Sally's dancing, Sarah's behaviour was a mild naughtiness, but it appeared worse somehow, though Kate could not explain to herself why she thought so.

Kate was suddenly aware that Johann was speaking to her.

'I was saying to Sally,' said Johann, now that he had her attention, 'that the schoolhouse will be too small for our needs. I have decided to rent a cottage on the road by the trout fisheries: a thatched, four-roomed place that will suit us better.'

'That sounds nice,' said Kate. 'How lovely for you, Sally.'

'I am also,' said Johann, 'going to provide for my parents-in-law. They have been given the means to purchase a caravan and two horses, with which they intend going back to a life on the road. They seemed delighted by the prospect.'

No doubt they were, thought Kate, but it was also a very convenient way of making sure his in-laws were not in the vicinity for any length of time. It was the perfect arrangement. Sally herself was young and would learn the basic refinements necessary to make her acceptable to Johann's class, and in this her comeliness would help, for the beautiful can be forgiven much. Her uncouth relatives, however, would embarrass the Reverend Haagan with their presence. Still, if they were happy, why should Kate criticise? Johann, like most gentlemen, considered himself to be a good provider, and his motives for purchasing the caravan were probably mixed, good and bad; but she couldn't help saying saucily, 'That will be perfect, for both you and your parents-in-law.'

He was unabashed. 'Yes, it will, won't it?'

He fell quiet for a moment, staring out over the valley. It was only when Sally nudged him that he was prompted into saying something more; and that turned out to be the something on which the whole conversation had been hanging.

'Ah, yes, the reason I am being jostled by my pretty wife is because I have a proposition to make to you, Kate. Sally and I talked this over last evening...'

'You had *time*?' interrupted Kate wickedly.

Johann frowned, showing he was not amused, before continuing with what he was about to impart. 'As I was saying, we spoke about a matter which we hope you will consider. Since the schoolhouse will be empty and the rent is paid by the church, we wondered whether you would not prefer to live there, rather than in your home by the waves. You would be doing me a favour by occupying the school premises. A house soon deteriorates without a tenant.'

'Oh,' said Kate, 'I couldn't possibly afford the rent.'

'Well, we were rather thinking it might come out of your salary as assistant schoolteacher. The amount is not large, but is sufficient to cover the cost of rent and food for one person.'

'Schoolteacher?' Kate flushed, both with pleasure at the picture it presented, and with confusion. 'How can I be a schoolteacher? I don't know anything.'

Johann nodded his head vigorously. 'Yes you do. You had a reasonable grounding until the age of fifteen, I know, which I improved upon when you took lessons with me before your cockling days. We have the summer recess ahead, during which I shall instruct you further. And once you begin assisting me in my classroom you will learn *how* to teach, and to maintain discipline, and so on. Eventually, I shall put you in charge of the little ones, while I take the older children separately. I shall be there to give you help and guidance, and you will soon, with the aid of books and study, be in a position to teach geography, history and such subjects. In the meantime, the alphabet and basic reading and writing needs to be pushed into their turnip heads. I have to warn you, much of an infant teacher's life consists of wiping noses and other less savoury parts of the anatomy, but I'm sure you can cope with that.

'You will be doing my dear wife an enormous favour, for it is traditionally the post offered to the spouse of the priest in charge of the school. Sally has not the desire nor presently the ability to become a teacher. We hope to do something about her illiteracy, but certainly she will not be in any position to pass on skills to children for some time yet.

'Now, I realise you have never taught before, but as I say, I see no great obstacles. What do you say to this proposition?'

Kate did not know what to say. She murmured something about needing time to think, and moved away from the dancers and revellers to a spot a little further down the slope. There she sat, her arms hugging her knees, looking out over the broad, shallow valley. There was mustard growing in many of the fields, just beginning to show its flowers. Next month, in June, the whole sweep of the valley, down to the banks of the Crouch and up the other side, would be a blinding blaze of startlingly bright yellow.

Kate could see the little schoolhouse, about half-way across the valley, nestled amongst some tied farm hovels. It looked a peaceful little dwelling, next to the two-roomed school itself, with a great battered old oak throwing a shadow over its south-west corner. That oak had to withstand hordes of children climbing up into branches every school day of the year.

She did not really need time to think about whether she would accept Johann's offer or not. She would be the most foolish woman in the world to refuse it. She was being offered a comfortable home and decent work. No longer would she have to drag the sledge out on to the mud, risking her life against the tides. She would have a warm little room to live in and a sheltered work place. She had needed the time to savour her good fortune rather than to weigh her decision.

Down in the valley, a horseman was making his way across a meadow knee-deep in wild flowers. Even at that distance, she recognised the squire's son, Howard Pritchard, for there were few with wealth enough to ride a thoroughbred in this corner of Essex.

Seeing this member of the gentry made Kate's thoughts turn back to Johann and Sally. She wondered whether the priest would be ostracised by his kind for marrying a peasant girl. Then it struck her that there were so few 'of his kind' in the area that the couple would probably not need to worry about acceptance at all, at least locally.

There was the squire and his family, quite rich, for the arable land yielded more per acre than in many areas of the country, it being rich alluvium. There were two or three farmers, but no gentlemen amongst them. They were common men who had made good, over the centuries, and now formed a kind of middle-layer society between the peasant and the shabby genteel. They kept to themselves. There was the Reverend William Josiah Potts, whose wife was dead, and who was so old he neither cared about nor gave consideration to polite society. Finally, there were the shellfish farmers, such as Kate had been, who had the money to educate their families, but still considered themselves common river folk with no pretensions.

The squire's wife and daughters might be a bit sniffy with Sally, but Kate did not believe Sally would be bothered with them a great deal. The gypsy girl was no social climber, and in any case she could give as good as she got in that direction. The squire himself was quite a rough man, not at all polished by his education, which had been administered by a tutor in his own house. He had not been away to university, he loved riding to the hounds and all the country sports, gave not a damn about books unless they were concerning modern farming methods (and these he devoured), cared nothing for genteel entertainments, and had been heard to call Johann 'a pretty, posturing sort of a chap' even though Johann wore fairly plain clothes and was nothing at all like a London dandy or macaroni. Sally, therefore, with her straight talking and blunt speech, might just turn out to be the kind of neighbour's wife the squire would take to. Kate was sure the elderly squire would think her a splendid example of womanhood, with her lovely face and figure and down-to-earth manner of speech.

Howard, the squire's son, was a quiet, serious young man. It was common knowledge that he had been away to Oxford, but had been sent home because of a respiratory illness. The management of his father's estates seemed to be his main concern, though there were reports that he sometimes went up to London to visit the theatre, or to one of the clubs such as White's.

According to the tenant farmers, whereas the squire was more interested in what to grow and how to grow it, Howard was more concerned about the accounts and investments made with the profits. The squire attended to improvements in the land and farming equipment, while Howard worried about increasing their crop yield and seeking out available markets for their produce. Between them they made a very effective team, keeping other local farmers on their toes, and deterring any land sharks trying to gain a foothold in their corner of Essex. They helped any local farmer in trouble, but made sure that man followed their advice in future.

The squire's son, Howard, was not married and seemed likely to remain a confirmed bachelor. He was too withdrawn and introverted to find a woman himself and was not handsome enough to draw them to him unasked. It seemed he preferred it that way. Kate was sure he would not deliberately snub Sally; he probably wouldn't even notice that she was any different from the other ladies of his acquaintance, and would doubtless merely offer her the same grunt with which he greeted and dismissed all females, from his sisters to the peasant girls that worked on his land.

Having thus satisfied herself about her friends' future in flatlands society, Kate went back to Johann and Sally to tell them that she was most grateful for the offer of the schoolhouse and job, and that she would of course accept.

They were both delighted.

A phaeton arrived at four o'clock, just when the locals were getting a little rowdy on the cider and apple wine, and Johann took his bride away to his parents' home; he wanted the three of them to become better acquainted. His parents had been a little stunned by his choice of a wife, but Johann knew that if he allowed the three of them to spend some time together, they would soon take to Sally, and come to regard her – if not as a fine catch for a daughter-in-law – at least with a certain respect for her toughness and forthright manner.

His father, Johann knew, would admire these qualities in her: he was a no-nonsense engineer who reckoned Johann was rather too soft and easy-going; and he would no doubt regard a woman of Sally's mettle as just the kind of wife needed to put a bit of backbone into his son.

His mother was an unassuming person, who liked to cook, sew and care for her menfolk. She was gentle and delicate with a mild manner of speaking. Sally's sometimes abrasive ways might alarm her a little, but once she found how soft the girl was underneath, Johann was sure she would warm to her. At least he hoped so.

Chapter Nineteen

Kate moved into the schoolhouse shortly after the wedding and, apart from missing Simon a great deal, was happier than she had been for a very long time. She was able, with her increased earnings, to pay for her Sister Liz to attend a good residential school near Ipswich, where she could study to become a teacher herself.

Jack Rockmansted came to see her, and again tried to persuade her to come to work for him, but she thanked him and declined, saying she was now settled in her new work.

Kate had one recent bad piece of news to impart to Simon which made her worry about his homecoming. She had told him that two of his brothers, Peter and Luke, had been arrested; now she heard they had been sentenced to be transported to Tasmania. She knew this news would distress Simon, and for this reason she did not include it in her letters. She wanted to tell him in person, so that she could be there to offer him comfort. The third brother, Joseph, had managed to flee to France and had not been heard of since the arrest of Peter and Luke.

Sally and Kate were able to see each other quite often. As the love between the two women grew, they found it strange to remember that they were once sworn enemies.

'What if you had never saved my mother?' Sally said one day, in an agony of remorse. 'And I just kept on treatin' you the way I did. I was so rotten to you.'

The two women were enjoying a quiet Sunday afternoon in the Haagan house, while Johann was out somewhere on work in the parish. Sally had taken the opportunity to get out her china tea set and was enjoying the experience of entertaining a friend in style.

'You were just protecting your livelihood,' said Kate, 'and your family; like a fox chasing away intruders on her territory. It was natural, for you were starving.'

'So you think I'm a vixen, eh?' laughed Sally, pouring the tea.

'Well, you *were* pretty wild, you know, when you were a cockle girl!'

Sally looked up quickly. 'I still am really,' she confided. 'All this . . .' she indicated the delicate china tea set, the Arabian coffee table, the silk cushions on the sofa, '. . . is not really me. I don't deserve it. I don't even know the names of some of these things. I mean, what's that box seat on legs called?'

She pointed to a piece of wooden furniture which they could see in the hallway through the open door.

'I think it's called a "settle",' said Kate, 'but I'm not quite sure myself.'

'Well if you don't know for certain,' said Sally, 'nobody does.'

Kate laughed. 'You seem to think I'm some sort of *lady*,' said Kate. 'I'm not, you know. I was given a little schooling, but I'm just as ignorant about the kind of society Johann moves in as you are. I haven't seen half of these furnishings before.'

'No? Really?'

'Sally,' said Kate, 'there's not just two levels in the social world, yours and mine. There are dozens. We're both right at the bottom of the scale. Even the squire is not a true aristocrat. He's only a rough country gentleman. They would probably scorn his company in London or Bath.'

Kate saw a look of pain go over Sally's face. 'Well what chance do I stand then, eh?' she said.

Kate took her friend's hand in hers. 'Sally, you're as good as any of them, from Queen Victoria down to the cockle girls on the mud, and don't you forget it.'

'I'll try not to,' replied Sally, 'but if I forget, you'll be here to remind me, won't you?'

'Always,' confirmed Kate.

Kate knew that Johann liked the idea that Sally had a close friend who was also quite dear to him. It made them all very comfortable in each other's company. He had expressed the hope that when he eventually met Simon he would like him too, and vice versa, so the four of them could become good friends. Simon sounded a bit of a rough diamond, he had told Kate, but she had explained that her man had been very young when he left home to go to sea. Johann had nodded and said that the voyages Simon was experiencing might not necessarily add any embellishments to his character, but no doubt they would give him some maturity, and help him to appreciate good fellowship.

At the school, Kate learned very quickly what was required of her. She managed to assist Johann in his teaching; at the same time she studied his methods, and refined them for her own future use. She also spent her evenings reading and studying for her own self-improvement. Over the next nine months she made so much progress that Johann told her she might even be able to work as a governess if she ever wanted to.

'I've known governesses who had not half your wit and will, and certainly not your grasp of subjects like geography. They are all skilled at embroidery and watercolours, but half of them don't know where Tahiti is situated and believe Tipperary to be a form of ladies' millinery.'

'I'm sure they don't,' laughed Kate, who enjoyed geography because it allowed her to find all those places mentioned in Simon's letters and to trace his voyages across the globe. Somehow it made him seem less distant from her when she could reach out and touch the South China Sea or the Pacific Ocean with her forefinger.

Sally, on the other hand, struggled to learn to read and write. It seemed a hopeless task, for what she learned on one evening, she forgot by the following morning. Johann was sometimes delighted by her progress, then devastated when she slipped back to her original ignorance within a short period of time. It seemed her brain was not fashioned for literacy.

'Generations of illiterate gypsies have bred out the need to read and write,' he complained to Kate, 'and my poor Sally, though she tries so hard to improve herself, has not the capacity to retain any of this learning.'

With her speech there was a marked improvement, however, and through constant elocution lessons Sally managed to fall into a pattern of good diction and enunciation with a great deal more ease. Sometimes Sally's grammar failed her, though, especially when she was excited or upset. She was a natural actress, extroverted and liking attention, so she performed her set speeches the way someone would on a stage. It was a very effective method. Her memory for vocabulary was good, almost remarkable, and Johann could not understand how she could keep words and their meanings in her head when he gave them to her orally, yet was unable to recognise written words.

The fact was Sally actually enjoyed being 'the vicar's wife' and acting out her part in public. She was alert for new phrases and idioms, gathering them in her memory when she met the ladies of the parish, as Johann would collect material in a notebook for his sermons. It gave Sally a sense of satisfaction to be able to pull out the platitude expected of her when asked a question by one of the ladies. She could roll clichés out endlessly.

'I can copy the best of them,' she said to Kate.

And it was true: she was an excellent mimic.

On arithmetic she could not be touched. In this subject her gypsy instincts seemed much like those of any other businessman: she could mentally calculate the most intricate sums of money and come up with an accurate answer every time.

At one time Sally's uncles used to sell meadow turf to gentlemen for their lawns: clearly they had passed the skills required for this on to their young, for Sally could look at a patch of ground, tell you instantly how many one-by-two-feet pieces of turf it would take to cover that particular area, and in the next moment have the total cost ready at a half-pence per oblong of meadow turf.

When Johann complained that this particular talent had very little relevance to the work of a priest and schoolteacher, Kate quickly pointed out to him that although he did not sell turves, there were many other aspects of his lifestyle in which Sally's skills would be useful.

'What about buying books for the school children, or new slates, or anything in bulk. These are tasks you can trust your new wife to handle with complete confidence.'

'Yes,' said Johann, sarcastically, 'and she can also judge at a glance the number of occupied coffins a graveyard will take without overflowing its sacred ground.'

Kate chided him for being flippant, but saw in the humour a fondness for Sally which she had not expected to appear in him so soon. Already his infatuation for Sally's beauty was deepening into an admiration more spiritual, more appropriate to man's love for his wife.

Though she saw Sally quite often, Kate spent many evenings alone, and these were the long hours when she dreamed of Simon's homecoming. Sometimes she went for a walk over the marshes, where she and her absent lover had spent their happy courtship, finding wader's nests and shore bird's holes. The oystercatcher's plaintive cry often had her looking upwards, startled by the sharp sound, wondering whether her fiancé was safe and well and on his way home to England. She saw, too, when the tide was low, the ribs of wrecked craft perhaps centuries old, sticking up from mud like the ribs of some long disappeared race of dragon creatures; and these rotting hulks worried her, made her mind dwell on shipwrecks and other disasters at sea. Simon was already late in returning, though inquiries had revealed that his ship had still not arrived at Southampton. What if he had been captured and marooned by pirates, or had been the victim of some terrible storm, and would now have to spend his life on some desert island, like Defoe's Robinson Crusoe? If she were told he was dead, that would be terrible enough, but to be told he was missing, presumed alive, somewhere in cannibal country, why that would be even worse, for she would be forever wondering. She tortured herself with these fears while wandering along the dykes and sea walls, her freckled milky complexion prey to the gnats.

Then there were other times, when the damselflies and dragonflies and the song of the frogs captured her attention, reminding her how much her heart was buried in the marsh country. This land of reeds and rushes, where the grass snake made its home and the lizard lived out its days, was her mysterious birthplace too. She was as much a part of it as the dunlin and plover. Even of the mudflats, after the tide had retreated leaving the creeks wet and slimy and rivers with their streaks of silver.

On certain evenings, Kate and Sally got together, sometimes under the guidance of Johann, sometimes on their own. These evenings were devoted to their education, for they found it easier to work together, even though they were at different levels. There were areas where both of them needed all the help they could get.

'What do you think of Mr Wordsworth's poetry?' asked Sally of Kate.

Johann was not present at the time: he was out visiting a sick child. The weather was stormy and close, and the mother was worried that the humid atmosphere was making the child's fever worse. Johann had gone with the woman to offer comfort to the family. Kate and Sally had both said they would go with him, but he had rejected this offer.

'You need to study,' he had said.

So they were asking questions of one another.

'I prefer his friend, Mr Coleridge,' said Kate. 'He's not so wishy-washy. Poems like "Kubla Khan" are really mysterious and deep. Mr Wordsworth's poems are mostly about flowers and man communing with nature.'

Sally looked a little put out. 'I quite like nature,' she said.

'So do I,' Kate agreed, 'but I like some mystical feelings there too. Now what about this one, from Mr Keats, Sally? Listen:

> *O what can ail thee, knight-at-arms,*
> *Alone and palely loitering;*
> *The sedge is wither'd from the lake,*
> *And no birds sing . . .'*

Kate read the whole poem to Sally, who sat there looking dreamy.

When Kate had finished reading, Sally said, 'Oh, that's lovely – and so sad. "Palely loitering". That's what Johann does: loiters around, looking pale.'

The image of Johann languishing after a fairy struck Kate as enormously funny. She burst out laughing. Sally stared at her in astonishment and asked what was the matter.

'Just the picture of Johann clanking around in armour, following this beautiful creature over the marshes,' cried Kate.

Sally wrinkled her brow for a moment, then said, 'I don't think that's funny. I'd kill 'im.'

This made Kate laugh even more and it was catching; soon Sally started to giggle, then she too went into fits of laughter. Soon both women had rolled off the cushions they had been sitting on, and on to the floor, hysterical. They were still in a state of absolute collapse when Johann walked into the room. It must have been raining outside, because he was wearing dripping oilskins.

He stared at the women, astonished. 'What on earth is going on here?' he said.

They looked up, saw him in the yellow mariner's oilskins, and looked at each other again before resuming their laughter.

Johann put his hands on his hips. 'Well, this is extraordinary bad manners, both of you. I'm not a man to be laughed at, I assure you.'

Sally sniffled and managed to make a straight face for a moment. 'Sorry dahlin',' she said. 'Go and . . . go and take your armour off an' if I smell any fairy dust on you, you're in for a row.'

Kate shrieked at this and buried her face in one of the cushions. Johann looked completely at a loss: first affronted, and then bewildered. In the end he stomped out of the room and into the scullery at the back to remove his oilskins and boots. By the time he returned to the room the women had composed themselves.

'I shan't ask what that was all about,' he said stiffly, 'for it was obviously a private joke, with me as the brunt, and I'm not fond of jokes at the best of times.'

Kate said, 'Oh, don't go all starchy on us. Can't you abide a little humour, even at your expense? We were comparing you to the knight in Keats's poem "*La Belle Dame Sans Merci*", that's all. You came off credibly well, though Sally says if you go off with any fairies, she's going to chop your head off.'

'Chop somethin' off,' murmured Sally, too softly for Johann to hear, which started both women giggling again.

Johann was gradually melting. 'And how did I fare in this comparison?' he asked.

'Oh, quite well,' replied Sally, recovering quickly. 'We thought you could loiter very palely indeed, which was why we was laughing.'

'Why we *were* laughing,' he corrected.

'Oh, was you laughing too?'

He threw up his hands in despair and raised his eyebrows at Kate, but it was plain he was not displeased at being compared to a knight-at-arms, which had Kate wondering about the vanity of men, even though they might be priests. There was something about that conceit which vaguely disturbed her, but she was too full of merriment to give it much heed.

The rest of the evening was spent with Johann reading poetry to them and then explaining the meaning of the verse, which tended to rob the lines of their magic for Kate, initially at least. Still, she enjoyed learning, developing an insight into the cryptic language of the poets, and there would come a time when she appreciated the ability to make the same sort of analysis.

PART TWO

Chapter Twenty

On a spring day in 1841, Simon Wentworth was discharged from his ship at Southampton. He had been away for two years and five months.

Simon made his way north by post coach to London, and went straight to Billingsgate, where he picked up a carter he knew would be going to the Roche estuary. The carter had delivered fish to Billingsgate market, but was carrying barrels of sherry wine on the return trip, destined for various inns in the flatlands. The first thing he said to Simon was that he had not seen him for at least a month or three, and he was sorry to hear about his brothers.

'A month?' said Simon, raising his eyebrows. 'I've been away for over two years.'

'Oh,' the carter said, undisturbed by his error, 'it were most certainly a while ago that I last saw 'ee.'

It was then that Simon got an inkling of what was in store for him. His fellow Essexmen lived an uneventful life. Days came and went with monotonous regularity and time moved to a different clock from the one Simon had known recently. In a place where things happened so slowly they might as well not have happened at all, time became compressed into a solid grey lump rather than the long line of events that travellers experienced. Within that lump there was so little change that yesteryear and yesterday were next door to one another.

Simon said, 'You mentioned something about my brothers.'

'Ar, you know they was arrested?'

'No, I didn't,' said Simon coldly. 'Tell me what happened.'

'Well, they was caught. Peter and Luke. Young Joseph, well he runned off to France, so they says. Not bin seen since. The other two, well they'm on their way to 'Stralee.'

'Australia? Damn, I knew they'd be caught in the end. But Joseph got away? Let's hope he can stay out of trouble in future, so I've got *some* family left.'

Simon did not feel as upset as the carter obviously expected him to be, for he had always known that his brothers' freedom was limited. They would never have given up smuggling while they remained at liberty, and those who smuggled with frequency were always caught in the end. Still, at least they were alive and hadn't been hanged. That was very fortunate, in the circumstances.

'You bin away off to sea, then?' said the carter, breaking the silence.

'Yes,' said Simon. 'I've been to the China wars and with Sir James Brooke, in Borneo land.'

The carter shook his head, almost sadly. 'Didn't knows we had any Chinee wars and I an't never heard on this Brooke. Where's Borneo land at? Near to France, is it?'

Simon realised it would be hopeless going into long explanations, for the carter would have no idea what he was talking about. Though he had been prepared for this kind of reaction from his friends, it was still a surprise to him, for the names and foreign places were so familiar to him, it was hard to imagine that others had no conception of them or their whereabouts. Most people he knew in the flatlands had not been more than fifteen miles from their homes. This carter, who visited London, was an international traveller by comparison, and if *he* did not understand, how could Simon hope to make others in the creeks aware of where he had been and what he had done?

'No, it's a ways beyond France,' said Simon. 'But tell me what news you have, here in England. I'm told the prime minister has resigned?'

The carter seemed pleased to be asked this, for he puffed out his chest, flicked his horse with his whip, and proceeded to tell Simon all about the country's affairs, followed by local gossip. Simon let him rattle on, hoping to hear something about Kate, and he was not disappointed, though the news shocked him dreadfully.

'Now Ed'ard Fernlee, poor ole fool, he went an killed hisself arter his oysters poisined some folks around Prittlewell.'

'Edward is *dead*?'

'Oh ar. Found dead as a mackerel in his own oyster beds he were, swallerin' mud. Some says he just died of a broken heart, arter his livin' were took from him by the water-serjint. His daughter, that there Katey, she looked arter 'im right well, but he went an' died on her anyways.'

'How did they live?' asked Simon, appalled.

'Well, Katey Fernlee, as I recall, went for to work at Leigh, a-cockling or triggerin' or some-'at. Hard work that there cocklin'. Not some-'at I should wish my daughter to do, God bless 'er, but she's fine now, a schoolteacher she is, with that there Dutchee-sounding priest.'

'Your daughter is a schoolteacher?'

The carter chuckled and flicked the reins of his nag. 'No, bless 'ee, not 'er. Kate Fernlee.'

'Kate is a schoolteacher?'

'That's what I bin tellin' 'ee.'

Simon absorbed this information with some difficulty. It seemed that things did happen in the flatlands; which, to those who lived through them, must seem almost as momentous as the world events which he himself had been experiencing. Edward Fernlee had died in mysterious circumstances after his livelihood had been taken from him by the law. *For selling poisoned oysters?* Contaminated, more likely. Thus far the story was shocking but believable. Yet the carter had said Kate was a schoolteacher. Was that possible? She had written in earlier letters that she was taking lessons from a priest, a Reverend Johann Haagan. Why, he thought in surprise, that must be the Dutchman the carter was talking about. Why had Kate gone to work with the priest then?

'This Dutch priest, is he married?' asked Simon.

The carter frowned. 'He was wed recent.'

'Where? Where was that?'

'Oh, local. St Andrew's at Ashingdon, I do believe.'

Simon heaved a sigh of relief. He had been thinking the unthinkable. Yet was it so unbelievable? He had been away a long time and this priest, a clever man it seemed, was new to the district. A single man with a good income. It would not have been any great wonder if Kate had fallen for such a man, especially since she had probably not received any of Simon's recent letters, perhaps none for as long as a year or so. There were no postal services going around Cape Horn. But Kate would surely have been wed at Paglesham Church End, not at Ashingdon? The relief flooded through him.

'Ar, Ashingdon it were,' said the carter. 'I do recall it were unusual, for the vicar, ole Potts at Paglesham, he were sick that month and not able to wed the couple, so they upped and went to St Andrew's, not hardly bein' able to wait, so to speak, until ole Potts were back on his feet. I heard it were a good do, wi' lots on apple wine an' cider.'

These words chilled Simon to the marrow. He did not dare ask the carter for the name of the bride, for he dreaded the answer. It was surely Kate, *his* Kate. Why did she not wait for him? They had ... they had ... well, they were joined in more than spirit. Oh Kate, he thought, could you do this to me? Why did I go away to sea and leave you to your troubles? I should have been here by your side. Of course, you had to turn to someone. You lost your oyster farm and your father, and *he* was there to comfort you. Of course you took that comfort, needing it – comfort which should have come from me. But, oh Kate, *did you have to marry him?*

He said very little more to the carter as they meandered slowly through the villages. Finally they travelled through Stambridge and along the road past the school. With a thick lump in his throat, Simon stared through the windows as they passed and saw a blond-haired man writing something on a board and, not far away from him, bending over a pupil, was his darling Kate, her burnished copper hair glinting in the sunlight that shafted the school room. She straightened, still looking down at the pupil, a smile on her face, and Simon saw how beautiful she had become. Achingly beautiful. When he had left she had been a girl of nineteen, a very pretty girl. Now she was a woman of twenty-two, and her prettiness had blossomed into such loveliness it pierced his heart like an arrow.

Simon wanted to run to her, demand explanations, find out where he stood. What was she doing there, with that soft looking creature with the straw-coloured hair? Was she not *Simon*'s fiancé? Yet how many times had other sailors warned him that she would not be waiting for him on his return? Of course he had scoffed at their warnings, had told them Kate was not like any other woman, that she was loyal and faithful, and that they loved each other so much they would each rather die than turn to anyone else. But she had been through so much, it seemed, and who was he to blame her for seeking solace in another? The plain fact of the matter was that he had not been there when he was most needed. What a miserable man he was to be sure. Perhaps it would be better if he just turned around and went back to sea? She would never know that he had come home to be humiliated by her defection, and he could stay away for so long that by the time he did come home it would not matter to either of them. They could laugh about it together, if they ever met accidentally.

The cart trundled by, leaving the school behind.

By the time they reached the Plough and Sail Inn, though, Simon was beginning to get angry. He *was* due an explanation. She had been promised to him. She had vowed to wait until his return. If she told him she thought he was dead, then that was fair, for he could well have been. He had suffered two wounds in the wars, one of them serious enough to threaten his survival. The pirate's bullet had passed through his chest and missed his vital organs by a fraction, coming out of his back and leaving a huge wound just below the shoulder blade. If she told him that, then he would simply nod and agree.

He left the carter and went straight to her cottage, determined to sit on the doorstep until she came home. Then, when he was actually before the door, he decided to knock, for Sarah and Elizabeth were still unaccounted for and perhaps if they were at home they could enlighten him.

He placed his seabag between his feet and knocked.

There was an answering grunt from somewhere in the cottage. The curtains were pushed aside and an old woman's face appeared at the window. 'What do you want?' she called.

'I . . . can you open the door, please?'

Instead, she opened the window a fraction, seeming fearful that he might leap through and do her a mischief.

'What? What is it?'

Simon said, 'Is this not the Fernlee cottage?'

'Fernlee?'

'Kate Fernlee. She lives here, does she not?'

Light seemed to dawn on the old woman's face. 'Oh, Kate? No, we live here now. Moved over from Burnham when the cottage came vacant. Kate, she lives at the schoolhouse now, down the road.'

The words struck him like a blow in the face, and Simon mumbled a thank you before stumbling away along the winding path. It was true, then. Kate lived with that floppy-haired creature who called himself a priest.

What was he to do? Go back to sea? Damn it, he *still* wanted to see her. He was owed that much. Yet what good would it do, except to cause hurt to both of them? Perhaps he ought to go to his own home? Then he could decide what to do next.

He took the dyke path along the river, then broke away into the marshes, walking deep into the dengies. Around him were the familiar scents, sights and sounds of the flatlands, though they did not cheer him in the least. He reached the clapboard house, in the heart of the dengies, and found it empty. At least he did not need to throw out any squatters. He wondered if Joseph would come back, once he heard his brother Simon was home?

The house inside smelled of brandy and fried fish, so Simon guessed his brother *had* been home recently. Surely the fool was not making regular trips again? Perhaps he had just returned to collect some of his belongings? He hoped that was the explanation. Joseph would do well to stay in France until the excise men had forgotten about him. Perhaps it was not Joseph at all, but some passing fisherman using the house in the heart of the marshes for a temporary overnight stop?

Simon glanced around his old home. It had not been a clean dwelling since their mother had died; it had looked what it was, a house for bachelors. Now dust covered every surface and insets and other creatures had taken up residence in dark corners. There were cooking utensils lying around that were black with use, the fat and grease on them hardened to a brittle quality. The blankets on the beds did not look as if they had been washed in a thousand years. Curtains at the windows were hanging like dead animal skins, full of dust and cobwebs. The floors were caked in river mud that had become brick clay.

Simon, used to swabbing decks and cleaning bilges, set to work. He found a broken broom, fixed the handle, and swept the place from top to bottom; then spent the rest of the day cleaning the house thoroughly.

When evening came, and the bats left the loft to go out in search of mosquitoes and gnats, Simon rooted around in the outhouse and found a lamp and some oil. He lit the lantern and sat with it on the porch. There he remained for a while, looking out over the marshes as the sun went down. A red glow crept over the sea of reeds, awakening some of the hidden creatures at their roots. The frogs and crickets began to form into their choirs.

The sounds that they made seemed melancholy to Simon, as if these creatures were not welcoming him home, but asking what he had come back for? His fiancée had married someone else, two of his brothers were convicted felons on their way to South Australia, and his third brother was likely to be caught any day unless he stayed in France. But Simon knew that Joseph would find it difficult to settle in a foreign land, and that once he heard his brother was home, he would probably return.

Simon went back into the sparsely furnished house and rooted through some of the drawers in the Welsh dresser. The crockery that had graced its shelves when his mother was alive had long since been broken or sold, and the brothers had eaten directly out of the iron pots and pans when Simon was last home. In one of the drawers he found some fishing twine and hooks and some old worms that had dried to pieces of string. He discarded the worms and from his seabag he took some bread and cheese. He made a ball with this, using some water from the rain barrel. Thus equipped with line, hook and bait, he set forth towards the creek, lantern swinging on his arm.

The next two hours were spent in fishing for dabs and smelt. He caught three dabs the size of his hand and about a dozen smelt not much larger than sardines. These he took home and cooked for his supper. One of the dabs he left to have with biscuits for his breakfast.

He chose Peter's bed to sleep in, because it was the longest, but first stripped it of its blankets. Out of his seabag he took his own blanket, purchased from the Iban Indians of Sarawak. It had a hornbill design in its pattern. Tired and dispirited, he slipped into a heavy sleep just before midnight.

Simon woke suddenly about three o'clock in the morning, thinking he heard a noise. When he listened hard, however, all he could hear was the sound of the wind around the eaves. He climbed out of bed and went out on to the porch. There was a warm southerly building up, which was forcing the reeds back in an unnatural direction, they being more used to winds from the east. A nightjar sounded somewhere inland.

Simon listened again, wondering what it was that had woken him, but on hearing nothing went back inside again. He climbed back into bed and closed his eyes.

The next moment the front door flew open as if it had been kicked. A dozen men rushed into the room, their boots thundering on the floorboards. Simon jumped out of bed instantly, only to be faced by several muskets with their bayonets attached. The muzzles were all pointed at him, the soldiers behind them ready to fire.

A stocky sergeant-at-arms entered with a small man in civilian clothes. They both carried lanterns, and both seemed very pleased with themselves.

'Got you at last, my lad,' said the civilian, smugly.

'What's the meaning of this?' cried Simon.

He was prodded with one of the bayonets and the sergeant said, 'Don't you take that tone with the officer, or we might find we have damaged you a little before you go to jail.'

Simon was not to be intimidated. 'What's the meaning of this, I say? You can poke me all you like with your prickers, I want to know what's going on.'

The sergeant drew a pistol from his waistband, stepped forward, and clouted Simon across the jaw with it, sending him spinning off his feet and on to the bed.

'I warned you, didn't I?' cried the sergeant, furiously.

The man in civilian clothes stepped forward. 'That's enough, sergeant, I want him fit for the magistrate in the morning.'

'I'd like to take him outside and shoot him, so I would,' growled the sergeant. 'They're too soft on these felons these days. Send them off to a sunny island? I'd hang 'em all from the nearest tree.'

Simon wiped his bloody mouth on the back of his hand. 'Felon?' he said, quietly. 'I'm no felon. I'm a seaman in Her Majesty's Navy.'

They seemed not to hear this statement, or took little notice of it. The civilian stepped forward and ordered a soldier to shackle Simon's hands and feet. Once this had been done he seemed happier. Then he said,

'Joseph Wentworth, you are under arrest for smuggling contraband into the United Kingdom. You are not obliged to say anything at this time, but will be taken to the holding prison at Chelmsford, where you will stand trial.'

Simon rattled his chains and laughed. 'An excise man! I might have guessed. Well, you've made your biggest mistake in a career of mistakes. My name is not Joseph Wentworth. I am *Simon* Wentworth, and Joseph, Peter and Luke are my brothers. I have never been involved in smuggling in my life. I have served on three separate Royal Navy ships in the last three years, and have received commendations from all three captains. You'll be smirking on the other side of your face when I get word to my officers.'

There was stunned silence for a while, then the sergeant shook his head slowly. 'No, no, laddie. No one's seen nor heard of any fourth brother. You're him, you're Joseph all right.' He turned to the excise officer. 'Slippery as eels, these Wentworths.'

'We'll see about this,' said Simon. 'Come on then, what are you waiting for? Take me away. I want to speak to the magistrate. And I'll not forget that blow you gave me, sergeant, which you'll get back soon enough. I always pay my debts in full.'

The officer seemed a little unsure now, but the sergeant was all bluster. He said that Simon was lying, and that a night in the jail would soon change his story. This seemed to give the excise officer the confidence he needed, and he ordered the sergeant to bring the prisoner.

They led Simon away.

After walking him back to the dyke and then along it, he was put in a coach and taken to Chelmsford. The officer and sergeant rode with him in the coach, as well as one armed soldier. They arrived in Chelmsford two hours later and Simon was thrown into a cell. He asked for pen and paper immediately, saying he could prove who he was by getting a message to anyone in the Paglesham area.

'They know me there. Ask the Reverend Potts, he'll speak out for me.'

The sergeant's smirking face came to the bars. 'Oh, I'm sure your friends would stand up for you, you rogue, but we're not having any of that.'

'Are you saying a *priest* would *lie* for me?'

'No, because he won't get the chance. You'll be up before the magistrate tomorrow, then back in here until you come up for trial. There won't be no visitors for you, laddie, I'll see to that.' His voice fell to a whisper. 'You see, I don't care which one you are. I've got you, laddie, and I'm keeping you, until you join Her Majesty's Navy again – in the stinking hold of one of its prison ships. Think on that before you decide you owe me a blow on the jaw, laddie.'

Chapter Twenty-one

Simon spent a miserable night in the cell, pondering on all his troubles. Towards dawn he fell asleep, only to be woken by a rat crawling into one of his pockets after crumbs. He threw the beast across the cell floor and it scampered away into some hole behind the brickwork. Having spent three years on board ship, rats and cockroaches were no newer to Simon than the dirty bare surroundings in which he found himself. Life on a Royal Navy vessel had been harsh and hard, with the added dangers of military action on top, so one night in a prison cell was no great punishment to an able seaman.

Still, there were harder things than physical discomforts to bear: things that injured a man's spirit. It appeared that the woman to whom he had been betrothed was married to some other man. As if that was not insult enough to his soul, here he was, victim of a case of mistaken identity, ready to be brought to trial for his brother's crimes. He began to wonder whether it might not have been better to die in one of the battles he had fought out in the Far East. His only hope was that he could manage to persuade the magistrate (who would otherwise bind him over for trial at the assizes) that he was Simon and not Joseph. After all, no one had any real proof of his identity; but then nor did he. He could be anyone . . .

After a breakfast of stale cheese and water, he was collected by the guards and taken to the courtroom, where the magistrate was Justice John Billsbody, a local gentleman farmer. He looked down on Simon through thick-lensed spectacles, while shuffling through the papers before him. Then he called for the sergeant who had made the arrest.

The stocky sergeant entered the courtroom with two of his soldiers.

'Sergeant,' said Billsbody, peering over his glasses, 'this is the man you brought in last night? The man accused of smuggling in the Paglesham creeks?'

'Yes, Your Worship, this is the man.'

'And where is the excise officer present at the arrest?' asked Billsbody.

'He's not available at this time, sir, but he will be for the trial.'

Billsbody leaned forward, looking down on Simon. 'Have you anything relevant to say, young man? Smuggling is a very serious crime.' He held up the papers through which he had been rifling. 'It seems your whole family is engaged in this dastardly business. Is there no honest man among you all?'

'Yes, Your Worship, there is – one of the four brothers is named Simon, and he is following a career in the Royal Navy.'

Billsbody nodded. 'I'm glad to hear it, glad to hear it, but *you*, young man, do not seem to share this solitary brother's concern for a virtuous life.'

Simon smiled at the magistrate. 'Oh, but I do, Your Worship, for I am he.'

The magistrate flicked his head, as if a fly had just landed on his nose. He peered down again at the papers, picked one out, and held it up, looking first at what was on it, then at Simon.

'I have here a likeness of the eldest Wentworth. Your features appear to be very similar.'

'Yes, Your Worship.'

'Then you do not deny you are indeed one of the Wentworth family?'

'No, Your Worship, I do not, for we are indeed brothers. But I have been arrested as Joseph Wentworth, when I am in fact Simon Wentworth. I arrived home only yesterday, having come up from Southampton from my ship, which docked the evening before.'

The magistrate turned to the sergeant. 'What do you say to this, sergeant? Have you made a wrongful arrest?'

The sergeant smirked and locked his hands behind his back.

'Your Worship, if I was a common criminal, which thanks to my regard for law and order, I am not – why, I should say I was my brother, too, if I thought it would get me let off.'

Billsbody shook his head in frustration, still fumbling with his papers, as if the answer to all his problems lay somewhere amongst them. 'Well, well,' he said, 'what are we to do? Do either of you have any witnesses? You sergeant?'

'Not as such, Your Worship.'

'What about you, the prisoner?'

'No, Your Worship, but if you will allow me to take off my shirt,' said Simon, 'you may see the wound I obtained in a battle with Dyak pirates off the coast of Borneo, whilst serving with Captain Tellins on board *HMS Spinola*.'

'What'll that prove?' growled the sergeant. 'He could have been shot by anyone, but most like it was the customs and excise who gave him a bullet for his trouble.'

'What we need,' said the magistrate coming to a definite decision, 'is a witness or witnesses to identify this man. I'm afraid it's not good enough, sergeant, for you to *believe* you have the right fellow. I'm sure you are sincere in that belief, but we cannot have the wrong man coming up for trial. I should indeed look a fool, should I not, if that occurred?'

'Yes, Your Worship,' said the sergeant through gritted teeth, 'you'd look a fool.'

'So,' said Billsbody, shuffling through the papers again, 'we have to send for somebody from . . . where is it? The Pagleshams?' A sudden thought seemed to strike him. 'Is that anywhere near the village of Stambridge?'

Simon nodded. 'Yes, Your Worship. Very near.'

The magistrate's face lit up. 'Ah, in that case, we may be lucky. Do you by chance know a man by the name of John Rockmansted, a mussel farmer from that district?'

'I do indeed, Your Worship,' said Simon. 'I have spoken to Jack Rockmansted, as he is called, many times.'

'Good. Good. I saw Mr Rockmansted on my way in to the court this morning. If you hurry, sergeant, I think you'll find him down by the fish market. Go and ask for him there – he is a well-known personage around the market – bring him to me immediately.'

The sergeant scowled and stamped out of the courtroom, flanked by his two soldiers, and Simon was returned to his cell, where he sat and waited.

Jack Rockmansted was half-way through bargaining with some stall owners when the sergeant accosted him and told him he was needed at the courts. He finished his business before accompanying the sergeant.

'What is this?' he asked. 'I'm a busy man. It'll need to be quick.'

'The magistrate, Mr John Billsbody, would like a word with you,' scowled the sergeant.

'Billsbody, that old fool?' grunted Rockmansted.

The mussel farmer was first taken to the magistrate, who explained how he could help the court, and then down to the cells. Jack Rockmansted went up to the barred window of the cell pointed out by the sergeant, and looked inside. Simon Wentworth was there, sitting in the corner of the damp cell, and he looked up into Rockmansted's eyes.

Jack Rockmansted nodded. 'I know this man,' he said to the sergeant.

'Do you mind if I have a word with him first? In private?'

The sergeant shrugged and went to join his men, who were lounging against the wall chatting to the turnkey.

'Simon Wentworth,' said Jack Rockmansted softly. 'They have you for your brother's crimes?'

Simon stood up and went to the window. 'They have indeed, until you inform them of their mistake.'

'Which I shall certainly do. I only hope they believe me, for the magistrate seemed very certain he had the right man. He said to me that all they wanted was my confirmation of their own certainty.'

Simon looked angry. 'I thought he was very doubtful when I was in front of him, but I'm not sure of anything these days. I come home from three years at sea to find my promised bride wed to another man, two brothers on their way to Tasmania, another a fugitive from the law, and now I myself have been arrested for crimes I did not commit . . .'

Jack Rockmansted nodded, slowly digesting the fact that Simon Wentworth believed his bride-to-be had married someone else. So far as Jack knew, she was in fact still waiting for this ninny to return from the high seas. Whom did Wentworth think she had wed? This was a most peculiar circumstance and one which Jack believed he could turn to his advantage.

Something was stirring inside Jack Rockmansted and he allowed it to begin to grow. For some time he had been planning for the future, and the flowering of his schemes depended a lot on what happened to the man before him, Simon Wentworth. It might have been better if Wentworth had not returned, had drowned or been killed like so many other sailors, but that had not happened and he was here. Yet, somehow, fate had delivered him into Jack's hands. He let out a long sigh, breaking the silence that had settled between them.

'Yes, Kate Fernlee wed. It must have been a shock to you. How did you find out?'

Simon snorted. 'Why, I saw her with my own eyes, in that schoolroom as I passed it yesterday on Dag Willis's cart, smiling up into that blasted man's face. They told me at the old Fernlee cottage that she was living at the schoolhouse, and then I knew for sure.'

Rockmansted stood in silence for a while, assimilating this revealing piece of information. Who would have been in the classroom with her? Only the priest, surely? But the priest had recently married a cockling wench. Was that where the mistake had arisen? Wentworth had heard about the wedding and believed it was Kate Fernlee who had married Haagan?

Jack shook his head, as if in sympathy with Simon's feelings. 'It must have been a great blow,' said Rockmansted slowly, 'to come home to find her married to such a man. I did not attend the wedding myself, not being a close family friend, but I heard it took place – at St Andrew's I think I heard tell?'

'That's what I was told,' nodded Simon. 'She married the teacher at Ashingdon.'

Jack Rockmansted made noises of sympathy. 'So, you have been cast aside for a schoolteaching clergyman? It must have been a tragic discovery.'

Simon said nothing but, if it were possible, looked even more downcast.

Jack said, 'Well, I had better get back to the magistrate. I must say though, he seems a queer old stick. He appears to think you're leading him a dance, wasting his time, and was quite sharp with me. I sincerely hope I can persuade him of his error.'

'So do I,' said Simon laconically.

Jack left the cell door and walked towards the group in the corner. The sergeant straightened when Rockmansted came towards him. His mouth was a thin line.

'Well?' he muttered.

Rockmansted looked him in the eyes. 'I think we had better go and inform Billsbody that he has an unmitigated rogue in custody, don't you? On top of his other crimes, Joseph Wentworth should be charged with impersonating his brother."

A smile broke out over the sergeant's broad face.

Having informed the magistrate that the man he had seen in the cells was none other than Joseph Wentworth, Jack went to the inn and collected his horse from the ostler. Then he rode back through Rettendon turnpike to Ashingdon and took the road to Paglesham. He made straight for the schoolhouse. There he found Kate giving lessons to the smaller children. He was relieved to see that the priest did not seem to be about.

Taking off his hat, he kicked his boots on the step and entered. 'Miss Fernlee,' he said, 'may I speak with you?'

Kate looked up, a half smile on her face. 'Yes, what is it?'

'In private if you please,' said Jack.

She indicated she was busy. 'I can't leave my pupils.'

'It's about Simon Wentworth.'

Her face went ashen. She put an older pupil in charge of the class and then followed Jack outside, into the schoolyard.

'Is he hurt? Is Simon injured?'

Jack shook his head. 'No, not hurt.'

'Oh God!' she said in an agonised voice. 'He's dead, isn't he? He's been killed.'

'No, not dead either. Nothing so bad as that. What he is, is been and gone, that's what.'

She flinched as if someone had slapped her. 'I don't understand. Please tell me what you mean.'

Jack took one of her hands and squeezed it gently, though she seemed reluctant to allow this intimacy. He looked into those beautiful blue eyes and put on a pitying expression. For a moment he just held her gaze. Then he spoke. 'I have to tell you something, but you must promise not to cry on me, because I can't bear it. I'm an older man, but that don't mean my feelings is harder than that of a young man's. I've always had a fond thought for you, Kate, and I hate to see you hurt like this.'

'Please,' she said coldly, 'please tell me what it is.'

He gave a heavy sigh, then launched into his speech. 'This morning, out on the Chelmsford road, I met Simon Wentworth. I think he was heading for the post coach at the turnpike. I would have passed him by, for we have little to say to each other, him and me, but he motioned for me to stop. When we had exchanged the greetings of two men who know each other only in passing, he asked me for a favour.

'"What would that be, Mr Wentworth?" I says to him, for I thought it strange he should ask *me*, of all people, for a favour, when the two of us have not said more than ten words to each other in our lives.

'I want you to carry a message for me,' he says, 'to Miss Catherine Fernlee. Tell her I am sorry for her father's death, for he was a good man, but I am no longer able to marry her because of what's happened.'"

Kate stepped back from Jack Rockmansted and her eyes narrowed. 'What is this you're saying? Simon came home and didn't bother to come to see me? I don't believe it.'

'I can see how you might be thinking it isn't true, after you waiting more than two years for the lad. But then I've got no cause to carry wrongful messages. Why, you only have to ask Dag Willis, who carried him on his cart, or the people at your old cottage, for he knocked on their door thinking you still lived there.'

Kate shook her head as if bewildered. 'Simon is home? Where is he, then?'

'Gone away again, to sea. That's what I've been trying to tell you. He said he had thought a great deal while he was away, and when he heard the Fernlees had poisoned people with their oysters, he did not feel he wanted to be joined to such a family. Now I told him it was none of your faults, that it was an accident of the tides, plain and simple, but he said that's as may be, he had made up his mind.

'"Anyways, it's been a long time," he told to me, "and I've grown a deal since I left. I'm no longer the boy Kate knew, but a man with different thoughts, different ideas. I have been right round the world, and seen many things, and am not yet ready to be tied down. Be so good as to tell her I'm as sorry as I could be, but things have changed and I must go away again."'

There were noises coming from the schoolroom.

Kate said, almost in a whisper, 'I must go back in. Thank you for the message, Mr Rockmansted.'

Jack lifted his hat to her. 'My sad duty, Miss Fernlee. I'm sorry I had to be the bearer of bad news, instead of good, the which I would have delivered with more pleasure, you can be sure.'

She turned from him then and went inside. She seemed to him to be smaller than before, as if she had been crushed by some enormous weight. He waited until he heard her voice, which sounded cracked, and then he left, satisfied that he was on his way to seeing his schemes fulfilled. He did not feel bad about himself, why should he? There were many adages he could turn to which absolved a man in love from blame. Why should he feel guilty at doing anything he could to possess Kate Fernlee?

Chapter Twenty-two

Somehow Kate managed to get through to noon, when she dismissed the children. She felt sick and dizzy, and went to her room in the schoolhouse to lie down for a while. Johann was still out with the older children, and would not be back until three o'clock or thereabouts. They had gone to one of the farms on Potton Island to study the summer grazing meadows where the squire kept his cattle. They were then going on to inspect some newly fashioned pigsties. Johann felt strongly that children in a rural community should be aware of what was being done with modern farming methods, so that they did not fall behind other agricultural areas.

Kate lay on her bed and stared at the ceiling until the giddiness and sick feeling passed. The despair was like a creeping poison, travelling through her veins and arteries, turning all her energy to lethargy. There were other emotions there, like anger and frustration, but these were crowded into a corner, unable at this time to influence that terrible flood of hopelessness which swamped her being. Never before, not even on the death of her father, had she felt such melancholy. She would not have cared one bit if someone had told her that the world was going to end in half a day.

When she felt she could at last stand, she rose and put on a shawl before setting off down the lane. She went straight to her old cottage and, without any hesitation, knocked on the door. It was an old man who answered. 'Yes?'

'I'm Kate Fernlee. I used to live here. Can you tell me if there was a man here, yesterday, inquiring after me?'

The old man shook his head. 'Weren't here yesterday. That was me wife answered the knock.'

'Then someone was here?'

'That's right, they was. A man asked after the Fernlee sisters, so me wife told me. You one o' they? Ah, here she is, a-comin' now.'

At that moment an old woman came down the winding path from the road, using a stick to help her along. Kate knew her from church, though she had not realised before now that she was the wife of the man who had taken over the Fernlee cottage.

Kate waited until she reached the step before speaking. 'I'm sorry to bother you, but was there a man here yesterday, asking after me?' Kate said to her.

The old woman looked up from her study of the path and where she placed her feet. 'Oh, Kate.' She smiled, seemingly unaware of Kate's distress. 'I was meaning to speak to you at church. There was a young man here, yes. In the Navy, I shouldn't wonder, for he had a seaman's bag with him, just like our Timothy's when he comes home. Asked if you lived here, and I told him no, you lived down at the schoolhouse now.'

'I said about her sisters,' interrupted the old man. 'I told her he asked for the Fernlee girls.'

The old woman shook her head. 'No, Alfred, you don't listen. I never said about the sisters, I said he asked for Kate.' She turned back to Kate. 'I thought he may have wanted to speak to your sisters, but he seemed to be all of a hip-hop and wanting to be away, so I didn't get a chance to tell him they were at Canewdon.'

'Did he say anything else?' asked Kate, forcing herself not to wring her hands.

The old woman shook her head. 'Not that I recall. Just – was Kate Fernlee in the house at that time?'

Kate thanked the couple and left them arguing on the step about whether the sisters had been mentioned at all.

So Simon had been there, looking for her. Then why had he not come to the schoolhouse immediately afterwards? Surely if he felt the same way about her he would have come looking for her yesterday evening? Or this morning? Could it be that he was too exhausted, or too shy? No, no, neither of those would have kept *her* away, so why should they keep him? Oh, where *was* he? Why hadn't he tried to see her?

Next, she hurried to the house of Dag Willis. His wife said he was putting his horse in the stables, so Kate made her way to the familiar stalls where she had kept her own horse, Damson, when her father was alive. There she found Dag Willis removing the horse's harness. He did not stop for Kate, but once the horse was in its stall and munching away on hay, he gave her his attention.

'Mr Willis, did you give a ride to Simon Wentworth yesterday?'

'Oh, ay. I did that. Home from the seas, he was.'

'Did you pass the school?'

'Ay, we did that. You was teachin' at the time. Saw 'ee through the glass we did. He was lookin' right strong at 'ee, as I recall.'

Dag chuckled at the thought and lit his pipe.

'He saw me. You're sure of that?'

'Oh, ay. We both on us saw 'ee. I noticed on him staring, like, and I looks too, and sees it was you what catched his eye. He were bright red in the face, and looked away quick like, when he sees that I catched him at it. And no wonder, pretty lass like 'ee. I remember thinking to meself, her's one pretty lass, that there Miss Katey Fernlee.'

Her heart sank to the very depths of which it was capable. Simon had been there. He had seen her through the window and had not even attempted to call in. No doubt he had gone to the cottage knowing she was not there, but thinking her sisters were still living at the house, and hoping to leave a message with them. No doubt that message was the same one he had passed to her through Jack Rockmansted. It was all true. Simon no longer wanted her, needed her, loved her. He had gone away, seen the world, and found excitement in other lands. He had grown out of the country girl he had left behind, matured beyond the rustic people of Paglesham, and found he could not go through with his promises. Could she blame him for that?

Dag winked at her over the top of his pipe. 'You'm lookin' for him, is it?'

'No,' she said dully, 'I just wanted to know if he arrived home safely. It doesn't really matter. He's gone away again and I doubt whether he'll be back.'

Dag removed his pipe and looked serious. 'I just thort on some-'at. Wasn't you and him sort of promised?'

'Not really,' said Kate.

She thanked Dag for his information and walked away, feeling another emotion now: that of intense humiliation. She had been rejected. The man had asked for her hand when he knew few women, had gone away and seen what the world had to offer, and had decided she was to be found wanting. Kate Fernlee was not good enough, not when compared to women outside Paglesham. She was all right for naïve young fishermen who knew no better, but not for a worldly man. She was a common girl, not exotic enough for a travelling man who had seen the East, with its perfumed beauties and alluring mysterious females. Kate had seen pictures of Eastern women, who were small and dainty like Sally, with large dark eyes and dusky complexions. Such women could bewitch a simple country boy by merely crooking their little fingers. Now, other men and women would look on her and feel sorry for her, pity her, because she had been jilted.

The feeling devastated her, but it also allowed the anger to release itself, and this was a good thing. She was able to concentrate on her fury instead of her despair. Dishonour! How *dare* he look down on her in such a way? Not even having the courage to meet her face to face and tell her himself. He left messages with virtual strangers. What must Jack Rockmansted be thinking of her? How could she face *him* again? She had been cast aside like a used rag, a worthless piece of rubbish. She had waited, loyal to him, for three years. She was past her best, her complexion already beginning to show the signs of too much time spent outdoors in inclement weather.

She was twenty-two; most country girls were married by that time. Not that she wanted a man now: they could all go hang themselves so far as she was concerned. She doubted that one of them was truly honourable in his attentions towards a woman.

Kate intended to make her way back to the schoolhouse, but instead found herself at the Haagan cottage. She knocked on the door and a few moments later Sally's day-girl, Fanny, answered.

'Oh Miss Fernlee,' shrieked the girl, 'you'm as white as a sheet. Are you ill, miss?'

Sally came up behind Fanny and gasped. 'What's the matter, Kate?'

Kate could hold back no longer and collapsed into Sally's arms, sobbing, and allowed herself to be steered into the house and sat in a chair. For a few moments she could not control her tears, which had Sally hopping around, agitated beyond reason, thinking something terrible had happened to Johann. Fanny began to get hysterical, and Sally banished her to the scullery before turning to Kate.

'Kate, what is it? You *must* tell me.'

'It's Simon,' said Kate, wiping her face on the duster which had somehow transferred itself from Fanny's hand to Kate's. It left dirty streaks down her cheeks.

'Oh, lord, is he dead?'

'Worse than that,' cried Kate, the anger rising above the despair again. 'He came home to tell me he no longer wanted to marry me, and has gone back to sea again.'

Sally put her arms around her friend and hugged her. 'Oh, my poor Kate. You waited so long. You loved him so, din't you?'

'I still do, damn his eyes,' said Kate savagely. 'I wish I hated him. I *will* hate him. You must teach me to hate him, Sally, for I can't go on feeling like this for the rest of my life. I must learn to despise the sound of his name.'

'So you shall,' said Sally, sounding almost as angry as Kate, 'for he doesn't deserve less. I never met him meself, but I think he's the biggest scoundrel that ever trod upon Essex ground.'

'Oh, but he isn't,' wailed Kate, fresh tears rolling down her face. 'He's kind and good, and gentle and sweet – at least he was when he left. What's happened to him in those China wars? Have they torn his heart out? The Simon I knew would never have sent someone else with a message. He wasn't a coward. He would have told me himself. Who is this new Simon? I don't want him anyway.'

Sally's eyes opened wide. 'You mean you haven't seen him?'

Kate shook her head mournfully. 'No. He saw me, but I didn't see him. He was with Dag Willis, and Dag said he saw Simon go bright red in the face, then turn and look away. What's that if it isn't guilt? And he went to the cottage when he knew I wasn't there, to leave a message with my sisters. When he found they had moved, he saw Jack Rockmansted, and asked him to tell me he was going back to sea and didn't want to see me again.'

'Oh, Kate, I'm so sorry. I could call him all the names under the sun, but that won't help you. What you've got to do is put him behind you, forget 'im. Such men ain't – aren't worth a thought. Any decent man would be proud to have you for a wife, and I don't understand his thinkin'.'

'I don't *want* any other man. I wanted Simon.'

There was a sound from the doorway and both women looked up to see that Johann had arrived home. Sally went to him and said something quickly and Johann nodded, looked at Kate in that frightened way men do when they sense a highly emotional atmosphere.

'I'll be in my study if you need me,' he said, nodding to Kate as he left the room.

Sally came back to Kate and took her hand, holding it and squeezing it. 'I know you think this is the end of the world, Kate, but it ain't – isn't...'

'Oh stop correcting your English,' cried Kate, 'it's driving me mad.'

Sally was not in the least put out. 'Sorry, it's not a good time for things like that, is it, but I got into the habit.'

Kate squeezed her friend's hand back. 'No,' she said quietly, '*I'm* sorry. I'm putting on a great tragedy, when I should be grateful for your sympathy. I needed to talk to you, Sally, and you were here. Thank you for that. Of course I'll get over it. No one ever really died for love, not in real life. I must concentrate on my work at the school, with Johann, and not dwell too much on what might have been.'

'We can talk as much as you like,' said Sally, 'there ain't – *ain't* much I can do for you.'

Both women laughed at Sally's attempt at humour and Kate dried her eyes on the duster before realising what it was in her hand. They laughed again, and she went into the scullery, where Fanny was desperately quiet, trying to hear what was being said in the living-room. She told Kate she was sorry to hear about her troubles and Kate smiled at the girl.

'That's all right, thank you Fanny. Have you got a wet cloth I can wipe my face with, before the Reverend Haagan comes out of his study and sees this strange creature in his house and thinks it's a monster from the marshes.'

When she had cleaned her face, Kate went back to the living-room to find Johann had emerged. He turned to Kate and said seriously, 'I am most dreadfully sorry to hear this. If he were a gentleman, I should have no hesitation in calling him out.'

'That would be a fine thing, a priest duelling, wouldn't it?'

Johann smiled. 'Well, the bishop would be a little shocked, I must admit.'

Kate said, 'What I should like us all to do, after this little outburst of mine, is to try and forget what has happened. I have to put this part of my life behind me and look to the future. I should appreciate it if it wasn't mentioned again.'

'Just as you wish, Kate,' said Johann, taking her hand. He took Sally's fingers in the other hand and led both women to the table. 'Now let us all sit down to supper together and talk of more pleasant things. Fanny,' he called, 'you can bring in the roast suckling pig and French wine now.'

Fanny appeared in the doorway, her face wearing a bewildered expression. 'They an't no roast pig, sir, nor French wine. Only beetroot and a bit of ham and cheese, with tea to drink.'

'No roast pig?' said Johann cheerfully. 'Well, never mind, beetroot will be just as appetising. I have always remarked upon the similarity in taste between beetroot and roast suckling pig.'

Fanny looked indignant. 'You'm funnin' me, sir.'

Johann raised his eyebrow and looked at Sally and Kate. 'Now, would I do such a thing to our Fanny?'

'Yes, you would,' said Sally, 'now stop teasing her. Fanny, could you bring the beetroot and make sizzlin' noises when you do, so that master here thinks he's gettin' roast pig? We must humour him, 'cos he brings home the money.'

Thus, as best friends will, they did their best between them to put some cheer into Kate.

Chapter Twenty-three

Simon spent April and May of 1841 in jail before coming up in front of the judge and High Court jury. He tried to protest his innocence, but at the trial the sergeant and John Billsbody gave evidence that his identity had been firmly and irrevocably established as Joseph Wentworth, the notorious smuggler, and brother of two felons already in the penal colony of Tasmania. He was found guilty and sentenced to transportation, to join his brothers.

Transferred to the holding prison at Southampton, Simon spent two months alongside people who were bound for the hold of a ship. There was a general feeling amongst the prisoners that their lives were over, that they were in limbo simply awaiting death. The misery of the unknown lay before them.

They had heard stories about the terrible conditions under which they would be transported, locked in damp, fetid hulls where there was little air, terrible overcrowding, and where the stink of poor sanitary conditions was overpowering. Some, they knew, would die in those ships, of illness, accident, or at the hands of their fellow prisoners. Some of them were, after all, murderers, men without conscience. Within the prison community there would be a hierarchy established, unofficial rules to follow, leaders to appease. The women would fare even worse. There would be rape and degradation, any protectors with them beaten, perhaps killed. Over all this would be the harsh authority imposed by Her Majesty's prison service; the men recruited for such work were not known to be humanitarians.

Simon shared a cell with thirty other men and got to know a few of them well. There was Bates, who had already undergone transportation for stealing sheep, had escaped by stowing away in a Dutch ship, and had reached England by way of Holland. He had tried to see his wife but was turned over to the authorities by the man with whom she was now living. He now awaited re-transportation, this time to Tasmania.

'It's a rotten business, that's for certain,' said Bates.

At the other end of the voyage, he said, was a land where people died of disease, heat exhaustion and poor diets. Where living conditions were appalling and hope was buried too deep to recover.

Bates's friend was a doctor by the name of Philpotts, who had murdered his wife and had half-killed a guard who tried to steal the coat off his back. Philpotts was a portly, mild-looking man, who could hardly see without his spectacles. There were scars down his left cheek, like the claw-marks of a leopard, and he was blind in one eye. When Simon got to know him he inquired about these lesions.

'My wife,' he explained to Simon, who imagined that as a doctor he had probably poisoned his victim, or had done away with her by some efficient surgical method. 'We reached the point, each of us, where we loathed each other. You could have cut the hate into slices with a knife. Then one afternoon we had simply had enough and flew at one another. There was a terrible struggle – the doctor gave a little cough, as if the memory were painful – and we rolled around in the street, our hands around one another's throats. Since I was a little stronger than her, my pressure was more effective, and at the last she tried to tear out my tongue and claw my eyes from their sockets. As you can see, she was half-way there when some policemen pulled us apart. It was in the middle of the market-place, you see, and we'd gathered a crowd.'

Simon was shocked. 'What were you arguing over?'

'Whether or not haddock was an aid to the digestion. I, as a doctor, maintained . . . Well, it doesn't matter. I've forgotten which side of the argument I took in any case.'

'Good lord, you and your wife fought like two wildcats?'

The mild little doctor shrugged. 'We were mad, violently insane, both of us, which was why I was not sentenced to be hanged as I deserve to be. Even as my wife was dying she sank her teeth into the ankle of one of the policemen and bit through to the bone. He had to strike her with his truncheon to make her release him.'

'Are you sure that wasn't the death blow?' asked Simon, appalled by the terrible picture this scene conjured up.

The doctor shrugged. 'Possibly it was, but it was still my fault.'

'And the guard you injured?'

'I don't remember that, poor fellow.'

Bates, Philpotts and Simon teamed up together, while they were in the cell, as a matter of protection.

'You got to,' said Bates, for you can't all go to sleep at once. One of these beggars –' he indicated a motley crowd of hardened criminals from the streets of the East End of London – 'will have the boots off your feet.

They'll slit your throat to do it, too. One of us has to keep watch while the others sleep.'

Bates was a huge man, with a black bushy beard, who had been a blacksmith before he took to stealing cattle and sheep. Simon guessed Bates had befriended Philpotts because the doctor's medical training would come in useful on the voyage and afterwards in the prison camps. Simon liked Bates well enough, but he was not sure of the doctor. He thought that perhaps Philpotts had been right in his assessment of himself: that he was a violent man underneath his mild exterior.

The leader of the East End crew was a man called Dan Priggot. Priggot was large, but not in the barrel-chested way of Bates. The Eastender was a big-boned man, with heavy fists, and a face that had been flattened in many fights. He was about fifty, but still powerful, with cropped white hair. Several teeth were missing from the front of his mouth, and he sprayed people too close to him while he talked.

The third morning Simon was there, Priggot came over to Simon and gave him a painful kick on the thigh. 'Your turn to muck out the cell, sailor boy.'

The cell was strewn with straw, into which many of the occupants of the cell quietly urinated, rather than use the overflowing buckets. It was the job of one of the prisoners to scrape the straw into a corner every second day, so that it could be shovelled into a wheelbarrow and taken away. There was a plank of wood available to do this scraping, which Priggot had commandeered. Those not strong enough to demand the plank from him were charged a large fee for its use, or had to collect the stinking straw with their bare hands.

Simon sprang to his feet and stared into Priggot's eyes. 'You ever kick me again, bully boy, and I'll knock your head from your shoulders,' said Simon.

Priggot glanced over his shoulder and smiled at his cronies, who began jeering.

Bates sat up and said, 'He's with me, Priggot.'

'You stay out of this,' said Priggot. 'This is between me and 'im. So, sailor boy? You goin' to muck out the cell like I'm sayin'? You'll have to do it without the plank, o' course, 'cause that belongs to me. It's bare skin amongst the shit for you lad, 'less of course you pay me for the privilege. It'll cost a sailor boy at least a guinea, won't it lads?'

There was more jeering from the other side of the cell.

'I don't think so,' replied Simon. 'I think I'll do it another day, when I feel it's my turn, and I'll borrow your plank for nothing when I do.'

A rat ran across the floor and over Simon's left foot, but he did not dare take his eyes from Piggot. One of the other prisoners kicked the rat into the air and it hit a slop bucket, causing a spillage. Seeing this, Priggot laughed.

'Bit more for you to scrape up with your fingernails, eh?'

Simon could see that Priggot was getting ready to hit him as soon as Simon's attention wavered. Simon felt into his pocket, surreptitiously, with his left hand. Like a great many sailors, Simon carried with him a length of twine for lashing frayed rope ends, securing deck cargo, and other emergency repairs. It was also a weapon, tied in a noose until required for legitimate purposes.

Simon feigned a movement away from Priggot, whose fist flew out immediately. Simon stepped quickly to one side, whipped the noose over Priggot's wrist and spun him off his feet with a sharp yank on the end of the line. As Priggot crashed to the floor, Simon grabbed the man's other wrist, lashing the two hands together behind Priggot's back.

He leaned down close to the man's ear and whispered, 'Listen, bully boy, any more nonsense out of you and you'll wake up with this twine around your throat one morning, only it'll be too late to remove it. Your face will be blue and your tongue lolling out. Understand me?'

'I'll do you,' growled Priggot, his face in the stinking straw.

'No you won't, you'll behave yourself,' said Bates, now on his feet and facing the other members of the cell gang. 'And if you don't our doctor there will perform a little surgery on you, if you get my meaning? He keeps a piece of razor, special for the purpose. There's three of us and we're all nasty people, so leave us alone, or we'll work on you one by one.'

Priggot turned his head in the straw to stare at the mild little Dr Philpotts. Clearly it was this man he feared above all others. It showed in his eyes. Being a man of violence, he recognised in Philpotts someone who could get out of all control. Someone to whom intimidation meant a savage, unrestrained response.

'You leave us alone,' said Priggot, 'an' we'll not touch none of you?'

'That's agreed,' said Bates. 'Let him up, Wentworth.'

Simon untied the Eastender, who sat up, glared at him, then rejoined his fellows.

'We won't have no more trouble from him,' said Bates to Simon. 'He's scared to death of old Philpotts here.'

'I can't understand why,' said the doctor pleasantly. 'I have a most agreeable personality.'

These were Simon's companions, as he waited in the tiny, overcrowded cell, battling for a place to lay his head at night, having the rancid breath of some other man breathed up his nostrils from an inch away. He had to endure rats and fleas, the stink of the sewage buckets which were only emptied when they overflowed, the curses of the guards and the kicks of other captives.

He had known that once he was herded on to the boat with the others, the chances of his plea of innocence being listened to and believed at the other end of the journey in Tasmania were extremely remote. He had tried continually to get messages to people he knew, and had finally managed to persuade a drunken warden to accept a note for the Reverent Potts. As the days had passed, though, and no liberator appeared; and when the time had come for them all to be shackled and led in a long line of despairing humanity from the cells to the ship, he had known he was lost. He might see his brothers again, but it was doubtful he would see the shores of England.

The prisoners – women with small children, great hulking men, youths, young girls, every shape of common man and woman – shuffled in line towards the gangplank. Bates, standing next to Simon, was sympathetic.

'Hard luck, matey,' he said. 'It don't look like your note got through, after all.'

Simon was resigned as he hobbled forward, his hand on the next man's shoulder, the chains on his feet forcing tiny, painful steps.

'It cannot be helped, Bates. I don't mind the suffering so much now.'

'Ah, you've been crossed by a woman?' said the astute sheep stealer. 'That's bad.'

'Crossed? No, for I went away for over two years and expected too much of her. It's all my own fault.'

They had reached the bottom of the gangplank and a voice barked out from the deck above. 'Quiet in the line there! You want to be the first to be flogged on this ship? You want to make a noise? I'll help you find your voice, a little more high-pitched than the tones you use at the moment.'

Simon stopped in his tracks. That voice! He knew it well. His old master-at-arms, Mr Kettle, from *HMS Panther*. For a moment his heart soared. Then he recalled how much the master-at-arms had disliked him, had given him a hard time of it on board the *Panther*, for reasons unknown to Simon. Nevertheless, when he came to the top of the gangplank, he stared the master-at-arms in the eye.

'You know me, Mr Kettle?'

The master-at-arms stared into his face. 'Do I? Move along there, or you'll feel my boot.'

'You know me, Mr Kettle, I say. Able Seaman Wentworth, from the *Panther*. We took Aden, you remember?'

Mr Kettle stared hard into his face. 'Wentworth,' he said after a moment. 'I'm sorry to see you here. I don't like to see Navy men gone bad.'

'I didn't go bad, Mr Kettle . . .'

An officer roared from the quarterdeck, 'Get those prisoners moving, Mr Kettle.'

Simon was pushed forward, but shouted over his shoulder, 'Check the manifest, Mr Kettle. Mistaken identity. They have me as Joseph Wentworth.' Then Simon was forced on by the rest of the line, down into the hold.

As he gazed around at the tiny, cramped space allocated him by a sailor, Simon started to wonder whether his statement would mean anything at all to the master-at-arms, for he had always been simply 'Wentworth' to men like him. It was doubtful if the master-at-arms even knew his first name, even if he did, he might well dismiss the claim that he was the victim of mistaken identity, or not care more likely, for there was no love lost between the two of them.

Later came the unmistakeable sounds of a ship making ready for sea. Simon knew them only too well. Then the sensation of being afloat on the tide. He knew they were under way and his heart slipped back into despair. His rescue would not come now. It was pitch black in the hold and there was a sense of fear amongst the other prisoners. Women, and men, were whimpering. Children were crying. Simon reassured those nearest him.

'The darkness is unpleasant,' he said, 'but you have no need to fear anything at the moment. There's a slight swell beneath the ship which accounts for the rocking motion. There's a strong northerly blowing, which will carry us swiftly down to the Bay of Biscay, where we shall experience a little rough weather, no doubt, but we are all in God's hands, and the captain's and both are highly skilled at keeping one of these solid craft afloat. You are in good hands. There is nothing to fear.'

Someone cried, 'God bless you, sailor: and others passed on his assurances to their neighbours, gradually they began to settle a little, to comfort each other rather than lose their minds to unknown terrors.

Shortly afterwards, Simon heard the hatch being opened, and two men descended, bearing a lamp. At the bottom they paused, and one of them called, 'Wentworth?'

'Here!' cried Simon, his heart beating fast. 'Over here.'

The lamp was brought forward as the men stepped between the tightly packed bodies. Finally they reached him. It was the master-at-arms accompanied by the first officer.

'Is this the man, Mr Kettle?' asked the lieutenant.

The master-at-arms said, 'This is he, Able Seaman Simon Wentworth. I know him from my old ship. He's a good sailor. The manifest has him down as Joseph Wentworth.'

'My brother,' explained Simon. 'He skipped to France and I was taken in his place.'

The lieutenant said, 'You're sure about this, Master-at-Arms?'

'I'd stake my life on it, sir. This is a man with whom I served, and a good man he is too. There's been some mistake, some injustice. We should put it to rights.'

'Release him, then, and bring him to the captain. If the captain's satisfied, then Wentworth can be taken on as one of the crew. We can always use an extra man.'

Simon felt limp with relief. At last someone had recognised the injustice done to him. And who should that be but his old enemy, Mr Kettle? As he was led up out of the hold, rubbing his wrists where the shackles had been, Simon said to the master-at-arms, 'I thought you might leave me here anyway, Mr Kettle, for I believed you hated me. I'm ashamed of that thought and ask your forgiveness.'

'Leave you here? Good God, man, you're a sailor. Don't you know I hate all *new* able seamen, for they need licking into shape and are a blasted nuisance. But you're a seasoned seaman now, having served your apprenticeship. What do you believe me to be anyway? Some monster?'

'I used to think so at one time,' said Simon with the first smile he had managed in months.

The master-at-arms laughed. 'That's what you were meant to believe, to keep you in line, to get you in shape. Now, a word about this captain. Show him you're willing, and he'll treat you as fair and square as any officer . . .'

Simon went before the captain, who listened to the story and asked many questions, but in the end satisfied himself that Simon was telling the truth. He promised that when they arrived in Tasmania, Simon would be cleared of all charges. In the meantime, he had heard that Simon was willing to join his crew. Was that correct?

'Willing and very able, sir!'

'Good man. See him to his quarters, Master-at-Arms!'

Simon thanked the captain – and Mr Kettle – profusely, and promised them he would not let them down. The master-at-arms told him that he had taken Captain Haines's attention, on board the *Panther*, with his diligence and gunmanship, so he had his own self to thank too.

Simon was still feeling bitter over what had happened concerning Kate; seeing nothing for him in Essex, he decided that he was destined to spend his life at sea.

As Mr Kettle said to him later, 'Women are the very devil, Wentworth, the very devil. A sailor can't put his trust in women. The minute your back is turned, they seek comfort elsewhere, that's certain. Put your trust in your comrades and the sea. They deserve it. They'll not let you down.'

This seemed very sound advice.

He was determined that one day he would get even with that sergeant, and the magistrate, for they must have been in league to keep him behind bars. Jack Rockmansted had obviously tried his best, but of course once he had gone that pair of evil blackguards had conspired to see that Simon was transported. Why were men like that? Why did they take a sudden dislike to their fellows and dispense with justice in order to satisfy some low instinct? And what made a woman so fickle that she could not wait a year or two for a man? It was all of a piece. All of a piece.

In the meantime, he was going to make a true sailor of himself, and make the Navy proud to have him amongst its ranks. To hell with marriage and a miserable life on the marshes. Here was a life on the ocean waiting to be lived.

Kate allowed three months to pass like a bad dream. She yearned for Simon, mourned for him, until she looked so sick and wasted that her friends were concerned for her health. Much of her free time was spent in retracing the old walks she used to take with her former lover, along the dykes, in amongst the creeks. There they had played as very young children, chasing the oystercatchers away from the shellfish beds, disliking each other then, as boys and girls of that age often do. Simon had called her 'copper-knob' for which she hated him. In turn she had accused him of being a 'ratter', the old Essex nickname for smuggler. (Later, he told her that it was probably one of the reasons he had never become a smuggler, because of the scorn she managed to invest in the word.)

Then he had come to her one day and offered her a bunch of sea lavender, picked from Lion Creek where it grew in rich mauve clumps. She had been tempted to toss the sea lavender away, but something made her suddenly very shy in his presence. It was the way he was acting, as if to look at her was painful for him, and so he had to stare at his feet an awful lot while she was there.

So they had come to love each other, very deeply she had thought, though now, as she stared across the crazed waterland with its poa-grass islands, its bladder-wrack creeks, she was inclined to think that perhaps she had been wrong. It hurt her now, to smell the sea lavender in bloom.

The yearning was replaced in time by a hollow ache, which she imagined would remain with her for the rest of her life. She did not know it then, thinking it just another stage in her recovery from being abandoned, but this ache would never fully go away. It would, even years later, jump out on her and let her know it was still there, in the middle of the night when she had woken suddenly from an unremembered dream, or while out walking in the sunlight, with the world seemingly happy around her. At such times she would be so brimful of sorrow that it would take all her reserves of emotional strength to stop from crying out, or bursting into tears. Something valuable had gone from her life and she would miss it always, would never be free of its loss completely.

It did not do to dwell on these thoughts at such times, for then she really would have sunk into despair. What she had to do, what she *did*, was push the feeling down inside her, somewhere deep so that it could not bother her, and continue with her life. It was the only way she could survive.

Kate enjoyed her work at the school of course, and six months after she'd given up on Simon, Jack Rockmansted paid her a visit and asked her if she would go for a walk with him one Sunday after church. Jack had suddenly begun attending the services at Paglesham Church End because, he said, a certain business took him to the area every seventh day and there was no reason not to attend.

Johann encouraged her to accept the offer, saying it would do her good to have different company for a change. 'It must be boring for you, seeing just Sally and me all the time'

'Not a bit of it,' she had replied, 'Sally's good company.'

Johann was by now used to the way Kate would make fun of him, and laughed at this retort.

So she went on the walk, and found Jack to be discursive, though sometimes a little vulgar. She was now used to Johann, with his smooth and gentle manners, and men like Jack seemed quite crude and rough-hewn in comparison. However, he was not an unacceptable companion. He talked mostly about shellfish and business, but that was what Kate had been raised on, and could give as good as she received. She quite liked getting back to her roots and exchanging ideas about the best methods to farm mussels and oysters, though Jack Rockmansted knew little about the latter. There were no long embarrassing silences, for both had much to say on the subject, and she did indeed feel she had found a man in whom she could confide certain things.

Jack's business along the Roche was doing extremely well; he also had property on Foulness and in other areas. He had the reputation of being hardheaded in his transactions, but said himself that if a man was to make his mark he could not afford to be soft with his competitors.

'Otherwise they'll stamp his guts into the mud, and no one will mourn for his losses except himself.'

He told Kate he had always admired her beauty and her business sense. He said he was a good deal older than her, some thirteen years, and had watched her grow 'from a spat' to the fine woman she was today.

'But our difference in ages is not so vast we can't appreciate each other, Kate, now is it? It's not as if I was some dodderin' old fool of sixty. I think we might do well, together, in a lot of ways.'

This was clearly an initial opening to an offer for marriage, and Kate suddenly stopped in her tracks, wondering whether she wanted him to go on. She was surprised that he was proceeding so fast, though of course he would never have asked her to go for a walk in the first place if he had not *some* intentions towards her. He was not the kind of man who would take rejection easily, but she did not want to make any decisions at all, for the present.

However, Jack needed no signals to tell him not to proceed any further that day. He seemed to know instinctively that she was full of uncertainties. He said, 'I don't want you to say nothing yet, but just think on it a while, let it simmer there in that head of yours. You should always obey your head, not your heart, for you can't trust a heart, Kate.'

'*That* I believe,' she answered, feeling the familiar hollow ache make itself known in her breast and having to force it down once more, away from herself.

They said no more to each other on the subject that day, and Jack went home without arranging another meeting, but there was an air of unspoken agreement between them that suggested that, if nothing more was said, then Kate might well consider seriously an approach with a firm offer for marriage.

Chapter Twenty-four

Kate spent many days and nights wrestling with herself over whether she should marry Jack Rockmansted or not. One evening she would go to bed convinced that she should not, only to wake up the next morning persuaded that she should. She went over his merits and demerits a thousand times, like someone obsessed with an imaginary illness, going over the symptoms they believed they were suffering. Each time she did so, she came out with a different answer.

Sally and Johann were certain that she should be married, though Sally was not convinced that Jack Rockmansted was the man for her. Johann, on the other hand, said he had heard no ill of the mussel farmer, except that he was hardheaded and unemotional when it came to business. There were people who hated him because of his transactions with them. There were those who claimed they had been cheated, though all businessmen collect such enemies amongst disgruntled rivals. He was a tough negotiator, a man who took advantage of every opportunity, a difficult man to better in commerce.

'But what of that?' said Johann. 'I would consider such traits an advantage if one was considering marriage to him. An ambitious and successful husband ensures that the family will never be wanting.'

There was a strong voice in Kate which told her there was no real reason to be married at all, unless it were to the right man. This was where all her arguments *for* marrying Jack Rockmansted fell down, for he was definitely not the right man. The right man had gone from her, leaving her jilted.

Thus, while these arguments swayed back and forth in her mind, six weeks passed. She said nothing, she did nothing. In the end she procrastinated for so long that Jack Rockmansted actually believed she wanted an offer. He had received no indication otherwise, and consequently he came to her one night after she had finished with some pupils who required extra help.

She invited him into her little room, knowing full well why he was here, and sat him in a chair while she made him some tea. The cup and saucer looked awkward in his huge hand as he tried to stir it with the little spoon. He took one or two sips and then turned to her.

'Kate, I have a desire to be married. I should like to be married to *you*.'

She sat down on the edge of her bed, there being no other place in the room to sit. 'I thought you were going to ask me,' she said simply.

'Well? When is it to be?'

He had not said, 'What is your answer?' He had said, 'When?' He had indeed taken her silence as consent, and so the offer was simply a matter of form. Kate realised then that she had actually done this to herself on purpose, knowing in the back of her mind that if she waited long enough, the decision would be made for her. She knew it was impossible to turn him down now. It would be quite outrageous of her to do so, having led him by her silence into making an offer. So she had subconsciously engineered a *fait accompli*, placing herself in an irretrievable position.

She stared at his big-boned face with its large ridged nose, small mouth and deeply-set eyes, and tried not to compare his features with Simon's. Simon's looks had now, after so many years absence, taken on a mythical quality in Kate's mind. She had idealised him, she decided firmly; she should not compare the two. Jack was not unhandsome, though his features had an iron quality to them. She thought she could live with this man, perhaps bear his children.

'Next year,' she said, 'January 1843.'

'That will make it a winter wedding.'

'Yes. I want no fuss. Just one or two people to attend the ceremony and a small reception afterwards. Nothing elaborate.'

He nodded in approval. 'Suits me. I don't like all the flummery attached to these things. We're of a like mind, Kate. But why so long?'

'I would like to see two or three of my pupils to the end of their schooling, which comes at Christmas.' This was simply an excuse. Kate actually wanted to delay the wedding as long as possible, but a few months seemed the most she could get away with. Anything might happen between now and the new year.

He shrugged and stood up, picking up his hat. 'If that's the way you wish to do it, but you'll have to say goodbye to the school when we are married. I don't want my wife working here when she should be with me.'

'I accept that.'

'Good. We shall see each other in church of a Sunday, and I shall call on you here once or twice before December, but you understand I'm a busy man.'

'Of course.'

'Then I'll say goodbye for now.' He stepped towards the door, turning at the last minute to stoop and kiss her cheek. 'You're an attractive woman, Kate. I shall be the envy of all in the estuary.' His eyes were dark and impenetrable to her. 'We shall deal well together.' Then he was gone, striding towards his horse.

When she was alone again, Kate's heart began racing. What had she done? But there had been no choice, she had left herself no way out. She was to be Mrs Jack Rockmansted, the wife of the richest mussel farmer in the district. She would probably want for nothing in material terms. It remained to be seen if she went short of anything else. Certainly he did not seem a man full of affection, but many estuary men were tough creatures, not wanting anyone to see that they had any softness about them whatsoever. It was as if they feared that the moment they showed any gentleness, they would be pounced on by their fellow creatures and torn to pieces. Perhaps he could be quite tender in lovemaking?

She stunned herself the next second by picturing herself in bed with Jack. It was such an unlikely scene for her it seemed doubtful that it would ever happen. But of course, it would, in January. Then the body which she had offered to Simon, wholly and completely, would belong to Jack.

She lay on her bed and closed her eyes, trying to visualise Jack's naked body on top of hers, pressing down on her. She tried to imagine him entering her. She tried to conceive of him whispering sweet things in her ear, and herself murmuring them to him.

Her eyes opened quickly, as if some violent motion of the earth had startled her to wakefulness, and the perspiration sprang to her forehead.

All she could see in her mind was Simon's face.

For the next couple of months Kate worked and prayed, thinking that Simon might change his mind and come to her. She thought that if he did they would have to run away together, to escape Jack Rockmansted's fury. December came around all too soon, however. She spent her Christmas with Johann and Sally, who seemed to be happier for her than she was for herself. The closer the wedding date came, the more frightened she became of what was to happen to her.

Then, just two days before she was due to be married, Kate awoke to find herself composed and ready. She was resolved. A calmness had overcome the panic within her and she knew she was going to be fine. She was to be Mrs Jack Rockmansted, and that was inevitable. Thus she would make the best of what was to come, and follow her head, pushing that hollow feeling deep, deep down inside her where it could not touch her.

* * *

The world was like an old bone the day she married Jack Rockmansted: hard, unyielding, but brittle. It was the coldest day in January. There was a freezing easterly blowing across the marshes, and the guests and couple were dressed in thick coats. Johann married them, having first requested the honour of doing so and having obtained the Reverend Potts's consent.

After the ceremony, Jack kissed Kate for the first time on her lips. They were both cold-faced, so it was not a great success. Then they walked from the church, the old frozen leaves crackling beneath the soles of their feet. Under the lych-gate she almost slipped on a patch of ice, but was caught from behind by Johann. A pony and trap, decorated by Sally with white ribbons, was waiting to take them to the Haagan's cottage, where a feast had been laid. The intended symbol of purity inherent in Sally's adornments, however, was lost against the hoar frost on the fields and around the trees.

The wedding meal was a subdued affair. Jack said they could not stay too late as he had some business to attend to.

'On your *wedding* night?' Sally exclaimed, half-way to raising a glass to toast the couple.

'Business don't recognise celebrations,' said Jack. 'I've no choice in the matter. My wife understands that, don't you, my Kate?'

My Kate. The words stunned her. She was Jack Rockmansted's wife, his to love and to cherish if he so wished. His to hold. No one else's. She was not Simon's, but Jack's. He alone was to possess her, call her his own. Simon was now gone for ever. There would be no more watching for figures walking along the road, hoping for a familiar gait, a recognisable silhouette, for even if Simon returned, contrite over his behaviour, swearing undying love, she could no longer run into his arms, crying, wanting him.

What have I done?

Jack's arm was around her now, squeezing her shoulders, his tone admonishing. 'Did you hear what I said, Kate? You don't mind me transacting a little business tonight? I shall not be at all late.'

She brought herself back to present company. 'No, business comes first,' she agreed.

In a way she was thankful, for it would give her time to prepare her mind for the ordeal to come.

Sally made disapproving noises, and even Johann seemed a little surprised. The others of the company, some dozen guests, which included Kate's sisters and aunt and uncle, made no comment. None of Jack's people were there. He had not even invited his brother Timothy, saying he would only disgrace the Rockmansted name by getting drunk or making advances to other men's wives and daughters.

So, at around eight o'clock, Jack stood up and took out his pocket watch. 'Time to be leaving,' he said.

Kate managed a few words with each of her sisters before she left.

'How are your studies coming on?' she asked Liz.

'Fine,' she answered, Liz was now a thin seventeen-year-old with a narrow face; not pretty, but not plain either. She was what people would call *interesting*, and young men would be attracted to her for reasons other than any superficial beauty. 'Miss Jameson said I should obtain my certificate without too much difficulty.'

'Glad to hear it,' smiled Kate.

Then Liz's brow furrowed, and she asked, 'Are you going to be all right?'

'With Jack, you mean?' Kate gave a false little laugh. 'I married him, didn't I? I'll be absolutely fine.'

'But not *happy*?'

'Don't you approve of Jack, Liz?'

Liz said quickly, 'I don't trust him and I never will. I'm sorry Kate, he's your husband, but that's what I think.'

Sarah, who had now joined them, said, 'He's a man and no man is to be trusted, so one's as good as the other. Kate is looking out for herself, aren't you Kate?'

Kate was beginning to feel attacked. 'Sarah, I'm not a mercenary.'

Sarah arched a brow. 'Do you *love* him, Kate?'

Kate hesitated for too long before she blurted, 'I don't think I need to answer that, do I, not on my wedding day. It's obvious, isn't it?'

Liz said, 'Oh, Kate, I'm so sorry,' and turned away with tears in her eyes.

Kate felt like crying herself, but she bit back the tears and spoke to Sarah instead. 'Are you well, Sarah?'

Sarah, now nineteen, was composed, almost serene. 'Perfectly well, thank you Kate. Congratulations on your match. I'm sure you've done the right thing.'

That's more than I am, thought Kate, but kept this to herself.

'You're looking very beautiful these days, Sarah. Your hair's much darker than mine and your skin's flawless. No freckles?'

Sarah smiled. 'None that I know of.'

'And your fiancé? Still content to wait?'

'Not for a great deal longer,' confessed Sarah, 'but I'm in no real hurry now. Funny, I used to be – but now it's going to happen I'm putting it off for as long as possible. You know my reasons.'

Kate gave her sister a kiss on the cheek in answer. Kate felt dreadful because Sarah's question had penetrated to the centre of her emotions. *Do you love him?* Why hadn't she ever asked this question of herself? Why indeed had she married this man, this stranger to her heart? To punish Simon, wherever he was? So that she could cock a snoot at Simon's rejection of her? Perhaps it was because she didn't want to end up an old maid? Maybe a comfortable life with one man was better than living a lonely existence? Perhaps it was a very complex reason, involving positive answers to all these questions, and many more besides? She knew, yet she didn't know, for it was all too complicated to result in any one simple answer. There was a simple answer to Sarah's question, though. The fact was, she did not love her husband. Who knew, though? If everything went well between them, and they were comfortable together, that in itself might prove enough, mightn't it?

The protests over their departure continued, but Kate was eventually given her coat and there were kisses all round. Sally began crying as she saw the couple to the door.

'Don't you let him keep you from us,' whispered Sally, just before she left. 'You're my best friend.'

'Bless you, Sally, I won't,' Kate murmured, feeling a great warmth for the girl she had once hated.

Then they were out in the cold, the wind biting Kate's cheeks.

They set off in the pony and trap. The lanes were dark, and though there was a lamp on the side of the trap, Jack obviously had to concentrate in order to negotiate the bends. Kate did not speak to him, nor he to her, during the whole trip. There was a sadness in her, not so much for a lost love, for she was not thinking of Simon at this precise moment, but more for a lost opportunity. She had been happy, teaching at the school, close to her friends. She was a little angry with herself for complying with the expectations of others. Every woman should be married, if at all possible – that was the expectation. And so she had married, a man she did not love. But she couldn't blame other people's expectations: the choice had been hers in the end. She had chosen, for a multitude of half-formed reasons, to forswear the life of the maiden teacher for that of a married woman.

By the time they arrived at the Rockmansted cottage, Kate was frozen right through. They were met at the door by a toothless old woman who seemed irritated that she had needed to stay awake for them. She stepped reluctantly aside as Kate went through the doorway, and Kate caught a whiff of the woman's rank body odour.

Jack introduced the old woman as Meg. 'She keeps house for my brother and me – or did. Now you're here, she won't need to stay.'

The look on the old woman's face told Kate that this communication had not reached Meg's ears before this moment. There was an expression of stunned disbelief, followed by one of terrible anguish. She actually let out a faint cry. Kate guessed that the elderly housekeeper had nowhere else to go and was counting on spending her last days at the cottage. Jack was turning her out into the winter, most likely to starve or die of the cold. Was it possible that her new husband could do such a thing?

Kate said, 'Jack, I shall need all the help I can get for the moment, if we can afford to keep her.'

'I'll work for nothin,' cried Meg. 'Please, master. I'll eat on'y scraps.'

'You eat like a damn horse,' growled Jack, removing his scarf. 'The larder can't keep up with that belly of yours.'

The old woman fell to her knees.

'Oh, please Gawd, don't let him. Don't let him.'

'Jack?' said Kate, putting a hand on his shoulder. 'Can she stay? You can't turn her out into the cold.'

'She's got a brother around the marshes somewhere. She won't need to go far,' said Jack.

'He won't have me,' cried Meg. 'He don't know me now his mind's gone flyin' out in old age. Anyways, I don't want to live on that rotten old sunk tub of his'n. It's all water at the bottom, where the tide comes in. I'll die in that there old boat, with the damp an' all. It stinks o' creek in that boat.'

'So do you, you unwashed sow,' said Jack, taking a lamp from the table and carrying it towards the stairs under which Meg slept. 'I don't know how we've put up with the smell of you. But if Kate wants you to stay, then I suppose I shall have to let you, won't I? Come Kate, I'll show you our room.'

Kate pulled the sobbing old woman to her feet and then followed Jack up the rickety staircase. The first door pointed out was Timothy's room.

'If he brings any trollops in here, you have my permission to throw them out by their hair,' said Jack. 'He's been turning the place into a bawdy house for too long now. With a respectable woman here he'll have to curb those damned licentious ways of his.'

The next room along was their room, Jack's and hers, and he flung open the door to let her enter.

There was a large double bed, wooden-framed, with a quilt cover and two soft-looking goosedown pillows. The oak headboard had corn sheaves and corn dollies carved into its panels. Some thin, rather old curtains hung at the small window, beneath which stood a combined chest-of-drawers and dressing-table. An oval mirror was fixed above this piece of furniture, its quicksilver intact. There was a stool in one corner and a thick-limbed chair in the other. A small worn rug with an unidentifiable pattern, and a large heavy wardrobe, completed the furniture.

Jack lit a candle by the bed, then moved to the door, having to squeeze past her awkwardly. 'I hope I shan't be too late,' he said. 'I have to meet a man at the Cherry Tree Inn. I shan't be the worse for drink, though. I'm not a man who drowns himself in ale.'

Then he was gone, taking the lamp, and leaving Kate with the shadows thrown by the candlelight. She was tired and made herself ready for bed. She opened a small valise which Jack had transported to the house earlier, along with her other luggage, and found her nightdress. As she pulled the garment from the case, it caught on a corner, accidentally pulling open a flap in the lid. Her letters from Simon fell out, spilling on to the bed. For a few seconds she was shocked by what had happened. There was something symbolic about Simon's words tumbling on to her marriage bed, a silent protest against what was about to happen there.

Kate gathered them up quickly before someone came to her room and saw them. She did not want Jack to know that she still kept Simon's letters. Before she returned them to their hiding place, though, she lingered a while with them, staring at the handwritten address on the folded sheets.

Miss Catherine Fernlee
Paglesham
Essex

These letters were to another woman, she thought. To a Miss Fernlee. She was Mrs Rockmansted: Miss Fernlee and Mrs Rockmansted were different people. They had met, just briefly, not long ago before an altar, and really did not know each other. That was how it had to be.

Her eyes rested on the handwriting, a last pang of longing running through her, then put the letters away.

Just as she was crawling beneath the quilt, the door opened a fraction, and Meg's face could be seen peering through. The old woman hissed at her. 'Just 'cause you spoke up for me, don't think I shall like you for it, miss hoity-toity. I'll have you gone from here, see if I don't.'

The door closed to a thin crack, but Kate knew that Meg was still outside. 'Meg,' she said, 'don't make an enemy of me. He would throw you out tomorrow if I asked him. I'm mistress here now, and you can stay, but I won't be abused because you're jealous of me. I'm his wife, you're his housekeeper.'

Meg opened the door again and, in the candlelight, gave her a toothless smile and a mock curtsy. 'An't the on'y one what'll be jealous,' said Meg, then the door was closed and she was gone.

Kate wondered what she meant by that, but it was too late to concern herself with mysteries and she was exhausted. No doubt she would find out soon enough.

After staring at the white walls of the bedroom for a time, she blew out the candle, and fell into a doze, from which she awoke when there was a scuffling on the landing outside. A man's drunken voice whispered something and there was an answering giggle. Timothy had brought home one of his 'trollops'. Shortly afterwards she heard some urgent sounds coming from the next room, followed by silence. Kate again fell asleep.

Much later she woke again, this time abruptly, as rough hands fondled her breasts under the nightdress.

'Wha . . .?' she said, stiffening.

'It's only me,' said a hoarse voice, which she recognised as Jack's. 'I'm here now.'

She was aware that she was cold and realised he had thrown the quilt back. A moment later her nightdress was pushed up to her neck, the force of the movement driving her arms up in a V-shape, so that she was like a child imitating a tree. A hard body climbed on top of hers and then there was a blunt pain as he began to force himself into her.

'I'm not ready,' she tried to say, but he pushed up and began his movements, the coarse hair on his chest rasping against her tender breasts.

A moment later he emitted a loud grunt, and his whole weight seemed to collapse on to her chest, crushing her. Unable to breathe properly, she began to panic, and she wriggled sideways. He grunted again and his weight rolled off her.

She lay there in the darkness, waiting for him to speak, but within minutes she heard the sound of heavy breathing. Gently, so as not to wake him, she reached down for the quilt and pulled it up over them both.

Once she was warm and snug again, things did not seem so alarming. If only he had woken her first, so that she could have prepared herself for him. Perhaps he had not wanted to wake her because he had been so late?

She had felt nothing, of course, except the hands, the body on hers, the rough entry. Nothing pleasurable. There had been no time.

Outside an owl hooted, and Jack turned in bed. She could feel his hot breath on her shoulder.

Next time. Next time it would be better. She did not find his body repellent. It was lean and hard, and could be enjoyed, she was sure. There was no strong spiritual love in her for this man, but they could surely appreciate the bed together? Next time then. Next time. Things would be all right, she was sure, next time.

Why then was she crying?

Chapter Twenty-five

Kate woke to sounds of movement in the room and opened her eyes slowly. Jack was busy dressing at the end of the bed, pulling his leather belt through the loops of a pair of breeches. She watched as he buckled it. Then he glanced up to catch her staring at him. He fixed her with his own stare for a few moments. Then he continued with his dressing, pulling on his boots from a standing position.

'I'm going to the beds,' he said. 'You can stay around the house, get used to things here. Meg will show you what you want to see – her or Molly.'

'Who's Molly?'

'Day-girl. Does ten times as much as the old woman. Meg's worse than useless these days.'

He reached for his topcoat, which was draped over the end of the bed. 'I'll be back this evening.'

She said softly, 'Jack?'

He looked at her. 'What?'

She shook her head, unable to say what was in her mind or her heart. 'Nothing.'

'This evening, then.'

With that he stomped across the room, opened the door, and went out, leaving it ajar. She heard him clumping down the stairs and calling for Meg. There was a scampering then, on the stairs, on the landing, and then a face appeared at the door at bed level.

It was a dog – no – two dogs. Narrow-faced, sharp-toothed. Lurchers by the look of them. They regarded her silently for a moment, then one of them bared its teeth and a low growl began deep in its throat. As Kate stiffened, staring at them, wide-eyed, both dogs began snarling. Then Jack's harsh tones called out.

'Bess! Dagger! Get you down here, *now*, damn-ye.'

The two faces were instantly gone, and the sound of claws scratching on wooden flooring was heard once again as the lurchers obeyed the call.

Kate breathed a sigh of relief. Was that what Meg meant the evening before, about she not being the only jealous one in the house?

She lay there for a few more minutes, looking at the frost patterns on the window panes: delicate, intricate fairy artistry fashioned from nature's ephemeral crystal. The light of the day beyond was brighter than usual for a January day and seemed to hold a little hope for the future. When she sat up higher in bed she could see the black skeletons of the trees in the yard crazing the sky. It would be beautiful out there in the spring, green and flourishing.

She turned her attention to the room.

There was a plain ceramic bowl on the dressing-table, with a tin jug standing by it. She stared at these items with disapproval, thinking she would have to get her own set soon, in a pretty rose or cornflower pattern.

Kate got out of bed, emptied the used water in the bowl left by Jack out of the window, and filled the bowl with what was left in the jug. She washed using the hard block soap, combed her thick auburn hair, and then dressed in a plain black frock. She tied her hair back with a black velveteen ribbon. As was her custom, and many were like her, she wore no shoes in the house in winter. Her feet were hardened to the cold. In the summer months she hardly wore them out of doors either. Finally, she pinched her cheeks, to put a bit of colour into them. Then she descended the stairs.

Meg was in the kitchen, stirring something that looked like porridge. She looked up as Kate entered and gave her a false, toothless smile.

Kate said, 'Good morning, Meg.'

Meg started curtsying the way she had the night before and simpering, 'Ma'am,' in a mocking voice.

Kate flared, her temper boiling over. It was time to put her foot down, or this behaviour would never cease. The house was promising, the humanity inside it less so.

'You do that once more, Meg, and I'll slap your silly face,' she snapped.

The smile disappeared instantly and a sly look came into the old woman's eyes.

Kate said, 'While you're in this house, I will respect you, Meg, but I want the same kind of respect in return. You will not make a fool of me. You'll treat me as politely as I treat you. Do you understand?'

Meg said nothing.

'Do you understand, Meg?'

Before the old woman could reply, a young girl burst into the kitchen, shouting, 'Meg, they say he's married. He told me nothing, Meg . . .'

The girl stopped in her tracks and stared at Kate.

Meg gave her another of her toothless smiles.

'And here she is, lovey. The wife of our lord 'n' master.'

The girl gave Kate such a look of hatred Kate almost staggered back into the parlour. No, she had been wrong, Meg had not been talking about the dogs when she spoke of another jealousy, she had been talking of this girl. The girl's eyes were like flints. Meg cackled softly.

Suddenly the girl's face seemed to collapse in on itself, as if the knowledge of her master's deceit had created a vacuum within her which threatened to destroy her. Kate's heart went out to her, wondering why Jack had not told the girl he was getting married when it was so obvious she was in love with him. He surely could not be so blind as to be ignorant of this girl's feelings. Yet how could he be so cruel?

Kate stretched out a hand as if to touch the girl, saying, 'My name is Kate...'

The girl gave a cry like an injured bird, then turned and ran from the kitchen, out into the yard.

Meg cackled again.

'Shut up, Meg,' said Kate fiercely, 'or by heaven I *will* have you turned out. Do you hear? I've had enough of this silly behaviour. Is this how the household acts all the time? You should be ashamed of yourselves.'

Then she felt a soft touch on her left buttock and a man's voice murmured in her ear, 'Hello, the little bride's come.'

She whirled and slapped the hand away with a stinging blow, her face still suffused with anger, to find Timothy standing in behind her.

'The bride isn't *little*, she's a grown woman, and she has claws. If you're simply going to add to this stupid menagerie, you can leave without breakfast. *I'm* in charge of the kitchen now, and what I say here is law. Where's your bedmate?'

Timothy looked as if he had been poked in the eye with a sharp stick. 'Upstairs,' he said, quietly.

'Well, get her out of here. I don't want to see her face in my kitchen either, not today, though what you do is your own affair after this morning. If they stay, then they help around the kitchen afterwards. I'm not having them treat this place like an inn, nor me like a landlady. Get her out. When she's gone, you can come down to eat, but not before.'

'Listen...' he said, his face hardening.

'No, *you* listen, Timothy Rockmansted. I've had enough for one morning. I'm your older brother's wife. That gives me a certain amount of sway around here. If you want a comfortable life, you can have it, but you have to make sure I'm happy with you, do you understand? I can make life sweet and easy, or I can make it hell. You're like a bunch of animals, at each other's throats, playing your nasty tricks. Get her out, then we'll talk, lay down a few rules for each other. One of them is "no touching", so you can mull on that for a start, while you tromp back up the stairs. I'm your brother's wife, not your strumpet.'

She whirled on Meg again, who jumped several inches in the air. 'And you, go and find that silly girl, what's her name?'

'Molly.'

'Go and find Molly, and bring her in here. Tell her if she doesn't come this instant, she'll never set foot in this house again and she can look for another job.'

Meg whined, 'I an't got no shoes . . .'

'NOW!' yelled Kate.

Meg went scuttling out of the kitchen, into the yard.

Timothy gave Kate one more wide-eyed look, this time with a touch of amusement in it, then muttered, 'There's going to be some changes, I can see that.' Then he too was gone, up the stairs.

When the household was all assembled before her – Meg, Molly, the yard boy – Kate gave them a lecture on what she expected from them in the way of courtesy. Things, she said, were not now the same. Circumstances had changed. The older brother of the house had married and she was his wife and they had all better get used to it. Being his wife, she was in charge of the house, and far from being treated like an unwelcome stranger – as was her first experience – they had better get used to the idea that she would be running the household. The first thing, she said, was a spring clean throughout, never mind it was January. The two bachelors had obviously not cared a great deal for the state of the home, but she was a married woman with a wife's responsibilities, and she *did* care.

'Molly has clearly tried to keep the place clean, but as everyone else is careless of things, she was fighting against the tide. Well, Molly and me together are going to straighten the whole place from top to bottom. Meg, you will do the kitchen. Get every pot and pan and throw them all out into the yard. Then scrub this place from top to bottom. It's filthy. When you get it clean, then start on the pots and pans. The yard boy can help you.'

The yard boy's eyes were round with fright at this terrible fiery-haired dragon-lady who was now the boss of the house. Kate had dragged him in, bewildered, with the rest when she saw him hanging around the stables. She felt sorry for him, but was now determined to lay down the law before anyone else started walking all over her.

Meg looked about to argue again.

Kate said, 'I don't want any ifs and buts, Meg. You do as you're told for once. When we get straight, then I'll relax a little, but you shouldn't have allowed the place to get in this state in the first instance. And another thing, you'll take a bath . . .'

Meg gasped and took a step backwards, real fear in her eyes. 'People dies of chest coughs with baths,' she whined.

Timothy had entered the kitchen now, and he leaned on the doorjamb with folded arms and let out a belly laugh.

'I take a bath every week,' said Kate, 'and I'm not dead yet. Why should the rest of us suffer the foul smell you carry around with you. You'll take a bath and like it.'

Kate turned to Molly. 'Now, Molly, you and me have got to work together. I know you don't like me, but that doesn't matter. I won't ask you to. But, if you continue to look at me with that sullen face, as if you're about to stick a knife in me, you'll have to go. You won't see your precious master again, not in here.' Kate smiled at her. 'Who knows, if you stay you might win him off me, behind my back.'

Molly glared, her eyes blazing. 'You comes in 'ere,' she shouted, 'shoutin' orders . . .'

'Right,' interrupted Kate, 'that's it. Out.'

She pointed towards the door. Molly's expression changed immediately to panic. She looked at Timothy who shrugged his shoulders.

'No good looking to me, lass. Like she says, she's the lady around the house now.'

'I'll see Master Jack . . .'

'If Master Jack objects to you leaving, he will be given the choice: either you go, or I go,' said Kate. 'Which do you think he'll choose, considering the fact that he married me and not you, Molly? I don't want to be cruel, but he's *my* husband and you can't have him now. I think I'm being generous in allowing you to stay. Now, what's it to be? Shall we work together, or will you walk out of that door?'

Molly looked shattered as the truth obviously dawned on her. She lowered her head, making Kate's heart bleed for the young girl. However, Kate knew it would be stupid to show weakness now, just when she had them on the run. If she let them see how little confidence she really had, they would stamp her into the mud without a second thought.

'I'll stay, ma'am,' she murmured.

'Good, I'm glad, for I think we'll work well together. But don't call me ma'am. My name is Kate.'

With this, she sent them about their various tasks, telling Molly to start upstairs in the bedrooms.

Then she turned to Timothy, who put out his hands as if to ward off any attack. 'All right, Kate, you've told 'em where to go. You've got some spunk, woman, I'll give you that. But don't try givin' me no orders...'

'I wouldn't dream of it... Tim. All I want to establish is our treatment of each other. I expect to be respected, by you of all people. We can be friends, or we can be enemies. I don't want to have to look over my shoulder to see where your hands are all the time, and I do want to be spoken to as if I'm a real person. What do you say?'

He smiled. 'It's certain I don't want you for an enemy, Kate, for you'd turn me to porridge in a very short time.'

He stretched out his arm. 'Will you shake my hand? I ain't never had a woman friend before and there'll be some novelty in it.'

'Respect? On both sides?'

He laughed and she warmed to him. 'Respect,' he agreed.

They shook hands.

Tim said, 'You're some kind of woman, Kate,' he murmured. 'Handsome as the devil and full of spirit. If my brother hadn't got to you first, and if I was ever contemplatin' wedlock, why you'd be top of my list for a wife.'

'Yes, Tim,' she replied, 'but you would not be top of my list for a husband. You're a rake and you know it. You'd make the worst husband in the world.'

'That I would,' he agreed, and Kate couldn't help smiling at his candour.

He left then, for the mussel beds, and Kate threw herself into the housework alongside Molly with such energy that they all thought she intended to exhaust herself by the end of the day.

The house was really a lot larger than Kate had first thought, for beyond the two bedrooms she already knew of, there were four others. One of them was twice as large as the room she and Jack now occupied. She had the bed and all the furniture moved from her present bedroom into this one. It had the advantage of space and it was three doors down from Tim's room, so she would not need to hear what went on in his room when he brought home one of his women.

Downstairs, there was the parlour, living-room, kitchen and scullery. There was also a front room which overlooked the road, but this was not used for anything except to gather dust on its ancient furniture. It was a chilling room with an atmosphere of doom about it. Kate went through a number of possible uses for it in her head before deciding just to clean the place out and leave it as it was, looking as if someone had died there.

Outside there were various outhouses and the stables, where Tim and Jack kept two horses and a pony. One horse was a wagon-puller and the other was for riding. The pony was for the trap. Molly said Jack was considering getting a third horse, another rider, now that the business was doing so well. There was no groom. The yard boy looked after the mucking out of the stables, and Molly did all the rest: the grooming, the feeding and taking care of all the animals' needs. It was she who ordered the oats and hay and saw to it that the tack was kept in good condition. Molly even led the horses to the blacksmith when they needed shoeing, though she never rode, not even in the trap. Any problems with the wagons or cart were dealt with by Tim.

Kate wondered about Molly's dedication to her duties when the girl did not appear to be fond of the animals for their own sake. It was obvious that Molly had Jack in mind above all things. Molly wanted to please her master constantly and the only way of doing that was to do one's work well. Enterprise was rewarded, laziness was chastised. There was no middle way with Jack Rockmansted, who considered his own brother (a man who worked as hard as any normal person) a good-for-nothing layabout.

When Jack came home that evening, the two dogs weaving patterns around his legs, he stepped inside the door and looked about him with a strange expression on his face. His supper was on the table, steam rising from the plate. Tim was already tucking into his. Meg had been scrubbed along with the rest of the household and was looking subdued and not like herself at all. Molly was cleaning boots in the corner of the scullery and looked up at Jack with dark, sorrowful eyes. The yard boy, exhausted, was asleep under the kitchen table.

Bess and Dagger slunk away from Jack's legs and settled down, one either side of the yard boy's warm body. Kate eyed the dogs, a little wary of what their reaction to her might be, but they did not appear to notice her. Perhaps that morning's incident had been caused because she had been caught in their master's bedroom? Well, that would not happen again, now its location had changed.

'What's to do?' Jack said. 'Has the queen been to see us yet?'

Tim nodded his approval of this remark. 'See, brother, you have got a sense of humour if you try hard enough. What's to do is your wife, who's had us all running about cleaning and fixing things, until – as you can see by the yard lad – we're all fit to drop. I think we must be due to sell the old house, for it's now ripe and clean enough to go on the market.'

Jack was silent, gazing around him with that iron expression of his.

Molly stared, a look of smug expectation on her face as if she thought she knew what would happen; that Jack would explode in wrath because someone had dared to interfere with his household without his say-so. Meg glanced up too, probably hoping for revenge for her scrubbing.

'Well, and not before time,' said Jack, slapping the side of his boot with his whip.

He sat down at the table, looking across at his wife.

Meg made a face and Molly sighed. They both returned to their separate tasks.

Jack said, 'We'll be eating in the parlour next, if my new wife has anything to do with it.'

'The kitchen's good enough in the winter, it's warmer than the rest of the house,' she said. 'We don't need to go lighting fires unnecessarily.'

'Frugal,' said Jack with his mouth full of stew. 'I like that. A good choice I made for a wife, you'll all agree to that, then?'

No one answered this except Tim. 'You're right there, brother,' he said. 'Shame you saw her first.'

Jack looked up quickly with narrowed eyes, first staring at Tim, and then at Kate.

Kate knew what was going through his mind.

She said, 'Tim and I have come to an agreement. If he lays one finger on me, I tell you, Jack, and you shoot him through the brains. He agreed this was quite fair.'

Tim dropped his spoon and laughed uproariously at this.

Jack went back to his own food, saying, 'I don't see what's so funny. I bloody well will blow your brains out, brother, if I get wind of you botherin' Kate.' This made Tim laugh even harder and, in the end, choking, he left the room saying he was going to the inn, though without a doubt the company would be much duller there, for his brother and sister-in-law had turned out to be the finest team of jesters he had heard in a long time.

Jack finished his dinner in silence after that, under the disappointed glances of Molly and Meg, who still had faint hopes that he might put this female intruder in her place and restore them to their former positions in the house. No such reaction was forthcoming, however, and the evening ended peacefully.

In bed that night, Kate waited expectantly, but there was not even a repeat performance of the previous night's activities, let alone an enhanced one. Jack merely expressed surprise that they had changed rooms, saying he had slept in the other one since a boy, and did not know if he could get used to new surroundings. He undressed and, without a glance at Kate, climbed into bed and fell asleep almost immediately.

Kate, although not ecstatically happy, was at least more comfortable in her mind than she had been the night before. She was beginning to see that if she filled her life with work and kept busy, there would be no time to contemplate the might-have-beens. Her hopes and dreams were all in the past now, and this was reality: this man, this house, this life.

She fell asleep herself soon afterwards, physically weary and mentally spent.

The following morning, Kate was woken by Jack. 'We need to go to the mussel beds. There are more posts required.'

Although Kate had not worked mussel beds before, she knew what Jack was talking about, for the various trades and activities on the tidal rivers shared a common language. There were certain small secrets of the trade – like which part of the river grew the best molluscs – but everyone concerned with the river knew the life-cycles of its edible shellfish.

In the wild, anchors for mussels were provided by rocks, old wrecks, pier supports, and other objects below the low-tide mark. Only the fan mussel could attach itself to mud, burying its pointed end in the silt. In river farming, musselmen hammered wooden posts into the mud in order to provide their edible mussels with anchors to which they would cling by a lock of hair, or byssal, which hardened in the water to guy-rope strength. This was new work to Kate, whose oysters required no such mooring.

Meg and Molly were elbowing each other for room in the scullery when Kate entered. Jack was sitting, spooning down some hot porridge. He motioned for Kate to take the seat beside him. 'Get something hot inside you. It'll be cold out on the mud.'

She helped herself to some of Meg's grey porridge, not letting her mind dwell too much on what extra ingredients it might contain.

'Who's in charge when you ain't in the house?' simpered Meg, with a crafty nudge at Molly. The words were directed at Kate.

'The horse,' said Kate, without pausing in her eating. 'The horse is in charge.'

'Which horse?' cried Meg.

'Any horse,' said Kate, 'but if all the stalls are empty, one of the dogs will do.'

Jack roared with laughter, while Meg gnashed on her gums.

'By God, Kate, you have a rare sense of humour,' Jack said.

Kate had no doubt that once she was out of the house, the occupants would be scheming and plotting against her, trying to oust her from her position as head of the household. She could do little about this except to confuse them with her intentions.

Wrapped well against the wind, Kate left the house with Jack and walked to the river. The fields were covered in frost and hard beneath her feet. She actually felt better, out here in the open country, despite the frozen landscape. Great castles of cloud towered the sky and there was a soft light over the water.

By the areas of river cordoned off for the Rockmansted beds, men and women were stacking oak posts on the banks. Kate threw herself into the work, enjoying the expense of physical energy which she had missed while teaching in school. She knew some of the workers and exchanged greetings while they toiled under the watchful eye of Jack, himself no slouch when it came to lifting and carrying the posts.

It seemed logical that she should team up with her husband, one carrying a post out and holding it in position, while the second hammered it into the mud. Jack placed her with Jiz Fowler, however, choosing a man for his team-mate. This hurt Kate a little, but she shrugged her shoulders and quickly forgot it. Grabbing an oakwood post, she went out into the freezing mud, sinking immediately to her knees. It was hard going but no one complained. They just got on with the job.

'Hold 'er steady, Mizz Rockmansted,' said Jiz as he swung the huge wooden mallet to strike the post on its head.

'Kate,' she replied. 'Mrs Rockmansted takes all day to spit out. If you were to shout "Look out, Mrs Rockmansted," I might be struck dead before it was all said. Just call me Kate.'

Bitterns flew up from the surrounding marshlands at the sound of mallets hitting timber, their booming calls freezing the other birds to statues.

The first strike of the hammer almost took the post out of Kate's hands, which would have disgraced her. It jarred her body through, until she learned to hold it with a light balanced touch, simply allowing the force of the hammer to direct it to its muddy footing.

The work went on until the tide forced them back to the banks of the river again. Kate sat on the dyke, exhausted by the morning's activity, watching the brown, brackish water swill around the multitude of posts, standing as if awaiting a messiah to deliver them from their fate. Within thirty minutes they were drowned beneath the swiftly moving flood.

'Well, Kate,' said Jack, his hand on her shoulder for an instant, 'you haven't forgot where you come from. Now you'd best be getting back to the house, to attend to your duties there, eh?'

'Yes, Jack,' she said in a leaden voice.

Kate did not want to leave the open air for the confines of the house, where she would have to deal with Meg and Molly and the other dissidents. However, she made no argument and walked through an avenue of sycamores to the cottage.

There was a flurry of activity as she opened the door, and she found Meg rushing around with a feather duster, attacking the furniture as if it were covered in flies.

'Well, Meg,' said Kate, taking off her coat, 'you look as though you deserve a drink of tea.'

'Oh, yes, I do, m'm,' cried Meg. 'I worked ever so hard.'

'Let's have one together then, and you can take a cup to Molly out in the yard.'

'Oh, good,' Meg said.

Kate did not want to have to rule them with an iron fist, but hoped the women would soften a little towards her if she played into their hands occasionally. Kate would brook no insults or cheap tricks, however, and intended to come down hard on anyone who overstepped the mark.

Three weeks after the wedding, Kate visited Sally. The two women went walking along the dykes. There was a sombre sky overhead and a long, running sea which forced itself down the river so that the high water chopped at the grassy paths. The two women were cautious about their footsteps, but not about confiding their feelings about their lives.

'How do you find marriage then, Kate?' asked Sally.

Kate thought about the preceding weeks, which had been not so much miserable as loveless. They consisted of a series of grey, lustreless days. She had settled into an acceptance of the life she had found herself in.

'Marriage isn't so bad,' she said. 'It's living with a man that's not so wonderful.'

Sally gave Kate a wry smile on hearing this ironic statement. 'Can you stand it?' she asked her friend.

Kate nodded, staring out over the wild surface of the river. 'Oh yes. It's not *awful*. It's not anything, really. It's just a way of going from day to day.'

Sally hooked her arm in Kate's. 'Well, you've got me. We've got each other, ain't we?'

Kate wondered if this was a hidden reference to Sally's own marriage. She asked, 'What about you and Johann?'

'We're all right. He works too hard, but I can keep busy too, see? An' everythin's nice when we get in bed at night, if you know what I mean.'

Kate did know what she meant and was instantly envious. Her own private life was simply an intermittent series of being taken quickly and then put aside. She had objected, tried to make Jack understand she wanted to enjoy it too, but he either did not comprehend or did not want to. He was never violent, but neither was he very gentle. There was never any passion in his couplings, just a brief burst of energy.

Sally added, 'Sometimes he goes to sleep with his arm still round me, cozy and warm, an' that's good.'

'It must be,' sighed Kate, who could not even imagine Jack cuddling her, let alone falling asleep in that position.

'Never mind, Kate. It'll get better, you know. It does. When we first married, me an' Johann, we just did it, without thinkin' about what it was we was doing. Then we started to . . . well, I'm a bit shy to talk of it, even to you, but our love-making got better in certain ways.'

Kate could not even call what Jack did to her 'love-making', for there seemed to be little love involved. He had recently compared the thrill of their coupling to shooting a pigeon on the wing, but she was not sure if it was meant to be a compliment or an insult. She had felt at the time that this was better than nothing at all, but she doubted Sally would think so. Kate kept quiet about it.

When Kate left Sally at a point on the dyke from which they could both reach their homes fairly easily, she hurried back to the cottage to find a triumphant Meg and Molly waiting for her. Meg broke the news.

'Master's home, out back. He'm in a rage wi' you, missis. You went off wi'out tellin' 'im, an' ee come home for to take you to the mussel working.'

Kate took a deep breath, feeling angry herself.

Just at that moment, Jack came through the doorway to the parlour.

Molly cried, 'Here she is!' and pointed a finger at Kate.

Jack's face went red. 'Where the hell have you been?'

Kate stuck out her chin. 'With Sally. I had no work to do . . .'

'There's plenty of work at the beds,' snapped Jack, 'if you'd have been so kind as to come and ask.'

Kate flared at last. 'I might have gone to see Sally, whether there was any work or not, if I felt like it. I'm not your slave, Jack Rockmansted, and don't you forget it. If you're thinking of putting me down further in front of the servants, forget it, because one more word and I'll leave by that door.'

Kate was so furious she could feel the tears burning down her cheeks.

She wiped them away quickly with the back of her hand. Jack stepped forward, his eyes blazing with anger, and raised his hand.

Meg said, 'Ow...' and stepped back quickly, as if Jack were going to strike her instead. Molly simply looked on with black, impenetrable eyes.

'Do it,' Kate snarled at Jack. 'I'll make you regret it. I'm not one of your frightened workers. I'll find a way to repay you, so help me, if it takes a lifetime.'

Jack's hand froze. The redness drained from his face slowly. Then he let his arm fall. He stepped back and leaned against the mantel, letting out a hard laugh.

'Damn me, you're a fiery one. I knew that when I married you. Damn me, Kate.'

That night, when Jack came to her in bed, she enjoyed it for the first time. He was no less rough, but there was passion behind the act, as if he were desperate to find his way to her soul somehow and the only way he could see to do it was between the sheets. There was the sense that if he could make her enjoy his body, then perhaps she would give him a little something of that spirit which she only showed when she was angry.

He said afterwards, quietly in the dark, with despair on the edge of his voice, 'You think so little of me. You think I give you so little of myself. But Kate, you give me *nothing* of you at all.'

And she knew it was true. She knew she allowed nothing of her soul to this man, whom she did not love, nor could she ever let it go to him. It was her fault, too, that they were strangers to one another. She was like a rock. She would remain so, she knew, for no matter how kind, how gentle, how loving he became towards her, she could not let him have any part of her that was not flesh or intellect. Jack had obviously sensed this from the beginning, and had resolved to offer just as little in return. This was why they were as they were and would be for the rest of their lives.

One thing came out of the scene in the parlour which served to assist Kate in her daily life. Meg and Molly were so impressed by her performance in front of Jack that they were even less trouble to her than before. It seemed that no one had ever stood up to Jack in that way without receiving a blow of some kind: Meg and Molly had realised just how powerful was this young woman who had entered their household.

Chapter Twenty-six

Kate's married life settled into a pattern of managing the home, helping out when necessary at the mussel beds, and occasionally seeing her sisters and friends. She was neither happy nor miserable, but existed in some state between these two. All her feelings for Simon were gradually forced into a hard shell somewhere deep inside her; but she knew the covering could prove fragile, and she learned not to try to crack it.

The dogs, Bess and Dagger, soon became used to her, and after a time she became their favourite, as they learned she was never too busy to give them some friendly attention. They made straight for her legs when Jack brought them home in the evening, and settled around her ankles, waiting to be petted.

Kate's relationship with Jack did not improve from that which was established in the early days of their marriage, nor did it degenerate. He showed little emotion when he was with her, and indeed she remained just as inaccessible herself. Jack was a stern, unfrivolous man, who was not interested in much beyond the betterment of his business. He was never unkind to Kate, and after the incident in the parlour treated her with all the respect due a wife, but there was little tenderness and affection in him.

A year after their marriage, Kate gave birth to a son. It was a bitterly cold winter's day, and Kate was at the mussel beds when the first pains began. She let go of her gathering basket and clutched at the nearest upright person for support. This happened to be Jiz Fowler.

Jiz, on being gripped painfully by the arm, then looking into Kate's distorted face, thought he was being attacked for some reason.

'Help here!' he cried, trying to peel away Kate's fingers. 'She's gone mad on us!'

Jack, who was a few feet away, knew exactly what was happening when he saw Kate's expression. He waded swiftly through the ankle-deep water to grab hold of her, just as Jiz tore himself from Kate's grasp.

'You old fool,' he shouted at Jiz, 'she's giving birth.'

This intelligence seemed to do nothing to improve matters for Jiz, who scrambled out of the way so that two women could reach Kate.

'I'm all right,' she gasped. 'Just get me to somewhere dry.'

The women helped her to the bank while Jack went for the wagon, hitched to the mill. He was back in a few minutes and Kate was loaded like a sack of millet on to the back of the cart. Then Jack took her back to the cottage, where Meg and Molly were waiting to fuss over her, a young mussel girl having run on ahead with the news.

'Is it really comin',' cried Molly, an expression of terrible anguish on her face, 'the baby?' Kate realised what was the matter with Molly, even in her pain, for she knew that this was the infant Molly had wanted to give Jack since the age of sixteen. 'Oh Lord,' Molly wailed, tearfully, 'it's comin'. The baby's comin'.'

Meg said, 'Get an hold on yerself, biddy, an' gi'n me a hand here to get the missis to bed.'

A change instantly came over Molly and she almost leapt into action, supporting Kate on the side opposite Jack as they helped her up the narrow wooden staircase.

Once in bed, Kate allowed herself to yell. Jack left the room to allow Meg inside. Kate knew that Meg would act as a midwife and that she had delivered dozens of babies.

Molly sat down by the bedside, holding Kate's hand and stroking her hair back from her forehead. 'It'll be fine, missis, you see. We got you now. Meg knows what to do . . .' Then a screech. 'Wash your 'ands, Meg,' Molly shrieked at the old woman.

Meg had been rolling up the sleeves of her filthy dress and looked as if she had no intention of going near the washbasin.

'Me 'ands is clean,' sniffed Meg.

'Wash 'em anyway, you old sow,' cried Molly. 'You'll make the baby dirty when 'e comes.'

Kate was too far gone to trouble herself with such niceties. Between the labour pains she lay back and sweated, then threw herself into a fit of yelling when they burst upon her again. She felt as though the whole of her bottom half was going to separate from her body.

The actual birth came four hours later. Kate wished Sally was there, but no one had sent for her friend. Kate produced a boy who just over-balanced seven pound bags of sugar on the scales. He was a healthy infant, with a great bellow to him, which Jack loved.

'Listen to that, will you?' cried Jack proudly. 'That's a musselman's lungs that is.'

The child was called James, a name agreed upon by both parents, each of whom had a James in their lineage.

A post-birth infection, about which she remembered nothing, almost killed Kate and ensured that he would never have any brothers or sisters, but Kate adored Jamie and for once happiness flooded through her as she contemplated her future. At last she had someone to love who might love her in return. She felt such a joy in her heart it extended to others, especially Jack, who mellowed under this shower of attention.

Jack too thought the world of his son, and was so solicitous towards Kate during her illness, and so distraught at the news that she could never again have children, that she realised why he had married her in the first place. Jack had needed children to ensure his immortality, to work with him in the business and to give him the kind of love and affection that needed only the minimum of returns. Nevertheless, Kate had provided him with a single healthy heir, and Jack was grateful for that much.

Jamie became for a time the centre of her world, and Kate came close to smothering the child with all the love and affection that had been bottled in her breast since Simon left to go to sea. Luckily, common sense rescued her: gradually she learnt to control her feelings, forcing herself not to become anxious when he was out of her sight, and to trust to God and others that he was safe. It was hard, but Kate was made of strong stuff.

Jamie was one of very few who could bring a smile to Jack's face. Kate knew by that rare smile as he beheld his infant son, that she had pleased her husband beyond measure; for a while there were even wisps of affection in Jack's behaviour, though this did not last long. They were like seed threads in the wind and were soon gone.

Kate was worried about what Molly's reaction would be to the son born of her beloved and her rival, but she need not have worried, for Molly's heart was melted by the mere sight of the boy. Her bitterness towards Kate did not extend to anyone else; in fact she was a naturally warm and affectionate creature whose love for Jack had warped her judgement in one direction only. Molly took to Jamie as if he were her own son, and was forever begging Kate to let her look after him. 'He looks like Jack, don't he?' she said.

Kate thought her son's dark looks favoured his uncle Tim rather than his father, but did not spoil Molly's dreams of eventually having a Jack who would love her, if only as a surrogate aunt. When Meg died, the spring after Jamie was born, Molly came to live in the house, taking the old woman's place. Kate felt it was a little dangerous, emotionally, to have Molly resident in the house, but she had not the heart to turn the woman out.

It was not Molly's fault that she loved a man not worth a moment's affection. Such a wasted love, too, for Molly was an attractive woman, who might have had a number of men in the district for a husband, if she showed any signs of encouraging them. There were some men who craved such love and were unable to find it, and there was Molly lavishing it on another woman's husband, turning it into shiny boots, into well-made beds, into clean shirts. Love had become attendance, which was ignored by the recipient. Kate was never sure whether Jack was ignorant of Molly's feeling for him – just too thick-skinned to notice – or knew of it and cunningly used it to his material advantage.

Kate did not allow Molly too much time with Jamie, for she was a loving and dutiful mother herself, and did not intend to lose her son to another woman. She guarded her hours with Jamie jealously and, when he grew to walking age, would take him along the dykes and through the creeks, showing him the wildlife that was to be found there. Jamie was fascinated by the variety and numbers of birds that inhabited the flatlands, and by the age of six knew most of them by name. He was especially keen on the geese, which came down to winter on the mudflats, and his father promised him that when he was ten they would go hunting together.

One day Kate took Jamie by the old Wentworth house, which was by then dilapidated and falling back into the marsh. She noticed that the clapboards had split in the sun, and the wind and the rain had taken their toll on the roof. One corner of the house had sunk into the mire. The doors and shutters flapped open, some hanging on one hinge only. It looked a very sad place and moved her deeply with its neglect. Kate thought: *I should be living there.* The decrepit state of the house seemed to symbolise the decline of the love between herself and Simon, now in ruins somewhere deep inside her.

As Kate stared at it, her six-year-old son obviously noticed something in her face and asked, 'What, Mamma? That house? Whose is it?'

'This, Jamie? Oh, a friend of Mamma's used to live here.'

Jamie looked at the tumbledown house and then at his mother again, as if wondering whether Mammas should have friends who had been kept secret from little boys.

'Are they my friend too?'

She smiled at her son. 'I would think he would like to be your friend, Jamie.' She turned back to the house. 'Oh, but look at his poor old clapboard cottage, falling to pieces . . .'

Over the years it had crumbled, begun falling apart. It would not be long before it collapsed completely and fell in a heap of debris into the marsh, to sink from sight for ever.

'Why are you crying, Mamma?' demanded Jamie.

She pulled herself up with a jerk. 'Wind in my eyes,' she said. 'C'mon, Jamie, time we went home. We have to make your pappa's supper.'

'Yes, Mamma, but don't cry any more.'

She squeezed his hand, proud of such perception in one so young.

On the way back to the cottage, the pair called on Sally and Johann. They now had two small boys of their own. Jamie went to play with his friends in the music room, while Kate sat and talked to hers in the parlour. Sally had tea and coffee, with small cakes, brought in to refresh Kate.

'Well,' said Sally with her tongue in her cheek, 'we are comfortable, are we not?'

Sally was a polished lady now, still illiterate, but able to hold her own very well in polite company. When she was with Kate, she often lapsed into her former accent, and occasionally indulged in an old-fashioned curse or swear word to relieve the boredom of being a vicar's wife. For Kate's amusement, Sally would mimic the other ladies of the parish, copying their mannerisms and speech – a thoroughly wicked vicar's wife indeed! Never in front of Johann, though, who was growing more stiff and correct as time went by.

'Yes, we are,' agreed her husband, who looked at his watch. 'Listen, ladies, I have to be at a meeting of the parish council in twenty minutes. Would you excuse me?'

He left a few minutes later.

Kate said, 'Isn't he taking himself a bit too seriously, your husband?'

Sally laughed. 'Oh, yes, he's getting a pompous bugger in his middle age. I won't let it get out of hand, though, you know me. Every so often I prick his pride, and though he hates it at the time, he's glad for it afterwards. If I didn't, he'd become insufferable, wouldn't he?'

'Yes, he would,' smiled Kate.

'What about you?' asked Sally. 'How's Jack?'

'Oh, he's getting a pompous bugger in his middle age,' replied Kate.

Both women laughed so loudly the children came in to see what was the matter.

Jack was in fact very proud of Jamie, and when his mother was not schooling him, Jack took the boy with him to the mussel beds, and out on the boats. They were very close, father and son, and sometimes Kate felt a twinge of jealousy when observing this relationship, for Jack showed he was capable of outward affection with the boy, if not with her.

Jack's business continued to flourish, though there were occasionally some nasty incidents where he had cut close to the line between being a hard businessman and actually cheating his rivals.

One day Kate learned that Jack had forced a smaller rival out of business by purchasing a right of way across a farmer's land, which the rival needed to cross to reach his mussel beds. Jack refused permission for the man to use the right of way, and the business was sold to the only person who had access to its beds: Jack Rockmansted.

Kate turned on Jack when he came home from work that evening. 'That was a vile act, to grab old Mr Wilkinson's beds. You didn't need them, Jack.'

Jamie was at the tea-table and Jack motioned for him to leave the room. Kate did not interfere with this move. She did not like arguing in front of Jamie either.

When Jamie had gone out to help Molly, Jack said, 'Listen, woman, you do not need to tell me my business.'

'It's my business too,' Kate snapped back. 'It's a family business.'

Jack's eyes narrowed and he picked up a fork to wave it in her face. 'Make no mistake, Kate, you have no share in my firm. I own Rockmansted Mussels and no one else. Not my brother, nor my wife. Me. I have the only say in what happens with regards to business, you understand that?'

'I understand it all right,' Kate said, 'but I don't agree with it. Why should I work my back off for *you*? I'm doing it for *us*, as a family – you, me and Jamie. If you don't agree to that you won't see me at the beds again, ever.'

'You suit yourself,' growled Jack, the anger showing in his eyes. He grabbed the pot of pickle on the table and ladled some on to his ham with the fork. 'You can rot in the house for all I care.'

'And I'll make sure Jamie doesn't work there either,' she added quietly.

'What?' he exploded, dropping the pickle jar and half-rising out of his seat.

'You can't threaten me, Jack,' Kate said simply. 'Haven't you learned that yet?'

He sat down again after a moment, then said, 'Kate, the Wilkinson thing was good business.'

'It was a deadly business, Jack. Wilkinson has a family, just as you have. He needs to earn his daily bread, just as you do. You're just greedy, that's all.'

'Well, it's done now,' sulked Jack. 'I can't give it back to him, can I?'

'No, Jack, you can't, for he's gone away now, but... *remember* in the future. Ask yourself if what you are doing is humane.'

'Oh, one of these blasted Humanists, are you?'

'I just want people to respect Jamie and me, and if they think my husband and his father is crook, they won't, will they?'

'No one calls me a crook,' roared Jack. 'Who did that?'

'Just about everyone, after the Wilkinson thing.'

'Well they can bloody well go to the blazes,' cried Jack, rising from his chair and storming out of the room.

There were not many people who would be prepared to stand up for Jack Rockmansted when St Peter eventually asked for recommendations, and a few were looking forward to the afterlife precisely in order that they might see the man they hated cast down into the pit. Jack had told Kate he was no angel, but pointed out that angels did not make good businessmen.

'I don't give a damn what they think of me, so long as they don't get in my way,' he told her later that week.

'Don't you think one or two friends might stand you in good stead, if the business ever does falter?' she had said.

'I don't intend to let it,' was his reply.

As Jack grew older, he became more morose and dark-tempered, though never with Jamie. His son was the centre of his life and he hoped, as most fathers do, that one day his boy would become the man he was himself, only more astute, able to manage the business even better than his father.

Kate, on the other hand, secretly harboured the hope that Jamie would not go into the mussel business, but become a lawyer or a doctor: a professional of some sort. She was determined to get him to university so that he might have the choice of his career; and she schooled him towards this end. When she could no longer teach him anything, she insisted that Jack engage a tutor from London.

Jack was preparing for bed, pulling his nightshirt over his head, when Kate approached him with the idea. She found he was more vulnerable without his clothes on, and she herself could view him as slightly ridiculous, instead of someone imposing and overbearing. A man half-in, half-out of his nightshirt makes an absurd figure.

'What does he need a tutor for?' growled Jack, forcing his left arm through the hole.

'Because we want him to be an astute businessman,' she suggested.

'Why can't you teach him?'

'I've gone as far as I can go with him. Now it needs someone with more knowledge than I can offer.'

'And who might this someone be?'

Kate said, 'A Mr Broding. Hopefully he can teach Jamie enough to get him into university.'

'What for?' cried an exasperated Jack, still searching for the second armhole. 'He's not going to be a preacher.'

'University education gives people the right contacts for the business world. Besides, they get a rounded education at university these days. You don't want Jamie to remain as ignorant as us, do you?'

'I'm not ignorant.'

Kate came back quickly, 'Which foreign countries do we have to fear in the mussel business, now that steam shipping is getting overseas goods to our markets more quickly?'

'How would I know?'

'Well Jamie will – if he goes to college.'

Jack finally found his armhole and thrust his arm through it with a look of finality.

'Do what you want, Kate. If it makes him any better at business then of course I'm for it, you know that.'

'Thank you, Jack,' she said.

Mr Broding, a quiet young man from Cambridge, was eventually hired.

Broding and Jamie got on well together and, to Kate's satisfaction, Jamie did indeed prove to be a bright scholar: not brilliant, but worthy and a hard worker. Jack rarely spoke to the tutor, except to inquire after his son's progress and to suggest that perhaps subjects like poetry were of little use to a boy who was to become the manager of a mussel farm. These suggestions were quietly ignored.

The three of them were sitting quietly in the parlour one evening: father, mother and thirteen-year-old son. Jack was poring over his accounts and Jamie working on some calculations, when Kate announced firmly that she wanted Jamie to go to London to finish his schooling.

'I want our son to have the education of a gentleman,' she said.

Jack looked up sharply from his papers. 'A gentleman is it?' he cried, obviously not at all enthusiastic about these plans for his son. 'You would have him better than his father, would you? Molly says the boy already knows more than the rest of us put together.'

'Molly can keep her nose out of where it does not belong,' said Kate, 'for Jamie is *my* son, not hers. Molly is a good woman, but she is no authority on the use and advantages of learning. I tell you, Jack, you had better do as I ask, or there will be a divided family.'

'Threaten *me?*' roared Jack, standing and raising his hand to strike her, at which point Jamie rushed to his mother's side.

'NO!' he shouted at his father. 'Don't hit Mother, for she is only trying to do what is best for me, you know that, Father.'

Jack looked as if he was about to hit both of them, then must have thought better of his actions, and lowered his hand.

'I won't be threatened,' he said. 'Kate, don't try to take my son away from me. You force a wedge between us. First this schooling in London, then university. I'll never see the boy. Is it your hope that when he comes home he will be ashamed of his father? I'll not let that happen.'

Kate sighed. 'You make me out to be such a devious woman, Jack. He's our son and I would do nothing to turn him against you. I shall miss him too, dreadfully. I just want him to have a better chance than we had. Giving him an education does not mean he will scorn his parents; Jamie is not that kind of boy. He can still work at whatever he desires. Education is no hindrance to manual labour: he won't lose his physical strength just because his head is filled with learning.'

'I don't trust you, Kate. You're up to something.'

'I'm up to *nothing*. Ask Jamie himself what he wants.'

Jack looked towards his son. 'Well, boy?'

'I would like to go to London, Father, if you approve.'

Jack shook his head and sighed. 'I don't know. I don't know. I feel no goodwill come of you leaving home. What if you get into bad ways up there in the city – gambling and drinking.'

'Father,' laughed Jamie, 'I'm only thirteen. The schools in London are quite strict, so Johann has told me, and will not allow such things. I doubt we shall be allowed out on the streets on our own. I'm going there to work, Father, not to play.'

Kate said quietly, 'You must learn to trust people. Don't you know your own son yet, Jack?'

Jack nodded slowly. 'You seem to have made up your minds between you – you, Haagan and your mother. The whole world seems to have conspired against me. Well, I'll allow it.' Jack slumped back into his chair.

Jamie put an arm around his father's broad shoulders. 'Thank you, Father. You won't regret it, I promise you. I'll make you proud of me.'

Jack nodded again and patted his son's hand.

That night, Kate went to bed first, and was between the covers when Jack came into the room. 'Thank you, Jack.'

He looked at her silently, then gathered his night clothes under one arm and, without another word, left the room. He never came back to her bed after that night, but moved into his old room next to Timothy. There was no argument between them about it; they never talked about it. Jamie mentioned it once, in an innocent way, but Kate told him they had agreed to sleep in separate rooms because she was growing restless and fidgety as time went on.

'I keep your father awake sometimes and he needs his sleep – he works hard.'

Jamie accepted this without a murmur.

As for the rest of the household, if they were surprised, they did not show it. Timothy's philandering ways were catching up on him and he had been savagely beaten one night behind the inn by the husband of one of his bedfellows. The attack had left him with a crippled right leg, and an ever-present pain in his kidneys which occasionally laid him low for two days at a time. If the change in his brother's marital circumstances seemed strange to him, he did not comment on the fact.

Molly said or did nothing to indicate that she was aware of the alteration, though of course Kate realised she must have been. If she had shown the slightest interest in the adjustments that had taken place, Kate would have sent her packing, for she could not have borne any sneers by Molly.

Life simply went on as if nothing had happened.

One evening, a week after Jack had moved to the spare room, Kate went to the cupboard under the stairs and took out her old valise. She carried it to her bedroom and there opened the lid and unclipped the inner flap. Her old letters, tied around with a scarlet ribbon, fell out. She undid the ribbon and held the now yellowing papers in her hands.

Kate began reading.

My Dearest Darling Kate, It is impossible to say how much I miss you for I think of you constantly . . .

She re-read all of them, then tied them up again and put them back in the lid of the valise. There were no tears for a lost love, and certainly no tears for Jack. In a way she was relieved that he had vacated her bed. It meant she could concentrate on herself, for once Jamie had gone to London she would have less to do. She would make Jack his meals, see that his house was kept clean and assist at the mussel beds, but any free time she would devote to improving herself. There were books to be read, plenty of them. Kate thought she had neglected her mind for too long. She knew now that any feelings she had once had for Jack were now gone.

Chapter Twenty-seven

The Reverend Johann Haagan had not thus far regretted marrying a common cockle girl. Certainly he was in love with Sally to the very depths of his soul and physical being; but that love did not wipe out all thoughts of ambition, or his yearning for another way of life, another society. He loved Sally, but he was also wistfully desirous of ascending the ladders of society towards success.

Johann was stuck in a professional backwater in Paglesham, and wanted to get a post as assistant to a bishop in some diocese somewhere – anywhere. However, to obtain such a post (which might always lead to promotion, perhaps to the bishop's chair itself), one had to have influence. One had to *know* someone. Johann, in his Essex estuary flatlands, stood very little chance of cultivating any friendships which might be of advantage to him. There was the squire, of course, who would occasionally invite him to dinner, but the kind of guests he was likely to meet there would be sportsmen not clerics. Squire Pritchard would not dream of extending his hospitality to anyone who could not shoot the eyes out of a partridge at twenty yards. Sportsmen of course might be other things, like politicians and nobility, but the squire was not quite at that level of society. His guests tended to be other squires or rich merchants and businessmen. These kind of men were not terribly useful when one wanted to reach bishops and lords.

Johann was not altogether a miserable man, however, merely a wistful one. He continued to dote on his dreams, especially whenever he felt he was a social misfit or an outsider in his environment, but came to tolerate the mud country and appreciate its inhabitants for what they were. When his children came along, he threw himself into fatherhood with such abandon that Sally was fearful for his job. She told him he could not spend *all* his time with his family: he had parishioners who needed his guidance, his help. Johann reluctantly agreed with her, privately thinking that his parishioners could go to wherever they might, if it was going to interfere with his enjoyment of his family.

The physical relationship between Johann and Sally was all they could have wished it to be. If ever they found themselves seriously out of sorts with each other, it would all be put right between the sheets that night. They could not possibly avoid touching one another in bed, for the particular chemistry which had first drawn them together could not be ignored. Once they were holding each other, no matter what gripes they had or how much they thought they hated each other, they would end up making passionate love in their usual desperate fashion. Afterwards they would hold each other in such tenderness and gratitude they would *always* talk. Once they were talking, in reasonable tones and with tolerant minds, they made up their differences.

Thus they could have a flaming row in the morning, not be speaking to each other all day long (or firing insults), and be the best of friends as they fell asleep, holding hands or one cuddling the other, fitting together like two spoons in a drawer. Johann loved Sally's svelte form and Sally told him she adored his smooth hairless body and silky locks.

'I could write poetry to your naked form,' he told her, 'if such a thing were not a sin.'

'Would it be a sin?' she asked, surprise in her tone.

'It would be for a vicar, and even if God did not label it as such, the moral burghers of our county and church certainly would. I should be unfrocked and cast out like a demon, into the snows of unemployment and disgrace.'

'Then I shall write a poem to *your* nakedness,' she told him, running her hands over his smooth chest, 'if I ever learn to write.'

For the first time in his life, Johann was relieved that his wife could not scratch more than a few letters of the alphabet. He doubted that those whom he wished to impress with his suit for promotion would make much distinction between a vicar and his wife in such circumstances.

One Sunday in May in the year of 1856, Johann was preaching from the pulpit about the Evil One being abroad in the world, a sermon his congregation never tired of, their imaginations being more attuned to supernatural threats than theological arguments. They were on the whole a simple, superstitious lot, who believed in monsters that lived below the slime of the estuary: it was much easier for them to envisage the Devil as a walking, talking abomination, than as a small voice of conscience inside them telling them not to covet their neighbour's mussel bed. The idea that Satan could be stalking their souls across the marshes seemed rather to appeal to them, in a horribly fascinating kind of way.

Johann was full of fire that morning, concentrating not so much on what he was saying as the intonation and emphasis with which he said it. When he reached the words 'Evil One', and quoted a particularly strong passage from Revelations, he looked down into his congregation and stopped in mid-sentence.

He quickly recovered himself when he noticed the open mouths of his surprised parishioners, and went back to his tirade. However, he never did quite recapture the flavour of his earlier style and failed to finish on his usual crescendo of abuse hurled at the Devil and all his works.

After the service he went to the steps of the church to shake hands with his departing congregation, as was his custom. He was shaking violently, and had to bite his own lip to keep himself from running away and observing the people from a distance.

Sally went with the children to the vestry, so he did not have to see her, but Kate and Jamie came through the doors after the back row of pews had emptied. Kate looked at Johann's face and saw something was wrong immediately.

'Johann,' she said, 'are you ill?'

'No, no, not ill. I'll explain later,' he murmured, then hurried her on, shaking more hands, wishing people well, thanking them for coming to his service.

Finally the moment he had been dreading arrived.

An old man came through the doors with a youngish woman on his arm. Johann knew he had been right, although he had not looked at her again after that first glance from the pulpit. It was Edwina and her father.

Edwina looked absolutely beautiful, in a white dress with white gloves and hat. Her small heart-shaped face seemed not a day older than when he had seen her last. She was the epitome of delicate loveliness, a princess grown. His heart was beating against his ribs so hard he thought he might injure himself. He had often imagined this meeting, how he would feel, and it was nothing like his dreams. In his imaginings he was cool, calm and completely at one with himself. In fact he had fallen apart, an embarrassed and shaken wreck, ready to begin gibbering at the first sign of her speaking to him.

She came towards him, having to move slowly because her father was frail and arthritic, his movements awkward. She had that delightful smile on her face: the smile that had haunted his nights so many years ago. Johann took a deep breath, smoothed down his cassock, and held out his arm, shaking Lord Rushmore's hand first and inquiring after his health.

'You know me, sir?' said the bent old man, his sharp blue eyes peering into Johann's face.

'Of course he does, Father,' said Edwina, rescuing Johann, 'you remember the Reverend Johann Haagan? He went to Cambridge with Robert. We had him as our guest a few years ago.' She looked Johann directly in the eye. 'Many years ago,' she corrected herself.

'Don't remember,' grumbled the old man, leaning on his stick and looking out over the fields by the church.

Edwina said, 'Father's memory is not good these days, Reverend Haagan. Please do forgive him. He hardly knows his own daughter sometimes.'

Lord Rushmore did not seem to hear this remark. He appeared to be somewhere else, somewhere too remote for others to follow. Johann found it quite sad, for the last time he had seen Lord Rushmore the old man had been full of fire, denouncing some local farmer for stripping hedges from a favourite hunting course, saying there would soon be nothing for one's hunter to jump but ditches all over the country. It had not seemed to matter that the farmer was increasing his wheat yield by enlarging his fields. The fox hunting was more important.

'Edwina,' said Johann, taking her small gloved left hand in his own, and holding it between his two palms, 'how have you been all these years?'

She smiled that smile again. 'Oh, tolerably well. My husband died, you know? He broke his neck while out riding.'

'Oh, I'm dreadfully sorry.'

'It was over a year ago. I'm fully recovered from my mourning now. Robert of course is no longer in England. He went to Father's estates in the West Indies and has married a woman of local colour.'

'Robert?' cried Johann. 'Robert married a . . .' He was going to say 'commoner' but Edwina broke in with, 'Yes, a light-skinned negress – a mulatto I believe they're called. Extraordinary, don't you think, considering?'

He knew what she meant, for Robert had been the one who had objected most vehemently to their relationship, had told them both that he would allow Edwina to marry 'a common foreigner' over his dead body, and brought all his influence to bear in order to separate them. This man, who had talked about noble blood being watered by common fluid, and had invoked all the arguments of the aristocracy against marriage with lowly creatures – particularly pastors with a Dutch ancestry – had himself ignored all his own rules. Sex and love had flattened his so-called honourable name.

'I'm told,' said Edwina in a throaty voice and leaning forward, 'that she is a remarkably sensual creature, irresistible.'

'I have a feeling she must be, if Robert has thrown away all his arguments of ancient lineage being sullied by commoners and foreign blood.'

She nodded. 'He wrote to me, not six months ago, and begged my forgiveness. Said he should never have intervened in our... our friendship. Said he regretted completely ever forcing me to marry our cousin, Courtney Delamain, now deceased. I wrote back and told him he could never be forgiven, for he had destroyed two people who would have been happy but for his interference.'

'Want to go home,' grumbled Lord Rushmore, shuffling his feet impatiently.

Edwina turned to him. 'So we shall, Father.' Then to Johann again. 'I understand you're married yourself now, Johann. Perhaps you and your wife would like to call on us at Gusted Hall? Father has purchased the property for me, as a birthday present, and we've decided to live there for a while, haven't we, Father?'

'Home,' he said.

'I'm not sure my wife Sally is up to travelling all the way up to Hockley,' said Johann, 'having recently given birth to our third child. However, I'm due to visit an old friend in the area, so perhaps I could accept your kind invitation on my own?'

'That would be nice. When may you come?'

'Tomorrow, if that's convenient? At 11 o'clock.'

'I shall look forward to it.'

A carriage drew up outside the church gates and Edwina walked towards it, helping her father along the gravel path. Johann stood and watched her, noting how confident were her footsteps, how very... aristocratic, her movements. He was so absorbed in this thought that he failed to hear Sally speaking to him the first time and she had to touch his cheek. He jumped a few inches in the air.

'Din't mean to scare you,' laughed Sally, offering him their new baby, Celia, to hold. 'Who's that?'

He took the child in his arms. 'Who's what?'

'That old gentleman you was speaking to?'

'Oh, Lord Rushmore. I knew his son. We were friends at one time – educated together.'

Sally stared after the couple as they climbed into their coach. Her eyes were wide. 'That's a real lord?'

'Yes, and his daughter. She's recently lost her husband – died in an accident – I've... I've promised to talk with her about it. She seems quite distressed.'

'So she should be, poor dear,' said Sally, shaking her head. 'That's a dreadful thing to happen to her. Why's she not bin to church before?'

'Why? Oh, they've only recently moved to the area. To Gusted Hall, near Hockley.'

'And they came all this way to church?' said Sally, raising her eyebrows.

'I think they came because they heard I was vicar here,' replied Johann. 'The son is now in the West Indies and Lord Rushmore wanted to pass on Robert's good wishes to me. I doubt they'll come again.'

'Oh, what a shame,' said Sally, 'it would be nice for you to have a lord friend. You've always wanted someone like that to help you with your career. Still, maybe you can go and visit them in their house, eh?'

'Yes, I intend to,' answered Johann, 'in a little while.'

Chapter Twenty-eight

Johann visited Gusted Hall as he had promised to do, almost turning his horse around a dozen times during the ride to the house to return to his loving and unknowing wife. He knew exactly what was going on, of course, and had in effect already lied to Sally. He kept telling himself he was just curious to discover what purpose there was behind Edwina's settling so near to his parish. Yet, there could be only one reason, save that of an accident, which it certainly seemed not to be. She had moved here deliberately in order to be near to him.

In truth, she must already have put a lot of thought and planning into her scheme, for she must have contacted agents to find her a suitable house in the area, persuaded her father to buy it for her, and finally persuaded him to escort her to the place, since it would not have done for her to come alone. Though Edwina Delamain was a widow and would therefore be permitted much more licence than a single lady, such a move – alone to an area where she had no relatives or friends – would have brought her intentions into question. As it was, Johann was amazed at the boldness, perhaps even the brazenness, of her actions. Ladies of quality, even widows, did not chase over the countryside after married men. Lord Rushmore, it appeared, was virtually senile and was therefore putty in her hands, but there would be others who would question her motives if they knew Johann lived close by.

Johann was of course immediately gratified by her actions, his nature as susceptible to flattery as that of most men. He reminded himself that he was the father of three children, and the husband of a most loving and beautiful wife. He had accepted that his wife was, and probably always would be, illiterate, though her social graces had improved beyond measure under his guidance, yet as soon as he had come under the influence of Edwina's gracious manners and accents, he had caught himself feeling ashamed of his wife and regretting her unorthodox background.

Gusted Hall was a large, low, rambling house in some gently sloping woodlands. Built sometime in the seventeenth century, it was fashioned of dark oak beams and solid stone floors. It was a traditional country house, with all the quirks of such a dwelling, from its tall twisted chimneys that strove to reach above the trees, to the undulating gardens that fell away from the uneven walls of the single-storey building. It was full of small rooms with low ceilings joined together by a maze of passageways. The windows were leaded, with diamond-shaped panes, bulging inwards at the bottom and outwards at the top, where the incoming and outgoing flows of hot and cold air had forced the lead to bend. No one part of the large house was formed of straight lines, for every floor, wall, sill and door seemed to have warped with age, yet the whole effect was of a charming house of old wood, handmade slates and Spanish tiles.

The garden itself was made up of rockeries and moss gardens, and uneven flower beds that flowed like a tidal flood away from the dwelling and into the countryside around, almost as if it were following the lead of the house in scorning straight lines. The edges melted either into woodland or low, ivy-covered drystone walls that seemed to have grown from the earth rather than to have been built by human hands. In the woodlands around there were shaded walks along which in season one could find bluebells and harebells, cuckoo pints and honey fungus. There were secret creatures in its thickets and bracken: squirrels, foxes, badgers, owls, wood pigeons, hawks and doves. Wood and field mice ate the bracket mushrooms and rabbits gambolled on the mossy banks of a deep narrow stream.

It was the kind of house in which a poet might work and die. It was the kind of house Johann would have given his soul to possess.

He rode along the winding path to the stables, situated some way from the house, and felt he was in heaven. Leaving his horse with the stable hands, he made his way to the front door of the dwelling and was met by the butler, who showed him into a small room lined with dark, leatherbound books on rosewood shelves. There he sat, upon an eighteenth-century oak chair breathing in the scent of old polished leather, and waiting to be shown into the drawing-room where sat the lovely widow who required his attention.

When the butler returned and showed him to the drawing-room, the Austrian movement of a grandfather clock chimed his entrance, almost as if it was only incidentally eleven o'clock, and had in fact been waiting for Johann to walk past its Romanised face in order to herald the coming of the pastor.

Edwina rose from a fragile-looking Queen Anne chair as he entered, a slim delicate hand outstretched. She was wearing a full, light-blue dress which showed her fair hair and pale skin to their best advantage. Her smile was sweet and full of promise. He could tell even at that first glance that she was happy to see him. His heart felt as if a hand had enclosed it and was squeezing it hard.

'Johann,' she said, 'how wonderful of you to come.'

'My very great pleasure,' he murmured, noticing that her father was not present.

'Please sit down,' she offered, as the butler left the room and closed the door behind him.

Edwina now sat on the sofa, her small white hands clasped on her lap. Johann took the chair opposite hers, so that he could study her pale complexion in the light from the drawing-room French windows. She looked petite and delicate and completely at ease, as he remembered her in similar situations. With her flounced dress spread around her, she was like a white flower, a blossom which has floated down and settled gently on the sofa. A smile hovered around her pretty mouth as she spoke to him.

'Do I pass muster, Colonel?'

He jerked upright. 'Oh, I'm sorry. Lost in a reverie for a moment.'

'So, how *do* you find me?'

He paused only a moment before smiling himself. 'As beautiful as ever, Edwina. How could you ever be anything else?'

'Oh, I shall probably be an ugly old woman one of these days: one of those dowagers with wrinkled skin.' She growled these words softly and mockingly.

'Never,' he laughed, feeling completely at ease himself now. 'You will simply fade into an ethereal being, retaining your beauty to the last.'

Edwina reached out and touched his hand with her silken fingers. 'You were always such a flatterer, Johann, but . . .' her expression became a little more serious, '. . . I loved you for it.'

They remained in the room together for nearly three hours.

Over the next few months, Johann visited Gusted Hall at least twice a week, inventing all kinds of excuses for Sally and others, and sinking deeper and deeper into a mire far worse than the cockle girls had to contend with out on the mudflats. He found himself living in some kind of dream world, divorced from reality most of the time, whereby his mind was a kind of grey, miserable place full of shadows. Certainly he was not happy, but at the same time he could not let go of either side of his life, and worked in some desperate measure to reconcile himself to the status quo. Guilt flooded through him every time he was with his family, and yearning whenever he was with Edwina. Selfishly, he wanted both worlds, and was not prepared to give up either.

He knew if he let Edwina go he would then have to confess to Sally, throw himself on her mercy. While the affair was in flood, it occupied his mind; but once it was resolved, one way or another, he knew he would not be able to help himself. He would have to tell Sally. It was to her he would turn for absolution.

Never having tested the forgiving side of Sally, he did not know what to expect, but guessed she was not of an excusing nature when it came to male indiscretions. Why indeed should she be? If her family found out, they would kill him, he knew, for they were a proud and fiery race, who believed in the honour retribution restored.

If he left Sally, and the thought threw him into the kind of cold sweat that fever chills bring, he would have to live the rest of his life without his children, without ever seeing Sally again, and without honour. He would certainly have to leave the Church: but at the moment that seemed the least of his concerns. What he could not imagine was never seeing Sally again. She had become so much a part of him that sometimes when he turned to share something with his companion he was surprised to see Edwina standing there instead of his wife. The truth was that Sally was so enmeshed in his soul that, even if he left her, he knew he would never be entirely free of her.

So he continued to live in his twilight world of deceit and misery, wanting a life with Edwina, yet not strong enough nor able to cast off his family. He preached hollow words from the pulpit on Sundays, and prayed for forgiveness from his God, knowing he would sin again, knowing that sin was in his mind, even as he confessed his trespasses. The ancient wood of the front pew became used to his elbows, the hassock embroidered by Kate's sister, Sarah, become familiar with his knees. Polished and hollowed by the agitated bodies of a million sinners, the pew seemed to fit Johann's shape as if he were already unfrocked and an ordinary member of the congregation. The church bells seemed to clang out their disapproval loudly in his ears: 'cheat', 'fool', 'rogue', they seemed to say; and he knew he was all these and more.

One day in autumn, he rode to Gusted Hall, prepared to end the affair with Edwina. He loved her, of that there was no doubt, for he knew now that one may love two people with equal fervour. It was not a case of loving Sally more, for they were not two sacks of potatoes to be weighed. It was not a case of one being better than the other, for their qualities could not be compared like two sets of teeth. The only thing he was sure of was that they were both better than he was, a selfish, deceitful, egotistical man who wanted them both.

What they were offering him, of course, were two very different ways of life. With Edwina, providing he was able to obtain a divorce and marry her, he would have the social life he had always craved. Edwina was quite wealthy in her own right. There would be balls, and London clubs, and shoots, and riding to the hounds. He would have his own hunter, his own dogs, a wardrobe the envy of everyone he knew. With Sally he would continue to have someone who could charge him with violent passion while making love, he would have a comfortable existence, a loving family, but he would remain low on those twin establishment ladders of society and success that he yearned to climb.

The only thing that stopped him from deciding upon a life with Edwina was that Sally would not be there to share it with him. It was this realisation which eventually made up his mind for him. He could not possibly live without Sally. She was too full of life, joy and enthusiasm for him to do without. Edwina was nice, but a little too intense and serious about life. Where Sally's mouth was ever ready for a smile, Edwina's was more often glum. Perhaps it was the current circumstances that caused Edwina to be unhappy, but he was inclined to believe that this was her normal state of being. So, he was to tell her goodbye.

His heart was pounding and his stomach felt hollow as he handed over his horse to the groom at the stables. Edwina saw him coming along the path from the casement window, and opened the door herself, not waiting for the butler. He stepped inside to observe that same anxious look on her face which she had worn from about their third meeting. He gave her a brief hug and she pulled away, knowing something was wrong.

'What is it?' she asked.

He tried to laugh, not feeling quite ready to unburden himself. 'Nothing. Nothing, my love.'

She turned away from him then, staring at the wall, clenching her small hands. 'I don't like this, Johann. We have to do something to be together all the time. I don't feel guilty about asking you. You proposed to *me* before you did to her. If it weren't for my brother Robert, we would be married today.'

'That's what I've come to see you about . . .'

She whirled, her eyes sparkling, her mood instantly changed. She was at once full of light and colour. The smile was back on her mouth and her eyes were wide with joy.

'Oh, Johann. I *knew* you would come to me one day. I just *knew* it.'

She wrapped her arms around his neck. 'I wanted it to be for ever, and it is to be so . . .'

A shock wave went through him at this point. He could not understand how quickly his intentions had got twisted around. It was as if he had just made a promise to her, and now had to do something about it. Quite the opposite, in fact, from that which he had set out to do this morning.

'. . . we can live together at last, in *our* house, sleeping in *our* bed. We can hold each other all night long and make love in the real darkness, instead of in the afternoon, behind curtains. We can live like ordinary people, and you can meet my friends, and I can meet yours. It will be wonderful.'

He peeled her arms slowly from around his neck. 'Edwina, please. We have to talk. I have other things to consider than just my own happiness – *our* happiness. There are children involved.'

'Oh, they'll forgive you in time, Johann. You'll be able to see them. She won't be able to prevent that.'

'No, no. Oh God, this is getting out of hand . . .'

Her voice came through somewhat colder now. 'I should have thought it had got out of hand a long time ago, when you first paid me that visit.'

'*You* came to me first. You came to the church with your father. If you had not turned up like that, in my congregation, I should never have come looking for you. It was you who engineered our meeting again, knowing I was married, knowing my situation.'

'And you were just too weak to resist my evil charms, is that it? What am I, some kind of Morgan le Fay? *La Belle Dame Sans Merci*? Have I bewitched you?'

He took her hands in his own.

'Edwina, you know I love you. You know I've always loved you. I can't help myself, that's the problem. I am a bad man, corrupt to my soul, because I *want* you so desperately. But I can't have you now. Events have overtaken that love.'

'I feel sick,' said Edwina, turning away.

'Please don't say that,' cried Johann, distressed.

'You love *her*, don't you?'

'Edwina, I have never said any different. Of course I love her – she's my wife. We've shared so much together, not the least of which was the birth of our children. I watched her go through the agony of those births, and felt for her to the roots of my spirit. We have laughed and cried, and shared a hundred quarrels, a thousand moments of happiness. Am I now to say that all this meant nothing? It would not be true. It would not. The end does not alter what has gone before. I've betrayed her trust, her love, but that does not alter history.'

'How can you love two women?' she cried, frantic now.

'It would take me a million years to explain it and I still would not get you to understand, because there is no logic to any of it, no easy explanation, only *feelings*. I can't spread my emotions out on the floor for inspection. I don't even understand them myself... I must go, Edwina.'

She looked at him sorrowfully and forced a weak smile. 'All right. When shall I see you again? Thursday?'

He was stunned by her lack of comprehension. It seemed she thought they were going to go on as before. Worse, he realised, he was going to allow it. All his strength of resolve had been used up. He had nothing left for today. He could not let her go today.

'Thursday,' he said, kissing her.

He turned away from her, leaving by the front door which had been open the whole while. Just as she reached it, she ran up from behind and spun him round, kissing him fiercely on the lips, and afterwards saying breathlessly, 'I don't *care* who sees us. Let the servants talk.'

He nodded and turned again, striding down the path, only to stop in horror; for at the end of the garden, by the trees, stood Kate Rockmansted with an arm hooked through a wicker basket. She was staring at him as if she had seen what had gone on just inside the portal. He did not know what to do for the moment, and stepped back towards the house. Edwina, standing just inside, saw his face, and then looked towards the wood.

'It's all right,' she told him in a whisper, 'it's only the woman who delivers the mussels.'

Johann felt weak, his face breaking out into a sweat. All was now lost. Kate had witnessed his infidelity. She would of course tell Sally and Sally would demand... what would she demand? He did not know. He could only imagine, and those imaginings were nothing beside the fact that he had to face her, see what was in her eyes. It was horrible. What had he done? What had he done? He had betrayed the most precious human being that had ever come into his life: betrayed her for a few dreams of yesteryear, trying to recapture his youth's ideals. How could he hurt people like this – Sally, Edwina – and still call himself an honourable man? He could not. He was worse than those people he reviled from the pulpit. The Devil might be in his soul, but the Devil was not to blame, only Johann Haagan.

When he looked again, Kate was gone.

Chapter Twenty-nine

On his fifteenth birthday, Jamie received a sporting gun from his father. It was February and Jamie was home from school for one week. Jamie was delighted with his birthday present and spent the first hour cleaning his new possession thoroughly, although it was a brand new rifle and as clean and oiled as it could be. He polished the rosewood stock, used the pull-through to clean the inside of the barrel, and carefully applied a dab of light oil to the working parts. He loved the deadly beauty of the weapon, the smooth wooden butt, the gunmetal-blue barrel, the comfortable trigger which seemed curved to fit his finger.

His mother was unhappy about the gift, but made only a token protest, for she knew that it would fall on deaf ears anyway.

'Kate,' Jack said to her, 'he is almost grown to a man, and knows how to handle the weapon.'

'He's *not* a man,' she said, out of her son's earshot, 'he's still a boy. If he comes to any harm, Jack, I'll blame you. I'll never forgive you, you know that.'

Jack sniffed in contempt. 'As if that would bother me.'

Their marriage had reached the point where they spoke to each other only when they had to. They were two indifferent people, enemies almost, living under the same roof. Kate had lost her youthful bloom long ago and was now a woman in her late thirties, still very attractive, with her wild auburn hair and wide blue eyes, but slimmer, with her bone structure more evident. Sixteen years with Jack had hardened her features a little, robbing her of that flush of innocent enthusiasm for life in general. Her son was her main concern in the world.

In the days when they had been communicating, Kate had asked Jack, 'If you hate me so much, why did you marry me in the first place?' It was a question which had bewildered her for a long time and she genuinely wanted to know the answer.

He had stared at her for a long time before answering. 'The truth, Kate? I wanted you because you were proud, like me, with a strong spirit. I could see that in you. I wanted a wife with both beauty and strength of character. There's not many of them in the estuary. They're either sharp-tongued fishwives, or they look like mud-hoppers.'

He paused before adding one more thing. 'And Kate, I wanted you, most of all, because I thought I could never get you.'

'Was it love?' she asked, almost plaintively.

'I don't know what that word's supposed to mean, but don't you go looking at me in that contemptuous manner. You never loved *me* neither, Kate, nor did I ever get anything that I didn't have to take. Even my son weren't given to me willingly. You'd have preferred a different father for him, don't you deny it. You always treated me as second-best.'

'Yes, I suppose I did. I'm sorry.'

'Don't be, for I soon tired of your beauty, your spirit and your damned fine ways. Your friends made me sick to my stomach, and these days I can't abide much about you at all. You Fernlees must be all the same, for I hear that childless sister of yours, Sarah, is mightily reluctant to hand out favours to her husband. Not that I blame the woman, for he's a toad of the first calling, as a man would have to be to discuss such things about his wife in the public house.'

So there it was. He had wanted her because she had been unobtainable; once he had her, familiarity had bred contempt. And now she was judged no better than her sister, who had married for security and parcelled out love to her husband when she felt in an especially good mood.

Between Jack's shallow view on love and Kate's own inability to give anything of herself to him, they had never stood a chance.

'It doesn't matter what I do then, does it?' she had said in conclusion.

Jack had narrowed his eyes and replied through tight lips, 'As to that, you're still my wife, and as such I don't want no talk of cuckolding to reach my ears. I won't be made to look a fool for nobody. I'll kill you first, in spite of you being the boy's mother.'

Kate had no doubt he meant it. His terrible pride was everything to him.

Jack, however, did not practise what he preached. He needed a faithful wife, but obviously did not see why he should remain loyal too. Men were the masters, and as such were entitled to break their own rules.

Kate had recently become aware that Molly was sleeping with her husband on occasion. There was nothing said, for though Jack and Kate slept in their separate rooms, Kate would not have stood any crowing from Molly and both she and Jack knew it. The hired woman was discreet about her midnight visits. Kate had at first thought it was some village woman visiting Timothy, but she was familiar with the different notes of the creaking doors, and realised eventually that it was Jack's room which the padding feet entered. Going to his door one night she had listened and heard Molly's voice whispering to her husband. So Molly had at last achieved her ambition.

Kate silently wished her good luck. She no longer felt strongly enough about her husband to object to the liaison. The two women got on fairly well together now, working around the cottage and on the mussel beds, and there was no need to spoil the relationship just because of a worthless creature like Jack. They were like two sisters who share the same house, not close, but tolerant of each other, knowing each other's moods and foibles, and respecting them. There was no sharing of secrets, but there was conversation on practical matters such as marketing and chores. Occasionally Molly would try to interfere with Jamie's upbringing, but at these times Kate would put her firmly in her place, and the hired woman would accept that she had stepped out of line. Kate realised how hard it was for Molly, wanting to be the mother of her lover's son, and knowing it was impossible.

Jack himself was more withdrawn and dour than he had ever been. His only interest remained his business, which was extremely successful, for he now owned virtually all the mussel beds in the Roche. He had also approached the Court of Conservancy for the lease of the old Fernlee oyster beds, but since he wanted them for mussels the court refused the request, saying they were prime oyster beds but would not produce large healthy muscles. They informed him that they preferred to wait for an oyster farmer to offer for the beds. Since Jack would have no oyster farmer come within five miles of the Roche, and made it known that he would drive any such intruder out at the muzzle end of a gun if they tried to reopen the oyster beds, they stayed unused. He had a hatred of oyster farmers that was difficult for Kate to understand, until she discovered that the Rockmansted family had once owned mussel beds along the Crouch and had been forced out of business, and down into the smaller Roche, by oyster families. It was history, but people like Jack never forgave.

Jack also owned land on Foulness, Potton and Canvey. He was convinced that one day summer visitors would tire of Southend seafront and go looking for the peace and quiet that the islands had to offer. He believed the rich and well-born would come to him for land on which to build their summer residences. So far, however, only artists and birdwatchers had approached him, and these he had sent away with fleas in their ears, for they were generally not well off. He wanted to see grand houses on the islands, not artist's shacks or bird-watcher's hides.

Jack's moroseness no longer bothered Kate. She managed his house for him, helped to manage the business, but there was no real contact between the two of them. For Jamie's sake, they put on a pretence of being a couple when he was home from school, but they were in effect two single bodies dwelling in the same house.

Jamie loved both his parents and would have been devastated had he known the truth. When he came home the three of them went out for walks together (watched by the distressed Molly from the window of the cottage as they left), and for picnics along the banks of the Roche. He swam in its waters with his father, helped with the mussels on work days, and took the edge off his mother's sadness with his bright talk. At school he was not a brilliant scholar, but he was adequate, and would one day, it was hoped, go to university and obtain a modest degree. He had plans to become a lawyer which, after some terrible rows, even his father now approved of, for he would be able to help with Jack's many complex transactions.

After her argument with Jack over the gun, Kate received a visitor. Sally had brought two of the children and suggested a walk by the river. Kate gladly accepted. She didn't often have such a pleasant reason to get out and about away from the house and business.

The tide was out as they strolled along the dyke; the pong of the decayed mud was strong. There were many birds feeding on the tidal flats, which the children kept pointing out to one another, Celia, the youngest, waving her arms in an attempt to make them fly away. Kate found her friend unusually quiet and, while the children were running ahead, out of earshot, asked her what was the matter.

'It's Johann,' said Sally, her hands deep in the pockets of her coat and her head hunched between her shoulders. 'He's seein' another woman.'

'Oh,' said Kate.

Ever since she'd seen Johann compromising himself at the manor house, Kate had been wrestling with her separate loyalties to both Johann and Sally. The dilemma it had presented her with was one she did not wish to confront; she had hoped that the cause would disappear without her having to do anything about it. Kate had in fact been expecting a visit, not from Sally, but from Johann who she was sure had seen her there.

'You don't sound surprised,' said Sally, after a moment.

Kate shook her head. 'I believe I saw something which I hoped I was mistaken about.'

Sally sighed. 'Well, I don't want to hear about it, 'cause it'll just make me as mad as fire, an' I want to stay calm on it. I love Johann now, more than I imagined I ever would, even though right at this minute I could strangle the bugger in his sleep. I hate him for doing this to me, to us, but I love him deeply. I don't want to lose him. Daft, ain't it?'

'No,' replied Kate, 'I understand.'

Sally said, 'I know who the woman is an' I'm not positive I'm going to win, Kate. She's got money, fine looks, and she's a lady as well. I think she's one of his friends from before he met me. You know how he always wanted to marry into the upper classes.'

'I knew,' said Kate, looking at Sally sideways, 'but I didn't know you did.'

'Peter!' called Sally. 'Don't throw stones at the birds dah'lin', they don't like it.'

The children looked around, dropped their stones, then ran on ahead, giggling.

Sally continued, 'You don't live with a man for years and not get to know what his ambitions was when he was younger. Anyway,' she stopped and sighed, 'I'm just goin' to wait it out, I think. If I say somethin' it'll just cause an argument and he'll have his excuse then, won't he? I don't want him to go like that, 'cause he'll regret it as much as me. Johann's all worked up at the moment: his greatest ambition is there for the taking; only his family stands in the way. But when he gets it, he won't want it. I know him. And even if he did, he wouldn't enjoy it, 'cause he'd feel so guilty about me and the kids. So it's best he stays, for his sake as well as ours, ain't it, Kate?'

'I don't honestly know,' replied Kate, feeling at a loss.

'Well, I think it is,' said Sally, giving her friend a brave smile. 'In fact, I *know* it is.'

When Kate got back from the walk she took out Simon's letters for the third time since Jack had moved out of their room. She pored over their contents, as if hoping to find an answer to Sally's problem in them. Kate was surprised at the freshness of the words in the missives. They were like poetry to her: they still retained a certain magic. But they held none of the answers she wanted, as she might have guessed.

The day after his birthday, Jamie rose early, crept downstairs, and took his new shotgun from the corner of the kitchen. He intended hunting wild geese out on the mudflats. One of the lurchers, Sabre, pricked up its ears. Bess and Dagger were long dead and had been replaced by two similar dogs, but Jamie did not want them with him today. They were not as obedient with him as they were with his father, and he was not confident of keeping them quiet out on the flats. They might run around chasing gulls and then he would not get within a mile of a goose.

Jamie left the house and walked along the winding, grassy path down to the river. There he took the dyke, following it through the creeks towards the Maplin Sands, where he intended to go out on to the North Sea mud.

There was a thick mist over the river, which was on the retreat, running out to sea. Boats loomed through veils of vapour and disappeared again, like the ghosts of craft from another era. They made Jamie think of the trireme of Odysseus, on his way home from the Trojan war, lost upon the Aegean, and for a while he imagined he was Odysseus himself, striding along an unknown shore – perhaps the home of Circe the witch, or even the land of the Cyclops. The mists were favourable to such thoughts, as shore beacons would suddenly come bursting through the fog to stand in his way, and Jamie would have to battle with them before being permitted to pass. On the ebb tide the gulls were crying out faintly, like sirens calling him to strange islands, where he would be forced to stay for ever if he were not the strong-minded warrior he knew himself to be. Once, he saw the great Achilles striding towards him on the dyke (a fisherman on his way home) only to pass him without a word, for ghosts cannot talk to living souls, even when the latter are visiting their underworld.

When Jamie reached the shore of the sea, the tide was almost out, and without hesitation the youth stepped on to the mud, sinking to his ankles. He cocked his loaded gun and began to move cautiously forward, knowing that there were thousands of geese out there somewhere feeding on the mud. He could hear their honking as they informed one another of their rightful territories. All he had to do was find a group of them and then he could shoot his first game.

Crabs ran from his squelching footsteps and mudskippers wriggled out of his way. The mist had closed in again before he was two hundred yards from the shore, but he was confident of his sense of direction. He could hear the horns of the boats across the sound, and knew that they lay to the south-east. With one compass point at his disposal, he had all the others, more or less. If he walked in a westerly direction he would eventually reach land.

Somehow the geese managed to evade him. When their honking grew louder he knew he was close to them, but always when he reached the spot where there was evidence of them having been feeding it was empty.

They had moved on. Their footprints went out in all directions; he would follow one set only to lose the spoor in a large tidal pool. Sometimes he heard a goose taking to the air, just before it came into range of his shotgun. Once he fired up into the mist, frustrated by his failure to locate the creatures, but nothing dropped down from the heavens at his feet to reward him.

Jamie must have covered a great deal of the mudflats in his search for game, but the geese taunted him with their calls, and led him a merry dance around in circles, over rays of water, gulfs of mud, and areas of broken shells, until he did not know up from down, let alone west from east. The mudflats, he knew, were legendary for claiming the lives of visitors to the area: hunters, fishermen, wildlife observers. But he was no visitor, he told himself, he was a local. He knew the sea and its way. He could hear the horns of the ships, but the fog distorted the direction. He would have to wait for the incoming tide and run from it, taking the same direction that it took itself, for that way would lie land. He began to regret not bringing at least one of the lurchers, for their sense of direction was instinctive.

The fog became so thick he walked straight into the side of a sunken boat that had become exposed by the low tide. He struck his nose on one of the rotten, algae-covered ribs of the old craft and it bled profusely for a while, until he managed to stem the flow by holding his head back, though he had to swallow a great deal of warm blood in the process. To teach it a lesson, he used the boat rib for close-quarter target practice.

He decided to walk back to the shore, for he was aware it was getting late. This he set out to do, but somehow kept coming across his own footsteps in the mud. He was not sure whether they were earlier prints or ones just made. He kept trying to gauge the direction of the horns from the boats, but found it difficult in the mist: one minute they seemed to come from behind him, and the next they seemed to be in front. It was as if they were taunting him.

Finally, he felt the cold water washing about his feet, and looked down to see the swirling flood tide. Suddenly panic-stricken, he began striding quickly away from the inflowing water, forgetting that the tide did not come in as a direct line from the east, but curved round in crescents. The mud sucked at his feet, and the faster he tried to walk, the deeper he sank into the mire. This was not like the Leigh part of the Thames estuary. The mud was firmer in the North Sea: an older mud with more consistency than the silt that came down the Thames. So Jamie was able to retrieve his feet, but only with great effort. Each foot came out with a slow, sucking movement that pulled on his muscles and drained his strength. Each step took an age. Twice he slipped over, falling into the freezing water and chilling himself to the bone.

Just when he felt he ought to be close to the shore, he came across another flow of water, coming directly towards him. He was close to tears, exhausted and frightened. Then he remembered, remembered how the rays came in like horns. He had fallen for the sea's oldest trick, the one it used to catch the ignorant visitor, to trap the unwary within its clutches. Jamie thought of all those times he had heard of people being drowned, held by the mud until the tide covered them, and he cried out in fear. 'Help, please help me!' Lifting his gun, he fired it in an attempt to attract attention to his plight. The sound of the shot echoed eerily around him.

He stared about him miserably, into the mist. A gull carked nearby, and for a moment he thought it was a human voice.

'Help!' he screamed again. 'Somebody help me!'

There was no answering sound except that of the rhonking geese, the creaking of their wings as they took to the air, travelling over his head towards the mainland. Now that the mud was being covered, they were no longer interested in remaining on the flats. They would seek inland fields and creeks, in which to wait for another tidal retreat.

The water was rising, had reached Jamie's waist as he struggled to move in the direction taken by the geese. Fortunately he was on a hard piece of ground, a layer of shells beneath, and was able to make slow though awkward progress. The sea was faster, though, and seemed to mock his efforts at escape. Before long he was up to his chest, the icy temperature of the water causing his muscles to seize and his blood to thicken. His chest constricted, labouring with each breath, and his consciousness seemed to be slipping away from him. He thought of his mother and father, still in the warm cottage, wondering where he was but not worrying because they would believe he could take care of himself. He pictured them being told of his death, his mother collapsing in tears, his father breaking like a toy doll in the middle.

'Help me,' he mumbled. 'God help me.'

Each step was tortuous now, his feet and legs numb, his muscles unresponding. There was a pain in his breast which was like a red-hot knife. For some reason he still clutched his gun, holding it above his head with one aching arm. If he threw his birthday present away, he would be lost for sure, because that would mean he had given up hope.

The water reached his chin.

'Oh my,' he whispered, the exposure causing his eyes to glaze, 'I am really going to die . . .'

He began to float, but he was fast losing consciousness. Nothing would move: not his arms, not his legs. He began to swallow water. The gun finally slipped from his grasp, splashing into the water and sinking to the bottom. The current reached out and grabbed Jamie, trying to pull him down to join his weapon.

Suddenly he was almost strangled as his collar tightened around his neck. It was a moment before he realised he was being wrenched from the water. Someone had him by the jacket and was hauling him out of the water and, blessedly, into a rowing boat. He was landed like a fish, in the bottom of the craft, and lay there gasping. Quickly wrapping him in a dry blanket, his rescuer began pounding his limbs until they began to hurt. As the blood eventually seeped back in to his hands and feet, Jamie screamed in agony, cursing the man, for it was as if someone were driving nails into his limbs. Then he was left alone as his saviour rowed for the shore, and feeling slowly crept back into his frozen body.

Once they reached the shore, he was half-dragged, half-carried to a clapboard house. Inside, there was a fire roaring in the stove, and he was propped in a chair, still wrapped around by the blanket, and given a drink. The man gruffly told him to strip, and gave Jamie some dry clothes, much too large for him, to put on. When he had done so, he looked properly at his rescuer for the first time, and realised it was the fisherman who had passed him on the dyke in the early morning.

'I'm very grateful indeed, sir,' Jamie said to him.

'So you should be,' replied the man. 'Stupid young tyke. You put me in danger too.'

Jamie stiffened, unused to being spoken to so harshly. 'I'm not a tyke. I'm fifteen years old and from a good family, sir!'

'Then you should know better than to go out on the mud on a misty day. You deserve a good thrashing – and so do your parents for letting you go.'

Jamie stared into the man's lean tanned face with its penetrating brown eyes. The features were strong and without compromise. It was an intelligent face, but one hardened to life. Jamie was a little frightened by the steel in this strange fisherman's eyes, as if he did not give a damn about any man or his son. He recalled a story his mother had told him, of a smuggler, a desperate character called Joseph Wentworth, who had evaded the law and escaped to France. Perhaps this was he, returned from those foreign shores?

'I'm sorry, sir,' he said. 'You're quite right, it was extremely foolish of me. However, my parents are not to blame, for they do not know where I am. I crept out before dawn to go hunting geese, hoping to surprise them with some game. It was my birthday yesterday and my father gave me a sporting rifle. Now it is lost, in the mud, and I shall have to tell him.'

The man's eyes softened. 'Just so long as you know you've been foolish,' he said. 'Don't do it again.'

'I won't, I can assure you, sir.'

The man busied himself in the corner of the room while Jamie got dry. He seemed to be making several band lines, which were long lines with about fifty hooks hanging from them. They would be strung out between two low posts at ebb tide, so that when the water returned it would cover them. Then, on the next ebb tide, the fisherman would walk out to the band line and retrieve any fish he might have caught.

'I think I had better go home now, sir,' said Jamie. 'I have to tell my father I have lost my gun. I fear he will be very angry, but it's something that has to be done.'

'Who is your father?'

'Jack Rockmansted, sir. A mussel farmer. I am James Rockmansted, but everyone calls me Jamie.'

The man grunted and, after biting through a piece of catgut, said, 'The biggest musselman in these parts, I understand.'

'Yes sir. He and my mother Kate have built the business up from small beginnings to what it is today.'

The man's head lifted sharply from his task and a dark look suddenly swept across his features. 'Kate? Kate who?'

Jamie was taken aback and a little puzzled, he was going to answer, 'Why, Kate Rockmansted, of course,' before he realised what the man was really asking. It took Jamie a moment to remember his mother's maiden name.

'Kate Fernlee, sir. Her maiden name was Catherine Fernlee.'

The man stood upright and seemed stunned. 'You are Kate's son? Of course, I see the likeness now. You have her eyes.' He stared so intently at Jamie that Jamie had to turn away. Then the man's voice sounded both distantly angry and somewhat puzzled. 'I was given to understand Kate Fernlee married a schoolteacher-cum-priest. A man by the name of Haagan.'

Jamie was now convinced he was talking to Joseph Wentworth, for the man had clearly been out of the district for many, many years. He seemed quite inquisitive about Jamie's family, but that was not unusual, for Jamie knew that if local folk ever left the area, they always wanted to know what had gone on in their absence. When you lived in a region like the flatlands, they became part of you; you had to know all the missing history or you did not feel whole. Jamie felt this way even when he came home from his London school: he could not imagine what it was like for this man, who had been away longer than Jamie had lived on the earth. So he sympathised with the curiosity, knowing it had to be fed and watered.

'You must have been out of the country for a long while, sir. My mother married Jack Rockmansted. Reverend Haagan is my mother's friend and he is married to Sally, who was a gypsy and a cockler before she became his wife. Reverend Haagan is now the vicar at Paglesham Church End and no longer teaches school: that is done by my old schoolteacher, the Reverend J.A. Smith . . .'

'Yes, yes,' said the man impatiently, 'but you say she married Jack Rockmansted. Did the priest divorce her then? I don't understand.'

'You seem confused, sir. My mother was *never* married to the Reverend Haagan. Molly told me my mother was engaged to a sailor, who came home just after Sally and Johann – that's the Reverend Haagan, begging your pardon, sir – were married themselves. He made no attempt to see my mother and indeed left the county to go back to a life on the ocean. I believe that man was your brother, sir, if you are, as I suspect, Joseph Wentworth, the notorious smuggler – a fact I don't mind, for you saved my life and I shall keep your presence here a secret, of that you can be sure. Your brother was unkind to my mother, but of course we are all glad he never came home, for I should not be here otherwise, and my mother and father would not have found that they loved each other, would they?'

Jamie smiled, he hoped reassuringly, at the smuggler before him.

The man did indeed seem to be put out of sorts by these revelations and the discovery of his identity, for he went very pale and said, 'Well, I'll be damned,' in a tone which was almost a whisper.

'I don't wish to malign your brother, Mr Wentworth, but he was not a very honourable man. If I were you I should have nothing more to do with him. And, if I may be so bold as to offer advice to a man many years my senior, I should say that you must keep clear of smuggling until I have taken the law. Once I am a barrister, I shall repay you the debt I owe you by defending you in court. Much time has passed since the offences for which you are sought were committed, and I think we can argue that you have paid for your crimes with the misery of exile in France. What do you think?'

'I'll be double damned, that's what I think,' said the man in the same tone of voice.

'Please think it over,' said Jamie seriously. 'I'm sure we can find some way of gaining the sympathy of the court and setting you at liberty, so that you need not be hiding away like this, fearful of the law for the rest of your life.'

The man seemed to gather some inner reserves of strength and drew himself up. He stepped across the room and put his hands on Jamie's shoulders.

'Jamie,' he said, 'you're a good lad – a very fine lad – if a little foolish today. I might wish you were my son, but that causes so many complications in my head you wouldn't believe the tangle. When you go home from here, please say nothing of my presence.'

'I promise I will not, Mr Wentworth.'

'Good. Good lad, Jamie. And I shall look for your gun when the tide goes out. I've a pretty good chance of finding it again, for there is a shell bed beneath the place where you were standing which will prevent it from sinking deeper. If there had not been, we should not be talking at the moment, for you would have been drowned.' He shook his head. 'What a fool I've been,' he said, more it seemed to himself than to Jamie. 'And now it's too late. Far too late. Perhaps I should go away again, this minute?'

Jamie said, 'No, I should like you to stay, sir. You saved my life and I wish to do the same for you.'

The man laughed. 'Maybe you shall. Now, off you go. I don't know how you'll explain the temporary absence of your gun, but give me until the next ebb tide, and it'll be standing in your porch.'

'I am most truly grateful, Mr Wentworth, really I am,' said Jamie fervently. 'I'm due back to school in two days and my father will be asking me about the gun before I leave. I can make excuses before tomorrow morning, though, if you're sure you can find it again?'

'It'll be there. Now shake my hand, boy, and get you gone, back to your parents. If I catch you hunting on the flats in the mist again, I shall drown you myself.'

'Yes, sir. Thank you, sir.'

Jamie left then, going out of the house and taking the path across the marshes to the dyke. Once there he hurried home, telling his worried parents on arrival that he had merely been for a walk, and apologised for causing them anxiety. He spent a nervous day with his father at the mussel beds and went to bed that night with a prayer on his lips.

The following morning he rose early and went downstairs.

Propped against the front porch, as clean and shiny as if it had been purchased yesterday, was his rifle.

Chapter Thirty

Simon walked into Rochford after leaving the boy's gun in the porch. He had reached the point where he felt the need to restore his house to its former state. Repairs on the place were long overdue, for no one had been near the clapboard cottage since his brothers had been transported. Two of them were dead now, and the other free.

Joseph had become embroiled in the French underworld, and had been killed on the Marseille waterfront. Simon did not know the exact circumstances of his death, but he understood that Joseph had been in some kind of smuggling gang which ran goods between Tunis and Marseille. A rival gang had followed three of them one night and Joseph had been stabbed. His body had been found floating in Marseille harbour the next morning.

Peter had died in Tasmania, of a common heart attack.

Only Luke was left, and Luke had gone to Queensland at the end of his sentence. As far as Simon knew, he was now the owner of a fishing boat, making his living in the tropical waters off the shores of Australia. It seemed that Luke had no intention of returning to Essex.

So the house was Simon's, to do with as he wished. The first thing was to get it into a state of good repair, then decide whether he wanted to live there or sell it.

In Rochford he purchased hammer and nails, saw, spokeshave, plane and paint. At a timber yard behind the Ship Inn he ordered weatherboarding, floor planks and clapboard planks with feathered edges for the outside. A four-by-four inch piece of lumber was needed to replace one of the porch posts, and some smaller spars for the roof and supports.

He left the tools at the timber yard, to be delivered along with the wood when a wagon was going out towards Paglesham marshes. Davey Spills, the timber man, told Simon it would be in the next three or four days.

Payment was in cash, for Simon was quite well off, having spent little of his pay while in the navy, and having been awarded a small pension to keep him day by day. After nearly twenty years on Her Majesty's ships, he had risen to the rank of master-at-arms, and had been discharged with honour. He had been respected by his subordinates as well as by his superiors, for his authority had not been upheld by force, but by his firm attitude towards his men, his absolute fairness, and his willingness to share in the manual labour when it was necessary. He was modest about his achievements, but liked to believe he had been just in his dealings with most men, except those who were lazy, incompetent or negligent in their duties. He knew there were friends he had made during his naval years who would have stood by him to the death if so required.

Having made his purchases, Simon went into the Ship and had a pint of ale, sitting in a corner away from the light. He was not anxious to be seen and recognised by anyone who might pass on to the Rockmansted household the information that he was home. It was his intention to stay away from Kate and her husband, so as not to cause any trouble.

Damn but the boy had had his mother's eyes! Seeing those eyes had caused something to stir inside Simon which he had thought long dead. Over the years he had worked Kate out of his system, both mentally and physically, and for a considerable time now had felt free of her. He had tried other women, of course, especially in the beginning, but found you cannot displace love from your heart by attempting to put a love of an inferior quality in its place. There had been women he had grown fond of and might have made a life with if Kate's features had not still been haunting him. In the end, he settled for brief encounters, as sailors are wont to do, with women who were content with such affairs. Even these had grown fewer over the last few years.

He had thought himself immune to Kate now, and had a little speech prepared in case he met her accidentally on the road, about how things had worked out for the best because he had had his career in the navy to consider, and that he hoped she was happy with her priest husband. In his mind he was cool and unruffled when giving this little speech, and able to look into her eyes without feeling anything whatsoever.

Yet, he had seen but a copy of those eyes yesterday, and his stomach had turned over, his heart had begun beating like a drum, and his hands had started shaking. What about when he saw the real thing? Could he honestly say he was going to look into her face and feel nothing? More likely, he would gibber like an idiot, his own face red with embarrassment, his hands twitching like elder twigs in the wind.

Rockmansted! The man had tricked Simon into leaving without even contacting Kate. He had told Simon that she was already married and promised to get him out of prison. Now it was obvious that Jack

Rockmansted had left Simon in jail on purpose in order to have Kate for himself. What a fool Simon had been, not to have checked once he came out of prison! Although perhaps even then it would have been too late. In those early days, he would probably have killed Jack Rockmansted, or been killed himself. One of them would have had to die, and the loss of Kate under such circumstances would have been unbearable.

Now? Too much time had passed. He hated the man for what he had done to him, but it was no longer a killing matter. There did not even seem much point in letting Kate know the truth, for what good would it do? The boy was fifteen; she must have been married to Jack Rockmansted for at least that many years. She was *his* wife, and as such had no doubt grown to love him. If Simon went barging in with accusations that were decades old it would do no good to anyone. She would not thank him for it. The past was long dead, and while Simon owed Jack Rockmansted payment for leaving him to rot in prison, he could not expect to influence Kate any longer, for he was a different man from the one she had known. He was a craggy middle-aged ex-sailor, with all the brittleness of a confirmed bachelor.

Kate had raised a fine son, though, he thought with envy. Young Jamie could have been his boy. He would not have been ashamed of such a youth, of that he was sure.

Simon tried to picture Kate after over two decades of hard work. She would not be the pretty lass he left on the dyke that day he had marched away to sea. No doubt, he told himself, she was a worn creature now. Perhaps he would not even recognise her? Why, he would have difficulty in recognising himself these days! His hair was certainly thinner, and the salt and sun had leathered his skin, leaving creases around the corners of his eyes and on his brow. She would probably think him a poor substitute for that handsome young man she had said goodbye to in the thirties.

By the time he had finished his ale, Simon had convinced himself that he and Kate would hardly know one another, let alone care what each other thought. He paid for his drink and set out along the road, walking back to Paglesham through Stambridge.

When he reached his cottage on the marshes, someone was waiting for him. It was Jamie. He looked scrubbed and clean, unlike yesterday, and wore fine clothes. On his head was a tall hat and there were polished leather shoes on his feet. He looked a little older in his city clothes than he had when Simon had fished him dripping wet from the sea. His cheeks looked a little raw from being cut by the February east wind that came in sharp thin sheets across the saltings, but those blue eyes were bright and warm.

'I'm on my way back to school in London, Mr Wentworth, and I thought to come and thank you for saving my life yesterday.'

Simon smiled at this eager youngster, who had yesteryear's eyes and tomorrow's face.

'Think nothing of it, lad, for I just happened to be there. What I would like you to do is remember the lesson. Don't go out on the mud alone, especially in the mist.'

'I've already taken that to heart.'

'Good.'

They both stood there in awkward silence. Out on the marshes the oystercatchers were calling to each other in their shrill tongues. Jamie moved towards the porch stairs. As he stepped down on to the path, Simon said to him, 'You made no mention of me to your parents, I hope?'

Jamie flushed at this question and Simon knew he had not kept his word. 'I... I told my mother you were here, but I said nothing about you rescuing me.'

Simon sighed heavily. 'What did you say to her?'

'I just told her Joseph Wentworth was back in his house on the marshes.'

'Joseph Wentworth. That's all?'

'That's all I said,' gushed Jamie, 'I swear it. I... I wasn't thinking. She caught me in an unguarded moment, while my mind was on other things, and asked me if I had seen anyone on my walk. I told her I had gone walking, you see, which was not so much a lie because I had. I just didn't say anything about taking my gun with me. Did I do very wrong? She promised she would not call the excise man.'

Simon smiled inwardly. 'She promised that, did she?'

'Yes. I said to her that I had given you my word that I would tell no one of your presence, and that if she called the excise man, and told them you were here, I should lose all my honour. She said, "I would never be the cause of you losing your honour, son." She asked me how you looked.'

This was a little more dangerous.

'And what did you tell her?'

'I said you looked well enough, for a man of your age, of course.'

It was more than Simon could do to prevent himself from bursting out with laughter at this naïve remark. 'Well, thank you. I'll take my ancient bones inside my shack now, and rest them in my favourite chair.'

Jamie's face dropped. 'Oh, I didn't mean to insult you, sir. I just meant, well, you are something near to my father's age.'

'Not really. Your father could give me at least ten years, if not more.'

'Then I apologise.'

Simon shook his head. 'It doesn't matter, it's of no consequence. Now, before you go back to school, remember – I want no one else told of my presence. Especially your father. You may believe your father is a man of honour, which well he might be, but he may also feel it to be his duty to inform the law of my presence. Any honest man, who has no debt to me, would consider informing the police that a criminal has returned to the area. Your mother knows, but I remember her as a very secretive woman in any case, and she would not inform upon the kin of Simon Wentworth. My brother Simon and your mother were very close before he went away to sea, and she would do nothing to harm his family, I am sure.'

The boy came back then, and stood at the bottom of the steps, looking up at him. 'When I told her you were here, she asked me about your brother Simon, whether he might be coming home too. I said I did not know, but would ask you if I saw you again. She told me to stay away from you, saying you were not a fit person for a young man to know. I suppose she still thinks you a smuggler and a desperate man. I wish I could tell her you saved my life, Mr Wentworth.'

'No,' said Simon sharply. 'You must not.'

Jamie hung his head for a moment. 'Then I will not, if you wish it to remain a secret. Can I ask you, though, where your brother Simon is?'

'Away at sea. Probably cruising around some tropical islands like the Filippinos, or Tahiti.'

'Will he ever return?'

'I don't believe so. I expect any day to hear that he has been eaten by cannibals, or drowned at sea, for it is the kind of death which would suit his wretched soul. Your mother broke his heart, boy, and he never recovered the pieces. He went out looking for a way to lose himself on the ocean and has been trying ever since . . . so I believe.'

Jamie visibly stiffened a little. 'I did not hear it that way, as I told you. I heard that he abandoned my mother.'

'Well, it doesn't matter which way it was, for it is all history now, and in the dark past. Perhaps both of them, your mother and my brother, have cause to grieve a little over those times, and no doubt they both believe themselves to be in the right, for as you will learn, lovers who break up never consider it to be their fault. They always blame the other person.'

'Why? If it *is* their fault?'

'Why? Because . . . I don't know why, boy. It's just that way, I'm afraid.'

'But what if there's nothing to blame them for?'

'Why, you tell them they have changed, that they are not the same person you once knew, that you believe they no longer love you, even if they say they do. You blame them for changing, that's what you do . . . Now on your way, James, for I am a busy man, and need to set my lines today, or I'll not eat.'

'Yes, sir. I'm sorry to delay you. Perhaps I can come and see you when I return for the holidays?'

'Not if your mother forbids it.'

'But she doesn't understand . . .'

'All the same, it would be better if we shook hands now, and called it quits.'

Jamie nodded. 'If we must.'

They shook hands solemnly.

'Now,' said Simon, 'on your way, boy, and do your mother proud at that school of yours, because she deserves it.'

'Yes, sir.'

The boy left him then, running along the path to the dyke. He turned and waved once, and when Simon went into the house he had a lump in his throat. *If he were my son,* he thought, *I should be as pleased as anything.* For a brief moment he entertained the thought that Jamie *might* be his son: that Kate had kept him secret from the world and her husband had adopted the boy for his own. But Jamie himself had told him that he was fifteen years of age, so such a thing could not be.

'Damn Jack Rockmansted's eyes,' growled Simon to himself, as he took out his band lines. 'I could slit his throat from ear to ear, even today.'

He sat in the light of the window and began tying on hooks that were missing from the band line. They were of many different sizes, to catch all kinds of fish. Most of those he caught were dabs and plaice, though he occasionally found eels, pollacks and black bream. Some he sold to the fishmonger in Rochford and others he ate himself. It was a living, for the time being, which satisfied him.

He left the house at the turn of the tide and walked to the dyke, where his dinghy was moored. He went out on the tide with the rowing boat and, when it was far enough out, he allowed the boat to settle on the mud. There he dug for lugworms and ragworms, with which to bait the hooks. Once this was done, and the band lines set between posts, he remained on the mud in the vicinity of the lines, occasionally walking up and down waving a rag until the tide returned. This was necessary in order to chase away the gulls and terns, for they would have stripped his lines clear of bait had he left them uncovered by water.

Once the water was ankle-deep, he climbed back in his boat and waited for the tide to lift it high enough off the mud for him to be able to row. Then he followed the water in, as it swept back reclaiming the territory it had temporarily vacated. Simon would follow the same procedure on the next tide, recovering the hooked fish before the water was shallow enough for the gulls to dive on them and rob him of his catch. His family had fished this way for several centuries, at one time setting out as many as fifty band lines. It was expensive in hooks, but there was not the necessity to repair nets every time he went out fishing.

He loved the excitement of rowing out on the ebb tide, wondering what his catch would consist of, and what size the fish would be, reaching down into the unknown and coming up with those live bars of silver, flashing in the daylight, or glinting under the beams of the moon! Even a disappointing catch merely whetted his appetite for the next time, or the time after that, when he might hit a shoal and come up with hooks full of flapping silver fish. The unseen world below the waves, releasing its treasures, its bounty: there was little to match such a life.

Simon went home to bed and tried to dream of a boat full of silver fish; instead his mind travelled to a warm shack below a dyke where there was clean straw on the floor, to make love to a woman for the thousandth dreamtime, as he had done for real just once, a million years ago in the past. He woke as Kate's face was looking into his own; alone, he stared into the cold darkness.

Chapter Thirty-one

After Jamie had gone back to school in London, Kate's life settled once more into a routine of working, eating and sleeping, with little consolation from her hollow marriage. It was not that she was miserable – though she was certainly not happy – but that her world was dull when her son was not there. He added sparkle and effervescence, and even Jack paid some attention to family matters when Jamie was around. She did not want to cling to Jamie though, using him as a substitute husband in a sham marriage: he had his own life to lead.

Two days after Jamie had gone, she was combing her tangled auburn hair (some acknowledged grey creeping in at the temples), when she spied someone walking down the path to the front door. There was a knock and she heard Molly hurry from the kitchen to answer. Then came the inevitable shout up the stairs.

'Kate, somebody calling for you.'

Kate sighed heavily, not looking forward to this meeting at all. She tied up her hair with a piece of clean yellow rag and then descended the stairs. She had to lift her pale lemon dress with its several petticoats, because it attracted the dirt like a magnet collects iron filings.

The Reverend Johann Haagan was waiting for her in the parlour, hat in hand. He looked a little agitated and seemed anxious that Molly should leave the room before he spoke. Molly, who was dusting furniture, seemed oblivious of this need, so Kate stepped in. 'Molly, would you make the Reverend some tea, please?'

Molly paused, the duster in mid-flick, and raised her eyebrows. 'If you want, but I an't finished in 'ere yet.'

'I know, but he looks thirsty, and he's ridden quite a way.'

Johann cleared his throat and said, 'I would appreciate it, Molly.'

Molly shrugged as if to say these quirky habits were not to her liking, but if people wanted to indulge in tea in the middle of the morning it was up to them. 'All right then, I'll finish 'ere later, Kate.'

'Thank you, Molly.'

The servant left the room and Johann, whose hat brim was soiled where his damp fingers had been turning it round and round, sat down heavily in an armchair and threw the hat on the floor.

'You know why I'm here, Kate,' he said.

'I'm trying to think. It is not to discuss Lord Tennyson's new volume of poetry, I suppose? I have to say I have read "Maud" and find it very dark and confusing.'

'Don't mock me, Kate, please. It took a lot of strength of will to come here today.'

'A pity that strength of will was not used before now, to avert the situation which led you to visit me today.'

She studied the effect these words had on Johann, trying to ascertain his mood. He must have been shocked, of course, to be discovered with another woman in his arms by his wife's best friend. But did that mean he intended to give up the woman, his wife, or continue to divide his life in two? Kate did not see it as her mission to guide him along any of these paths. He had to make up his own mind; though she could not help but feel angry at his betrayal of her best friend, and her manner towards him was stiff and cold.

Johann sensed her anger. 'Please don't think of me too harshly, Kate. May I explain?'

'If you feel you must,' Kate replied tersely.

Johann leaned forward, making a spire out of his fingers and studying it intently while he spoke. 'The woman you saw, Kate, was the lady I courted in my youth, after leaving university. Her brother Robert objected to our romance and, as I have told you in earlier conversations, forced me to leave her. If I had not gone, I would have had to kill him – a terrible thing for a priest, you will admit.'

'A terrible thing for *anyone*.'

'Yes, of course. Well, I went, as you know, and Edwina married someone else, a marriage of convenience. He was somewhat older than her and he died in a riding accident, so she tells me. She had not, at the time of his death, recovered from our own affair of the heart, and she came seeking me in Essex with her invalid father. I looked up from my sermon one Sunday to find her not ten feet away, staring up into my eyes. You can imagine my shock.'

'I think I can.'

'In that state, then, she pursued me. I know that sounds weak and even a little egotistic, but it's true.'

Kate shook her head. 'And you were the reluctant quarry. You fought against it, furiously, but you were overcome by insurmountable odds.'

The spire was broken and Johann clenched his fists. 'You're not making this easy for me.'

'Am I supposed to?'

'No, but you could be more of a friend.'

'Sally is my friend too. I have to take sides in this and I'm afraid I choose the side of the innocent party. My own marriage has not been what it should, and Sally has supported me all through the years. Should I desert her now, for a man who goes chasing skirts, and fashions elaborate excuses for doing what my dear brother-in-law calls "wenching"?'

'Don't compare me with Timothy Rockmansted!' shouted Johann, half-rising from his seat.

At this moment, Molly entered with the tea on a tray and a blank expression on her features, though she must have heard at least some of what was being said. Abruptly Johann sat down again, muttering inaudibly.

Once Molly had left the room again, Kate said, 'I'm sorry, I should not have said what I did. Johann, I don't know why you're here, because I have not and would not pass on what I saw that day to Sally. Not out of any consideration for you, I have to add, but because it would hurt her to know any details. She knows, you realise that?'

Johann had been in the process of lifting his cup of tea from the tray, but his hand shook so badly that the cup and saucer began to rattle and he put them down again.

'What was that?' he said.

'I said Sally knows about your affair. She has known for a long time. I believe she has remained silent about it because she hopes it will fade away of its own accord, and you will go back to being the loving husband and father you were before this woman came to the neighbourhood.'

'I have never neglected my duties as a family man,' he said, 'even after all this began.'

'You've changed though, considerably. How else did she guess something was going on? No one told her. Sally guessed a long time ago, Johann, but not wanting to lose you she kept it to herself, locked it away, hoping it would not damage your life together.'

Johann buried his face in his hands for a moment. He emerged again and said, 'But Sally has such an evil temper. I would have thought the instant she knew I had been unfaithful to her, she would have attacked me with a kitchen knife, or worse. You know yourself how savage she can get with people.'

'You're not people, Johann. You're her husband. She loves you. She's afraid of losing you. She's afraid of breaking her family apart. Do you not understand one little thing about women?'

He looked at her bleakly. 'Obviously not. What am I to do, Kate?'

'I can't advise you on that. You have to face up to your own problems and solve them yourself. You must surely have spoken to God about this? You of all people. You're a priest, for heaven's sakes, Johann. Did you go into this by putting God aside and regarding his laws as nothing? *Thou shalt not commit adultery.* Did you even think about it?'

'Edwina had me bewitched,' he moaned.

'That's a feeble excuse and you know it. It's always the woman's fault isn't it? Men can't help themselves, poor things, they have no resistance against female temptations. You know that's a weak man's argument. Please, Johann, take responsibility for your actions.'

He nodded dumbly. 'I shall go home now, and do what I should have done a long time ago. I shall face Sally with the truth and beg her forgiveness.'

'Do as you feel you must,' said Kate, not willing even to give him this much support. Whatever he had done, it was up to him to sort it out. He wanted to be propped and shored up. Well, Kate was not going to do him that kind of favour. She had suffered with Sally, and she was not going to do the same with him: his actions had been the cause of it all.

She gave him his hat and saw him to the door. He gave her one last pathetic look and then strode off in the direction of his house. Kate watched him disappear behind the hedgerows.

Molly came up behind her. 'He's gone then?' she said.

'Yes, Molly.'

'A priest an' all,' said Molly in a disapproving tone.

Kate sighed. 'You're in no position to throw stones, Molly.'

'No,' admitted Molly with candour, 'no I an't.'

With that the two women parted to go about their household chores, coming the closest they would ever get to talking about the man who had shared both their beds.

Johann walked home in a sombre mood. True to his indecisive nature, he still did not know what to do. He still wanted both women, and did not want to let go of either. He knew it was a selfish and arrogant way to be, but he could not help his emotions. Not for the first time did he wish he were two people and able to have both lives. Despair closed around his heart like winter ice.

There had been a heavy frost in the night and the crisp grass on the edge of the road made swishing sounds as he walked through it. In the stark, hoary hedgerows, he could see the birds' nests of last season, bare and empty. They seemed symbolic, somehow, of a broken and dispersed family. So too, the holes in the now exposed banks of the ditch, which had been vacated by summer creatures. Yet he kept remembering the words of his mistress, telling him how happy he would make her if he left his wife and family and came to her.

Above him, the cumulo-nimbus clouds gathered in tall dark towers, threatening either hail, sleet, snow or rain. They loured over the horizon, as if watching him, waiting for the moment to let go a deluge and make his misery complete.

When he arrived at the cottage, Sally was alone, the children having been taken out for a walk by the nanny. He saw her through the window, cutting something out of paper, a panel shape which she would use to make a section of a new dress. He watched her work, her slim fingers moving nimbly. Something ached inside him. He felt himself to be a pathetic and wretched creature beside this woman.

He opened the door and entered. She looked up at him and smiled. He stood there, still in his hat and coat, the door open to the darkening elements.

'Sally,' he said, 'I have something dreadful to tell you. I have been unfaithful to you.'

Her face dropped then, unhappiness spreading across her lovely features. 'I know,' she said. 'I've cried about it. But I've stopped all that now. You can't keep on cryin' for ever, can you? What do you want to do?'

'Sally, I don't know. I think I have to leave.'

She lifted her head then, looking more regal than any *lady* of his acquaintance. Her features had a defiant look to them as she tilted her chin. 'Well, you'd better go then, if you have to. I don't want you to, but I can't stop you, can I?'

In the face of this noble woman he felt utterly humble. There were no recriminations, no insults or abuse, no scenes of tragedy. Only a quiet insistence that he make up his mind at last and do what he had to do. She sat on the rug before the fire, slim, dark and sensual, and mocked his stupidity with her simple directness. If she had argued, or been angry, he could have coped with it more easily: an angry confrontation would have been much more to his liking. She did not. She stayed calm and serene and called for a decision.

He started weeping then. 'I'm so sorry, Sally. I would beg your forgiveness, but I'm not worth it.'

'No, you're not worth it at the moment, for to be truthful, Johann, you look a bit silly. Maybe if you stay, we'll find you're worth a bit more than you seem to be at the moment, eh?'

He fell on his knees beside her and took her hand in his own. 'Do you think we could go on, knowing what I've done, and still be happy?'

She smiled at him. 'Well, you haven't killed nobody, have you? Not yet, anyhow.' She gave a little laconic laugh. 'Me neither, though I come close to it, once or twice. I nearly killed you and her, both, if I could've got me hands on her.'

'Oh, God, I'm sorry.'

'Does this mean you're staying then?'

'Yes,' he said in a small voice, thinking she was now going to erupt with all the passion of which he knew she was capable.

'In that case, you can go and tell her goodbye, can't you?' she said, still calm, 'an' I don't want you back in here until that's done. You can't keep making promises all round and breaking 'em the next minute. Go and tell her, or stay there, one or the other.'

His heart was pounding in his chest as he stood up. 'Yes, I will have to, won't I?'

'Now, Johann.'

'Now,' he agreed.

Chapter Thirty-two

At the time Sally was battling to save her marriage to her dithering, procrastinating husband, Kate received one of the greatest shocks of her life.

It was ten o'clock in the morning, and Kate was on her way to Rochford market using the pony and cart. She had with her on the cart several barrels of dried mussels to sell. These were inferior but by no means inedible stock which could not be sold to regular customers. They were either too small or a little past their prime gathering date, but would make excellent soup for those who liked it.

The market square was crowded and sectioned off into straw-strewn pig, sheep and cattle pens. Men clustered around these pens, poking, feeling and studying the animal flesh within them, arguing over prices, while the domestic stock itself was squealing or snorting, running around and crashing into barriers, stamping hooves on the cobbled ground, and generally adding to the racket. The smell of dung was in the air, a stench so familiar that the locals hardly knew it was there.

There were horses for sale and several dark-faced, dark-eyed gypsies were wandering around, some holding a stick conspicuously in their right hand to indicate that they were selling rather than buying. Kate knew you had to be sharp if you bargained with a gypsy, for they were reputed to be the world's canniest horse traders. There were gypsy women too, with their embroidered fabrics for sale, and local farmers' wives selling bottled fruit, honey, jam, winter vegetables and other fare. It was a busy, colourful spectacle: Kate never failed to feel invigorated by a visit to the marketplace.

There was a sharp nip in the air this morning, animals and humans alike were emitting clouds of vaporous breath. Kate led her pony to the horse trough, where someone had already broken the thin layer of ice on the surface. Sprigs of steam blew from the pony's nostrils as he lapped up the water.

A gypsy sidled up to Kate, offering to buy her beast from her. She politely refused, and the man nodded and moved away, his lurcher at his heels. Landowners like the squire maintained that the gypsies were thieves and rogues who stole anything they could get their hands on, but Kate and other country folk knew them to be as honest as any others. It was true that there were thieves amongst them, but no more than in any other community. They poached on the squire's land, but that was not regarded as a crime so much as a bending of rules set by rich and powerful men, and therefore legitimate as far as most country folk were concerned. The hare and the rabbit were put there by God to feed ordinary people, and if a pheasant found its way into the sack, well, hard luck on the bird and the landowner. The locals and gypsies alike saw the squire as being a borrower rather than an owner of land, water and sky. God was the holder of the property; so long as you thanked Him properly, before meals, the Lord would surely not mind you taking what you needed to fill your children's bellies.

Kate got her business over with fairly quickly, selling by the whole barrelful, rather than having to parcel out the contents. One barrel might keep a large family in soup for the whole winter, and the dried mussels were cheap enough. Two of the barrels were purchased by the owners of Wick Farm and Southchurch Hall, and another three by the manager of Sutton Hall. She kept a single barrel for the vicar of St Andrew's Minster, at Ashingdon, which she was to deliver directly to the vicarage next to the church.

Kate then wandered around the market, nodding to acquaintances, noting who was there and who was not, in case Jack wanted to know – for business purposes. Standing in a small group were John Nottidge, Sam Keble and Nehemiah Rogers, three rival mussel farmers from old established Essex families, Nehemiah Rogers being a descendant of the notorious Fleet parson, John Rogers, who was burned at the stake in the sixteenth century. Ernest Fothergill and John Imrie were talking earnestly together, while John Forward and Tom Larkin snared John Gibson in passing and pointed to William Pulley, the blacksmith, working away in a shower of sparks at his open forge, beating out an iron rhythm on shoe and anvil as masterfully as any musician. Martin Brethon, the cooper, was plying his trade just off the alley, hooping old barrels, selling new ones. Josiah Church, the wheelwright, stood at the entrance to South Street, his wheels stacked like a pile of giant coins beside him.

When she felt she had stayed long enough, Kate left the square and headed towards home.

On her way to Ashingdon, a short distance of two miles from Rochford square, she passed one of Jack's men on the road. Jiz Fowler was hunched and morose as she drew up alongside him. He looked at her and a scowl crossed his features. He seemed to be walking aimlessly, with no purpose in mind, and she asked him if he would like a lift on the cart.

'Yes, missis, thank'ee missis,' he growled, swinging himself up beside her.

Kate was not particularly fond of Jiz Fowler. He was a crabby-looking man with grey matted hair, and smelled constantly of shellfish. His face was always covered in a layer of grime and she had once, as a young and cheeky girl, asked him whether he ever washed.

'Not the top 'alf, for the bottom 'alf on me gets washed every time I wades out to the mussels. Me legs and waist is as clean as a whistle, and if them bits is cleaned twice as offen as others clean 'em, why, I can't be blamed for not worriting about the top 'alf on me body, can I?' was his reply.

She put up with smell now without complaint because she sensed that Jiz Fowler was not in a good mood. 'Shouldn't you be at work, Jiz?' she said, flicking the pony's rump with a switch. The cart rolled forward.

Jiz looked at her with a dark expression. 'Yor 'usband, damn his soul, 'as put me out.'

Kate was puzzled. 'What do you mean, put you out?'

'I mean,' said Jiz, the tears suddenly springing to his eyes and his previously threatening expression collapsing into dirty creases, 'I ain't got no job no more. Thirty-seven year I worked for that man, an' now I'm gettin' old, he throws me out on me backside. It ain't right.'

Kate was shocked at the news. While she had little time for Jiz Fowler as a man, he had certainly been one of Jack's most hard and loyal workers over the years, and had been one of Jack's father's main musselmen. Surely Jack could not have thrown the old man out simply because he could not work as hard as he used to? In Kate's eyes, you did not do that to ageing employees.

'Did you steal something, Jiz?'

No,' he groaned, the uncharacteristic tears streaming down his cheeks and making pale channels through the dirt, 'I ain't done nuthin', truly I ain't, missis. He jus' said I was gettin' too slow. Me! Who worked his fingers to the bone for that... beg pardon, that *skulker*. Why I did so many shady things for that man, 'e owes me my livin'.'

'What do you mean, "shady things"?'

Jiz shook his head and looked at her slyly. 'Ah, Missis Kate, you don't know the 'alf of it, you don't. That there man o' yourn 'as done some terrible things to folk around 'ere, including your good self. He's cheated widders out of their land and bought the roofs from over the 'eads of the poor and needy, 'e has.'

Kate was aware that Jack often cut close to the line between the legal and the criminal, but she had always regarded him as an unethical businessman rather than an outright scoundrel. She said this to Jiz Fowler, who half agreed with her, but said there were some things that Jack had done which could definitely be regarded as a crime.

'One of them things was on your own dad's oyster beds, missis, and I'll tell you that for owt.'

Suddenly, Jiz clamped up, thinking he had said enough, for Jack had a wicked temper and if he gave too much away Jack would hunt him down and then God knew what would happen. He did not believe Jack Rockmansted was beyond murder, if he felt he had been slighted enough.

Kate, however, wanted to know more, and stopped the cart. 'What about my father, Jiz? Come on, out with it.'

Kate's heart had gone cold. She had a faint inkling of what Jiz Fowler was talking about, a tiny suspicion, for now that she knew how her husband operated on others, it was of course fairly obvious how he might have been instrumental in the downfall of her own father's business. She wanted to know, now, what the man had done to Edward.

'Jiz, if you don't tell me what you're talking about right now, I shall go straight to the constable and have you arrested.'

This was an idle threat, but Jiz did not know that. The old man went pale and began visibly to shake. 'Don't do that, missis. None of it were my fault. He made me do 'un.'

'What did he make you do, Jiz?'

'I dunno.'

'Yes you do, and I'm going to the constable.'

'Oh, missis, don't do it. I'm an old man an' I'll die in that there jail, quick as quick. Me old bones won't take to livin' in stone cells.'

'Jiz, I *have* to know.'

And she did have to know. Now that some dark beast had been woken from its sleep, she had to know what it looked like, what it had done to her and her family. Jiz Fowler could describe that beast to her in all its detail.

Jiz Fowler, more terrified of jail even than what Jack Rockmansted might do to him, told her what had happened. He had poisoned her father's oyster beds, he told her, with sewage taken from the typhus ward of Rochford hospital. He and Jack Rockmansted had done it late at night, when the world was asleep. They had emptied buckets of the foul semi-fluids into the shallow waters of the beds at low tide, for three nights running, and the result was poisoned oysters.

Kate was shocked to the very core of her being. Jack Rockmansted had destroyed her family – not just her father's business, but her whole family – in order to drive out the oyster farming from the River Roche. The news stunned her and for a moment she could not think properly. Then, as her mind began to thaw, there came in the wake of the shock a terrible anger, a fury she had not felt before. This man, this *beast*, had done this thing to her, then made her his wife. If he had done that, what else had he done? What other terrible deeds had he perpetrated, against her as well as others? He was a monster, plain and simple. A devious, evil monster. How could she have lived with such a man? How could she have *slept* with him, borne his child?

'I couldn't but help it, missis,' Jiz was mumbling as the cart rolled on. 'It twern't my fault.'

She pitied the old man as well as despised him. He had been Jack's instrument all his life. But she couldn't kick him now he was down. She told him to be quiet, she was not going to do anything about it – well, about Jiz anyway.

She dropped Jiz Fowler off at the top of Ashingdon hill, made her delivery to the vicarage, and then went inside the church itself to pray. She knelt down between the piscina and the James II royal coat-of-arms, beneath the fourteenth-century window. There she prayed to God that she would not resort to violence when she faced her husband again. At the moment she felt like driving a knife into his heart, and ridding the world of him for ever.

For a time she prayed silently and, when she felt calmer, she climbed to her feet and stood next to the north window where a white light burned constantly above the fourteenth-century aumbry, a place where the sacred sacrament was reserved for the communion of the sick and dying. There was a statue of the Virgin Mary on a sill by the aumbry, which Kate touched with her fingertips, trying to gather some of the inner peace which was evident in Mary's expression.

She left the Viking-built church and climbed back on the cart, where the pony was waiting patiently to return to Stambridge. As she rode home Kate still felt full of vengeful thoughts and composed remarks which she intended to fling at her husband when next she encountered him.

Then suddenly she fell into a state of despair. What was she to do now? Jack Rockmansted was the father of her son, and if she gave up the father, would she see her son again? Jack was devious enough to poison the boy against her, as he had poisoned the waters of her own father's oyster beds.

Yet she could not continue to live with him, not in the same house. He would have to find her another place to live. He could afford it. She would write to Jamie and tell him . . . tell him what? That his father was a monster? How could she do that? Her hate for Jack did not extend far enough for her to contemplate turning his son against him, for that would destroy Jamie too.

In order to protect Jamie, she had to remain silent about Jack's deeds. She could not let the young man think his father was evil, or he might come to believe that there was something wrong with him too: the sins of the fathers visited on the sons. No, Kate would have to find some other way of explaining her absence from the house.

What a terrible mess this new knowledge had made of her life: but it could not be undone. She would charge Jack with the accusation, as stated by Jiz Fowler, and she would know by his eyes, by his face, the truth. There was a small ember of hope within her that he was innocent of the crime, but even as it glowed, she recognised that it was no more than a tiny, dying spark.

Chapter Thirty-three

Kate intended to confront her husband the moment he walked through the door that evening. She was not a woman to sit and brood, nor could she convince herself that Jiz Fowler had been lying, for she could not believe such a straightforward simple man could make up such a story. So, she prepared herself throughout the day for the ordeal, and when Jack entered the cottage, wet through from the rain, she pounced on him like an enraged panther.

'You poisoned my father's oysters!' she cried.

Jack stopped in his tracks, looking startled. 'What are you talking about, woman?'

He shook his coat, the water spraying the parlour floor. Rivulets ran from the brim of his hat, down on to the recently purchased rugs. He removed his outer garments carefully, and hung them up behind the door. Having gained time by these actions, he seemed to have composed himself, but Kate had watched him throughout, had read all the changes of expression his features had taken.

'It's *true*,' she cried. 'You destroyed my father's business. You murdered my father.'

'I did not murder your father. The old fool walked out into the marshes and killed himself.'

'He did it because he thought people had suffered through eating his oysters and his whole life collapsed around him. How could you do a thing like that? We were no real threat to you. Your business would still have prospered, even if we had continued to sell our oysters.'

Jack's expression changed now. He slammed a fist down on the table. 'You were in my river!' he thundered. 'That was justification enough for *anything*. If someone poisoned your damned oysters, it was your own fault. The Roche is a musselman's river. If you wanted to farm oysters, you should have leased parts of the Crouch, where all the other damned oystermen ply their blasted trade. Well, you took the consequences of intruding upon our river. It was your father's fault, damn him.'

'Your river,' snarled Kate. 'Who are you? The Lord Almighty? You own the earth, do you, you pompous ass?'

He stepped forward and struck her, sharply across the face with the back of his hand. As she went spinning away from him, he kicked at her legs with his booted foot. Kate cried out and crashed down on the grate, dangerously close to the fire.

Molly had heard the noise and entered the room from the kitchen a few moments later. She stared at Kate, who was struggling to get to her feet. An ugly welt had appeared on Kate's cheek. Jack was standing by, looking menacing. Molly helped Kate to her feet, saying, 'Jack, what have 'un done?'

'You shut your mouth, woman,' snapped Jack, 'and get back in the kitchen where you belong.'

'Don't talk like that, Jack,' wailed Molly.

'I'll talk to you how I like. You're a hired woman. Any more of your lip and you'll be out on the street.'

Molly stared at him, then ran through the open kitchen door and slammed it behind her.

Kate said, 'Brave man, fighting women.'

He raised his hand again but now she had hold of the poker which she had snatched from the grate. 'You touch me once more, Jack Rockmansted, and I swear I'll take your head off your shoulders.'

The hand was lowered slowly and Jack walked across the room, threw himself into a chair, and removed his boots. He seemed suddenly to be amused, for there was a smile around his lips. He warmed his hands by the fire. 'You don't know the half of it, woman,' he said, 'and you never will. One thing is certain. You're my wife. You'll do as I say. How you got to be my wife is neither here nor there, and I don't give a bloody tinker's damn what you think of me, but you'll do as you're told in my house.'

She lifted her head, sticking out her chin. 'I want another house,' she said.

He snorted, looking up at her. 'What?'

'I want a house of my own, away from you.'

'You can go to hell, woman, that's what you can do. If you think I'm going to fancy around buying little houses for you, so that you can nurse your black feelings against me in your own private cubby hole, you're wrong. You get nothing from me, you understand, *nothing*. I'm not throwing good money away on a cold witch like you. Why,' he laughed, 'you can't even satisfy a man in bed. Molly is ten times better at that than you ever was. Why do you think your precious Simon Wentworth never came back for you? He'd seen the world by then and known a few women, is my thinking, and he knew what he would be getting.'

'You leave Simon out of this.'

Jack stared at her without compassion. 'I could tell him how cold you are in bed.'

'Even if it was true, he wouldn't need you to tell him,' she said in sudden triumph.

It took a second for this to sink in, and his face clouded over. 'So that's how it was,' he growled. 'I got leavings.'

'If that's how you want to put it, yes.'

She thought he was going to spring from the chair and strike her again, but then he suddenly sniggered, holding his head, as if something had just fallen into place. She stepped forward, standing over him, and raised the poker, but he reached up and grabbed her arm, twisting the iron poker from her grasp.

'We'll have none of that, either, you poor excuse for a female. What we'll have is a little respect around here. I'm the master in my own house. If I kick you, you say "thank you, sir".'

'How can you sit there and call yourself a *man*,' said Kate. 'You're an animal. What do you think your son would think of you now? Do you believe Jamie would look on this scene and think his father a man or a beast?'

Jack looked up at her with a dark expression. 'So, you'd turn my son against me, would you? I suppose you plan to tell him all your lies, so that he loses his respect for his father. It won't work, the boy idolises me.'

Kate shook her head slowly. 'You think I would soil my son's fine mind with his father's dirt? He does think the world of you, but that's because he's ignorant of your crimes. When he discovers them, of his own accord, you'll have great difficulty in retaining any kind of respect, Jack Rockmansted. Someday he'll find out, though not from me. When he does, you'll walk the same path as my father did that last night, because both you and I know that Jamie is the only person you even half care about in this world. You don't care for Molly. You never cared for me. You only think about what's good for Jack Rockmansted. You're a self-centred creature without any true heart. But Jamie is part of Jack Rockmansted, isn't he? Flesh and blood. He's you, living again. And if he were to turn against you, it would be like your own hands trying to strangle you. One day it will happen, Jack, and without my help.'

With that she turned and left the room, ascending the stairs. Her heart was full of fury and her head spinning with plans. She intended to leave the house that night, when they were all asleep.

She was surprised at the top of the landing by Molly, who stood by the casement window.

'I'm sorry,' Molly said, 'what he said about you an' me, it an't true, Kate.'

Kate said wearily, 'Don't worry, Molly. Whatever he says to me now has no affect on me. It's not all your fault. I should take some of the blame, for I never made him welcome to my body, as you did to yours. He's all yours now, lass, to do with as you wish. I want nothing more of him.'

'I'm sorry,' whispered Molly.

Kate went into her room and locked the door. She immediately began packing a few clothes, wrapping them in a bundle, using a bedsheet as a bag. She heard Jack's feet on the stairs, in the hall. Someone tried the door handle, slowly and quietly, then when they found it locked, they went away. She guessed that he was satisfied she was in her room, and that he intended to lay down a few more laws the following morning. Well, she would not be there in the morning to listen to his ranting. Where she would be, heaven knew, but it would not be in Jack Rockmansted's cottage.

She sat on her bed and waited for the house to fall into sleep.

It was not true, what she had said to Molly, about not caring about Jack's words. His remarks about her being useless in bed had stung her to the quick. She wondered about it now, as she had often wondered in the past. Was she indeed a woman without feeling, without passion, when it came to making love? She had no real arts in that direction, having been taught none, but she had thought when she and Simon first made love that there was a natural passion in her which was enough to please a man. Now she doubted that, for why would Jack leave her bed for Molly's if her body, her love-making, was attractive? Perhaps she was one of those women whom men find cold and empty? Could it be that was why Simon never returned to her? Because she was no good at satisfying a man? What about the man satisfying *her*? Jack had certainly never done that. And Simon?

She found herself weeping then, crying for no reason at all, and a thousand reasons.

When the whole house was quiet, Kate carefully unlocked the bedroom door and went down the stairs, carrying her bundle. Tim was not yet in and she did not want to encounter him limping home drunk, or with some floosie on his arm, so she left by the back way. The lurcher under the scullery table got to their feet when she passed through, but her firm, 'Stay,' was enough to make them settle again, their wondering eyes on her as she opened the back door and slipped out into the night.

Once out on the moonlit road, she breathed more easily. Despite the ugliness she had been through that evening, she felt a sense of freedom surging through her breast. She had at last broken from him, asserted her independence, and was striking out on her own. The fields around her were mostly bare, though there were a few with winter cabbages in them. A hare broke from a furrow, zig-zagging over the ground towards a far ditch. Scarecrows flapped in the light wind. The rain had stopped, at least for the time being, and everything shone wetly under the moon.

She took the lane to Johann and Sally's cottage, but even before she reached it, she knew she could not stay with them. They had their own domestic troubles at the moment and they would not welcome a guest, she was sure. There was a light on in one of the rooms, for Kate could see it from a distance. Someone was up late, walking the night, or working by lamplight. No, she could not disturb her friends and place another burden on their shoulders, not at this time.

Where then could she go? To her sister Sarah's place? There was not enough room for another person. Her aunt and uncle in Canewdon were quite old now, and though they would welcome her, it would worry them too much to have her stay. Kate imagined they would be forever telling her to go back to her husband, without trying to understand that such a thing was impossible. Liz was now living in London, an unmarried schoolmistress there. Could she go to Liz? The trouble was, the first place Jack would look when he searched for her would be at the houses of relations. While she would fight tooth and nail not to return with him, Jack would have plenty of sympathetic people on his side to help persuade her to go back. The law would certainly take his part, him being a man, since for Jamie's sake she was not about to divulge what he had done to her father.

No, best to stay away from such houses and go somewhere Jack would never think of looking.

But where?

Kate found herself staring over the marshes. There were empty boats out there, which she might make into something in which she could live for a while. Then an idea struck her. Simon's old house! Why not see if it was habitable? That would be better than the rotting hull of an old fishing smack, whatever its condition.

She took the winding dyke along the edge of the Roche, disturbing the wildlife as she went. Kate was afraid of little except treading on a viper, which was highly unlikely in the winter, since they hibernated in groups, usually in holes in the dyke bank. The birds were quiet at night, either floating like silent boats on the tide, or hidden in the reeds and grasses, resting until the day came back. Even the oystercatchers were not around, to mock her retreat from her husband with their shrill tones.

Kate found the path across the salt marshes: a narrow strip of hardish mud lined by poa grass. It had begun to rain again, and she realised she had been so eager to get away that she had not put on a coat. The coat was in the bundle over her shoulder and, by the time she had retrieved it, she was soaked through to the skin. Her dress clung to her figure, emphasising the shape beneath. Wrapping her coat around her, she continued walking.

The tang of fish-salt-mud was in the air, along with the deeper, more ancient odour of the ooze back on the river banks. There were the skeletons of old wrecks on the skyline: grisly looking objects in the moonlight which might be taken for shapes of animate things. There before the dyke was built, when the marsh was part of the ocean, they remained frozen in their attitudes, their Dark Age forces buried deep in the rotting timbers. Whatever cargo they had been carrying at one time, whether grain, gold or warriors, was now a secret of the marshland.

Kate finally came to the house. It looked as if it had undergone some renovation in recent days. With a sinking feeling she suddenly remembered what Jamie had told her: that Joseph had returned and was living in the house. She would not be able to stay here after all.

Or would she?

Perhaps Joseph might rent her a room, at least for one night, until she could find somewhere else?

Kate stood, undecided, on the porch, studying the exterior of the house. Certain planks had been repaired and some painting had taken place. The porch had been refurbished, in a corner where it had begun sinking into the marsh. There was no light glowing in the shiplap cottage, however, and Kate wondered whether Joseph had gone away again. Presumably he was still a wanted man, though they must have all but forgotten him by now. It seemed like a thousand years ago that Joseph had run away, his brothers had been transported, and Simon had come and gone without even seeing her. A thousand years and a thousand lives.

Well, at least if he was not there she might still be able to borrow the cottage from Joseph without his knowledge. She was sure he would not mind if she left some money.

She climbed the steps, put her bundle on the floor by her feet, and stood before the door. The old iron lion's head knocker was still there, though rusted away until it resembled more closely an emaciated ginger tomcat.

Kate lifted this and knocked hard, hearing the sound echo through the wooden house.

There was no response at first. Then a light spat and flickered as someone lit a match. Joseph *was* inside. A lamp flared into brightness within. Finally, footsteps came towards the door. She hoped he had not been away so long that he had forgotten his brother's girl. Would he recognise her, with the grey in her hair, and her face changed by time?

'Who's there?' cried a harsh voice.

Her heart was hammering against her ribs. 'Kate Rockmansted.'

There was a long pause then, before she heard the bolts being drawn. The door opened and a man stood before her. She blinked, the lamplight being in her eyes, and stared at the man's shadowy face. This was not Joseph, surely?

'What do you want, Kate?' said the man, his voice softer and more familiar now that there was no wood between them. 'Why have you come here?'

Kate took a step back and gasped. 'Simon!' she cried. 'Oh God, it's you.'

Chapter Thirty-four

'You'd better come in.'

Kate stood in the doorway, uncertainly, wondering whether or not to run. This was the man who had jilted her, who had left her waiting for him while he went traipsing around the world in search of his so-called honour. This was the man who had come home and not bothered to call on her, to tell her he no longer wanted her. She had had enough of treacherous men for one night.

Simon broke the silence. 'You're all wet,' he said. 'Come in, before you catch your death.'

She stepped inside and he closed the door.

Turning to him, she said, 'I didn't know it was you, come back here to live. My son Jamie . . .'

'I know, I know,' he said, pulling a chair up for her beside the fire, which had all but died, 'he told you it was Joseph living here. I let him think that. It seemed best. Here, come and sit by the embers. I'll get some more logs.'

He went out the back and returned with an armful of logs, two of which he put on the fire. Then he guided her, his hands on her arms, to the chair. Mesmerised and confused, she sat down.

Simon left the room again and returned a little later with two steaming mugs. 'Soup,' he explained.

As she took one, she could not avoid looking into his eyes. A searing pain went through her heart. He had grown older, it was true, and his face was lined with the furrows a life at sea would give it. His hair had the beginnings of grey in it, just like her own, and he was fuller in the face, in the body. He looked a very strong man now and she guessed his naval career had been responsible for this change in him. He had left her a supple youth and had returned a hard, muscled man.

But his eyes, they hadn't changed at all.

'Thank you,' she said quietly, suddenly very shy in his presence.

'Now,' he said, 'only two questions. Why would you come looking for Joseph at this time of night, and how did you get that bruise on your face?'

'The bruise?' she touched it with her fingertips, finding it tender. 'I... I walked into a signpost, on my way here. I came to ask Joseph to rent me a room. There's been some trouble at home. I don't want to go back.'

'Why?'

'It's really none of your business, Simon.'

He nodded thoughtfully. 'You're right about that, but I have to say there are no signposts between here and Jack Rockmansted's house.'

She shrugged. 'Well, something then.'

He stood up and walked over to the window, staring out on to the black marshes. She studied his hands, clasped behind his back. They were small hands, for a man, but covered in scars. Twenty years at sea had marked him in more ways than one, she thought to herself.

She took a sip of the soup. It was good. The logs had caught now and were blazing, hissing out their blue-green gases, and warming her through. She was conscious of her wet clothes now and wanted to get them off.

'Can you leave the room for a minute, please?' she asked. 'I want to change.'

He turned from the window.

'Of course.'

When he had left the room she undid her bundle and managed to find a dry frock in the middle of her possessions. She stripped off the wet garments, dried herself on the sheet, then pulled on the frock. She then ran a comb through her wet hair, getting most of the moisture out. Then she returned to her place by the fire, feeling more like the woman she really was, instead of a drowned urchin come in out of the storm.

'You can come back in now,' she called.

He entered the room again and stared at her for a long while. 'I think I prefer you in wet things,' he finally muttered, 'you looked less like the Kate I knew in them.'

The subject had been opened now, like a raw wound splitting apart, and immediately Kate attacked him. 'You never came back to me,' she accused him. 'I waited and you never came.'

'I never came because I was in Chelmsford jail, awaiting transportation for a crime I did not commit. Your damned husband could have got me out, but he preferred to leave me there amongst the rats and roaches, to rot.'

She drew back from the fire, feeling a little faint. 'You *could* not come?'

'I heard... I thought you'd got married and he told me it was true. He lied of course, but I didn't get the chance to find that out, not then.

Obviously he wanted to keep me out of your way.

'When I first came home, I passed your schoolroom, and saw you with that priest fellow. Somehow talking with people, I got muddled, and ... and then it was too late. I was arrested as Joseph Wentworth. Jack Rockmansted was called to identify me, and he must have told them at the time that they had the right man, though I thought he'd spoken up for me and they just didn't believe him. They sent me for trial, I was convicted, and would have been transported to Australia if it wasn't for an old shipmate of mine. He finally got the authorities to see the truth of the matter.'

'You thought I was married to Johann?'

'Yes,' he turned away from her, 'I think that was the fellow's name.'

She shook her head, sadly. 'Simon, Simon. You didn't even try to talk with me.'

'You were married anyway, to Rockmansted ...'

'No, I wasn't married, not then. I didn't get married until a lot later, almost two years after that.'

He turned to face her again. His face was deathly white. 'Oh my God, Kate. What a stupid man I am.' He fell to his knees on the wooden floor. 'What you must have thought of me. What a blamed fool. If I had come home, took a boat back to shore – but they never would have let me. I had to go to Tasmania first, you ... and me ... I can't bear it. Twenty damn years at sea, scouring your memory from my mind, trying to hate you for marrying a man I thought was my superior in every way. How could I have compared? A clever man, with an education, with fine gentlemanly manners and looks, and money, and position ...'

'And you think those are things that matter to a woman already in love? What foolish creatures you men are.'

He climbed to his feet and flopped in the chair opposite her. 'Foolish indeed,' he agreed. 'All those wasted years.'

'And did you manage to hate me, Simon?'

He looked into her eyes. 'With great passion,' he admitted. 'If I couldn't love you, then I had to hate you. Kate Fernlee was my whole life in those days. I couldn't just turn what I had inside me to indifference. I had to fill the hole with something. Yes, I hated you. I hated you so much I wanted to kill you.'

'Good,' she smiled, 'because I felt the same way about you. I cursed you from dawn to dusk, some days. I wished I was a witch, so that I could strike you from a distance.'

'You are a witch, in some ways.'

An icicle pierced Kate's heart for a moment. 'A *cold* witch, you mean?'

He moved back in surprise at her tone. 'Cold? Why, no. Why should I think you were cold? I meant you bewitched me, Kate. Every damn woman I ever saw after that, could not compare. I looked at them and saw copies of you – poor copies, not worth the bother. They were all auburn-haired, blue-eyed creatures but, try as I might, I couldn't get any feelings for them.'

'There were quite a few then?'

'One or two.'

They were both silent after that, staring into the flames of the fire. Kate was thinking that Jack had a great deal to answer for. Not only had he destroyed her father, he had been instrumental in keeping Simon in jail, and had poisoned her former lover's mind against her. His deviousness seemed unbounded. He wove intricate plots in order to get just what he wanted out of life, and when he was tired of things, even wives, he just threw them aside like used rags.

She and Simon had talked about hate, and knew that love could be turned into such a feeling when the passion was strong enough. Yet she felt no hate for Jack, only a cold contempt for a man whose soul was bare of any real goodness. He was a selfish, unfeeling creature, of no worth. She wanted nothing more to do with him, ever, and only hoped he would not turn her son against her. It was a hollow hope, for Jack would not be as indifferent to her fate as she was to his.

'May I stay here?' she asked Simon, after a while. 'Just for the night. Until I can find somewhere else to live?'

'Of course,' he replied. 'You can have my bed. I'll sleep down here.'

'There must be other bedrooms.'

'I'd rather be down here.'

She shrugged, not knowing what to think. 'If you believe that's best. I don't really want to turn you out of your own room, though. I can just as easily sleep by the fireside as you.'

He shook his head emphatically. 'This is my house, we do things my way. I'm a crusty old bachelor – an ancient mariner. I like to give the orders on my own ship.'

'Not so old,' she said. 'So you never married?'

'I told you, they couldn't compare,' and with that he left the room. Kate sat deep in thought, the warm feeling inside having little to do with the blazing fire. *A cold lover, eh, Jack Rockmansted, and another man could not forget?* For the first time in many years, she felt some pride in herself, though her heart bled for Simon, who seemed to have been hurt beyond all help by the things that had conspired to keep them apart. Still, it was too late: they were two different people now. The Kate of yesteryear was gone, as was the Simon she had known. There was no way to repair the damage of the past, only to accept it. You couldn't turn back the clock and make things right again.

When he returned and told her the room was ready, she impulsively reached out and touched his hand. 'Do you still hate me, Simon?'

He stared down into her eyes. 'Hate you? No. How could I hate you, for you turn me upside-down with one look. I made a terrible mistake, Kate, and it's myself I should hate, not you.'

She shook her head, but finding nothing more to say, took a candle from the mantel and lit it in the flames from the logs. Then she bid Simon good night and climbed the stairs, the candle chasing away the shadows in front of her. At the top, she paused, and as if he had been expecting this halt he called up the stairs after her, 'Third room on the right.'

'Thank you,' she called back down to him.

'The uh... it's out the back, if you should want it during the night. Take a light, it's dark out there.'

'Yes,' she answered. 'Thank you.'

She found the room and on entering saw that he had put a pink bedspread on the bed, which she guessed must have been his mother's. Kate was touched at this thoughtfulness, this attempt at making her feel a little at home. She undressed and slipped between the blankets, feeling warm and comfortable. A few moments later, she heard him outside the door. She gripped the blankets tightly around her, but he did not enter the room. She heard him placing something down on the floor.

'Water and basin,' he said quietly through the door, and then she heard him going down the stairs.

Relaxing, she ran the day's events through her mind and marvelled at how much had happened in so short a time. For years life had gone by, grey days following on grey days, then suddenly, all in the space of a few hours, she had learned that her husband was a common criminal and that her childhood sweetheart had returned to his home without a wife. Her life had been turned upside-down and she wondered what the next day would bring. She certainly could not expect to stay with Simon, but she would have time to think, at least, and to prepare for the future.

Kate slipped into a half-sleep, with the wind and rain rattling at the shutters. It was not an annoying sound. It seemed comforting. She was aware of Simon walking around restlessly, in the room below, then on the porch. Poor Simon, she thought, he's had a shock too. He couldn't have been expecting his old fiancée to turn up on his doorstep in the middle of the night asking for sanctuary. Now, she guessed, he was trying to come to terms with the fact that he had her under his roof. She determined, in the morning, to absolve him from any responsibility for her: it was not fair to burden him like this; she must face her problems on her own.

It was so good to see him again, though, she thought, dreamily as sleep began to overcome her at last. He looks handsome and strong, just as I had imagined he would. He looks like Ulysses, returned to Ithaca, to reclaim his Penelope. But Simon's Penelope hadn't waited at the tapestry, weaving by day and unstitching by night, faithful to her lover-king. She had gone and married one of the dark suitors, and Telemachus was another man's son.

Chapter Thirty-five

The following morning the sharp piercing sound of an oystercatcher woke Kate from a deep sleep. There were more noises as she surfaced: ducks quacking in the yard, the sound of wood being chopped with an axe, the cries of kittiwakes. She opened her eyes slowly to find herself in a bright room. The curtains had been opened to let in the day and the weak, slanting rays of a March sun lit the white interior. The jug and bowl Simon had left outside the door last night were now in the room, standing on a low dresser.

She rose, washed her face, then looked out of the window. The whole spread of the dengies was before her, with few trees to interrupt the view. Beyond the sea of reeds was the ocean itself, with ships passing to and fro. It was a wonderful sight. There were birds out there in their hundreds, some on the shallows, others wheeling through the air. To her left was the Crouch, down which skiffs and ketches were moving, and in front, before the broad North Sea, was the Roche.

There was a movement down below, and she stood on tiptoe, looking downwards. Near the rain barrel, Simon was working, cutting logs with an axe. She watched his broad shoulders moving under his shirt as the axe rose and fell rhythmically. Wood chips flew up around him and landed amongst the ducks, making the scatter every so often, protesting loudly. The chickens too must have felt they were under siege, for they were still clustered about their coop, pecking at the dry yard. Smoke was billowing from the woodshed, the smell of hickory chips and smoking fish mingling in the morning air.

For some reason the scene below, and the whole ambience of the house, gave Kate a feeling of warmth and comfort. She had not felt so at peace with herself for many years: it was almost as if she had finally arrived at the place where she really belonged. If it was not heaven, then it was just outside the gates.

Kate left the window and dressed herself. Then she went down the wooden staircase to the kitchen below. There she found some hot tea on the stove and poured herself a cup. With this in hand, she stepped down into the scullery, a foot lower than the rest of the house, and out through the back door into the yard. The sun touched her with its winter warmth and she felt calm and at peace with herself.

She found Simon bent double, gathering the logs he had cut. He had on his working clothes and his hair was tousled like that of a young boy. He had not heard her approach.

'Good morning,' she said, shyly.

He looked up from his task and his craggy face gave way to a smile. 'Good mornin'. Did you sleep all right?'

'Very well, thank you.'

He grunted and stacked the logs against the side of the house, covering them with a tarpaulin. Then he dusted off his hands and said, 'Would you like some breakfast?'

'Yes please.'

They went back into the kitchen, where he had laid some cheese and sliced apple on the table. Simon deftly sandwiched these ingredients between thick slices of bread fresh from the oven, and placed a laden plate in front of Kate.

'Well,' he said, 'you must have been tired, for it's ten o'clock gone. I've visited your house and left a message with the woman there, as to where you are . . .'

She dropped the knife she was using with a clatter on her plate. 'You've what? Why did you do that?'

He stared at her grim-faced. 'I suppose I knew you would balk at that, but it had to be done. Consider, there would be worried people, wondering where you were. You were left in your bed and missing in the morning. They had to be told.'

She was angry now. 'I don't give a damn whether Jack worries or not.'

'Frankly, neither do I, Kate, but I'm not talking about Jack. What's the first thing that would come to mind in the household? That you'd gone out on to the mudflats gathering something – cockles, mussels, whelks, whatever – and not returned. They would send out search parties after you when you failed to come home – search parties of people willing to take risks in order to find you. Someone might have been killed, Kate, looking for you out on the mud.'

She hung her head and bit her lip, the anger gone. 'I didn't think of that.'

'No, well, you're not thinking too straight at the minute, because you've got your head full of bitterness against Jack. I'm just explainin' that it had to be done, you understand. You don't have to go to him. That's up to you.'

She looked up sharply. 'But I'm his wife. Most men would say he had a right to come and get me – take me back.'

'I'm not most men.' Simon bit into his sandwich ferociously.

Kate rose from the table to get some more tea, but he jumped up quickly, and poured it for her.

'I'm not used to this,' she said. 'It could destroy my nerves.'

'This is my house. I do the fetching and carrying here.'

She sat down again and clutched her cup with both hands. Kate was seriously worried about what Jack would do, now that he knew she was living at Simon's house. He would never believe they were not sleeping together, of course, not after what she had said to him. Even if he *didn't* believe it, he would certainly pretend otherwise. It was in his interest and in character for him to make her look bad. He would want to denounce her to neighbours, telling them she was living in sin.

'I'm really concerned about what Jack will do,' she said. 'I'm sure he'll come to fetch me.'

Simon took a swig of his tea. 'He's already been. I met him out on the marshes this morning. He was coming here for you.'

She opened her eyes wide in surprise. 'But . . . I didn't . . . didn't he want me to go with him?'

'Oh yes, but I said that was up to you and I wasn't going to wake you just to ask that. I said if he wanted to know, he would have to wait around for a good bit, because you were very tired when you went to bed.'

Simon took another large bite of his sandwich and nodded as he chewed.

Kate said, 'And what did he say to that?'

Simon's brow furrowed in thought. 'He said . . . now let me get this right. He growled at me in that dark way of his and said, "What the hell is it to you, you damned bootlegger." Yes, I think that's what he said.'

Kate's mouth fell open and she gaped at him.

Simon continued, 'So I said, "How would you like me to knock your head off and put it on backwards?" Something like that. Whereupon he attempted to plant a facer on me with his fist, at the same time as swinging his boot at my belly. The second action was a mistake on his part, I think, for it put him off balance and I merely had to tap him on the chin and he fell over into the mud.'

'He did not?' said Kate, faintly.

Simon shook his head. 'Well, I hate to contradict a lady, but I'm afraid he did, and then he made another mistake, for he drew out a pistol and aimed it at my chest.'

'Oh God,' Kate cried, her hands flying to her face.

Simon shook his head sadly. 'This meant I had to tap him again, with a wooden belaying pin – I carry one in my belt when I'm expecting company – and I think it discouraged him a little, for he climbed to his feet and went off, cursing and threatening me.'

Kate said, 'What are we to do?'

'What are we to do? Why, we go on as we wish. If you want to go back to your home, Kate, then I shall walk you there. If you want to stay here, why then you're very welcome. It's up to you. There's no need for histrionics of any kind, for I think Jack and I came to an understanding.'

'And what was that?' she said, almost whispering.

'The understanding was that if he put foot on my land again I would tear him in half.'

'Oh.'

'Yes. Now I'm sorry if that upsets you, for he is your husband and all, but I'm afraid to say he has the manners of Barbary ape.'

'No, I don't think it upsets me, but . . . can I come with you this morning? I don't want to be here alone if he comes back again.'

'I don't think he'll come back, but if you wish, you may accompany me to the band lines I have laid. Have you got anything at all warm to wear?'

'Not really,' she admitted. 'Perhaps you'll loan me some clothes.'

His head went back. 'What? Men's clothes? Breeches and such?'

She laughed at his conservative attitude. 'Yes, why not?'

He looked a little uncomfortable.

'I don't know why not, really, but it just doesn't seem right, a woman wearing a man's clothes. I never heard of such a thing before.'

'Oh, don't be such a prig.'

So, to Simon's disapproval, she kitted herself out in his breeches and shirt, and a warm sailor's jacket, and wore thick grey woollen socks under seaboots on her feet, and borrowed a long scarf which she wrapped around her head, until Simon said he was bound to declare that she looked for all intents and purposes like a man. She replied that it was better that way, for then he would not be tempted to take advantage of her. He blustered something about no such thing being in his mind and they set off over the marshes towards his boat.

They spent the next hour or so laying new band lines and collecting the old ones from the posts. Kate declared that it was very exciting, the number of fish they had caught, and she wondered why she had never thought of laying lines in this way when she was cockling.

'It's an old family way,' he said. 'Being the last of them, I think it's right I carry it on.'

She sympathised with him about his brothers, and learned what had happened to them all, including Joseph. Then she told him what had happened to her, once her father had been forbidden to trade in oysters. She skipped over the part when she was a cockling girl. It became clear as they talked that many of their letters had never reached their respective destinations.

Kate told him how Johann had given her the opportunity to become a schoolteacher.

'I loved it,' she said, 'but of course Jack made me give it up once we were married.'

Simon said that was a shame because he had always known she was cleverer than most of the men and women in and around the estuary. He said a person should do what they do best, and if teaching was what she liked, then it must be for her.

'It's too late now, though,' she replied. 'I don't want to go back to that. There's been too long a gap in between. But I would like to start some kind of business again.'

'What?' he asked her.

'Well, I only know oysters and mussels, and I can't trade in oysters. The order forbade all Fernlees from carrying out the business. And Jack has the mussel business in the Roche bound up tightly. There's no way in.'

They were walking back to the house now, the fish strung over their shoulders.

'That's a shame,' said Simon.

Jack was in a terrible rage over his beating by Simon.

'He's no doubt been saving that up for years,' Jack muttered to himself as he saddled one of his horses. 'That Wentworth never liked me. Not one jot.'

It was indicative of Jack's state of mind that he had conveniently forgotten all the wrongs he had done Simon Wentworth, including leaving him in prison for four months or more.

Once the horse was ready, Jack swung himself into the saddle and rode quickly to Rochford. There he found the offices of Smeddley and Drove, his solicitors. Jack hitched his horse to the rail by the trough and went into the solicitors' office. He found Mr Drove at his desk and explained what had happened to him.

'Enticement,' said Mr Drove, excitedly. 'The man enticed away your wife. We shall also sue for physical injury, for the blows you sustained. They cannot counter with trespassing, for you had every right to believe your wife had been abducted. A man is entitled to do all in his power to recover a lost wife. Now, Mr Rockmansted, is there anything in the past, in your dealings with Wentworth, which you might wish to tell me? Believe me, once an action starts they will dig out every piece of dirt against you they can find. So, anything at all, Mr Rockmansted?' Mr Drove sat with his pen poised over paper.

It was only now that Jack recalled all the wrongs he had perpetrated, not only against Simon Wentworth, but against others. As Mr Drove had said, once the action began there would be all sorts of things crawling out of the woodwork. Jack had no doubt that others would approach Simon, once they knew a court case was in progress, and provide him with ammunition. Wentworth would have enough with his wrongful imprisonment, in any case, should he be able to prove it.

Jack leaned forward and whipped the paper from beneath Drove's pen. 'Forget it,' he growled. 'I'll find some other way to deal with this.'

Drove looked startled. 'Mr Rockmansted . . .'

'I can't afford you,' said Jack, walking towards the door. 'You damned lawyers will bleed me dry, I know you will. I remember the last time.'

Then he was out of the offices and striding back to his horse. He had come to another swift decision. He would get the community on his side first, before trying anything else. He would go to church, denounce his wife and her lover. There would be much sympathy for a man whose wife had been taken from him by another, whether by force or – what was the word Drove had used? – Enticement. That was the way he would play this game: stir up general feeling against the pair and get the community on his, Jack's, side.

Then strike.

Kate remained at the house for the next three days. There were times when panic rose in her, like a black suffocating cloud, and she resolved to go back to her proper home. After all, she thought, there's still Jamie to consider. Jack would still be angry of course, but even after all that had happened, he was still her husband. People's tongues would be wagging by now and, whatever else had happened between her and Jack, they would regard her as being in the wrong. She had left her home and moved into the house of another man. Godfearing neighbours would cluck and tut and think her a wanton woman.

Kate's guilt drove her as far as a hundred yards from her old home, before she turned away and went to the Haagan household instead.

Johann was not there, but Sally seemed relieved to see her. Kate told her friend everything that had happened since she had left Jack, including the things that she had discovered in her talks with Simon. Sally was suitably horrified by the evil that Jack had wrought in his time.

'Thank goodness you're all right, anyway,' said Sally. 'The way that husband of yours has been talkin' I expected to see you murdered before now. He's been spreadin' it around that you've been kidnapped.'

'I'm in Simon's house of my own free will. I'm not going back to Jack, Sally. I almost did today, but it would be a mistake. I know it's wrong, living with another man, but we haven't done anything I'm ashamed of . . .'

'Can't think why not,' snorted Sally. 'I would've. Do you still love him?'

Kate laughed out loud. 'Good heavens, no. Simon and me? Still in *love*? That would be silly. It's been too many years. Simon . . . I've . . . well, we've both matured. Don't forget we were very young.'

'I see,' Sally said, 'you *are* still in love with him.'

Kate became exasperated with her friend. 'Didn't I just say I wasn't?'

'Yes, but it was the way you said it. I know when you're tellin' lies, Kate Fernlee. You haven't been to bed with him for some queer reason, but you still love him. If you *had* been to bed, you wouldn't even be considerin' going home again, I bet. Hasn't Simon made no approaches?'

'It's not as easy as that,' protested Kate, feeling that her friend was leading her out of her depth.

'Isn't it?' asked Sally, with a trace of bitterness in her tone now. 'You should speak to my husband. He didn't seem to have much trouble in doing it.'

Kate suddenly felt awful. She had intruded upon her friend during a crisis to pour out her own troubles. Why was she always so selfish?

'I'm sorry, Sally, I forgot you have problems too. I shouldn't have come here today.' She stood up, ready to leave.

Sally said, 'Sit down. Don't be daft. This is the one place you *should* come to when you're in trouble. So I've got a few troubles too? You know about those already. I want to help, Kate. That's what friends are for. If we both waited until neither of us had any problems, we'd never see each other, would we?'

Kate laughed sardonically. 'Isn't *that* true!'

'Well then,' said Sally. 'Look, you stay with this new man of yours. From what you've told me, Jack deserves to be in prison for what he's done to you and your family – and to Simon. No wonder Simon knocked him down. Jack ruined Simon's life too, you know. He destroyed Simon's relationship with you and had Simon shipped off to Australia as a criminal. If I was Simon I would have chopped his head off . . .'

'Or something,' smiled Kate.

'Or something. So you go back to Simon and make the best of the rest of your life. I'll get Johann to inform all those gossips just what the truth is behind all this.'

When Kate got back that evening, Simon did not question her, or ask where she had been. It was so refreshing to be with a man who was not suspicious about every little absence. Jack would have wanted to know precisely where she had been and how she had spent her time. It would not have been because Jack was concerned about her faithfulness either, but because he did not like his wife wasting her time, frittering it away on things other than important business or manual work.

Over a meal, Simon said to her, 'I've been thinking.'

'What?' she asked, knowing something important was coming. Did he want her to leave? Did he indeed want her to share his bed?

Simon said, 'You've been forbidden to trade in oysters, but I have not. Could you get hold of the lease to those beds you worked back in the late thirties?'

'Of course. There's payment outstanding, but once that was settled . . .'

'Good,' he said, his eyes on hers, 'then why don't we start up the company again, registered in *my* name?'

She stopped eating, her forkful of food half-way to her mouth, and stared up at him in the gloaming, trying to gauge the seriousness of his suggestion. There was no hint of amusement in his eyes and her heart began to patter a little faster with excitement. Could he really mean what he said?

'What would you want to get in on the oyster business for?' she asked. 'You don't know anything about it.'

'I don't know yet, but you could teach me.'

'Would you *want* to be taught by a woman?'

'If a woman knows more than me, why should I not? I have money, Kate, more than enough. What do we need to purchase, apart from settling the terms of the lease?'

Her heart was racing now. 'We would need a waggon and a horse, wicker baskets for gathering the oysters in, and barrels to transport them to London and other places. We would need a small room, for an office . . .'

'There are rooms enough here.'

'. . . and we would probably have to purchase some sick oysters.'

'We don't want no *sick* ones,' said Simon. 'I've got money enough to purchase good oysters.'

She laughed at his lack of knowledge. 'No, no. *Sick* oysters are those mature enough to produce spats – that's like eggs – which the oyster will shed and leave to grow into mature oysters themselves.'

He looked relieved and stood up, coming round to her side of the table. 'Good. I know this is soon, for this kind of thing, but I couldn't hold it back. I've been thinking about it all day long.'

She looked up into his eyes and then suddenly, impulsively, she stood up and kissed his cheek.

He remained there for a moment, staring at her, and then walked to the other side of the room, saying briskly, 'Well, there you are then, we're business partners . . .'

Just at that moment she wanted it to be more. She wanted him to come and take her in his arms and say, 'I can't stand it, Kate, I have to make love to you.' But he did not and they went to their separate rooms as usual, when the birds had fallen quiet and a peace was on the land. She lay in the pale darkness of her room, wanting his touch, wanting *him*.

Chapter Thirty-six

Jack Rockmansted went to church for the first time in many years and, during the sermon, stood up and publicly denounced his wife and her 'lover'.

'They are living in sin out there on the marshes – wallowing in carnal lust. It is disgraceful that a respectable man like myself should be put to such shame, seeing his own wife turned into a harlot by this smuggler . . .'

He ranted and raved, gaining some sympathy from the congregation, though the Stambridge minister was not altogether happy that his service had been interrupted for such a purpose, and strove to quieten the man who had not been near his church for as long as he could remember.

After the service, there was talk amongst the villagers of going in a body to the house on the marshes, and running the owner out of the county at the end of a shotgun but, like most vigilante estuary talk, it was never translated into action. Estuary people are fairly cool-blooded, and those wishing to start riots about this and that, quickly find apathy overtaking any initial enthusiasm amongst the flatlanders. Once the excitement of the denunciation was over, the parishioners all went home and became more interested in their Sunday roast than the iniquity of Kate Rockmansted and Simon Wentworth, though it provided good after-meal tattle.

Jack then wrote to his son, telling him that his mother had been enticed from her home by a man named Simon Wentworth, who now held her prisoner in his cottage on the marshes. He told his son that he had tried to release her from this man's clutches, but had been beaten by the man's gang of cut-throats: 'for he is a pirate, a brigand, and should be brought before the law.'

In the meantime, Kate was teaching Simon all she knew about oyster farming.

'Oysters can't live on sand or silt, such as we have in the Roche, so we must make them a bed of culch, composed of old oyster shells, tiles, stones and suchlike material. When this has been cleaned and bleached by exposure to sun, wind and rain, we spread it over the muddy bottom. The culch serves as a nursery for the young oysters.

'When the spats develop and are released, they grow hair-like projections, and use these to swim with for a while. When the heavy shell develops, of course, they can't move unless we move them. Oysters at this stage are known as "brood". At the end of the first year, we dredge them up and carry out a separating process called "singling". At a year old the oysters are about as big as a shilling, and if they weren't singled, they would crowd upon one another and their shells would become distorted.'

'I see,' said Simon, making notes while she spoke.

Kate continued with her lecture. 'It takes three to five years to develop an edible oyster. They need to be two-and-a-half to three inches in diameter, at which time the brood is moved to what we call "fattening-grounds". This is usually in April, May and June. By September, they're ready for market.'

'I understand. It's a long time to wait – five years – just to see a little profit.'

Kate nodded, saying, 'Yes, but then every year after that we will have oysters to sell, don't forget. And we might expect oh, fifty million eggs from one oyster in a single summer.'

Simon nodded. 'So, these shellfish believe in large families, and why not, if they can support 'em, though I think I would be a little frayed at the edges if I had so many children running around my ankles. And has our little oyster friend got any enemies?'

'Yes, the sting winkle . . . and Jack Rockmansted.'

They both laughed at this, though it was a serious consideration.

'What else do I need to know?' asked Simon, after he had made them some tea, and they sat drinking it by the fire.

'Something you might not approve of,' said Kate with a wicked glint in her eye.

'Oh, and what's that?'

'Well, you see our little oyster friend, as you call it, begins life as a male, but he changes sex, into a she . . .'

'So, all mature oysters are lady oysters?'

'No, for she changes back again, and then back again, several times during a season, as if the oyster doesn't quite know what it wants to be, a male or a female.'

'Hmmm. You're right. I don't altogether approve. It seems a little strange to me. Especially since it starts out as a male, for females can never make up their minds, but males are usually good solid creatures, with steady minds.'

'Is that so, Simon Wentworth?' she cried.

'It has been my experience.'

'You know all about women?'

'Not so much about women, but I know men are to be relied upon to steer straight course, to a determined point, without getting sidetracked by such issues as whether they would like to be a woman or not. Perish the thought.'

She nodded, suddenly serious. 'Being a woman is not much fun, unless you are lucky in your choice of men.'

'Or have nothing to do with them at all.'

'Or that,' she said, sipping her tea thoughtfully.

When they went to bed that night, they parted at the bottom of the stairs. They were still maintaining their original sleeping arrangements, she in the bedroom upstairs, and he in the parlour. They didn't discuss the fact that they were being accused of impropriety, although Simon at least was aware of what was being rumoured in the village. He took no notice of such gossip, and expected it to die down within a short while.

The next day, Kate went on a shopping expedition to Paglesham East End, to the old trading post where she used to shop when her father was alive. There was a lively March wind blowing across the marshes as she made her way to the village, and the jack hares were boxing each other out in the fields, battling for the best jills. It was the season of new life. The wild geese and redwings had gone back to their northern climes and summer visitors were appearing.

Kate reached the trading post at about nine o'clock in the morning. As she entered, she passed one of her old neighbours coming out. The neighbour stopped dead on being confronted by Kate's smile.

'Morning, Mrs Winchard,' said Kate.

Mrs Winchard pushed past Kate with a frown on her brow.

Kate shrugged, wondering what she had done to upset the old woman. Inside the store it smelled of its combined goods, with a musty-cheesy odour dominating all others. She went to the counter where stood Alan Huggins, the proprietor, guarding his barrels of pilchards, his sacks of wheat flour, his bottled fruit and dried fruit, his ropes, pulleys, spades, axes, and a multitude of other foodstuffs and equipment.

'Good morning, Mr Huggins,' said Kate, producing a list. 'I should like these goods, if you please.'

Alan Huggins folded his arms and did not even bother to look at the list.

'What is it?' asked Kate.

Alan Huggins said nothing, but his wife Jill came from behind a curtained doorway at the back of the store and snapped, 'We don't want no strumpets in here.'

Kate flushed. 'Who are you calling a *strumpet*?'

Mrs Huggins, twenty stones and as formidable as one of Her Majesty's ships-of-the-line, hove into the middle of the store.

'You'm livin' with a man what an't your husband. It an't Christian, and you knows that, Kate Rockmansted. When you goes back to your rightful home, *then* we'll serve your needs.'

Jill Huggins looked as if she knew she was standing on solid moral ground. It was her duty, as she saw it, to lay down the law to this wayward creature she had known since an infant. Kate had 'grown above herself' by obtaining an education and becoming a schoolteacher, and Jill Huggins intended to put her in her place. Alan and Jill Huggins had been the kindest of people when Kate had been looking after her sick father, extending his credit to her when she was short of money, offering assistance. Now, petty jealousy, old rivalry and simple envy were merging with self-righteousness to dominate any natural good-fellowship, and Jill Huggins was smug in her delivery of the ultimatum.

Kate was beside herself with fury. 'How *dare* you talk to me like that? You know nothing, *nothing*, of what has gone on between me and my husband. You know nothing about my situation now. You presume too much, Jill Huggins, on old acquaintance. If you persist in this injustice, you will certainly regret it.'

Perhaps Jill Huggins had been expecting Kate to wilt under her attack, for the storeman's wife looked shocked by this retaliation, and took a step backwards, almost tripping over a sack of flour.

Alan Huggins defended his wife. 'The whole village is talkin' about you an' Wentworth, and is up in arms about it,' he said.

Kate whirled on him. 'Then they had better pray for forgiveness, for they are sadly misguided in their thoughts. Simon Wentworth and myself reside under the same roof and nothing more. He was kind enough to take me in when I was homeless and you shall *not* smear his name with false accusations and slander.'

'You had a home already,' cried Jill Huggins.

'I had a home? I had a *house*, nothing more. My husband has been spreading rumour, has he? Did he tell you he has not been near my bed in years? Did he tell you that he and his housekeeper have been sleeping together. Did he tell you that? Did he tell you he is a cheat and liar, who left an innocent man in prison, and tricked a woman into marriage? Did he tell you those things? Come on, Jill Huggins, you *know* Jack Rockmansted. Just about everyone around here has been cheated by him in some way or another. Why do you take his side?'

'You'm his wife,' muttered Jill Huggins.

'And that's the whole of it, is it? He can treat people with contempt, tread their faces into the mud, swindle them out of their money and land, but if is wife leaves him because he is rotten to the core, those same citizens will rise up in indignation and restore his wife to him, to do with as he pleases, when he pleases.'

Kate looked at both of them furiously. 'You are silly, mind-fuddled fools,' she said. 'What are you afraid of? That husbands and wives all across the country will run away from their spouses? Is that it? Once the chain has been broken? Do you want to leave Alan, Jill?'

Jill Huggins drew herself up. 'No,' she said indignantly, 'certainly not.'

'Then what are you afraid of? Either of you?'

They were silent then, both of them. Kate then noticed several other villagers standing in the doorway of the trading post. No doubt they had been listening to the arguments, most of which had been coming from Kate. She regarded them sadly as they clustered around the door.

'I'm ashamed of you,' she said. 'You listen to rumour and you take it to be truth. You all know Jack Rockmansted. You all know me. I have never cheated or lied in my life. I shall tell you here and now that Simon Wentworth and I merely share the same roof, and that until now every propriety has been observed by him, and by me. However, I can't promise that will last, for I certainly do not intend to return to the man who is responsible for a lot of the misfortunes of others, including my own family. Now I shall leave you to fester in your silly gossip and buy my goods in Rochford . . .'

She pushed through them and out into the open air, still bristling with anger. A young hostler shouted something after her, but was shushed by the other villagers. She ignored them and continued along the lane. It was a long walk to Rochford, but her energy was fuelled by her simmering wrath. Only when she had gone about three miles did she finally weep; even then the tears were still hot with outrage.

By the time she returned to Simon, later that day, she had decided not to say anything to him about the incident. But he had already heard, having been to the fishermen's landing point along the Roche, where they had gleefully told him of the latest news, in which he was a star turn. Simon was a little feared by the fishermen, so there was no condemnation in their voices when they spoke of Kate. They merely told the story and awaited his reaction, which was to their minds disappointing. He neither ranted nor raved about the villagers, nor did he swear revenge, nor even grumbled about their accusations, defending himself. He merely nodded, saying, 'Well, people do talk, don't they? You would think they would have better things to do.'

'I hear you had a little trouble down at Paglesham,' he said to Kate that evening.

She looked up from her work. 'Did you? It was nothing.'

'It sounded like more than nothing.'

'Well, I wasn't bothered. I gave as good as I got.'

Simon nodded thoughtfully. 'They told me you said you could not promise we would not sleep together one day.'

She looked up at him again, quickly. 'It was just words,' she said, eventually. 'I was trying to shock them.'

'Oh,' said Simon, 'just words.'

'Yes.'

They were silent with one another, she going back to her work, he looking out of the window at the marshes. Finally he said in a low, drifting voice, as if he were speaking to the reeds below the window rather than her, 'Words have transformed poor nations into rich ones. Words have made gods of men and dust of gods. Words have built cities, raised ignorance to the heights of knowledge, destroyed armies. Words are what separate us from animals: civilisations have been founded on words. Words have been transformed into wonderful inventions, into beautiful works of art. Words are what bind a man and woman together in holy wedlock. The Bible is made of words. Words are politics and poetry. Words are life.'

He turned to look at her. '*Just* words?' he said.

Chapter Thirty-seven

'I've been thinking,' said Simon, 'that now we've got back the leases to your old oyster beds, we should expand somewhat.'

They were sitting on the porch, side by side, looking out over the marshes. The sky was streaked with purple, it being evening, and the wildlife was settling for the night. A lone tree on a distant dyke was noisy with starlings, chattering busily before they bedded down.

Kate said, 'We've laid the beds with mulch now in preparation for the spats. What are you suggesting? That we take up a few more yards either side of the beds?'

'When I was registering myself as an oyster farmer, I got speaking to the clerk. He told me there are much larger beds up near the Roche-Crouch fork, unsuitable for mussels, which I suppose is why they've not been taken up, but probably good for oysters, so far as he knew.'

Kate nodded. 'I know the beds. They were worked sometime around the beginning of the century, but they're quite large. They used to belong to the squire, but he's no oyster man. He never worked them right, not successfully.'

Simon stood up and paced the porch. 'I spoke on all that with the clerk. He said Squire Pritchard finally let his leases lapse and that they could be bought by anybody who wants them now. So, I went on and bought them, for seven years at first, but we can extend later, if they work out all right.'

Kate, who had been sitting back in her chair, suddenly rocked forward and stared at Simon intently. 'What are you saying?' she said. 'You bought the leases to the squire's old beds?'

'I think that's what I said,' grinned Simon.

Kate gasped. '*All* of them?'

'Yes. Didn't seem no point in buying pieces. If we're going to do this, we might as well do it properly.'

'Properly?' Kate frowned. 'You realise it doesn't end with just buying the leases? We'll need at least three twenty-ton dredging smacks to work those beds properly. You've suddenly taken us from running a small, safe business, into being one of the biggest businesses on the Roche. Once the oysters mature, we may need even *more* boats, and certainly we shall have to hire twenty to twenty-five men . . .'

Simon went to her and took her hands. He could see the worry swimming around in those blue eyes that had once stolen his heart from him. The locks of her hair, falling in copper-coloured waves over her shoulders, caught the dying rays of the sun. In the twilight she looked extremely beautiful, she had never looked more beautiful than she did now, even as a young nineteen-year-old girl. In those days, she had been pretty. Now she was like some ravishing Celtic queen that might ruin a conquering Roman general by robbing him of his wealth, his self-respect, his career, bewitching him with her beauty.

'Kate, Kate, stop getting so frantic. If we have to have these things, then we'll have them. I'll be guided by you.'

'But I've never handled anything as big as this before, you know that, Simon. What if we fail? All your money, the hard-earned pay you risked your life for at sea, might be lost on some bad tide. Twenty years of savings? Surely you haven't money enough, for they do not pay you so well in the navy.'

He squeezed her hands. 'What's twenty years, compared to one hour here beside you? As for the money, you forget, we fought pirates in the East. I had my share of the wealth we confiscated from those devils. The Sultan of Brunei rewarded us with gifts. So did Mr Brooke. Many others. I'm prepared to risk all this, for the sake of doing something worthwhile, doing it *well*.'

'You'd do all this for *me*?' she said, her bottom lip trembling. She stood up and moved to the porch rail, resting her hands on it, and stared at the big red ball of a sun which was slipping down into the calm sea beyond the marshes.

For the first time since she had been with him at his house, he felt brave enough to hug her, and so moved up behind her and, slipping his arms around her waist, placed his face next to hers.

'Don't cry, my darling Kate,' he whispered. 'You also forget I once loved you more than you can imagine. When we were parted my whole reason for living went sailing off somewhere, into a dark underground sea, but now it's come back again, loaded with treasure. I see we were meant to be parted, so that we would appreciate each other the more, for I find you the most fascinating of women still. Your beauty of spirit is beyond compare.'

She smiled through the brimming tears. 'My *spirit*. Ahhh, yes.'

'Not only your spirit. You are more wonderful to me now than you ever were.'

'This tired old body?'

'I ache for it,' he said seriously. 'I have never seen, in all my travels, a form as beautiful as that which I hold in my arms at this very moment. You have improved with the years, until I begin to wonder whether you might not be, in your very old age, the envy of all the maidens in the estuary.'

She turned in his arms so that she was facing him, and laughed. 'Where did you learn such charming flattery, Simon Wentworth? I had better not ask you of your experiences with oriental ladies.'

'Kate,' he said seriously, 'I have never told another woman I loved her.'

She looked into his eyes and saw that it was true. 'Oh,' she said, 'I'm going to start to cry in earnest now. You mustn't do this to me, Simon. My defences are all shot to pieces at the moment. I can't help myself.'

'Do you want me to let you go?'

'No,' she whispered into his shoulder. 'No, I don't think I do.'

A voice came out of the gloaming. 'Get away from her.'

The pair of them jumped apart, guilty at being caught locked together, whispering.

Then Simon recovered and said angrily, 'Who's there? Come on, show yourself, man.'

A slim figure stepped out of the murk. There was a gun in his hands: a sporting rifle. The weapon was pointed at Simon's chest.

Simon heard Kate cry, 'Jamie!'

Adjusting to the light, Simon stared, and saw that it was indeed Kate's son.

Jamie said, 'You told me your name was Joseph Wentworth. You lied to me. You just wanted to get my mother away from my father all the time. You're a conniving trickster, sir, and I am going to shoot you.'

'No!' cried Kate, and she started forward, but Simon gripped her arm, holding her there.

Simon said in a hard voice, 'I did not tell you I was Joseph, and you will apologise for your bad-mannered intrusion into the privacy of my home, young man. It was *you* who mistook me for my brother, not me who told you it was so. Furthermore, your mother left your father because of his treatment of her, and she will return to him when and if she feels he is showing any remorse.'

'How can she return now?' cried Jamie, his voice shrill. 'She has shown herself to be a . . .'

'Be careful,' interrupted Simon, forcefully. 'Do not call your mother any names you might regret for the rest of your life. She is your mother, and has done nothing wrong in the eyes of God or men, except to leave the home of a villain. However, I have to say that I love your mother and have always done so. I would do nothing to harm her and I will not let you hurt her either, if I can at all prevent it.'

The gun was still not lowered, but wavered menacingly before Simon's chest. Jamie said in a choked voice, 'You presume too much. You are not *family*. And my father is no villain, sir!'

Kate stepped forward now. 'It's time you grew up, Jamie,' she said quietly, 'and learned about your father. I didn't want to tell you this, but you force me to. Your father has done many wrongs, to many people, in his life. Some of those wrongs, perhaps the worst of them, were visited upon Mr Wentworth here. Your father left him to rot in prison, when he knew he was innocent of any crime. Your father allowed him to be transported to Tasmania, simply to get him out of the way, so that I would be available to him. He lied, he cheated, and he tricked me into marrying him. Now, you are our son, Jamie, and I love you, but sometimes you just have to see the world for what it is. It's hard to find that your own father is not the hero you always imagined him to be, but I'm afraid it's true.'

A sobbing sound came from Jamie. 'You would say that, when I catch you in the arms of a man who is not your husband . . .'

'It was an unguarded moment,' said Kate softly, 'and it will not happen again.'

'We were comforting one another,' Simon said, 'and before you kill me, I have to remind you that you owe me your life, young man. Now pull the trigger if you still feel you are in the right.'

Jamie stood there, the muzzle still pointed at Simon's chest, and then he suddenly gave a cry like a wounded animal and ran off into the darkness. Kate rushed after him. Instinctively Simon started to follow her, then reluctantly stopped himself: mother and son would have to work things out between them, without his presence.

What a tangled mess, Simon thought, as he trudged despondently into the house. In just a few more minutes he and Kate might have sealed their future with each other. And now? Now he had heard her promise to her son and was certain she would not break it. *It will not happen again.* He had lost her again, just as he had been on the point of finding her. Once more he had almost seized happiness with Kate, only to have it snatched from him at the last moment. Was this how his life was meant to be? A series of thwarted chances and broken dreams? So be it. If they simply lived together, were in each other's company for the rest of their lives, he could be content with that. He would have to be strong, but he would be content. For twenty years now he had been without even that, and had survived. She had brought joy back into his life by just being there, and if he had that, it would be enough.

God please, he prayed, don't let her go back to *him*. Don't let her son persuade her to go back to him. I'll never touch her again, just so long as she *stays*.

Half an hour went by, and finally he heard footsteps on the porch. The door opened and Kate and Jamie entered the room. Jamie's face was tear-streaked, but he came up to Simon directly and held out his hand.

'I'm sorry, sir,' he said. 'Will you shake my hand? I think I was wrong. I am unhappy and confused. It is a terrible thing when one's parents are split apart.'

'Of course it is,' said Simon, taking the proffered hand. 'I'm sorry you caught us in such circumstances. As your mother said, it was an unguarded moment. We were talking over old times and became a little emotional. We are very old friends, your mother and I, and are entitled to comfort each other when we are in distress.'

'You will forgive me if I remain disapproving,' said Jamie, 'but I am not unaware that you are basically a good man. You saved my life and I can't put that aside. I still owe you my gratitude for that action. As for my father? Well, he is still my father. I can't put that aside either.'

'But your mother is still your mother, too.'

'Yes, I know. It's difficult to know what is the right thing to do in such circumstances. One is never prepared, as a child, for such a world . . .'

'This is the *real* world, Jamie,' said Kate, her arms folded. 'The delightful world of the nursery has to be left behind.'

'It's the real world,' replied Jamie, 'but it doesn't have to be hell. I have many friends whose families are intact, whose parents love each other, whose fathers are good, honest men. Reality does not mean accepting that, once you are full grown, your whole world crumbles.'

'No,' said Kate, 'that's true, son. But when it does happen, we have to be strong, and accept that it is so.'

'I cannot leave my father,' said Jamie. 'Whatever he has done, I cannot abandon him, Mother.'

'I understand that,' she said quietly.

'I must go home now.'

'I'll go with you.'

They went through the door then, mother and son, without another glance at Simon. It was almost as if he were no longer there. He slumped into a chair and put his face into his hands. Would Kate return, or would she stay with her husband now? It was a time for decisions for her, that much Simon had deduced. Her son had come to seek her out, take her *home*, and she might not be able to resist this plea. What if Jack told her he was sorry? What if Jack promised to make amends and make things right between them? She had lived with the man for a long time, as his wife, and there must be some kind of bond between them. He surely had a strong hold over her, whatever he had done to her in the past. And, of course, Jamie would certainly encourage her return. In truth, Simon did not really stand a chance. They were a family, bound together by family history, and he was an outsider. A wife and a husband, and a son: how could he fight that? He could not. He might as well pack his bags now and go back to a life at sea, for he could not stay in the region if she did go back to Jack now.

In this miserable frame of mind, Simon made up his bed in the parlour and went to sleep.

Sometime in the night he heard a sound.

Someone was creeping across the floor to the bottom of the stairs. He could smell her womanly smell and his heart lifted for an instant, before he realised she might just be returning for her clothes.

'Is that you, Kate?'

'Yes, it's me. Go back to sleep.'

Just like that! As if he could.

'Did you see Jack?'

'Yes, I saw him.'

Simon's heart sank. 'Oh. What happened?'

'What happened? I told him to stop feeding Jamie lies or you would come and tap him with your billy pin again.'

'*Belaying* pin,' laughed Simon. 'You told him that?'

'Yes, but of course he'll take no notice. He cursed me with his foul language, in front of my own son. At least Jamie got to see what his father was really like for once. I think it shocked the poor boy. He tried to intervene when Jack took a step towards me, but Jack brushed him aside and told him if he got between "him and his business" again, he would disinherit him. Molly came down the stairs and Jack screamed at her. It was a madhouse.'

'You'll be staying here then?'

'If you don't mind.'

'No, we have a business to run, haven't we?'

'We certainly have. Jack's heard about your purchases, by the way, and he is incensed. He thinks we're trying to run him out of business and says that he'll see us dead first. Good night, Simon.'

Good night, my darling, he thought, but, 'Good night, Kate,' he said. 'Tomorrow we'll seek out some dredgers. I shall need your advice on those.'

She ascended the stairs and he heard her moving about in her room for a while before the house fell silent.

As Kate undressed for bed she thought about the scene in Jack's house and her stomach turned over. She had been scared stiff, she admitted that to herself now, but she had also managed to exorcise a lot of her guilt. If she had felt any remorse at leaving Jack before, it was gone now. Had Jamie not been there, Kate was convinced she would not be alive now. Jack would have killed her. She saw it in his face. There was a kind of madness there.

Had that set in recently, or had Jack been slowly going insane over the last few years? It was difficult to say, for she had not looked at him properly for a long time. Perhaps her leaving him really had turned his mind, though she could not believe she had that much power over him. After all, Jack had not been in love with her, ever. Had he?

Kate had also been afraid for Jamie when she left him with Jack, but her son had assured her he would be perfectly all right.

'I can handle Father,' he had said confidently. 'You two hate each other — which makes me very sad — and it brings out the very worst in him while you are around. But Father and I are able to deal with one another rationally when you are not present, Mother.'

She had kissed Jamie on the forehead and left them together, father and son, for it was not in her to try to turn Jamie against his father, even though she believed he was a dangerous man. What right had she to destroy probably the only love Jack had ever felt for another human being?

Chapter Thirty-eight

In the weeks that followed, until early summer, Simon and Kate worked on building up the business. They purchased three dredging smacks, employed twenty men, and began to court contacts. There were some 'wild' oysters to harvest from the old beds, which gave Simon some practice at what was to become his trade. Simon registered his name as an oyster trader with the Court of Conservancy, and they received a visit from the water-serjeant, a different man from the one who had visited Kate and Edward on that terrible day many years previously.

The water-serjeant told them that Jack Rockmansted had registered a series of complaints with the Court of Conservancy, mainly pointing out that his wife was not allowed to trade in oysters, but since the company was registered in the name of Wentworth the court ignored the complaints. There were members of that court who felt that twenty years was a long enough ban anyway, especially since the owner of the old business was now dead. There was little enough sympathy for the likes of Jack Rockmansted amongst any group of people in the district, and those on the bench of the court were no exception.

Jack Rockmansted continued to spread his poison around the county, trying to rouse public indignation against Kate and Simon, but he had made too many enemies in his lifetime to get very much support. There were those who frowned upon the idea of two unmarried people living in the same house, the squire being one of them, but none of them were actually prepared to do anything about the situation. They all felt that it was Rockmansted's business, and he ought to deal with it himself.

Jamie went back to London after pleading with his father not to carry out any of the black threats he was issuing against his mother and Simon Wentworth. Jack moaned that even his son was turning against him, and threatened to cut him off without a penny. Tim told his brother to let things lie, or Jack would destroy himself, but this received the same response as Molly's similar request, which was a mouthful of violent abuse.

'The man is bedding my wife!' cried Jack, his face suffused with hatred.

Tim said, 'You haven't been near her in five year or more, Jack, so what do you care?'

Jack slammed his fist down on the kitchen table, making the lurchers jump and slink from the room, thinking they had done something to upset their master. 'That's not the point. The point is, she's my wife.'

'I may be a reprobate,' Tim replied, 'and a womaniser, but I've never treated a woman the way you treated your wife. You can't ignore a woman's needs and expect her to *stay*. She might very well do so, Jack, but you can't expect it. You never showed her any respect. You have to show people respect, Jack.'

'Who the hell asked you for advice?' roared Jack in fury.

Tim's eyes narrowed at this. 'Don't be takin' that tone with *me*, Jack,' he said, 'for I wager I can knock you senseless if I have to. I may be a little crippled in the leg, but I could always take you, Jack, and you've always known it. You want to make an enemy of your own brother, just keep on abusin' me.'

Jack wisely kept his mouth shut after that when Tim was around, for his brother was right. Jack was afraid of him. Tim was a waster and always ready with a joke, but underneath he was a dangerous opponent. He had been in too many brawls over women not to have learned a few tricks with his feet and fists, whilst Jack had always used other men to do his dirty work whenever possible.

In the Wentworth household, things went on quietly, without too many frustrations. Kate and Simon had established a chaste relationship which, while not perfect in the eyes of either, served to keep tensions to a minimum. Kate had made her promise to her son, perhaps a little rashly, and while neither she nor Simon spoke of it, it was still there, hovering in the air between them. They touched each other as little as possible, and when it did happen by accident, there was always a few moments of silence, even though one of them might have been talking in full flood.

One Sunday afternoon in March, Kate received a visit from Johann, who seemed subdued and thoughtful. Simon, when he saw the conversation was going to become serious, went immediately out to the back, and began doing something in the yard. Kate offered Johann some tea.

'How is your family?' she asked, cautiously, once they were seated and sipping their tea.

Johann seemed stiff and awkward and he leaned forward before speaking. 'They're very well, Kate. Very well. I . . . er, this is not easy for me, but I wanted to say that I am no longer seeing Edwina. Her . . . she has gone away, at my request.'

Kate nodded. 'I'm sure that pleases Sally. Does this mean you will be remaining with your family?'

Johann screwed his hat in his hands. 'Sally has forgiven me and wants me stay.'

'It's more than you deserve, Johann. You treated her very badly.'

'I know,' he said in a low voice. 'I used to say I could not help myself, but I see now that I was just weak. A gentleman does not, should not, allow himself to get into such a situation. I had a low opinion of my wife and a high opinion of my ex-lover, and that is the worst part of it, for I was very wrong. Sally is the most noble and splendid of women. It is in her blood, naturally, not bred into her by generations of gentility. It is not a person's lineage which makes her estimable, but the quality of her character. I should have known that – I, of all people, a minister of the Church. I shall have to leave the clergy, of course . . .'

Kate put down her cup. 'Oh, don't be so dramatic, Johann, of course you don't have to do that.'

'What?' he cried, his pomposity wounded.

'You don't have to do anything of the sort,' said Kate, undeterred by his look. 'No one will ask you to do that, for you have at least been very discreet, and you'd be foolish to offer. You made a mistake, but if you're genuinely remorseful, then there is no need to make a big show of leaving the Church. You do love your grand gestures, don't you?'

He stood up, his crumpled hat in hand. 'I see it was a mistake to seek your advice,' he said.

'Sit down, you pompous idiot,' cried Kate, so loudly that Simon looked in at the window.

Johann did as he was told, waving Simon away from the glass irritably. Simon shrugged and went back to his yard tasks, thinking this priest friend of Kate's was more trouble than he was worth. He seemed to upset everyone with whom he came into contact.

'Think of this,' continued Kate. 'You have just put your wife through an ordeal, which fortunately, because of her strong character, she was able to come through. Many women would have blamed themselves, thinking it was their fault their husband was straying; thinking it was a lack of something in themselves that had sent their man into another woman's arms. When Jack went into Molly's bed – no, don't look away, I know women are not supposed to talk this way, but you and I are old friends, brother and sister almost, and should be able to speak of these things – when Jack went to Molly, I thought it was because I was at fault. I could not please him. Molly, I thought, was superior to me because she was able to satisfy Jack where I could not. I thought myself a poor creature, not able to make any man happy, and was even glad that I had never married Simon, for it would have hurt me more than I could bear to have been disappointing to *him*.

'That's the kind of thing that happens to a woman, inside, Johann, when her husband risks losing his family, friends and occupation, by seeking his pleasures elsewhere. She blames not the husband, but herself. Fortunately, Sally has a great deal of good sense, and in her straightforward way could see that it was not her fault, but yours. You are lucky she *was* able to do this, for it meant she could look on your disloyalty and betrayal compassionately.'

'Yes, you're right,' he admitted, his face reflecting the agony of his spirit.

'Now, would it be fair to her for you to resign your post and put the family into financial difficulties? Simply in order to salve your conscience and indulge your guilt? You have confessed to the Lord, you are contrite, what more is needed? Stay in the Church, Johann, and for once in your life try to let someone else have some of the attention. Sally deserves it. She has been more than the best of wives to you, has withstood the torment you have caused her to suffer, has even forgiven you for it; and now you have to make it up to her. You're not going to do that by resigning your post, now are you?'

'But won't this be the easy way out?'

'What of it? Do you have to take the hard way out and make your family suffer with you, just to prove you can do it? If you have to do penance, go up to your attic, take a whip with you, and flog yourself quietly, without an audience and without the whole world having to witness your repentance.'

Johann looked genuinely shocked. 'Kate! What are you saying?'

'I'm saying that if you need some kind of suffering to make you feel better or cleanse your soul, why not do it out of the sight of the world, and keep it secret. Grand gestures are for those who can afford them. You cannot. You are dependent on your work as a priest, are you not? Then don't be so foolish as to give it up without a struggle.'

He stared at her for a long time, his face showing his anger, but gradually the fury left his features and suddenly he smiled. 'You could always make me see how stupid I really am, Kate. You're right. I'm stuffed full of straw, aren't I?'

She smiled at him and touched his hand. 'You can be a good man when you take the trouble to step outside yourself and laugh at your own faults.'

His face wrinkled. 'Why are you so good to me, Kate?'

'Because I like you. You're an intelligent, thoughtful man, most of the time. And we all have our faults. I have dozens, you know, but I'm not going to display them for your benefit.'

Johann shook his head. 'You have none.'

'That's not true. I *do* have many faults. So does Sally. Don't get to thinking we're angels, because we aren't.'

'It's difficult not to think that.'

'That's because you're a man who knows very little about women. Strangely enough, of all the men I know, Jack is quite astute when it comes to knowing women. The trouble is, he uses that knowledge to put them down and control them, rather than to help them. Sad isn't it?'

'A terrible waste of insight.'

Simon came into the room then, knocking the dust off his boots. 'Have you two finished talking, for I'm fed up with trying to find things to do out there.'

Kate laughed. 'There's another *man* for you. Blunt and to the point, after his own fashion.'

Johann, who did not know this man very well, and thought him to be a little rough and ready for the likes of Kate, said, 'I'm sorry to be taking up so much of Kate's time.'

'That's nothing to do with me,' said Simon.

'Well, it is your home.'

'It's Kate's too, for as long as she wants it.'

Johann suddenly saw deep inside this man, who had been tricked out of his bride-to-be and into twenty hard years at sea, for there was no soft life to be had in Her Majesty's Navy, even priests knew that. He might not know women, but he knew men, and he realised he had misjudged this one on first meeting. Simon, he knew from Kate, did not share her bed, yet he was prepared to risk all his hard-earned cash to offer her his home. And to do so for the sake of a woman who had married another man. There must be something noble in Simon Wentworth, for all his rough ways.

'You must hate Jack Rockmansted,' Johann said suddenly to Simon.

'I did once,' admitted Simon, 'but he's such a pathetic creature I can no longer do it.'

Once Johann had gone, Simon talked to Kate about the business. Everything augured well for the future, so long as Jack stayed out of their affairs and just got on with his own. They did not want to hurt his business in any way, but they were certainly not going to curb their own because it displeased the mussel farmer.

They separated, as usual, for the night, Simon saying at the last moment, 'That man today, he'll need a new hat, for he destroyed the one in his hands before my very eyes.'

Kate laughed, ascending the stairs. 'He gets too emotional.'

'I'm glad I don't,' said Simon, 'for I only have two hats and can't afford an endless supply of them.'

Oh, but you do, thought Kate to herself sadly as she entered her room. *You just don't reveal it to me, my love.*

That evening, when she knew Johann would be at a service, Kate went to see Sally at her home. Sally revealed the fact that now she and Johann were reconciled she felt that Johann's unfaithfulness had helped strengthen her. Though she would rather not have gone through it all, she preferred to review the experience with a positive eye.

'Once he had her, he realised he didn't want her, but she was a tough one, I'll give her that. She went out fighting. The relief in Johann's face when he came back from telling her was enough to tell me that it'll never spring up again. He wanted her gone as much as I did, once the dreams had been shattered.'

Kate detected a certain satisfaction in Sally's tone, as if her friend was much more confident now than she had been before the affair. Perhaps it had not improved the marriage, for the wounds would still take time to heal, but it certainly seemed to have bolstered Sally's belief in herself. Kate mentioned this.

Sally said, 'I used to feel, oh I dunno, a bit stupid with Johann, and with you to a certain extent, Kate . . .'

'Me?'

'Yes. Not your fault of course, it was all in me head. You was both so much cleverer than me, so I thought. Now, with Johann, I know it's not just book-learning and manners and things that makes a good or even a clever person. It's other things, things I've got that he hasn't . . .'

'Honesty, loyalty, strength of character. I always knew that, Sally.'

'Yes, but *I* didn't. I don't say I'm *better* than him, but he's not better than me, like I thought he was. I thought he was a superior person, you know? But he's got his weaknesses and he needs someone like me to help him get over them. Not just this woman, but other things as well. He's afraid sometimes, of things that don't even worry me, and I can get rid of them fears. I can do that, Kate, 'cause I've got things he hasn't, see. I might not know which fork to use on fish, or how to greet a duchess, but I can certainly cut away nonsense when I see it, and get to the heart of the truth.'

'You don't need to tell me that, Sally, I've known it all along. I hadn't realised before now just how insecure you were; I think I failed you in that.'

'How could you,' smiled Sally, 'when I didn't know meself? You don't admit these things to yourself, do you? You just go around with a scared little lump in your tummy, thinkin', "I hope I don't make meself look daft today. I hope I don't make Johann ashamed of me." But not in words like that. Just *feelings*. Well, they're bloody gone now, and good riddance to the buggers. I never had 'em out on the mud, where I could easily have died, so what was I so worried about here, eh?'

So Kate left the house feeling that her friend had at last shed her insecurities about her background, her lack of education, and her hidden fears that she would somehow disgrace her husband. Sally was a changed, confident woman, while she, Kate, was . . . what? She felt like a bundle of problems and troubles at that very moment, but perhaps she too would win through and find new strength?

Chapter Thirty-nine

Hatred against his enemies festered in the mind of Jack Rockmansted over the passing months. Sleep would not come to him as his head spun with poisonous thoughts. He paced the floor at night, vowing revenge, using his expletives to damn those who had crossed him. Dawn would see him, sitting at the kitchen table with black-ringed eyes, still deep in bitter plans for the destruction of his enemies. Jack was convinced that his wife and her lover were trying to drive him out of business, ruin him for good.

'She's trying to get her own back,' he told himself. 'She wants to see me grovelling. Well, that won't happen. I won't let them grind me into the dirt. My name ain't Edward Fernlee, it's Jack Rockmansted. We'll see who gets trod into the mud.'

Molly pleaded with him to leave well enough alone, but he damned her too, and told her if she didn't keep her mouth shut she would be out on her backside.

'Don't you cross me too,' he snarled at her. 'I won't have it. I will not be brooked. People have to pay for coming up against me, and if you're not with me, then you're against me, and I'll destroy you along with them.'

With each new day came a fresh revelation about his enemies' activities. Their business was expanding at an alarming rate. Three smacks had been purchased and twenty men hired with the promise of more jobs to come in the neighbourhood. As more and more of the Roche was leased to the new oyster company, Wentworth Oyster Industries, Jack felt the pressure on his own business. He felt pressed in, crushed from all sides.

'They're not letting me breathe!' he screamed at the wall one night during supper and, as if his physical condition was following the same course as his business, he began to wheeze with fury.

He took to going out, in the night, to inspect what they had done during the day. There were the old beds, now mulched and ready for the spats. There were the vast new beds, at the confluence of the Roche and the Crouch, which made him writhe with annoyance. There seemed to be no stopping his wife in what he saw as her quest to dominate the river and drive him from its waters.

'Pirates, brigands, smugglers,' he muttered to himself. 'I'll see them dead first.'

In the villages and town, the talk was all centred around the new company and its owners. Most people listened to Jack Rockmansted respectfully, and commiserated with him on this new development, but none was prepared to go further than a few words. Certain people considered Kate a trollop for living with a man who was not her husband and the tongues clucked and the tongues wagged, but it was all talk. Others simply looked on with interest and privately considered that Jack Rockmansted was getting what had been coming to him for a long time.

After a visit from Jack, Squire Pritchard did consider making representations to the Court of Conservancy, to have a ban slapped on the new Company, but the Reverend Johann Haagan and his own son advised him against it. Both men counselled the squire not to become involved in a battle between two businesses, on behalf of one of them.

'Jack Rockmansted is just using you,' his son told him, 'to further his own interests.'

Once the squire realised he was being used, and could see it for himself, he was very much against assisting Jack Rockmansted in any way. 'The man thinks me a toy,' he said to his son. 'I'll be damned if I'll raise a finger on his behalf.'

When it became obvious that the squire was not interested in helping him, Jack Rockmansted hired London bully boys to intimidate the new oystermen of Kate and Simon's company. They waited on the tow paths and dykes for the workers to come along, and threatened them with violence if they did not find work elsewhere.

'I got a right to work where I wants,' said one oysterman.

'Oh, 'ave yer?' cried a burly ruffian. 'Well, I got the right to punch your face to mush if I feels like it.'

He struck the unfortunate oysterman on the side of the head, sending him spinning down the grassy bank of the dyke and into some cow dung. That particular rogue was not there the next day, when Simon met with the other hired scoundrels, who professed to be innocent of any crime themselves.

'Gone back to London,' they shrugged, grinning at Simon. 'Dunno where, though. 'Ave to go an' look, wontcha?'

'You touch any more of my men,' Simon said, his hand on his belaying pin, 'and you'll have me to battle with.'

'Well, well,' said one of them in mock fear, 'we'll 'ave to watch ourselves then, won't we, eh?'

When Simon walked back to his beds, he could hear them laughing behind him, and knew that he was going to have great difficulty in getting rid of them: they were obviously all replaceable parts of a large gang. As soon as one of them actually committed a crime by attacking one of Simon's men, he would disappear back to London.

The police were brought in, but this kind of coercion was difficult to prove and to stamp out. However, a week after it had begun, Sally's relatives arrived in the area, now part of a greater troupe of gypsies trading in horses, and they camped on the edge of the dengies. Johann received a visit from his father-in-law, who was told of recent events.

Sally's father had never ceased to be grateful to Kate for the many things she had done for the gypsy family, including saving Sally's mother's life and introducing their daughter to a man they considered to be very wealthy and who had given them several grandchildren. Kate was their benefactor, the cause of their change in fortune, and they felt they owed her an enormous debt.

'You leave this to me,' the gypsy told Johann.

The very next day after the gypsies had arrived they walked along the dykes of the Roche until they came across some six louts lounging around on the tow path. The gypsy men stopped, and began to pass the time of day amongst each other. The London ruffians did not know what to make of this development.

'Well, well,' said their leader. 'Wos all this then? A load o' pikeys, eh? Come out of your vans for a bit of fresh air 'ave we? Diddycoi's day out, is it?'

The gypsies did not answer, but soon an oysterman came along the path, walking to work. The louts began to bar his way. When the oysterman reached them, the gypsies stood up and surrounded him, walking along the tow path with the oysterman in the middle.

'Wos your bloody game?' cried the leader of the bullies, and proceeded try to strike the man over the shoulders of the gypsies, whereupon a great fight ensued, in which the ruffians were soundly beaten and sent back to Jack Rockmansted.

Jack raved and fumed over this new development, but the gang from London told him they couldn't fight with ''undreds of bleedin' pikeys' and left him to his anger.

Jack finally came to the realisation that he would have to take care of things himself; consequently he made his plans.

* * *

At the end of April a terrible storm blew up in the Atlantic Ocean. Many ships were lost during the day. High winds drove millions of tons of water into the North Sea and up the mouth of the Thames. Jack saw this as a wonderful opportunity to sneak out and wreak some destruction on the oyster beds and shipping of the new company. Any damage could be blamed on the storm afterwards.

He took with him an axe.

The night was a whirling mad turmoil of darkness, a maelstrom of wind and rain, which lashed Jack's fisherman's oilskins and impeded his progress. He bent his head into the thrashing wind which changed direction every moment. He plodded on through the muddy pools of the fields. He felt elated. Here at last was a chance to get back at his enemies, strike them where it hurt. They had played their last game with Jack Rockmansted. He would see them go under and stamp on the remains afterwards. That was the way it had always been, that was the way it would be again. No one had ever bested Jack Rockmansted in a head-to-head battle for supremacy of the flatlands.

As he approached the dyke, the rain ceased, though the wind continued its onslaught, crashing through the clumps of trees on the islands of raised ground, whipping the reeds back and forth over the marshes. He used the axe like a mountain climber's pick to scale the slippery slope of the twenty-foot-high dyke. When he reached the top he was amazed, for the tide was full in and the water level was at the top of the dyke. The moonlight shone on a vast flood where there should be only a river and some winding creeks. The poa-grassed islands had disappeared beneath the encroaching waters, now shining darkly and stretching as far as the eye could see. It would seem that the waves came all the way from France without interruption.

The wind was whipping up turrets of foam on the flood, driving them towards the dyke. Tons of water were slamming into the turf-and-stone defences of the Essex lowlands. Normally the water would not come quarter of the way up a dyke, occasionally perhaps up to six feet, but here it was, lapping over the top, spilling into the fields and dengies on the other side. It was an awesome sight, an awesome feeling to be witness to it.

Jack wondered about his mussel beds, whether they would survive this attack from the sea. The posts on which the mussels grew had their foundations firmly in the mud, but they had not had to withstand such a scouring as they would get from this tide when it retreated. He needed to make a decision: whether to go to his own beds and see what he could do there, or continue with his plan of wrecking the dredging smacks owned by his rivals.

Hate finally triumphed over all other emotions in his breast. He decided it was up to him to destroy his wife, for even his son – his own son! – had failed him in this matter. Standing on the top of the dyke like a black monolith in the gale, Jack saw that it was he alone who controlled the destiny. The wind and the rain, the water and waves, these were his servants, to assist him in this destruction of his enemies. Only the elements were with him, for the rest of humanity were cowards and recreants, not fit to stand beside such a great man as he. Who was it that produced these elemental agents for his use? Why, God, and therefore God must be on his side.

'God is with me!' he cried out, into the wind.

Jack continued along the dyke path until he came to the place where the smacks were moored. They were in what would have been a peaceful haven, had not the sea joined with the river and swollen the latter into a monster. Now the craft lolled against each other, crashing flanks when the wind and waves chopped against each other, causing conflicting eddies. The smacks were floating high in the water, their masts towering over the dyke. Wind whistled through the stanchions and stays, through the sheets and halyards: an aeolian harp playing eerie dirges and pibrochs. Funeral music, Jack thought, for the death of the Wentworth Oyster Industries.

The dark shapes of the vessels were like crowding beasts, nudging together, attempting to scale the last few inches of the dyke and reach safe ground. Jack began hacking at the mooring lines with the axe, until first one, then two, and finally the third smack broke loose, and went sliding off into the dark waters. Where they would end up, Jack did not care, but he hoped they would smash into some solid place, like a pier or jetty, and hole themselves. Or drift out to sea and be lost in the storm. It was all one to him.

Next he intended to smash down the wicker fences around the oyster beds, but on arriving at the beds he saw they were well under water. The wind continued to lash at his clothes and face with its unseen whips. Jack turned and stared out over the chaotic marshes, where the reeds danced crazily in the moonlight. He could see the lights of the cottage where *they* were most likely fornicating, speaking his name as they did so, laughing at his impotence in this war. Well, he would show them how impotent he was with his very next stroke!

He began hacking at the top of the dyke with the axe, to make a channel for the waters which were brimming the turf-and-stone wall. The axe rang out and let fly sparks whenever Jack struck rock, but gradually he managed to make a small channel for the water to go pouring on to marshland below. He stepped away as this breach rapidly grew in size, taking earth and stones with it, tumbling down into the lowlands. Millions of tons of water were behind that breach, which was quickly torn open, and widened, letting the flood rush towards the house not a quarter of a mile distant.

Jack laughed loudly. They would be drowned. He hoped they would be drowned. Soon a whole sea would be rushing, thundering over the landscape in a forceful wave, taller than the house, as the dykes gave way and fell apart. Such waves were stronger than steel: could bend girder bridges as if they were made of paper. They would smash the house to matchwood. Nothing could save them now. Jack imagined the pieces floating on the calm waters of a new day, the occupants of the house missing presumed dead, and congratulated himself on winning yet again. The crabs would be nipping at Wentworth's lips and eyelids before morning, and Jack Rockmansted would be free of his scheming wife for ever. His only regret was that she would never know it was him who had destroyed her.

Jack began walking home as whole sections of the dyke around the gap he had made came crashing down and the floodwaters surged through, cascading into the marshes with unstoppable power.

Unstoppable power... All along the dyke, far from the original breach, foundations began to crumble. The dyke, one long wall of earth and stone, was like a granite bridge: Jack had effectively removed the keystone. The structure was breached, and the pressure along the dyke was becoming insupportable: it began to collapse in on itself, as boulders shifted all the way along the formation.

The dyke began to loosen as the rocks shifted and strained in the direction of the breach. Boulders began to slip, letting in a trickle of floodwater around their bases, and earth and sand was washed away, first in grains, then in lumps, and finally in great blocks. Jack felt the dyke tremble under his feet and felt a flutter of fear pass through his breast.

He began to run.

Beneath his feet the dyke started to crumble, great gaps appeared behind him, the torrents rushing through, grateful for the release of the pressure holding them back. He looked behind him, then down at his feet, at the crumbling dyke. The fear flew up to his throat and increased to screaming panic. He was staring at certain death. A whole ocean heaved forward, breaking through the walls that had held it back for centuries, thundering triumphantly over the fallen blocks.

Jack dropped the axe and did not look down again, but fled for his life, his chest heaving with the effort of his run over slippery, muddy ground.

The moon went behind a cloud and all was darkness for a few moments. Jack stumbled and fell. He was on his feet again in a second, fleeing from the disintegration which threatened to overtake him. The earth was breaking into pieces, falling to bits under his feet. The mighty flood was carrying all away with it, to another world, a world of darkness and silence, deep and still and very cold.

He almost made it. He almost got to the Paglesham steps and to the solid stone walls and jetties of the fishermen's wharf. There he would have been safe, for this section was like a fortress, built to withstand any flood tide the sea cared to throw at it. He almost made this section, but his feet went from under him at the stile which separated turf-and-stone from solid brick and mortar, and he was swept away in a second, his heavy boots and oilskins dragging him beneath the tumultuous surface of the monster he had unleased.

Chapter Forty

The first wave that hit the house was low and full, and had limited force, since it had come from the initial breach in the dyke and had fanned out and spread as it progressed. When it reached the cottage it merely loosened the supports of the wooden structure. The clapboard dwelling had no foundations – few country houses did – and stood on six stilts of three stones each, which raised it a foot above the ground to keep it free of the damp marsh earth. Indeed at times it appeared that the house was held aloft by the mist that often layered the dengies.

Thus the first flood of water washed under the house, scouring away the sandy bases of the rock supports, rocking and tilting the house, and waking the occupants.

Simon still slept in the parlour, even though there were bedrooms available, for reasons which he had difficulty in explaining even to himself. He knew only that it was something to do with the need to remain in a distinctly separate part of the house from Kate during the night hours. The first jolt had him out of bed and on his feet, thinking there was an earthquake in progress, a phenomenon he had experienced in Japan. Then he remembered where he was and ran naked down the now sloping floor to the door.

As he opened it, the water gushed in over the floorboards, though it was only ankle-deep, and therefore not especially alarming. He stared at it swilling round his feet, scummy and foaming, without comprehension. Then Kate called from upstairs, obviously having been woken by the movement of the house, and he came to his senses. He turned and called to her, saying, 'There's a flood,' then stared out across the moonlight marshes at the distant dyke.

It was then he saw something glinting beneath the moon: something with an urgent pace to it. It was difficult to say exactly what it was, and for a moment Simon simply gazed, as one might at a forest that had begun to run, or a hill that flowed over the landscape. There was something unreal in the smooth advance of this shining giant that curved outwards and inwards in its concave motion.

Suddenly, the image became real for him, and he knew what it was that slid towards him. A great wave was sweeping towards the house, at least twenty feet high and backed by such a volume of water as would hit them like an avalanche of stone. He pushed the door shut, against the wishes of the flood which resisted his action, and turned to find Kate staring down from half-way up the stairs.

'What is it?' she cried.

Only mildly concerned with his nakedness, Simon ran to her, the water sloshing around his feet.

'Upstairs,' he said, 'quickly!'

The gravity of his tone must have impressed her, for she turned immediately and scrambled back up the flight of stairs. Simon was close behind her. They had just reached the landing when the giant wave hit the side of the house, slamming into the woodwork with unbelievable force. The whole weight of the ocean, millions of square miles, billions of gallons, was behind that shoulder of water. It knocked their legs from under them like skittles, and sent them tumbling together down the passageway.

Jack Rockmansted would have been correct – their house would have been turned to matchwood – if the dwelling had been fixed to solid ground. But the house was free-standing so, when the wave hit it, there was no resistance: the cottage was lifted up and carried with the force of the water like a boat. It floated on the flood tide.

The clapboard house and inhabitants were swept along as if the house were a wooden box. It struck standing objects in its path, spinning dizzily before resuming its inexorable journey. Floating debris clattered against its sides as the house was carried along by the flood tide: for the moment it seemed to be surviving each blow, but Simon and Kate knew that at any time the dwelling might hit an obstacle head on and break apart, throwing the pair of them into the rushing waters. If it did so, they would certainly drown.

It was a strange and unpleasant sensation to be inside the careering, floating house. Kate held Simon tightly, expecting at any moment that the house would shatter. She could not understand why it was floating like a boat in the first place, for her head was in as much turmoil as the flood beyond the window. The whole world had gone topsy-turvy in a few minutes, and she just wanted the motion to stop so that she could gather her faculties. Instead, everything raced crazily on the current, borne by the water surging inland.

The feeling was not an unfamiliar one for Simon, but Kate had never been to sea, had never experienced being at the mercy of the waters of the earth. It seemed to her that the world had come to an end and they were rushing to their deaths. She kept praying that it would be quick: she had a horror of drowning, having come so close to it herself when cockling, and having seen so many bloated, half-eaten victims of the river and sea.

Occasionally they struck a sunken object, like a wall or gate, which threatened to tip the house on its side. The force of each bump was felt throughout the whole house. However, though it swayed dangerously, and came close to turning over, it miraculously managed to keep upright.

Sometimes it scraped along slowly when it hit a piece of high ground, its underfloor catching on the ground. Simon hoped it would stick somewhere, come to a halt, so they could assess their situation.

It did not.

It continued to race with the current, over drowned lands, spinning occasionally, cracking submerged posts with walls.

Then, finally, the house jammed hard between the tops of two tall trees, and held there while the water careered on, carrying other debris with it. Flotsam struck the front wall of the house facing the flow with terrible-sounding crashes. A log came smashing through the downstairs front window and slammed into the dividing wall between the parlour and kitchen. Kate cried out in fear and Simon held on to the doorjamb of a bedroom to prevent himself being flung to the floor. Both of them prayed that nothing large – like another dwelling or a boat – would strike the house, for such an object would doubtless smash the clapboards to splinters.

Gradually, the flowing motion inland began to decrease as the flood tide ran out of motive force. Then, finally, it was still. After a short time the waters began to withdraw, back to their original position, almost with the same force as they had used to invade the land. Objects which had crashed into the front of the house, spun around its corners and continued on their journey, now returned to batter the back of the dwelling with equal vigour.

The withdrawal was not complete. There remained behind an amount of water level with the sea: some seven to ten feet in depth. When they stared out of the window, on to its moonlit surface, it looked calm and peaceful. It had become a great inland lake behind the dykes, and it would only retreat with the ebbing of the tide. Only then might shoring work begin on the walls that protected the lowlands.

The wind still whined around them as the house gradually sank and settled between the two great elms that had been responsible for arresting its progress. The water rose to the third stair from the top, and then went no further. Kate and Simon were safe upstairs.

Simon appraised the situation, watching the level of the water against a nearby oak until he saw that it was falling, though barely perceptibly. They would be trapped for some time, but it seemed that their lives were no longer in danger. Anything could happen, of course, but for the moment they could rest easy.

Kate, exhausted by fear, went into her bedroom and lay down on the bed. Her dresser had crashed on its side, the chair was lying in the corner, but the bed was intact, albeit at a crazy angle. She stared out of the low window at the waters surrounding the house. They looked eerie in the moonlight, but strangely beautiful. The world had been reshaped in the space of about fifteen minutes, and she was now a stranger in her own country. She knew not where she was, nor who was near them. There were no recognisable landmarks to pinpoint the position of the cottage on the landscape – or rather seascape – and there was a feeling of being lost in time and place. It was all very unreal, very dreamlike.

Trees she should have known, for there were few enough in the flatlands, stood with their heads above the flood and defied recognition. They looked like phantoms of themselves, in the moonlight, their reflections on the ghostly waters. She thought for a moment that perhaps they were dead, in some limbo place before going to heaven or hell, but then her practical mind won over her imagination and she knew this was not so. She closed her eyes and rested.

Simon too was staring out of the window, on the landing, but he knew where he was. He could see a church tower from his position, and realised they had been carried westwards for about a mile and a quarter, into Squire Pritchard's beet fields. He was feeling calm and safe now, but was very conscious of the fact that both of them, he and Kate, had missed death by the smallest of margins. They might easily have both been drowned. He was experiencing the kind of heightened perception which comes after narrowly escaping death, and was asking himself those questions, providing those answers, which such an experience engenders. *Why have I been concerning myself with petty worries, small issues, when death is so unavoidably near at all times? I should be living life to the second, not fretting over money, status, the opinions of others . . .*

Simon could suddenly see where the significant things lay and where the trivial things stood. He knew now what was important to him and what was not. It was all, for the moment, as clear as a windowpane. It might become fogged with time, but right at that moment he knew what made the world a wonderful place to live in and he thanked God for it.

Still naked, he went and stood in the doorway of Kate's bedroom, staring at her supine form in the moonlight. Then he went to her bedside. She looked so beautiful, lying there in repose, her hair spread out over the pillow. Her nightdress was wet and clinging to her full body. Desire surged through his veins in the wake of an overwhelming feeling of love for this woman who had been dominating his thoughts for as long as he could remember. Tenderness mingled with great passion in his breast. He wanted to hold her gently in his arms, he wanted to ravish her where she lay.

'Kate,' he said hoarsely. 'Kate, my darling?'

She opened her eyes and looked up into his, seeing what was in them. 'Yes, Simon?'

'I . . . I love you. I have always loved you. You drove me mad at sea and you drive me mad here. There's such a feeling in me . . . Kate, I can never explain it to you. It's like fire and ice in my veins. Does that sound like madness to you?'

She smiled at him, opening her arms. 'Oh no, for how can it when I feel the same thing?'

'Do you?' he cried. 'Do you still?'

'I have always, deep down, loved you my darling. I had to push it away from my heart, keep it away from my mind, for I never thought you would return it. I believed you had found you did not love me and had gone away for ever.'

'Oh my God,' he said, giving a choking cry. 'Oh my God, I love you so much, Kate. Those words, they're not enough to tell you. They just are not enough.'

He lowered himself into her arms and they held each other.

'Show me,' she whispered fiercely into his ear. 'Show me how you love me.'

Then his warm hands were now again on her body, like they had been so many, many seasons before, just once in a dreamland long ago, on the dry hay of a little hut. They touched and kissed, his lips roaming over her face, her shoulders, her breasts, her thighs. She delighted in that touch, in those kisses, wanting him never to stop, for the excitement in her was overwhelming, until she could not find her breath and had to grip him hard and cover him with her own kisses, her own touch.

The wind soughed around the eves as they moved together on that placid inland lake, borne by the waters of the world into a new dimension of feeling, of intensity, of happiness. She cried out, for the first time in her life, as the heat of her body suddenly exploded in a great flash-flood of feeling, the waves of carnal ecstasy washing through her body, rippling through her limbs as they had never done before. It frightened her with the strength, the magnitude of its force. More powerful than any sea that breached its walls, her feelings overcame her long-imprisoned enjoyment of physical love. She cried out, in a high, clear tone which might have been mistaken for the shrill call of a startled oystercatcher, on experiencing the sheer euphoria and delirium of having reached the heights of a feeling she never knew existed before this night.

Then, when her own enjoyment had settled into a delicious, warm emotion of spiritual love, she felt Simon's body reaching a similar plateau of feeling and clung to him, holding him tightly, loving him loving her. Then he relaxed and remained with her, whispering into her ear, 'Darling, my darling Kate, of all that's wonderful . . .'

She smiled to herself, not wanting to let him go until the doors of the house were battered down by rescuers, not caring if the archbishop himself found them in the position they were in at that moment. At last she had found her lost man, had found herself, and she was never going to let either of them go ever again.

Chapter Forty-one

When the flood subsided, taken away by the tide, the work of shoring up the dyke began. In such an emergency everyone in the district turned out, even the squire. Squire Pritchard directed operations and they were able to block the breach, using bags of sand and rocks, before the next tide. It would take time to restore the dyke to its previous strength, but for the time being it was safe against any ordinary tide.

A great deal of damage had been done, to crops, cattle and some outbuildings, but the people of the estuary country were used to floods, and they took it in their stride. There would be hardship for a while, but they would cope. One or two old hermits, living in stranded boats, had taken a voyage into the squire's fields, as Kate and Simon had, but it seemed that no one had actually been drowned, since the flood plain had been mostly over the dengies.

After the tide had retreated, Jack Rockmansted's body was discovered in the mud. Kate was upset that he should have died such a death, even though she had few feelings left for him.

The Rockmansted business fell into the hands of Jamie and Timothy. Jamie was determined to be a lawyer and therefore left the running of the business completely to his uncle who, now that the serious brother had gone, became more responsible in his attitude. It was as if before, when his brother was alive, he had no need to be accountable. Now that Jack was no longer there, Tim bent himself to the task of managing the company and even took himself a wife to help him manage the mussel company.

Tim also took it on himself to visit Kate and Simon, to say there would be no more battles between mussel and oyster. So far as he was concerned, the river was big enough for both.

Molly remained at the Rockmansted household, perhaps the only person besides Jamie who actually mourned the passing of Jack Rockmansted.

The clapboard Wentworth cottage, which had stood on the dengies for half a century, until its journey into Squire Pritchard's fields, had to be broken up. Kate approached the squire and asked to rent one of his cottages, similar to the one in which she and her sisters had spent their childhood, and the crusty old squire agreed, provided it was not used for 'carnal purposes'.

'Mr Simon Wentworth will have to find his own place,' said the squire meaningfully.

Kate said nothing, for she and Simon had already agreed that they would be married in the late autumn, a suitable time after Jack's death. The propriety was observed, not because they themselves were concerned about what people might think, but for Jamie's sake: Jamie had respected his father despite his misdeeds, and Kate was glad and proud that he was so loyal to his father's memory.

The three smacks which Jack had tried to destroy ended up almost intact at the far side of the dengies, stranded on the marshland, where the flood tide had carried them inland. There were repairs to do on them, but nothing very serious. The oyster beds themselves had undergone a battering from the flood itself, owing nothing to Jack's efforts, but Simon and Kate simply set to and re-mulched the beds, re-fenced the corrals.

Kate and Simon were married by the Reverend Johann Haagan, as planned, in the late autumn. The wedding took place in Paglesham church. It was a simple affair, which suited both parties concerned. Jamie came down from London and, though quiet himself, was respectful to Simon and wished the couple well. He still grieved for his father and, though he loved his mother well enough, he had mentioned before entering the church that he thought the wedding a little hasty.

When they had left the church and were standing in the churchyard, Kate said to her son, 'Simon and I are marrying more for purposes of business than anything else, Jamie. People don't like to deal with a couple unless they're married. We have to get the business under way as soon as possible, you understand that. Your father would have done.'

If Jamie realised he was not being told the whole truth, he did not reveal it, but he certainly looked happier on hearing the words. 'Of course, Mother, I realise Mr Wentworth is a good man, and you're right. To Father the business was everything. He might not have approved of your choice of groom, but certainly he would have endorsed your reasons for having the wedding so quickly after his death.'

Simon shook hands with his stepson at this point. 'I want us to be good friends, Jamie. I don't want to replace your father.'

In this he too had not told Jamie the whole truth.

'Oh, you know,' said Jamie, looking a little embarrassed. 'I shall need guidance from you. I'm still only a young man and you have much experience of the world.'

'Too damned much,' laughed Simon.

Sally came up to them at this point and threw some rice over their heads. 'Gotcha!' she cried.

Johann joined them a moment later after having changed out of his vestments. 'Well,' he said. 'This is a gathering of hopefuls, I must say. A young man on the threshold of his career, a newly married couple about to break all business records and –' he hooked his arm in Sally's and pulled her to him – 'a fusty old rector and his beautiful wife inviting them to dine with them this evening at the Plough and Sail, by way of a reception.'

Simon said, 'We hadn't planned anything special. We was just going to go home for a quiet ...'

Jamie interrupted with, 'Simon, Mother, we *must* accept Reverend Haagan's offer. I've heard that the Plough is offering quail, from Scotland, on their menu. May we try the quail, Reverend? It sounds quite exotic.'

Johann laughed. 'You can try the quail, young man, can't he, my dear?'

Sally smiled, 'Unless you'd rather I cooked you a hedgehog in clay, Jamie? If you like exotic food, gypsy hedgehog is extremely tasty.'

Jamie made a face and looked panic-stricken. 'If it's all the same to you, I'd rather not put you to the bother, Mrs Haagan. After all, you don't want to go cooking on a day like today. You have to enjoy yourself too.'

Kate laughed at this and put an arm around her friend's shoulders. 'Of course she doesn't want to cook. We'll save the hedgehog for another time. Come on, then, let's all go to the Plough and Sail. We accept your kind offer, Reverend Haagan.'

On the walk from Paglesham church to the Plough and Sail, Simon paid particular attention to Jamie, knowing how the wedding was affecting the young man, and told him privately that he would take good care of his mother, that they were old friends who needed the comfort of each other in such times.

'You know I would have married your mother before,' he told Jamie, 'but circumstances forced me to concede victory to my rival. Now we both have another chance for happiness. It would be foolish not to take it.'

Jamie pondered his words. He was still torn between loyalty to his father and the knowledge of what his father had done. Maybe it all worked out in the end: two men had fought for a woman, one had initially lost, and then the other. There seemed to be a balance in the thing: a kind of fairness.

He still grieved for his father, but no fault could be laid at the door of Mr Wentworth.

While Simon was talking to Jamie, Kate was speaking to her two sisters, who had fallen in one on either side of her.

Liz was now in her thirties, still unmarried, and arts' tutor to the children of a very grand London family.

'Are you happy, Liz?' asked Kate.

Liz, tall and thin, with humour lines around the corners of her mouth and eyes, replied, 'Oh yes, quite happy thank you, Kate. I have a good income, nice accommodations and I am pretty much my own person, you know.'

'What about men?' asked Sarah, from the other side of Kate.

'Men?' smiled Liz. 'And what about them?'

'Don't you want one?' asked Sarah.

'Well, yes, but not as a permanent feature in my life. I have a very nice man friend. We go to concerts, the ballet and opera together. We dine together occasionally. Sometimes we sleep together.'

Sarah's outraged, 'Elizabeth!' just made her younger sister's smile widen even further.

'Well, you did ask,' said Liz.

'As long as you're happy,' Kate said.

'I am, thank you. And I'm so grateful, Kate, that you allowed my education to go on beyond your own – or Sarah's.'

'Yes, it's more than I got,' complained Sarah.

Kate took her middle sister's hand in her own. 'I'm sorry you had such a time of it, Sarah.'

Sarah shrugged, 'You didn't have it so good either, Kate, with the cockling and all.'

'But I hate to see you so bitter, Sarah dear, about your life.'

Sarah laughed at this. 'Bitter? I'm not bitter. My husband treats me kindly - in fact, as you both know, I am the mistress in my house – and he seems to like me taking care of things.'

The other two sisters knew that Sarah ran both her husband's business and the household. All her husband was responsible for was actually doing his work. Sarah paid the bills, made decisions on the use of any profits, and generally managed all their affairs.

Kate nodded, 'Some men don't like responsibility.'

'My husband is one of those,' said Sarah, 'and it suits me fine. So, –' she let go of Kate's hand and linked their arms, while Liz did the same the other side – 'here we are, the Fernlee sisters, all right and tight and comfortable. The bad times are behind us, the good times ahead.'

'Well spoken, Sarah,' cried Liz.

'Amen to that,' laughed Kate, and the three of them strode out in front of the rest of the party, like close comrades returning from a foreign war together.

After a very satisfying meal, during which there was much chattering on trivial matters, with Jamie trying to explain to Johann the intricacies of hunting wild geese and how quail were that much smaller and would need an expert wildfowler to bring them down, and Sally drawing out Simon's adventures from him, they finally came to saying their goodbyes.

Sally kissed Kate and, with a widening of her eyes, whispered, 'At last, eh? You got 'im now. Hold on to him. You waited long enough.'

'Much too long,' said Kate, smiling.

Johann said, shaking her hand, 'Bless you, Kate. You deserve all the happiness you can get.'

'We all do,' she replied.

The couple set off for the cottage, leaving the rest of the party to finish the wine. Kate had her old valise with her, retrieved from the Rockmansted house and, while being trotted to her new home in the pony and trap, she opened the lid flap and took out the bundle of Simon's letters.

Reins in hand, Simon glanced to the side and asked, 'What're those?'

'Oh,' she smiled, running her hands over them, 'just some letters from a lover.'

Simon looked harder and then recognised his own handwriting. 'You kept them all this time?' he said, wonderingly.

Kate raised her eyebrows at him. 'Didn't you keep mine, Simon Wentworth?'

He looked a little uncomfortable at this and pretended to concentrate on his driving. 'It's difficult for a man at sea,' he said at last. 'We only had a small footlocker.'

'You could have thrown out those old boots you've had since you were nineteen.'

'Those boots? They're my fishing boots. I couldn't do without my fishing boots.'

'Oh, well,' she sighed, 'if they're more important than letters from me . . .'

He looked so crestfallen she laughed out loud. 'Oh, Wentworth, you're so gullible, it's no fun making jokes at you. Look!'

She tossed the letters away and they landed in the marsh and sank from sight.

Simon reined the pony and looked back, a puzzled expression on his face.

'Don't you want them any more?' he asked. 'After keeping them all these years?'

'I don't need them,' she replied, hugging him. 'I have you now, my darling husband.'

He hugged her back. 'My darling wife...'

They laughed together; laughed and laughed.